LAUREN L. GARCIA

Catalyst Moon: Storm

Book Three

Fabulous cover art courtesy of Fiona Jayde Media

Contact the author: lauren@laloga.com

Website: http://www.laloga.com

The Catalyst Moon saga:

Incursion (Book 1)

Breach (Book 2)

Storm (Book 3) <—you are here

Surrender (Book 4)

Sacrifice (Book 5)

Join my mailing list for freebies, new releases, and other fun stuff!
https://laloga.com/newsletter

First edition

This book was professionally typeset on Reedsy.
Find out more at reedsy.com

For Wade, my soul-bonded.

Contents

- Above all other things, this is a story about love. -

1

ONE

Snow drifted to Kali's shoulders and wind teased her hair, but cold could not touch her within the shelter of Stonewall's arms. She savored the press of their foreheads and the warm kiss of his breath against her lips. They were both foolish to stay, but here they were. *Together.*

She shifted closer, pine needles crunching beneath her boots. He inhaled as if about to speak when a thrall's scream pierced the air. The otherworldly, high-pitched shriek struck a nerve in her skull. She jerked away from Stonewall, heart clapping like thunder in sudden terror. They had to *run,* had to–

"Kali?" Stonewall's voice was quiet, confused, one hand on her elbow as if to pull her back to his chest.

Breath hitching, Kali searched the shadowy forest around them for sign of the thrall, but only saw the sleeping sentinels, the mages' tent, and the mage-made campfire, burning merrily in the filmy snowfall. Even Frost and the other horses stood beside the mage carriage, content in their slumber.

Warning crept up her spine to prick the base of her skull. *Sweet magic.* She could sense it in her own veins; like catching the delicious scent of something she had never tasted, but dearly desired to. A sense of *hunger* filled her, too sudden and severe to be her own. She looked into Stonewall's serious, almost-gold eyes. "You didn't hear that?"

Dark brows knitted as he glanced around them, one hand reaching for his sword. "No. What–"

Another thrall's scream cut him off. He must have heard this one, for he swore and drew his daggers, spinning to place her behind him while he scanned the tree line. The horses started awake, snorting and stamping in their tethers, while the four other sentinels scrambled out of their bedrolls and drew their weapons.

"Where in the blazing void are they?" Flint said as her eyes darted across the surrounding forest.

Her brother, Milo, surged to the horses and carriage. "We have to go – now!"

The sentinels looked to Stonewall, but their sergeant's gaze had fallen on Kali. Only when their eyes met again did that prickle of warning grow to a thrill, and she realized the truth. "No time," she whispered. "They're nearly upon us."

Fear flashed in Stonewall's eyes before the warrior in him took over. "Get in the carriage," he told her before looking toward the tent, where Sadira had emerged, her moonstone-pale hair glowing in the darkness. "You too, Sadira."

The campfire's gentle snapping sharpened to a roar as the other mage hurried to the mage-carriage. Of the sentinels, only Rook shot the renewed flames a wary glance as she nocked an arrow. The rest were converging on the carriage, where Milo had untied the horses so the panicked creatures could gallop into the darkness. With luck, they would survive the encounter and the sentinels could find their mounts again.

A third shriek echoed through the forest, sending Kali's heart into her throat as Stonewall pulled her to the carriage. But when he tried to shove her inside, she dug in her heels. "I must try and cure at least one!"

His mouth thinned but he offered no argument as he shoved on his helmet. "Protect the mages," he called to the other sentinels, who immediately drew closer to Kali and Sadira.

"After that display at Parsa," Rook muttered. "The mages ought to be protecting *us.*"

"The real danger is out there," Stonewall shot back. "Everyone will do their part."

"Aye," Kali managed. She looked at her fellow mage. "Sadira, will you help them?"

Sadira nodded and flexed her hands; little tongues of flame leapt to life in her palms.

Rook did not reply, only climbed up the side of the carriage to the roof with the grace of a cat and readied her bow and arrow. "There. To your right, Stonewall."

The group held its collective breath. Throat dry, Kali turned to face their enemies, shoulder-to-shoulder with Sadira. First one, then two, then three pairs of eyes, bright and burning as stars, floated through the darkness toward her and her allies. Never in her life had Kali been so glad to be surrounded by sentinels and near the shelter of a mage-carriage.

"Mara have mercy on us," Beacon murmured. Like his sentinel brethren, the mender had drawn his daggers rather than his sword, and had positioned his tall, lanky frame in front of Sadira.

Stonewall stood in front of Kali. While she was rigid with fear, his shoulders sank with his deep exhale as he slid into a ready stance, calm and collected – at least from behind. His presence relaxed Kali a tiny bit, so she managed a choked, "Remember: keep as many alive as you can."

Stonewall inclined his head toward her but addressed the other sentinels. "You heard her: try to disable the thralls, not kill them."

"Oh, aye," Flint muttered as the eerie stars materialized into shadowy shapes. "The sodding thralls' well-being is *my* biggest worry."

Milo's voice wavered, but only at first. "They were people once, *relah.* We must try to help them."

"I know," Flint replied. "I just hope *we* live to argue about it."

"Do the best you can," Stonewall said. "But your priority is to defend yourselves and each other. Kill as a last resort."

The thralls came on slow, powerful steps, circling the humans in the manner of hunting wolves. The creeping shadows and glowing eyes made

Kali yearn to run away. But running had never done her any good, and her knee was aching again, despite the metal brace. She had to stand and fight.

Focus, she told herself, trying to banish her terror. This might be her only opportunity to use her magic to save even *one* of those poor people. Fear was a luxury she couldn't afford.

A deep breath brought Kali a tiny measure of calm, enough for her to drop into the concentration necessary to perform magic. A new sense of eagerness swelled within at the mere thought of using her abilities, but she tried to ignore the feeling.

"Sadira?" she whispered.

"I am ready," the Zhee mage replied as the thralls drew closer. Some were armed in the manner of lower-tiered villagers, with only pitchforks and rusted axes. A few carried swords. Bits of cloth and leather covered every piece of metal that might have touched a thrall's skin, and a few folks wore gloves. This confirmed Kali's suspicion that the thralls were somehow connected to the supposedly mythical beings known as the Fata, who could not abide the touch of metal.

"A fireball would be *most* welcome right now," Beacon said.

If Sadira replied, Kali didn't hear. She was lost to magic. She closed her eyes out of habit and reached out with her senses to feel the particles—the tiny specks of energy that made up all things—of the nearest thrall, an older woman who was still several meters away. When Kali's awareness brushed the thrall, the creature screamed. Its shock sparked through Kali like lightning, though the feeling turned at once to a hunger, a *need* like she'd never known.

The feeling centered on Kali and came swiftly from not one thrall, but all of them. The sudden weight of the thralls' emotions hit Kali in the chest like a kick from a mule and she gasped aloud, fighting to maintain her control. If she lost herself to the strange emotions, she would lose control of her magic, and possibly her humanity. But how could she feel the *thrall's* emotions? Dimly, she sensed Stonewall moving in front of her, heard the song of steel as his daggers met a thrall's weapon, felt her other allies press closer. Unnatural heat coiled in the air, making sweat bead at her back and forehead, rolling down to sting the barely-healed slash at her throat, but she kept her eyes shut.

Sweet magic.

That strange foreign hunger spiked through Kali again, sharper than before, and it took every ounce of strength to resist the urge to grab Sadira, and–

Kali cut off the thought. *Focus.*

She wrenched her concentration back onto the first thrall's particles. As far as she knew, no other mage could do what as she was about to, but she had been practicing, so she began to siphon the woman's energy away, pulling it toward her as one would pull handfuls of coins across a table. *Not too much,* she cautioned herself. Not enough to kill; only weaken. Only enough to make the sentinels' jobs easier and hopefully incapacitate the poor woman before someone cut her down.

A few thralls screamed in fury, their anger resonating through Kali's body like a dozen plucked viol strings. But Kali's swam in the current of magic. Raw power flowed into her body and it was all she could do not to laugh in delight, because it felt so sodding *good*, because she felt strong and supple, and because there was nothing she could not do.

"Kali!" Stonewall's voice, thick with effort between clanging steel, brought her back to herself, slammed her into her crippled body like a face full of mud, and reminded her of her task.

She opened her eyes. The thrall had fallen before her, scuffing the loam and snow as she thrashed, trying to break Kali's grip. Stonewall had kept his place by her side, but faced two other thralls, working to keep himself between them and Kali. Arrows whistled down from atop the carriage. Beacon, Flint, and Milo stood shoulder to shoulder, each wielding daggers as if they'd been born with weapons in their hands. Sadira was busy too; at each approach attempt, little fires erupted at the hems of the thralls' coats.

Rook swore from the top of the carriage. "They're breaking off!"

Stonewall shouted something, but Kali did not hear. She knelt in the newly-fallen snow and grabbed at the woman's arms, but the thrall screamed and jerked out of her grip, not allowing her to get even a cursory look at the woman's particles. Even weakened by Kali's magic, the woman was far stronger than she looked. With the thrall in this frenzied state, Kali could do no more than try to hang on.

"I need more time," Kali cried.

Stonewall grunted and the clang of steel rang out again. One of the thralls he had been fighting screamed as he knocked it back. Chest heaving, he prepared to lunge at another thrall, pausing only to call back, "Hurry!"

* * *

There was no forest, nor wind, nor gently drifting snow. There were no daggers, nor blood pounding hot through Stonewall's veins. There was neither emotion, nor thought. There was only the fight. Stonewall did not watch his foe drop, only turned his attention to the next. Sadira's fire had caused some thralls to retreat, shrieking, but the rest either didn't care or were too stubborn to go down easily.

Stonewall had that in common with the thralls, at least.

When he found a moment, he shot a glance back at Kali, but she wasn't behind him. His heart stopped, then he looked down to see her kneeling over a thrall, her face tight with concentration. He had no time to wonder what she was attempting, for Rook shouted a warning and the battle was upon him again.

He tugged his dagger free of the thrall he'd been fighting only an arm's length from Kali. The creature gave one last gasp before crumpling to the ground. This battle was over. Stonewall's breath came fast and gore painted his armor, while his blood still sang with energy. Although he'd taken a few hits, he felt no pain.

Despite the chaos, he had not lost count of the thralls he and his squad faced. A dozen had tracked the group from the little village of Parsa. Three had fled after feeling the touch of Sadira's magic. Five had fallen by the sentinels' blades and arrows: sacrifices to keep Stonewall's allies safe. One remained under Kali's ministrations, writhing and shrieking in agony as the mage worked her magic. The burnie twins faced two thralls now, clearly struggling to defend themselves without killing their attackers. But the thralls were vicious and unrelenting; one way or another, the battle would not last much longer. Before Stonewall could intervene, Sadira offered her assistance, and the buckles on the thralls' belts glowed red, the scent of searing flesh mingling with that of spilled blood and new snow. Flint and Milo exchanged defeated looks and lunged for the last time, and the forest was silent.

Eleven. Stonewall's heart froze. "There's one more," he shouted to the others. "Rook, do you see–"

The mage-carriage rattled as something rammed into its other side. The carriage had no true windows, only ventilation slots near the roof, and one door that Stonewall and the others stood before. But whatever had rammed the thing did so with enough force to shove the vehicle forward, making Rook leap down and the other sentinels and Sadira dart out of the way. The carriage would have crushed Kali if Stonewall had not managed to snatch her to safety, but he could not save the thrall she had been trying to heal. The carriage groaned as it rocked in the dirt and dead leaves before toppling over onto the Parsan villager.

"No!" Kali cried, scrambling to her feet among the fresh snowfall.

Another thrall's scream cut off her words as the twelfth and final creature clambered over the fallen carriage to stalk toward them. It was a young woman, with arms bent at odd angles and a black and white cloak, tattered and bloody, swaying behind her. Even though her eyes burned like stars and her face was smeared with dirt and blood, Stonewall recognized her and his stomach dropped to his knees.

"The Cipher from Parsa," Milo whispered. "By the One!"

Kali lunged for the woman, but Stonewall grabbed her arm to let the others to subdue the monster. Kali twisted back to him, eyes flashing with fury. "Let me go!"

Surely it was his imagination that made her voice sound so harsh, almost piercing with hatred. He released her, stunned at the look on her face: pure rage, a mirror of the thrall. Kali turned away from him to the Cipher, one of the revered priestesses of the Circle clergy, who now lay struggling in the

7

snow and dirt beneath the sentinels' grasps. Despite what were clearly two broken arms, the young priestess fought against the sentinels, screaming with what Stonewall imagined was pain and anger. Rook and Flint held the thrall's shoulders while Beacon and Milo held her legs. Sadira stood to one side, body relaxed, face grim. All eyes turned to Kali, who stood still, chest heaving as if she had been running.

After a second of debate, Stonewall dared to touch her shoulder. "Can you help her?"

To his consternation, she looked back at him, tears streaking down cheeks smudged with dirt and blood. All traces of anger were gone and there was only earnestness in her voice. "I must try."

Kali limped forward. Stonewall followed. She knelt beside the possessed priestess, who snarled furiously up at her, struggling to break free of the sentinels' grips. Her round face was twisted with hatred, but Stonewall felt nothing but pity for the poor young woman. She was not herself. He knelt by Kali as well, ostensibly to keep her safe should the others lose their grips, but mostly because he wanted to be near Kali while she worked her magic. Stonewall had no magic of his own, of course, but he wanted to learn from Kali what he could.

Sadira knelt at Kali's other side and the three of them studied the Cipher before Kali placed her palms on each of the priestess' cheeks. "It's all right," she murmured, eyes closed. "Everything will be all right. Just relax."

The thrall screamed again, but this sound lacked that eerie resonance. Heartened, he exchanged glances with Sadira, whose face mirrored his own hopes. Kali was still concentrating, but he couldn't stop himself from placing a gloved hand against her back, hoping, somehow, to send her his strength, to help her fight this battle he could not see. Kali leaned into his touch, heartening him further still. No doubt the other sentinels would guess the connection between them, but in this moment, he didn't care.

"The hematite." Sadira pointed to the multitude of hematite rings and pendants the priestess wore. Hematite – the dispelling stone. It would prevent Kali's magic from working properly. The sight made his breath catch: this was proof that mages *couldn't* have created the thralls! As carefully as he could, given how the woman still writhed, Stonewall removed the jewelry and tucked the pieces into a pouch at his belt.

Kali's gentle murmurs continued, the words blending together beneath the thrall's cries, which indeed sounded more human than before. While the others watched the scene before them, Rook met Stonewall's gaze, a question in her eyes. He caught her meaning at once. They were too exposed here, should any other thralls find them, but Stonewall was reluctant to move.

Give her a few more moments, he thought, holding Rook's gaze and nodding to Kali. The petite sentinel frowned but resumed her watchful glances.

The thrall was quieter now, though she panted and writhed. But her movements lacked their initial frenzy. Was she better?

Before Stonewall could ask, the priestess shrieked again, making all the sentinels start. She jerked out of their grips as if she were made of stone, and leaped to her feet, eyes blazing, body aimed like a dagger – at Kali. "Sweet blood," the thrall hissed. "Give it to us. Now!"

The thrall moved before she'd finished speaking. She lunged at Kali, who only stared up, mouth agape, defeat written on her face. No time for hesitation. Stonewall stepped in front of Kali and grabbed the thrall, and dragged his dagger across the poor woman's throat.

I'm sorry, he thought as the thrall fell to the new snow, unmoving.

2

TWO

As Milo stared at the dead Cipher, disbelief shrank his guts like a rotting vine. The priestess was gone. Magic had done nothing for her. What good was it, then?

He looked at Mage Halcyon, who sat frozen, one hand to her bandaged throat. Mage Sadira knelt beside her, looping one arm around the dark-haired mage's shoulders, though her gaze, too, was on the dead priestess.

A sob escaped Rook. She tried and failed to choke it back, and pointed toward the dark forest. "Flint and I will try and find the horses."

"It's only the first snowfall of the year, but it still shouldn't be too hard to track them," Flint added. Only because Milo knew his twin so well did he recognize the haunted look in her blue eyes as she glanced his way before she and Rook slipped off.

The sergeant clenched his dagger, crimson clear in the still-blazing mage-fire from their campsite about twenty yards away. He looked at the blade, then at Beacon. "Will you...see to her?"

Beacon nodded. "Aye, and the...villagers. We ought to...I don't know, perform rites or something. We can't just leave them here."

"We can't take them all back with us," Stonewall replied, eyes flickering to the mages. "We'll say rites when the others return and do whatever else we can."

"Someone from the Circle can come for the...bodies," Milo heard himself say. "Right?" *Please don't let that task fall to us,* he added silently. *After* we *killed them.*

"I hope so," the sergeant replied.

Mage Sadira glanced at the mender. "Do you need our help?"

"No," Beacon replied. "Maybe get some food together?"

The Zhee mage helped Mage Halcyon to her feet, and the two women went slowly back to their camp. What warmth had filled the air retreated with the mages and Milo couldn't help but watch them go. Would they try to run? But neither one seemed interested in doing anything other than rummaging through the rations.

As Beacon leaned over the dead priestess, Stonewall nodded to mage-carriage, which lay on its side in the powdery snow and churned earth. "Come on, Mi. Let's see if we can salvage anything."

The front axle and one of the rear wheels were broken. The side where the thrall had shoved was splintered in places. While the sarge poked around the carriage's underside, Milo examined the trail in the patchy snowfall that the vehicle had left. Sweet Mara's mercy... The thrall had shoved the carriage well over a horse's length across the ground.

As Milo knelt in the snow, tracing the priestess' footprints, Stonewall came to stand beside him. "It can probably be salvaged, but not right now. Hopefully Rook and Flint will find the horses. Otherwise, it's going to be a long walk back to Whitewater City."

"How is this possible?" Milo asked, pointing to the footprints. "She is—was—such a bitty thing. How did she move the entire carriage?"

Stonewall knelt beside him, frowning down at the tracks in the snow. "She wasn't herself, Mi. She was...something else."

A bitter wind blew and Milo shivered. "What?"

"Kali has...an idea," the sergeant said slowly. "But I'm not sure I understand." At Milo's confused look, he shook his head. "It's best if I let her explain." He began to rise, but paused halfway up, shuddering hard enough to make his teeth chatter.

Milo rose as well. "You all right?"

He grimaced the instant the words left his mouth, for he had not added

11

a deferential "ser" at the end, and the One knew he'd made enough mistakes in the past day. Forgetting an honorific wasn't nearly the same as abandoning his post and allowing a mage to get harmed, but it could be considered insubordination. And even though Mage Halcyon was fine after Mage Sadira had healed her, Stonewall obviously had a...connection to the dark-haired woman.

Thank the One and all the gods, Stonewall didn't seem to notice—or care—about the informal address. "Aye," the sergeant said. "Just got a chill."

"Nox's kiss?" Milo offered.

Stonewall gave a humorless laugh. "I suppose." He swiped off the snow from his close-cropped dark hair and replaced his helmet. "Anyway, it's passed. Let's go help Beacon."

Heartfire. It was fitting, in a grim way, that Milo should spend the longest night of the year in such a fashion. At least the snowfall wasn't heavy or persistent. As the men collected the bodies of the Parsan villagers, Milo searched the shadowed forest for a sign of his twin. Just when he couldn't bear waiting any longer, the sound of hooves crunching on dried leaves reached him through the darkness. Relief swelled in his chest as he rushed forward to help Flint and Rook, who led only five horses.

Milo's stomach fell. "Where's Clove?"

"I'm sorry, Mi," Flint said, gripping his forearm. "We think the thralls found him."

Another loss. The carriage horses were *his* responsibility, too, and he'd failed to keep them safe. Numbness filled him and all he could do was nod mutely as Rook and Flint tethered their mounts and joined in the sentinels' task.

* * *

By the time Stonewall laid the last Parsan villager beside her neighbors, the first stirrings of dawn crept though the forest.

Men and women of all ages; they had been monsters briefly, but now lay silent beneath the intermittent snowfall and the branches gathered to protect the dead from scavengers. Stonewall's heart was leaden; *he* was responsible for their deaths. Yes, he and the others had acted in self-defense, but such action had been simpler when he had believed that thralls destroyed these people's humanity.

None of the sentinels spoke as they returned to their camp, where the Zhee mage knelt by the fire. At their approach, the flames sprang to new life, snapping eagerly at the darkness. A warmth like the sweetest summer day surrounded the group and Stonewall sighed with relief as he settled on his bedroll.

"Here."

He looked up to see Kali holding out some rations and some of the ptarmigan that Rook had caught for their supper. "Thanks," he said as he accepted the cloth bundle, though he was too worn to eat.

She glanced around and then laid her hand against his cheek. She said nothing—what could either of them say, right now?—but her touch comforted him enough to take a bite.

When everyone had food, Kali settled down across the fire from Stonewall, dark eyes fixed on the flames.

"We should say...something," Milo said, looking up. "Right? Or will the Circle do that when they come?"

Beacon cleared his throat before murmuring the words that all sentinels knew by heart. "Nox bring your spirit safely over the river. Tor guide your steps into the next life. The One keep you in all your days."

Stonewall and the rest of the squad joined in; even the mages bowed their heads. Stonewall could not say whether Sadira believed in the gods, but Kali did not, so it heartened him to hear her voice in cadence with the others. Outside the bubble of light and warmth cast by mage fire, snow fell in soft drifts and a bitter wind still blew.

Rook's face was wet. "I wish we could have saved even one."

"We had to protect ourselves first," Flint said gruffly. "They would have killed us. Right?"

She looked at Stonewall, but he had no answer for her. Milo toyed with his own rations and regarded Kali with uncertainty. "Do you know what's going on? Does it have something to do with magic?"

Kali clasped her hands and did not look at anyone. "I did some investigating at Parsa, and now I have…an idea of what's causing the thralls. And I don't think it has anything to do with mages."

"If you know anything," Beacon said. "You must tell us. We have to stop this."

She gave the mender a wan smile. "I'll tell you, but you probably won't believe me."

"Try us," Flint said.

All the sentinels stared at Kali, waiting, but she only looked at Stonewall, her thoughts plain: *Can I trust them?*

He answered without hesitation. "Please share what you've learned, Kali."

"Very well." She seemed to consider. "To the best of my knowledge, thralls are people who have been…taken over, somehow, by the Fata."

No one spoke until Flint exhaled. "Glimmer stories. She's raving mad."

"She's not," Stonewall replied with more force than he meant to. "She knows more than all of us, combined. Her magic…helps her see things we can't. Right?" He shot Kali a look he hoped wasn't too desperate.

She regarded him with fondness before nodding to Flint. "Yes, mages can…examine someone up close, much closer than with the naked eye. I did so to a woman at Parsa, and I saw…something else within her. Something foreign. And I've done…research on the Fata, which leads me to believe they're not only real, but they're controlling these thralls, somehow. With their own magic, if I had to guess, though it's dangerous to speculate too much at this stage—"

Sadira cleared her throat and Kali's cheeks colored as she continued. "I wanted to try and keep them," she gestured to the villagers, "alive, because I thought—I hoped—I could figure out a way to cure them."

"Great job," Flint muttered, poking her dagger against one of the burning logs.

Stonewall glared at the burnie, but Kali spread her hands as if acquiescing. "I failed – twice. I would try a third time, but we'd have to find another thrall."

"What was the..." Sadira tilted her head in thought. "Constable?"

Kali's brows knit. "Constable? I don't..."

"Why could you not cure the thralls?" Sadira clarified.

"Do you mean obstacle?" Kali asked, and Sadira nodded. "Their particles were...wild, frenzied. I couldn't get a good enough look to even see what the problem was, let alone do anything about it. All I knew is that there was something inside them that shouldn't be there."

"Particles?" Flint said, frowning. "What are those?"

"The place where magic lives," Stonewall and Rook said in unison. He glanced at the freckle-faced sentinel in surprise, but she only shrugged.

Kali nodded. "Particles are how we mages interact with magic. We can sense and manipulate them to achieve a desired end. We can also examine them to figure out what's going on with the body in which they reside."

"But particles are found everywhere, in all things," Sadira added. "Not just people. Fire, for example..." She pressed one fingertip to the end of the nearest log, and flames licked up anew.

Beacon's eyes were round as he looked between the mages. "Fascinating. I've always wondered *how* mages heal."

"Magic is extraordinary." Kali sighed. "When it works."

"Dunno anything about the Fata," Milo said, sitting upright. "But if we can find another thrall, could you try again? Maybe we could drug one. Beacon? What do you think?"

The mender ran a hand through his coppery hair. "I...suppose so, though we'd have to convince Talon to let us try."

Stonewall's heart sank at the truth in Beacon's words. Would Talon be willing to let him take Kali out of the bastion again? Before Heartfire, she'd made it clear that he was to keep his distance from his dark-haired mage, lest his squad suffer the consequences. But now, perhaps the emergency of a new thrall attack would set aside all other restrictions.

"Sarge?"

He glanced up to see all of them—even Kali—watching him. "It's worth trying," he said. "Though I'd not stake any hope of gaining the commander's permission." Before anyone could inquire further, he got to his feet. "It's light enough to travel. We'd best get underway."

But the trip back to Whitewater City led to a dilemma, one Stonewall found he was almost too eager to solve. Without the carriage and both its horses, they had five mounts and seven passengers. Rook could have easily accommodated another, but Stonewall wanted the scout to ride in her customary place ahead of the group, keeping an eye out for danger. Beacon was too tall; his horse couldn't reasonably carry the weight of another passenger and what supplies they'd salvaged from the carriage. Milo was also too large to warrant taking another rider.

Stonewall made certain *not* to look at Kali as the others began to mount up. "Flint, would you take Sadira? If that's all right," he added to the Zhee mage.

Sadira nodded and Flint brightened. "At least I'll be warm."

Only one more passenger to see to. Stonewall glanced at Kali, a flush creeping up his neck. *Ea's tits*, he thought, trying to fight back the feeling. *They'll know about us soon, if they haven't figured it out already.* But after nearly losing her—twice—last night, he found he didn't care so much any longer.

But even so, it would not do to flaunt anything, so he kept his voice professional. "Mage Halcyon, are you up to riding with me?"

"*With* you?" Kali replied, just as politely, though he could read the merriment in her eyes. "I suppose so. For old time's sake, if nothing else. We had to share a horse on our trip to Whitewater City," she explained to Sadira. "This horse, actually."

Frost, the dapple-gray mare who had accompanied Stonewall and Kali on their first journey together, twitched her ears toward the mage. Kali smiled as Stonewall helped her into the saddle. "I think she remembers me."

"How could anyone forget you?" he said quietly. Pink bloomed upon her cheeks and her smile widened, and when their eyes met his other troubles seemed far away.

Together.

Beacon offered to assist Sadira, but the Zhee mage swung easily into the saddle behind Flint. The group moved out, Rook taking point. Stonewall cast one final look at the carriage, and at the bodies of the Parsan villagers before mounting. Kali leaned into him; he slid his hands a little too close to her hips as he gathered Frost's reins.

"Careful, Sergeant," Kali murmured, pressing into to his armored chest.

Stonewall fought the urge to wrap his arm around her and instead nudged Frost into a quick walk. When they caught up with the others, Flint twisted around to give Stonewall and Kali a pointed look from behind her helmet. "So, how long have you two been fucking?"

Kali burst out laughing, startling a group of birds from their roost in a nearby pine.

Stonewall gritted his teeth and swore inwardly. "We're not-"

"It's wrong to lie, you know," Flint broke in. "Especially when you're terrible at it."

Kali's body shook with mirth but Stonewall could find *nothing* amusing about this conversation. "Drop it, Flint."

Beacon snorted. "I think you already have, ser."

Flint guffawed; Sadira shot Kali a somewhat startled look and Kali shook her head, still laughing. However, Rook rode ahead, back straight as the pines surrounding them, not looking back. No doubt she wasn't as amused as the others. Well, she and Stonewall had *that* in common, although he didn't blame anyone for wanting to blow off some steam after last night. He glanced over to see Milo gaping at him.

He had to dam this problem before it had a chance to flood. But how?

To his surprise, it was Kali who replied to Flint. "Does it matter?"

No one spoke, although many confused, thoughtful glances were exchanged. A flash of fear ran through Stonewall, hot as any hematite burn. Would any of them report him and Kali to Talon? *Stupid sod,* he scolded himself. He'd tried to prevent such a thing from happening before, and broken off their relationship, but he'd gotten carried away with Kali – again, for she had that effect on him. Now she would pay the price

At last Flint said, "No, I guess it doesn't."

"It's against protocol," Rook shot back. "With good reason, I might add."

"A lot of things we do are against protocol." Flint shrugged. "Besides, it's not wrong to care about someone. You can't control who you love."

The others gave Flint astonished looks, but her gaze was distant.

Love? Was it so obvious to them? Stonewall glanced down at Kali, still laughing even as she tugged her cloak over her dark hair.

"No, I can't," he said.

Beacon offered Stonewall a rueful look. "We thought there was... *someone.*"

"*You* thought it was Commander Talon," Milo replied.

"*Talon?*" Stonewall sputtered. Kali's laughter died and she looked back at him, one brow raised. But he had no answer for her and instead glanced between his squad-mates. "Talon?" he asked again. "She threatened to send the lot of you to the mines if I disobeyed her. I'd sooner kiss a dung beetle."

"The mines?" Rook said, incredulous.

Stonewall nodded and the others exchanged disturbed looks.

"Well, you being *with* Talon seemed like the most logical...err, option," Beacon said at last. "At the time, I mean."

Flint snickered. "Well, we *thought* you were too pious to plow a mage. Looks like we were wrong."

"Thank the stars," Kali said, sending both Flint and herself into laughter again.

Stonewall tightened his grip on the reins and tried to keep his voice calm. "Keep your heads on straight. Remember, not all of those thralls have been accounted for."

That settled them down, though Stonewall did not miss the speculative looks shot his and Kali's way. He pressed one hand to her side, both to keep her steady and to reassure himself that she was safe. She laid one of her hands over his; though they both wore gloves, he imagined he could feel the heat from her skin. *Together.*

Resolved filled him. He'd made a commitment to her, and to his squad. Somehow, he had to find a way to keep both in balance. Surely they had all been brought together for a reason.

18

3

THREE

Everything hurt.

The stone walls and floors of the garrison's detention area held no heat, but sweat trickled down Drake's body, stinging the multitude of cuts he'd earned over the course of Heartfire. Commander Talon's voice echoed in his ears. "Tell me what I want to know."

The sentinel commander had locked them both deep within one of the hematite-laced cells. They were alone.

Drake swallowed thickly; his throat was dry as parchment and his hands were numb from being raised above his head, wrapped in hematite cuffs, and chained to the wall. His legs, too, were cuffed, holding him in place. He was too exhausted to shiver, even though she'd stripped him of all but his pants. His head throbbed, his back ached, and his shoulder burned where the commander's sword had pierced him during the mages' escape... Was it last night? This morning? He had no way of knowing how much time had passed since the sentinels had brought him here. His bruises had bruises.

The sentinel commander shifted in place, glaring up at him. She was tall and sturdy, more so than most other women he knew, but she still had to look *up* to look him in the eye. Good. Drake met her gaze, ensuring that his own held nothing but resolve. Talon may have uncovered his own secrets, but she would never make him betray his friends – the *other* mages she so desperately sought.

Because he *was* a mage. He'd hidden from the truth for most of his life, but now, *finally,* had accepted the blood that ran through his veins. Admittedly, his timing could have been better, but even though Drake was shackled and bound, a part of him felt *free.*

"I know there are other renegade mages out there," Talon said at last. "Where are they? Where are your allies in the Assembly?" The refined lilt of her accent—Silverwood Province, he guessed—was tattered after their time together.

His silence only stoked her ire. Her face, shining with sweat, twisted into a visage of true fury. Once more, the dagger left its sheath at her hip and found its way to his throat faster than an indrawn breath. Talon pressed it to his skin, enough for him to feel the point with each beat of his pulse.

"Where have my mages gone?" she growled.

Hopefully far, far away from here. At least Eris could fly. The thought brought Drake no mirth when Eris' husband, Gideon—his own dear friend—was dead. "They're not *yours,*" Drake replied, the first words he'd spoken since his capture. "They're no one's. They're free."

Her brown eyes widened a fraction and she drew back, lowered the dagger. Drake knew one moment of relief before her gloved hand struck his jaw hard enough to make his vision spotty. His jaw went numb, briefly, before heat and pain flooded the area, pricking at his eyes.

"I know what you are, despite your sentinel mark," she said, lifting her dagger once more. "Traitor."

Drake steeled himself and met her gaze, and was silent again.

* * *

Commander Talon bit her tongue to keep from shouting at the as-yet unnamed renegade mage. Instead, she turned her attention back to her dagger, as if considering some new question while she wiped the blade on the sweat-soaked tunic she wore beneath her armor. Of course, she had no new questions. Not now, after she'd asked the same few again and again.

How had the mages orchestrated their escape? Where had they gone? And, perhaps the most pressing: would this happen again? If not at Whitewater, then in other bastions across the continent? Were the sentinels facing the beginning of a...rebellion?

Her stomach, already twisted into painful knots, contorted further. The throb that had begun at her temples the moment Foley had alerted her to the breach in the bastion wall sharpened. She took a deep breath to quell both the pain and the driving, clenching fear, but it did no good.

Footfalls by the door made her look up to see Captain Cobalt standing at the cell's threshold, helmet tucked under one arm, pale eyes fixed upon the renegade mage. Sensing that he was being watched, however, he met her gaze and straightened.

"All available squads have spent the night scouring the city and the surrounding area," he said without preamble. "The city guards are helping, too. After morning meal, I'll send our forces back out to continue the search, and widen it into the province. Furthermore, we've done a head count in the bastion: eleven mages have escaped."

"Including Gideon Echina?" Talon asked.

Cobalt shook his head. "No, ser. His is the only confirmed death. Lieutenant Faircloth of the city guard claims to have flung Eris Echina off of the bridge, but given her history of shape-changing, I think we should presume she's alive until we can prove otherwise. The rest got away."

The renegade mage sucked in his breath, but did not speak. Talon did not spare the dreg a glance.

"The breach?" she asked.

Cobalt's mouth tightened, tugging at the scar that ran down his left cheek. "Wren and Thom's squads are guarding it now. We'll need a mason to patch it up properly." Neither his voice nor his expression changed, but she detected weariness in the set of his shoulders. "We think it's an old blood run, but there's no telling how long it's been there."

Another failure, on her part as much as anyone else's. *But how could I have known?* "Rest-assured," Talon said. "We *will* find those mages, even if we have to burn the province to ashes." Already, she was cataloging possible destinations the renegades would have fled. They were not long gone. Perhaps she could salvage this situation. Foley might have some hints as well, though Talon was *greatly* interested to hear what the First Mage of Whitewater Bastion had to say about this mess. Yes, he had alerted her to the breach in the bastion wall, but not until the night of the mages' escape, allowing Eris and her allies plenty of time to flee into the chaos of Heartfire.

If Foley heard the slightest whisper of this beforehand, and didn't tell me... The throb in her temple increased and she gripped her dagger as if it would help her keep her feet.

"The remaining mages?" Talon asked.

"All but two have been collared and locked in their dorms: Mages Halcyon and Sadira. Sergeant Stonewall's squad has not yet returned from Parsa."

"Stonewall?" the prisoner choked, straining against his bonds, eyes darting between the sentinels.

Talon seized his weakness. "Friend of yours?"

The mage's green eyes widened, then he lowered his gaze and said nothing more. But the damage was done. Talon studied his face with new interest. The shape of his nose and jaw were both familiar, as was the lilt of his accent, which marked him as a native of Indigo-By-the-Sea Province. All together, they reminded her of...

The knots in her stomach twisted again. *Stonewall.* This mage knew the sergeant; gods above, they looked so similar, they might be related. Was Stonewall involved in the mage escape? Certainly, he had been *involved* with Mage Halcyon until Talon had ordered him to put a stop to his dalliances. At the time, she'd thought the young man was thinking with his cock and not his brain, but now, seeing this new connection, icy dread flooded her. A traitor from within could spell doom for everyone living in the garrison and bastion alike.

With effort, she kept her voice steady. "They should have been back hours ago."

"Aye, ser." The captain's reply was just as cool. "There's been no word from the sergeant, either. They might've run into similar trouble as we did."

Any other morning, or with any other sentinel, this situation would not yet be cause for alarm. Delays happened. Carriages broke, horses lost shoes, desperate bandits thought they could take on a sentinel squad and walk away. But given the situation, Talon could not quell a renewed flare of anxiety – and fury.

"If he's not back by midday," she said. "Send out a few scouts to look for him. We can't afford to let any other mages out of our grasp. In the meantime, the bastion is on lockdown. No mages are to leave for *any* reason." Foley would be beside himself, but Talon couldn't risk any more trouble from the mages. Perhaps later, when the dust had settled, she would reconsider. "Lock them in the dormitories and post guards at the exterior doors. They'll have their common room and latrines, at least, though we'll have to bring in food and water for now." Troublesome, to be sure, but at least there were less mages to tend. *There is balance in all things.*

Another thought struck her and she leveled a stern look at Cobalt. "Nor are *any* sentinels not assigned to guard duty allowed to enter without express permission from you or I. Even officers."

Satisfaction gleamed in Cobalt's eyes. "Consider it done, ser."

"Good. I'll speak to the Circle about our hematite stores. If we had been properly supplied, this *incident* might not have occurred."

Cobalt's relief was palpable as he gave a warrior's salute: arms crossing his chest, bowing deep. When he straightened, his gaze fell upon the renegade mage again, and then darted to the dagger still in Talon's grip. "Have you been able to learn anything more?"

She withdrew one of the vials of hematite, no larger than her little finger, and passed it to the captain. "He had six of these in his belt."

Cobalt examined the vial in the torchlight. "Ours?"

"I believe so," Talon said. "This mage matches Sergeant Gossan's description of the dreg who stole our shipment before Heartfire."

"What in the blazing void does a mage want with hematite?"

Talon reached up to turn the fellow's right wrist so Cobalt could see the sentinel mark beneath the cuff: line-drawn twin triangles with intersecting tips.

"A sentinel?" Cobalt immediately reined in his shock, squaring his shoulders and glaring at the dark-skinned mage. "I thought his fighting style looked familiar. But how–"

"I've asked that question, too," Talon interrupted, holding out her hand. After a second of hesitation, Cobalt passed the vial back to her and she stowed it in her belt pouch with the others. "But the mage has been uncooperative – so far." She moved to the cell door: iron alloyed with hematite. After she locked the door, the two of them started down the stone corridor.

"Perhaps High Commander Argent will have more luck with the dreg," Cobalt said.

There it was again: that wash of fear so cold it burned. Talon's instincts screamed at her to keep the mage escape a secret from Argent, but such an act would be considered insubordination at the very least. At the worst, her superior would view concealment of the truth as an act of treason – or incompetence. No, she had to let Argent know.

Hopefully the renegade mage's capture would mitigate any damage. If Talon could provide a link to the escaped mages—or the Assembly—Argent might be lenient with her for allowing mages to escape in the first place.

Maybe.

At the very least, she prayed her father would be safe from Argent's ire, should the High Commander ever decide to intervene. Foley had not fled, after all.

It took all of Talon's control to keep her voice from shaking. "Perhaps he will."

Cobalt walked a step behind her. "What will you do with the prisoner?"

"Nothing, for the moment. I think our magical friend needs some time to consider the reality of his situation. Perhaps, after a few days in our care, he'll be more inclined to cooperate."

Their boot steps echoed faintly on the stone walls and the captain's voice was all business. "What about the dead mage? Shall we give Gideon Echina

24

to the other mages for cremation?"

"No," Talon replied through clenched teeth. "Bring his body to the bastion and bury his corpse. Make the other mages watch you. No. Make *them* bury him."

Cobalt halted. "*Bury* him? Condemn him to the void for all time?"

So rarely was the captain at a loss, Talon had to pause just to witness the event. Surprise did not suit his stern, scarred face. "What does it matter?" she asked, more out of sheer curiosity than concern. She had too many burdens to trouble herself with his sensibilities, pious though they might be.

"Fire is the gateway to the next life," Cobalt replied at once, as if she had never heard those words. "Without cremation, Echina won't be sent to the gods. He won't be sent to his next life, where he could atone for his wrongdoing in this one. My feelings on mages aside, ser, that's an ill-fate to bestow upon anyone."

"Mages don't believe in the gods," Talon replied, continuing for the door that would lead back to the garrison proper. Two cinders stood guard; the older sentinels snapped to attention at her approach. "I want Gideon's death to serve as a warning to the others. Besides, we have cremations of our own to attend to. Or have you forgotten?"

The captain's jaw tightened. "I have not, ser. I'll have a new scar from the thrall attack at Parsa yesterday morning, and we lost many brothers and sisters to sacrifice. But what you're suggesting is–"

"Is an order," Talon interrupted. She shot the captain a final glance before stepping through the door. "Report to me when it's done."

Cobalt stared at her before saluting again. "As you say, Commander."

4

FOUR

new day dawns. Our sun sidles over the horizon: golden, warm, **A** *ever-watchful. The source of all life.*

    A shadow appears in the endless sky, marring the dawn, blotting out that warm, guarding light. It is no thunderhead, heavy with rain, but the winds stir and the world grows cool. An answering icy terror fills our veins. Our hearts leap out of our chests and we yearn to run from the shadow-cloud and the coming storm, but fear pins us in place. The shadow looms closer. We have only one way to hide.

Kali jerked awake with a gasp, blinking into the morning mist blanketing Whitewater City. Her heart raced as the strange vision faded into the river's constant roar. Or was she still dreaming? Stonewall's hand on her side brought her back to herself.

"You all right?" he murmured.

"Aye," she managed, rubbing her eyes. "Just woolgathering."

The delicate snowfall had retreated to the morning's assault. They were approaching the outer gates that led to the bridge crossing the White River. Beyond the closed gates, the province's capital city sat dark and silent while the river churned around it. Crows, mice, and other scavengers searched the cups and bits of food that littered the ground, and the air stank of wine; remnants of last night's festivities. A squad of city guards watched the sentinels pass through the outer gates with a little too much interest. One

26

of them, a lieutenant, judging by the insignia on his armored shoulder, signaled Stonewall and the others to approach. Behind him, the other city guards glowered. Kali twined her fingers in Frost's mane and pressed herself close to Stonewall's armored chest.

"What in Nox's void is going on?" Flint asked. "Why do those guards look like they've all eaten bad cheese?"

Kali's stomach turned to ice. Heartfire. Eris' escape. She had almost forgotten after all the insanity of Parsa. If Eris, Gideon, and the other mages had succeeded... Well, that would account for the guards' sour faces.

Stonewall glanced at the others. "No idea. But let me do the talking."

"Stonewall, I need to tell you–" Kali began, but the city guard lieutenant was already by their side, glaring up at her.

"Well met, ser," Stonewall said as he halted Frost. "Is everything all right?"

"It is now," the lieutenant replied. "Those dregs with you are mages, right? Thank the One, you've caught some of them! Did you see any more?"

Stonewall shifted in the saddle, no doubt at a loss.

Play along, Kali thought, willing him to catch on. *Let the guards think you caught some renegades.* Perhaps they could learn something useful before stepping back into the lycanthra's den.

"We've done our duty," Stonewall said at last. "What's the situation here?"

The guard removed his helmet, revealing a man in his middle years, blue eyes ringed with exhaustion. A network of fresh, bandaged scratches mingled with older, ugly pink scars that covered his face, as if the metal on his helmet had burned his flesh. "It's been a night for the histories, let me tell you. I still can't believe so many moon-bloods got away—and no one knows just *how*—but we've done the best we could, serla."

Stonewall had gone still. "I'm sure you have," he managed. "Can you give me an update on the bastion?"

"Full lockdown, from what I hear," the city guard replied. "You're about the last bunch to return. I imagine you're ready for some food and rest." He glanced between Kali and Sadira, eyes narrowing. "Did they put up a fight, serla?"

"They gave us no trouble," Stonewall said.

The lieutenant frowned. "Wish we could say the same. We had a beastly struggle right here at the gates." A thin, satisfied smile curved across his face. "Well, let no one say Ballard Faircloth don't pay his dues."

A knot tightened in Kali's stomach. "What do you mean?"

Faircloth glared at her, but Stonewall cleared his throat. "Good man. Was anyone else injured?"

The guard spat onto the stone walkway leading to the bridge. "Aye, you could say that. I flung one bitch down to the river. The other..." He squared his shoulders and patted his sword-hilt. "The other met his end on my blade. Almost makes me think I should try for the Burn."

Two mages dead; was one of them Eris? Kali's mouth fell open but she couldn't speak. Her head felt light and her vision swam and never had she been so grateful for Stonewall's solid presence at her back. Without him, she surely would have toppled to the ground.

She managed to catch Sadira's gaze, only to find her own shock mirrored in her friend's face. Had Sadira known about Eris' plans? Raw fear coursed through Kali's veins, relentless as the river below. Two mages killed... If not Eris, then two people Kali knew were dead. Two people who wanted nothing more than freedom. Something dark and hot burned within her throat, but she swallowed it down.

"Thank you for the information," Stonewall was saying to Lieutenant Faircloth. "But we'd best be on our way back."

Faircloth stepped aside. "Good luck."

"We'll need it," Flint replied as the sentinels rode past him.

No one spoke while they crossed the bridge, heading for the inner gates. Whitewater City loomed ahead, mist-shrouded and blotting out the sky. The White River's rush filled Kali's ears and damp air was colder than the chill within the forest. Frost's hooves clopped gently on the stones and Kali fought the urge to dig her heels into the mare's sides. She wanted to rush to the bastion and learn what had happened; she wanted to turn Frost around and flee with Stonewall. Was she a fool to have returned?

"You knew about the escape." Stonewall's voice was quiet, only meant for her ears.

Kali swallowed but said nothing.

"You didn't tell me," he added.

"It wasn't my secret to tell."

"Yesterday…when I came to the bastion to bring you to Parsa. Would you have gone with Eris if I hadn't?"

Tears pricked at her eyes, made hotter by the contrast of the winter wind. "I wanted to. I thought …" She took a breath to try and regain control of herself. "I thought it would be easier if I didn't have to be near you, after…" She trailed off, unable to voice the thought.

"Can't say I blame you," he replied after a second too long. "Will it make you angry if I say I'm glad you didn't leave? Only because I know you're alive."

Despite everything, Kali managed a smile. *Together.* "I'm glad I didn't leave, either."

They were almost across the bridge. Even now, the inner gate guards were stepping forward to assess these new travelers. Soon they would be back at Whitewater Bastion. Another wind bit through Kali's cloak and she shivered.

"Whatever happens when we return," Stonewall whispered in her ear. "I love you."

Kali twisted to try and look at him, pulling the hem of her hood aside so he could see her face as well. Behind his helmet, his expression contained its habitual sternness, but his gaze warmed her from within. "I love you, too," she replied.

* * *

The silence blanketing the city grew more oppressive as the group drew closer to the bastion. Although traces of last night's revelry still littered the streets, no one stirred, save a few hastily drawn curtains when Kali and the others passed. When they turned a street corner and Kali spotted the garrison's gates, the knots in her stomach tightened and her better sense urged, *Run.*

But she'd tried—twice—to convince Stonewall to leave this place. Admittedly, the first time had been in jest and the second had been the product of desperation, but she knew him well enough by now to realize he would not turn his back on his duty. Stonewall had built a life here, as had she. And in truth, she had to know what had happened last night. She had to know if Eris was dead.

A sentinel squad met them at the garrison gates. Their cured leather armor, dyed a dark gray and embedded with hematite, seemed dull in the wan midmorning light. Beneath their helmets, their gazes upon Kali and Sadira were suspicious. Little wonder, given the events of last night. Even so, Kali tried to keep her expression neutral and nonthreatening; perhaps through compliance she could gain information.

At a wordless gesture from the nearest sentinel, Stonewall and the others reined in their mounts. "Sergeant," the new sentinel said as she strode forward on long, lanky legs. "We were starting to get worried."

"We ran into some trouble at Parsa, Vigil," Stonewall said. "I must speak with Cobalt immediately."

"That's *Captain* Cobalt," Vigil replied. Kali rolled her eyes before she could stop herself, and the sentinel glared at her before looking at Stonewall again. "Where's the carriage?"

"Long story," Stonewall said. "I'm sure *Captain* Cobalt will be interested to hear it."

"If it's so important, you ought to tell the commander."

Stonewall tensed. "Aye."

Vigil frowned at him, but nodded to the guards at the garrison gates. As the gates swung open, she stepped aside and regarded Stonewall and his squad. "Everyone's just got back from the search. You lot missed all the fun over Heartfire."

"We had our own fun, Vig," Beacon replied as they entered the garrison's courtyard. "But we heard some of what happened here. Are there any injured?"

"Nothing hematite won't fix," Vigil said. "Assuming we get more."

"One of the city guards told us two mages were killed last night,"

Stonewall said.

Vigil shook her head. "We only found one body. The other one..." Her frown deepened. "Well, the river could have claimed her, but only the One knows what moon-bloods can do to save their skins."

Kali's breath caught. Vigil *must* be speaking of Eris. No other mage in this bastion could have saved herself from a fall off the bridge. Perhaps Eris had shifted to her crow from in the last second...

Or perhaps Vigil spoke of Adrie or someone else, because if one mage could shift, then surely *all* of them could – at least as far as Vigil was concerned.

"Which mage's body was found?" Kali asked.

Vigil stared at her, but did not respond. "Get them inside," she said to Stonewall. "The captain's waiting."

The gates closed behind them with a *clang* that resonated within Kali's chest, leaving the garrison's courtyard to stretch between her and the bastion gates. Her heart was racing again. She took a breath to steady herself as they crossed the yard.

Flint exhaled. "Feels like a sodding tomb in here."

"Don't speak of such things," Milo replied. "Besides, you've never even seen a tomb."

"Neither have you," Flint shot back.

More tears stung Kali's eyes and she ducked her head, clenching her fingers around Frost's mane until her hands ached. Stonewall cleared his throat. "Stop the bickering, burnies. For Tor's sake, now's not the time."

The twins fell silent, thank the stars. Kali exhaled and Stonewall rested a hand briefly on her side. Though he said nothing, his touch was enough to bring a sliver of calm, of courage. By the time they reached the bastion gates, Kali found the strength to raise her head and meet the waiting sentinels. As at the garrison gates, two sentinels stood guard on either side. Through the iron and hematite bars, in the bastion's courtyard, Kali could make out more sentinels and a few mages. The mages were...digging?

Her heart stuck in her throat. *What in Seren's light is going on?*

"Why are they not bound?" Captain Cobalt strode up, one hand on his

31

sword, fury in every step. "And where's the sodding carriage? Answer me, Sergeant."

Only because Kali was so close to Stonewall did she hear how he sucked in a breath. But his reply was calm. "It's a long story, ser. I'll go into it more once we've gotten them settled. The short answer is the carriage got damaged and I didn't see any reason to bind the mages on our return journey."

More sentinels broke from the main group overseeing the digging mages and joined their captain. Cobalt spoke to the sentinels at the gates, and then these opened as well, allowing the arrivals to enter. The resulting slam when the gates closed echoed through the bastion.

"Get them down," Cobalt replied, gesturing to Kali and Sadira. Some of the sentinels with him stepped forward and Kali tensed.

"We've handled them this far, ser," Stonewall replied as he dismounted. "We can–"

"Collar them," Cobalt interrupted.

Barely before Kali had a chance to register what was going on, one of the other sentinels shoved past Stonewall, grabbed her waist, and pulled her bodily from Frost's saddle. No sooner had her boots touched the flagstones had another sentinel come forward to take her arms. By Kali's next breath, a leather collar, embedded with hematite, tightened around her throat, leaving her world gray and dull.

Eris had been forced to wear one of these before her escape, so Kali knew without having to look that the clasp contained a tiny lock made of hematite. The blazing thing was *supposed* to keep her from manipulating particles. But Kali had proved that her magic, at least, could work on hematite when she had used magic to break Eris' collar, over a month ago. *Calm down,* Kali told herself. *You can break this one, too. Just not right now. Be patient.*

Even with this knowledge, the collar stole all color and life from Kali's world. She gasped at the loss, but couldn't take a proper breath.

Kali glanced at Sadira to see her friend had received the same treatment, with the collar fitted above the hematite torc that Sadira wore—by her own volition—to bind her powerful magic. Sadira's blue eyes met Kali's, and even the normally calm woman looked frightened. More sentinels, unfamiliar to Kali, closed around her, shoving Stonewall aside. Kali's heart was in her throat as she tried to peer between the gray armored figures, who all blended together in a haze of hematite.

Even Stonewall was lost in the mass, until he shouldered through the new sentinels, causing them to drop Kali's arms, and placed himself in front of her. Leashed fury laced his words. "Captain, these women were on a mercy mission and had *nothing* to do with the escape."

"Aye," Flint added. Kali thought she and her squad-mates had all dismounted by now, but it was difficult to make them out between the surrounding sentinels. "In fact, they were–"

"Not another word out of you, burnie," Cobalt broke in. "Sergeant, step away from the mage."

The day was fine, but clouds marred the horizon and the wind brought another promise of snow. Kali shivered as she tried to see between the armored figures surrounding her, to the center of the bastion's courtyard, where she could hear shovels scraping against the hard ground. But she was too sodding short and couldn't make out what the mages were digging. Something told her that was for the best.

Stonewall trembled. "With respect, ser, let me explain what happened at Parsa–"

"Explain it to Commander Talon," Cobalt said. "Step. Away. From. The mage. *Now*. Or I'll throw *you* down with the dreg in our cells."

Stonewall's hands tightened into fists. Kali's thoughts were sluggish—either from fear or hematite, she couldn't say—but it would do no good to have both of them imprisoned. Again, she tried to take a deep breath, but the collar dug into her skin.

"It's all right," she whispered. "I'll be fine." More than that, she could not say.

He inclined his head toward her, but did not move any more until his shoulders sank and he stepped away. Though he wore his helmet, she could read the thin line of his mouth better than any book.

"Lock them in the dormitories with the others," Cobalt was saying to his sentinels.

Someone grabbed Kali's arm again and began to haul her toward the large building that housed the dormitories. But Kali dug her heels in and looked at the sentinel captain. "Please tell us what's happened here. Who was killed?"

Cobalt stared down at her. "You and Eris were friends, were you not?"

Oh, no. Sweet Seren's light, no. A strange lightness filled Kali, as if her soul itself had detached from her body. Her reply was no more than an indrawn breath. "Yes."

The captain gave a silent signal. The sentinels who had blocked Kali's view stepped aside to reveal five mages at the center of the bastion courtyard. All wore collars like Kali and Sadira. Four wielded shovels and pickaxes. They had broken through the hoarfrost and now flung hard ground back up beside the pit. The fifth mage, Foley Clementa, stood to one side, hand and hook clasped, head bowed beneath his gray cloak. More sentinels surrounded the mages—of course—and two more stood beside a prone figure on the ground, where a thin sheet covered the distinctive human form. At another silent signal, one of those sentinels bent to draw back the sheet.

Gideon stared at the sky, face ashen, features fixed into a look of terror. Dead.

Kali tried to clap her hands over her mouth, but one of the other sentinels held her arms in place with a grip like iron. A cold unlike any Kali had ever known swept through her and she nearly collapsed; she was strangely thankful for the grip that kept her upright. Stunned, she looked away from the grim scene and her gaze fell upon Rook. Tears streamed down the petite sentinel's face, beneath her helmet.

Too overwhelmed to consider what Rook's weeping might mean, Kali looked away as tears stung her own eyes. If Eris was alive, she would be devastated. If she even knew. Or was she dead, too?

Kali bit her tongue to redirect her thoughts and then looked at the sentinel captain again. "What happened to Eris?"

He met her gaze steadily, his scarred face hard as any mountain. "Gone."

Anger swept through Kali, so cold it burned as it beat behind her ribs in a wild tattoo. "Dead?"

Cobalt ignored her and looked at Stonewall. "Twelve mages tried to escape the bastion last night. As far as we know, ten—possibly eleven—succeeded. We will find them in short order. As of this moment, the bastion is on lockdown. No one is to enter or leave without express permission from Commander Talon or myself. There will be no missions of any kind until further notice."

Sadira had gone still upon seeing Gid's corpse, but now she looked back at the captain. "But what about–"

"*No* missions until further notice," Cobalt ground out, glaring at the Zhee mage. He nodded to the sentinels who held Kali and Sadira. "Get them inside. Now."

A sentinel tried to wrench Kali forward, but she refused to be moved. Not yet. "But...a burial? Not a cremation?"

Cobalt's expression darkened. "I said, get them–"

"His spirit will be adrift forever," Rook broke in, making everyone look her way. Her brown eyes were wide and wet. "His soul will be lost. Ser, how can you condone this?"

"He's a mage," Cobalt replied through gritted teeth. "He doesn't believe in the gods. And what does it matter to you, anyway?"

"It's barbaric," Stonewall said. Beacon and Flint nodded, echoing his words. Milo's face was white and he looked to be on the verge of tears.

The captain took a deep, shaking breath, but his voice was firm. "We have our orders."

That familiar anger filled Kali's heart. Even Stonewall fell out of her thoughts as she focused on the pale-eyed, scarred sentinel who regarded Gideon's body with maddening indifference. Fury roiled within her, writhing into a hate so sudden and strong, she gasped. Despite the collar, despite the presence of sentinels and their hematite-laced blood and blades on all sides, her hands itched for magic.

Yes, sweet blood. Kill it.

"Gods or not, this is wrong," she managed. "You know this is wrong."

Cobalt gestured to the other sentinels. "Get them out of here."

5

FIVE

White filled Stonewall's vision as if he were caught at the center of a snowstorm. It was like being in battle; his body moved of its own accord. Only when a strong hand grabbed his shoulder did he realize he was stepping after Kali as the others took her and Sadira to the bastion. Beacon's touch snapped Stonewall out of his haze, though his hands hovered over his daggers.

"Something wrong, Sergeant?" Cobalt asked. The sentinels that the captain had gathered moved closer, blocking both Stonewall's view of Kali and the mages digging Gideon's grave. His *grave.*

What a mess to have come back to. But somehow, it paled in comparison to the mess they had left in Parsa.

Tor help me. Blinking, Stonewall lowered his hands. Behind him, someone exhaled. Although Stonewall couldn't make out Gideon's body, the sound of shovels scraping against dirt made his skin crawl. "Captain, I understand you have...other matters on your shoulders, but I must tell you what happened at Parsa – and after."

"Fine, but make it quick."

On their journey here, Stonewall had worked out how much he ought to disclose. "There were thralls at Parsa," he began.

"I know," Cobalt replied though clenched teeth. "I was there before you. I have the sodding stitches to prove it."

Out of the corner of his eye, Stonewall caught Flint's mouth opening, but he shot her a warning look. To his surprise, she snapped her jaw shut, though she still glowered at the captain. He gave the others a similar look, willing them to be quiet.

Four pairs of eyes met Stonewall's from beneath their helmets; four armored sentinels stood resolutely at his side. Some of the unease in his guts relaxed as he glanced back at Cobalt. "The thralls appeared *after* the mages healed the villagers. One moment, everything was normal; the next, a group of villagers had changed *into* thralls. They injured one of our mages. It was a battle to get out of there in one piece. We fled until we deemed it safe to stop, and made camp for the night to tend to the injured mage. More thralls found us that morning. We..." He swallowed. "We took care of them."

Cobalt frowned. "Were they Canderi?"

"No, ser. Parsan."

"Is there anyone left in that blazing village?"

"I don't think so, ser."

Cobalt ducked his chin. "Poor bastards."

"We had to leave the bodies." Stonewall gave the location as best he'd been able to reckon, and added, "Someone should...gather them."

"I'll send a message to the Circle." Cobalt regarded him. "There's more."

Before Stonewall replied, he injected as much calm confidence as he could into his tone. "One of our mages believes she can...cure thralls."

"*Cure* thralls?"

"Yes, ser."

The captain glanced around the courtyard, as if expecting an ambush – or a group of others in on some joke at his expense. "This mage...is it Halcyon?"

Stonewall's cheeks warmed but he kept his reply professional. "She's had a chance to...study them, to a degree. I know it sounds strange," he added as Cobalt scoffed, "but even if there's a slim hope that thralls can be cured, ser, we ought to look into it. A lot of people could be suffering needlessly."

"You know our orders, Sergeant," Cobalt replied. "The thralls are not our focus."

"Our orders are…" Stonewall trailed off at the warning in the captain's pale eyes. A chill passed through him; he should keep his mouth shut before he brought more trouble on himself or his friends. So he only nodded, shoulders sinking in defeat. "Yes, Captain."

Cobalt rubbed his forehead. "Why was it so important to tell *me* all of this now, not the commander?"

This, Stonewall had *not* thought through, for he'd deliberately avoided thinking of Talon. Not only had she tried to coerce him into ending his relationship with Kali by threatening Kali's life, she had made an advance on *him*. *"If you seek a release, you do not have to look for it in the bastion."*

Shame filled him, hot and fast as hematite, but infinitely less pleasant. Had he unknowingly encouraged her to make such an offer? He bit his tongue lest he shudder visibly. Talon was his superior officer; refusing her was likely a dangerous—and stupid—thing to do, but he saw no other choice. He still didn't. And he couldn't trust her.

But could he trust Cobalt? Stonewall met the captain's gaze again and saw the same sharp edge as always. No weariness; no sorrow. Just duty. Was that what Kali had seen when he'd tried to end their relationship?

How long could she survive here? How long would *he*?

"I wanted someone to know about a potential cure immediately," Stonewall said at last. "And with regards to Parsa, my squad acted in self-defense, but there could still be trouble for us."

"Trouble." Cobalt made a snorting sound that might have been a laugh on any other man. "Aye, because we've little enough of *that* to go around."

Had the captain made a joke? Stonewall kept his expression neutral. "How did the mages escape?"

His squad shifted, exchanging startled glances, though the captain seemed not to notice.

"A breach in the wall," Cobalt replied grimly. "An old blood run, by the look of it. It must have been built when the bastion was, but I've never seen it before, not even on old renderings."

"Ser, what's a blood run?" Milo asked.

"A sodding foolish idea," Cobalt replied.

Beacon cleared his throat. "The bastions were built to keep mages safe from the general population, who didn't fancy the notion of folks able to start fires and such with a wave of their hands. Those folks also believed mage blood would heal any ailment. Mages used to be hunted down and killed because people were frightened of their abilities. So when the queen's grandfather, King Solasar, had the bastions built, he ensured the mages would have an opportunity to flee, should angry, frightened folks storm the gates."

The burnie twins exchanged astonished glances. Stonewall knew how they felt. "The king *wanted* mages to be able to leave?"

"The Circle wouldn't allow that now," Rook said.

The mender shrugged. "It was a different time."

"How in Tor's name did the mages keep this blood run secret?" Stonewall asked the captain.

"No idea." Cobalt sighed. "The worst bit is, we only caught them at the end of their little escape. By then, the Echinas had made it to the outer gates. The other mages were already gone."

"Did they have outside help, ser?" Beacon asked.

Flint nodded. "Last time any mages got out, they got lost. Remember, Mi? Eris Echina didn't know one street from another when we chased her that night."

"Oh, they had help," Cobalt said. "One of those renegade mages we're always trying to root out. By the look of it, he's the same one who stole our last hematite shipment. Sod was acting as a fire-dancer during Heartfire. We also got wind of Sufani—and probably Assembly—folk helping as well, though the dreg in our cells has yet to confirm any of it."

"The renegade is here?" Stonewall asked.

"Aye, Talon's been…questioning him all night." Cobalt's face went blank and his next words were too calm. "Matter-of-fact, he's only said one thing of significance: your name."

Something like a warning prickled the back of Stonewall's neck. *"My name?"*

The captain nodded. "Know any mages from Indigo-By-the-Sea?"

All gazes fell upon Stonewall, but he was at a complete loss. *What in the blazing void is going on?* "No, ser," he managed. "I've never known any mages outside of a bastion. How did he know about the blood run?"

Cobalt's face darkened and his hand sought one of his daggers. "Perhaps you should ask the traitor, yourself."

"Traitor, ser?" Rook asked.

"The dreg used to be a sentinel," Cobalt replied, and Stonewall's heart skidded to a stop.

A sentinel from Indigo-By-the-Sea.

Drake.

Stonewall's vision swam. *No.* His brother had been dead for three sodding years. Whomever Talon held captive was a stranger, nothing more.

"Adding insult to injury," Cobalt was saying, "the dreg *knew* our habits and methods, and used them against us." He spat on the cold ground. "Brother in service, indeed."

Stonewall wanted to ask more questions, but his tongue felt frozen in his mouth. The old danger sense he'd developed as an orphan on the streets now trilled a warning, while *fight* and *run* warred within his body.

The rest of his squad shared his astonishment. Cobalt ignored them, looking back at the mages who had dug Gideon Echina's grave. Having finished their work, they now gathered around the dead mage's body in preparation to lower it into the cold ground.

"Get your report to Talon as soon as possible," Cobalt said to Stonewall. The captain turned abruptly and strode back to the grave site, tossing his next words over his armored shoulder. "In the meantime, follow protocol. Do your duty. Obey your oath."

* * *

None of the squad spoke again until they had reconvened in the stables to tend to their horses. Even then, talk was sparse and perfunctory as

41

the stablemaster, a cinder named Ferro, bustled around the newcomers and their mounts. Only after Ferro had taken their leather tack to the storeroom did Stonewall relax, inhaling the warm scents of horses and hay that were always comforting.

"Was it just me," Flint said as she ran a curry comb down her mount's chestnut neck. "Or did the captain think you were full of shit?"

Stonewall laughed, more out of relief to be in relative safety again than from true amusement. "At least he's consistent."

"Well, it doesn't matter what he thinks," Rook said from a stool beside her horse, Ox, as she brushed his back. "So long as the commander believes you."

Stonewall winced before he could stop himself. The others caught on at once. "What is it?" Beacon asked.

Stonewall briefly debated not sharing the whole story but decided it didn't warrant being kept secret any longer. Still, he chose his words carefully. "By now, you all know about Kali and me. What you don't know is that I…" *This* was harder to convey than he'd realized, but he powered through. "I tried to break it off with Kali not long before Heartfire."

"Why?" Milo asked, brows knitted.

"Because Talon told me she'd have Kali killed if our…relationship continued." The others exchanged stunned looks and Stonewall grimaced. Gods above, he could still see the stricken expression on Kali's face after he had tried to end things between them. Thank Tor they were both too stubborn—or too stupid—to keep apart.

Though Kali might regret that fact one day.

Stonewall shook off his doubts. They had made a commitment to each other, and he'd be damned if he faltered now. He'd chosen a path and he would not deviate from it. But they had both learned by now that they couldn't live here and be *together* as they wanted.

Better shake off that thought, too. It was too vast and too soon. Stonewall fixed his attention on the curry comb and Frost's gray and white dappled coat. "That same night, Talon made her…interest in me clear. I refused her."

Flint made a low whistle. "Ea's balls... Is that why she's had it out for you these past few weeks?"

Stonewall gave the young woman the best smile he could muster. "I'm sure it didn't help."

Flint didn't seem convinced. "Maybe. But she's been a real bitch lately, hasn't she? More so than usual."

"Don't be disrespectful," Milo said. "She's our commander."

"I *do* respect her," Flint replied, shrugging. "But she's still a bitch."

"How's *that* work?" Milo asked.

Beacon cleared his throat. "Did she really threaten us, too?"

"She did," Stonewall said. "I'm sorry. I didn't want the...situation with Kali to affect any of you."

Rook's gaze held nothing but compassion. "Talon's actions are not your fault, Stonewall. She should hold herself to a higher standard."

"Right," Beacon added. "Well, I can't say I'm especially pleased with the commander of late. That business with the Sufani... Capturing a civilian to send to Lasath for questioning." He trailed off, shuddering. "I'm glad you let her go, Stonewall, even if it meant we *failed* our mission."

"*Failed*," Flint echoed, snorting. "That's the official word, I guess."

"But not the *right* word," Milo added.

Stonewall nodded, but thoughts of that "failed" mission brought another face to mind: Drake. Stonewall had *sworn* he'd seen his dead brother among the assembled Sufani his squad had surprised that day. But surely the sight—and the sound of his brother's voice—were tricks of grief. He'd experienced them after Drake's death, though not in some time.

"That order came from Argent," Rook said suddenly. "Not Talon."

Stonewall regarded her. "How'd you know that?" When Talon had given him the order, she had not expressly stated it was from Argent, but it had been implied. But he'd not breathed a word of that to any of his squad.

A flush crept up Rook's freckled cheeks and she turned fully to her horse, brushing harder with each word. "I just assumed. It wasn't Talon's...style."

"Besides," Milo said. "The Sufani weren't exactly innocent if they were the same ones who stole our hematite."

"The Sufani aren't mages," Flint replied. "The sodding local guard should have taken care of them. Why'd *we* get sent?"

"Because of the hematite," Milo shot back.

Stonewall raised his hands. "That's in the past now. Parsa has laid a bigger issue at our feet."

"The Fata have, as well," Beacon replied. "Kali was right; the connection between them and the thralls fits. But it's not looking like Talon will hear you out."

"Where does that leave *us*?" Flint asked.

Beacon stroked his beard. "We might have to take matters into our own hands."

"How?" Rook asked. "Disobey a direct order?" She shook her head, light-brown hair falling loose from her braid. "Insubordination won't end well for us, if High Commander Argent gets involved. Which I've no doubt he will."

Forsworn. The word hung in the air like a storm cloud. Stonewall shivered despite himself. Receiving the label—and having one's sentinel mark burned away—was the worst fate that could befall any sentinel. A life without duty; a life without the camaraderie of the other sentinels or the benedictions of the gods. As the rumors went, it was the lack of purpose that killed quicker than the lack of hematite, though the latter was supposedly excruciating.

But despite the knowledge that had been hammered into Stonewall since he was a lad, anger stirred within his heart. Was coercion the only way Talon knew how to lead?

He would lead differently; he would not blackmail or cajole those under his command. He studied each member of his squad: Beacon, whose intelligence, calm nature, and good humor always shone a light in dark times; Rook, steadfast and quick-witted, always looking out for others; Milo, whose true strength lay not in his body, but in his relentless optimism and gentleness; Flint's cutting wit, bravery, and fierce loyalty. They were a good lot, and right now they were all looking to *him* to lead them through the trials to come.

All their lives were forfeit; it had been so the day they each had woken from their first Burn, the day they had all pledged themselves to the gods. Stonewall could not speak for the others, but what would he make of his life in the meantime?

A conversation with Kali, long since tucked away in the back of his mind, crept to the forefront:

"What does Tor ask of you?"

"Courage. Strength. Unwavering dedication to the path I have chosen."

Simple words, easily given. It would cost so much to live by them. Stonewall measured his next words. "I'm starting to think that some orders should not be followed."

The squad exchanged wary glances, tossing a few over their shoulders to make sure they were alone in the stables. During their conversation, the sentinels had drawn closer together, so that now they stood in a tight circle in the middle of the grooming area. The stables were still quiet, with only the occasional faint sound of a horse shifting in its stall.

Beacon spoke first, his voice hushed. "What are you saying, Stonewall?"

"We all swore an oath," Rook added, also in a whisper.

Courage, Stonewall told his racing heart. "We swore an oath to the *gods,*" he replied softly. "Not to Talon. Not to Argent or the queen. Not to the Circle – or even to the Pillars."

"But that doesn't mean we can do anything we like, simply because we don't agree with our orders," Rook replied. "What good is an oath if it can be twisted to suit whatever fancy catches your mind?"

"Is that what this business with the thralls is to you?" Stonewall replied. "A fancy?" As his conviction solidified, so too did his voice gain strength. "An oath made under duress—like our first Burn—is not to be trusted."

"Aye," Flint added. "And what about what Talon's done with Gideon Echina? I'm no fan of mages, but even *I* know that was wrong."

All color drained from Rook's face, leaving her freckles stark against pale skin, like drops of blood on parchment. She closed her eyes, lips moving in a silent prayer.

A sudden tread of boots made everyone tense. Stonewall glanced up to see Ferro guiding a piebald horse out of the stables. The stablemaster didn't seem to notice the squad at all as he patted the piebald's neck and spoke in low, soothing tones. Once he passed out of earshot, the squad exchanged glances again, faces tight with worry.

"After the last few days, I'm not...opposed to this sort of talk," Beacon added softly. "But we really shouldn't speak of such things here."

"We shouldn't speak of such things at *all*," Rook replied. "If Argent ever finds out–"

"Why are you so terrified of the High Commander?" Flint broke in, frowning at the other woman. "You know something we don't?"

Rook glanced away. "Talon is dangerous, but Argent is..." She shivered. "You don't want to get on his bad side."

"I have no doubt of that," Stonewall replied. "But I'm not certain how much longer I can keep to the path he and Talon are laying out, and still live with myself."

"Because of Mage Halcyon?" Milo asked.

"In part," Stonewall admitted. "But mostly..." He sighed. "Well, this might all be for nothing. Talon might hear me out. Argent might think it's grand that mages want to try and cure thralls."

"You should talk to Talon in person," Beacon offered. "Rather than just submit a report. Even if she has reasons not to like you, she'll hopefully at least listen."

"Sound advice," Stonewall said, although he had his doubts.

Rook swiped at her eyes and gave him a look he couldn't quite read. "Will you talk to her alone?"

His stomach knotted at the thought, but he was loathe to drag any of them into this mess any more than necessary. "Aye. It's for the best."

Flint rolled her eyes. "At least take one of us with you. In case she tries anything funny again."

Despite the jest in her tone, there was an undercurrent of concern that caught Stonewall off-guard. "I'll be fine," he told her. "Really."

Silence reigned until Beacon sighed deeply. "Sod it all, I could really use a burn right about now."

Despite the serious talk, Stonewall gave a weak chuckle. "Aye, me too."

The mender began collecting his grooming supplies, speaking in his normal jovial tone. "It's been a long day. Night. Whatever. Anyway, as squad mender, I say we all need some food and some general spirit lifting. The more spirits, the better."

The others caught on immediately. "Yes, please," Flint said brightly. "I'm starving enough to eat a horse. Not you, boy," she said to her mount. "But really... I could eat lunch, dinner, *and* breakfast."

"I've no doubt," Rook laughed, though her smile faded when she rubbed her arms. "I can't seem to get warm. It would be nice to sit by a fire for a while and just...be."

"You need a burn too, don't you?" Beacon asked her. When she didn't answer, he shot Stonewall a wry look. "Well, that makes two of us. What about you? Or were you just joking a second ago?"

Stonewall considered his own state: chilly, fatigued, yet restless. Probably a product of the previous night and their conversation, but not completely, for he could feel the urge building in the back of his mind. "It's not bad, yet," he said. "But I should probably take my dose in the next week or so."

"Might only be a half-dose," Beacon said grimly. "The rationing's hit us hard. Hopefully we'll get more, soon." He glanced at the burnie twins. "Don't tell me *you* lot need another burn just yet."

"Not us." Flint looked at her brother. "But don't tell me you're not hungry, *relah.*"

Milo shrugged. "I dunno. I guess."

That was troubling; the lad always had a hearty appetite. Stonewall made a mental note to keep an eye on Milo.

Beacon looked at Stonewall. "Ser, I know you like to eat alone, but..."

Despite the honorific, likely spoken out of habit, there was hope in Beacon's voice. Indeed, Rook, Milo, and even Flint regarded Stonewall in the same way. They *wanted* his company.

Stonewall felt a true smile curve his mouth. "I'm in."

* * *

Later, Stonewall said Rook's name as the squad parted ways outside the common room. She gestured to Flint. "Go ahead to the baths. I'll join you in a moment."

When the burnie slipped off, Rook glanced back at Stonewall, a question on her face. Gone was the nervousness she had shown during the squad's earlier discussion. Something inside of Stonewall eased a tiny bit.

"Are you going to tell Talon about...?" He waved a hand in the general direction of the bastion.

Rook did not play coy. She was forthright in her own way. "I've no plans to tell Talon anything."

That tight, coiled part of him eased a little more. "Thank y—"

"But you're an idiot," she interrupted, shaking her head. "To love one of *them*."

He decided to ignore the disdain in her voice. "No arguments there. I just don't want anyone else to be in danger because of it."

Rook's gaze went distant. "Love is the most dangerous foe you will ever face. For while the One shaped our souls, our hearts were not made for magic." She blinked as if to clear her eyes, and regarded him again. "Take me with you when you talk to Talon."

It wasn't a request, but neither was it a demand. Stonewall opened his mouth to object, but thought better of it. Sometimes, it was foolish to turn aside aid freely offered. And it would be good to have an ally with him the next time he spoke to the commander – whenever he could rally his courage.

So he nodded. "I'd appreciate that. Thanks."

Rook gave him a small smile. "You're smarter than you look."

Now he laughed outright. "Not by much."

6

SIX

Birdsong trickled through the darkness, reaching Eris in sleep – if indeed she had been sleeping. Lately, she could not tell the difference between sleep and wakefulness. The latter was usually more uncomfortable; the pressure on her bladder might have had a hand in rousing her this time, too. Her eyes opened reluctantly and fell upon the empty space beside her on the tiny bed.

She closed them again, willing herself back to her dreams, where she could see Gid again. But her body betrayed her, refusing to let her sink back into blissful unconsciousness until she'd attended to basic needs. With a sigh, Eris sat up, and for the first time in recent memory, examined her surroundings. She was in a small, rectangular-shaped room with a single round window above the bed, through which she could see a white sky. So it was daytime, wherever she was. The room was packed to bursting with boxes and baskets, cleverly fitted together to use every bit of available space. Scents of cedar, lavender, and her own less-than pleasant odor hung in the air. How long had she lain here? Where was *here*, exactly?

Sounds of conversation made her peer outside the window to see a Sufani camp. The brightly colored wagons sat around several fires, some with smoking meat or stew; others hosting the nomadic people swathed head to toe in jewel-toned robes. No sign of the other mages, or Leal, for that matter, though surely the Sufani woman was the reason Eris was in one of their wagons.

A small door at the opposite end of the wagon opened and a familiar figure peered inside. The moment Adrie Talar realized Eris was standing, relief swept across the older mage's face. Adrie slipped inside and shut the door behind her.

"Where are we?" Eris asked as Adrie bustled up, balancing a basket on her hip. Fair-haired, Adrie had about twenty summers on Eris. Round cheeks and clear blue eyes gave her a soft appearance, but her gaze upon Eris was discerning.

"According to Leal, somewhere in the outskirts of Whitewater Province," Adrie replied as she set the basket upon the bed. "Far away from Whitewater City, at any rate. We're with Leal's family."

"I gathered."

Adrie studied her. "How are you?"

Eris looked at the window, but saw only the smudges on the glass and nothing of the world beyond. "How do you think?'

"Three days," Adrie said. At Eris' bewildered look, she shook her head. "You were gone for *three* days after Heartfire. We thought..." She began to rummage through the basket. "Let's just say I've never been so relieved to have a sopping wet crow fall in my lap, though I could have done without you changing form immediately. The Sufani didn't know what to make of the naked woman that seemed to drop out of the sky."

Three days. For a mercy, Eris' memory of those days was hazy. Mostly she recalled the rush of wind through her feathers and the endless sky above. Perhaps crow impressions were simpler than human ones. But no matter how high or how far she had flown, she had not been able to escape her grief.

"How long have I been here?" Eris asked.

"Just a day. You found us yesterday morning."

One day? It felt like longer.

Adrie withdrew a clean set of clothes and various foodstuffs from the basket, chattering away to distract them both. "I've made myself useful here, as much as I can. Wish I'd been able to bring some of my good pots and pans, but I can always find more. I've some bread and cheese for you, and some sort of dried fruit Leal's mother gave us, though it's a bit tart for my liking. You must be famished."

"I have to piss," Eris said.

"No doubt." Adrie held out a clean tunic and a thick, dark-green cloak. "I'll show you to the women's latrine. It's hardly more than a secluded spot in the forest, but no snakes have bitten my ass, so I suppose that's the height of luxury out here."

Eris studied the tunic before glancing down at what she had been wearing: a cotton shirt that billowed to her knees and ripped wool leggings. She'd lost her original clothes when she'd shifted to crow-shape, so someone must have put her in these when she'd returned.

She looked back at Adrie. "It doesn't matter what I look like."

"But you look like you fell out of a tree. You're filthy and your hair is full of knots."

Eris ran a hand through her long black hair – or tried, as it was matted and tangled beyond repair. She pulled out a small black feather, which she twirled between her forefinger and thumb before shaking her head. "I don't care, Adrie. I just have to piss."

"You'll feel better with fresh clothes. And you'll need boots as well, if you're to be traipsing through the brambles." Adrie hesitated, then placed a gentle hand on Eris' arm. "I know it hurts, love, but you must take care of yourself – and the little one."

Dread swept through Eris' veins. How would shape-changing affect the new life growing in her womb? She closed her eyes in concentration and searched for the particles of her unborn child. If she'd harmed hers and Gid's baby with her magic…

"Everything's well," she said, eyes stinging with relief. "But I don't know if that will always be the case. I don't know of another mage who can shape-change."

"Nor do I," Adrie replied, offering the tunic again. "So you must take care."

Eris changed quickly and tugged on a sturdy but too-small pair of boots, then followed Adrie out of the caravan and into the pale daylight. The sky was white and heavy with snow; the clean, sharp scent promised nasty weather, and soon. Eris kept pace with Adrie as the other mage led them through the half a dozen or so scattered caravans and campfires, and the nomads who lived among them. All eyes followed the mages' progress, but Eris ignored them.

As Adrie had said, the latrine was rustic, but Eris didn't complain. Once she'd finished, the two mages made their way back to the main body of the camp. Now, Eris found some interest in the faces they passed; she didn't care about the Sufani, only the other mages from Whitewater Bastion who had escaped with her and–

"Where are the others?' she asked.

Adrie pointed ahead, to a caravan Eris had not noticed before, tucked away at the perimeter. "They're together, mostly. Everyone's been worried about you, but I've tried to keep them at bay. I thought…you might not want company right now."

The hesitation in Adrie's voice made Eris look at her. "Thank you," she said, managing to sound like she meant it. "But I'd like to see them."

Adrie frowned. "Now? Are you certain? Don't you want something to–"

"I can eat and talk to my friends at the same time," Eris interrupted. Sod it all, she spoke too harshly, and the other mage's frown deepened. Eris tried and failed to find an apology, and instead added, "I need to know they're all right."

Brightness welled in Adrie's eyes but her reply was brisk. "Aye. Of course. They're all fine, for what it's worth."

A prickle of unease ran up Eris' spine. "What's wrong?"

Adrie glanced around at the Sufani who watched the mages, stepping aside to give both women a wide berth. The mages passed by a male Sufani holding a small child; the child waved, but the man grabbed her arm and turned them both away, speaking to her in low, harsh tones.

"They don't like us," Adrie whispered. "Well, some of them don't. Apparently, Leal's parents lead this group, but Leal never asked for permission to bring the lot of us back here. She argued with her mother and father for hours after we arrived. I'm not sure they've exchanged more than a handful of words since."

Eris' unease flared into anger so hot and fierce it caught her by surprise. Yet, she was *not* surprised to learn that even these Sufani nomads—considered outcasts by most of Aredia—did not want mages in their midst. "Have the Sufani been hostile to you or the others?"

"No, nothing like that." Adrie sighed. "Well, you can see how they feel about us."

Eris glanced to her other side, where a trio of Sufani women watched her and Adrie's progress through their camp. At her look, the women shifted uncomfortably, muttering to one another. Eris scowled at them before facing forward. "The feeling is mutual."

The other mages had clustered together around the wagon they must have used to escape the city, which made Eris wonder whose caravan she had recuperated in. But before she could puzzle that out, Cai spotted her. The brown-haired young man, who had been Gideon's closest friend in the bastion, nudged the mages beside him and they all rose to greet her. The next thing Eris knew, Cai had bounded forward and swept her into a massive embrace, pulling her off her feet. When he set her down, he gripped her shoulders and met her gaze. His tan skin was flushed and his eyes were red-rimmed.

"Those sodding guards," he said between clenched teeth. "Eris, I swear to you… I'll avenge his death."

Eris' throat tightened and she could do no more than nod in reply. Marcen greeted her next, fair skin seeming gray in the morning light. He offered her a quick hug, adding in a whisper, "I'm so sorry."

"Me too," Eris managed.

Sirvat embraced her then, the pregnant mage's swollen belly brushing against Eris, reminding her of her own condition. Eris made her way through the remaining seven mages, who all expressed their condolences over Gideon and offered either promises of revenge or words of sympathy. Eris accepted both, but neither stuck in her mind. Revenge or sympathy… Neither would bring her husband back to life.

Someone handed her a bowl of broth and a hunk of bread, and she sat beside the fire among her allies as they shared their experiences on Heartfire. "Cai wanted to turn back for you and Gideon," Adrie said, seated beside Eris. "But there were too many city guards and sentinels. And...we truly thought you were dead."

"That sodding guard flung you over the bridge," Cai said when Adrie trailed off. Unlike the others, he paced back and forth by the fire. "No one saw you change, so we feared the worst until you found us yesterday."

"How *did* you find us?" Marcen asked.

Despite the chunks of vegetables and the scent of spices, the soup tasted like nothing. The bread was hard. Eris almost set both aside until she thought of her unborn child. Resolutely, she dipped the bread into the broth and let the liquid soak through.

"I don't know," she admitted. "I don't remember much after..."

The fire danced before her, snapping at the chill air. Had the hemies burned Gideon's body? Or had they buried her husband in the ground to rot away, to be eaten by worms and maggots? Tears pricked her eyes and she stared down at the squash and potatoes floating in her bowl. A warm hand on her back made her look up to see Marcen's soft smile. Despite herself, Eris found the expression comforting, because Mar was *alive.* Her friends were alive – and free.

All but one.

Movement in the forest caught Eris' attention: a pearly gray mourning dove, cooing softly in the shadows of an oak tree. Unexpectedly, images of Kali came to Eris' mind's eye: Kali grinning at her when they were girls in Starwatch Bastion, after having pilfered sweetrolls from the kitchens; Kali weeping in the garden at Whitewater Bastion only a few days ago, wracked with grief over some sodding sentinel she'd been foolish enough to love.

"We couldn't have made it out of the city without Leal," Adrie was saying. "After Drake got captured, she ensured we all reached the caravan safely, then drove us herself until we reached her family."

Drake. Eris had not forgotten the renegade mage, but the sound of his name brought more memories flooding back: Drake fighting alone with nothing but a spear to keep the sodding sentinels at bay so Eris and Gid could escape; Drake leading them through the city streets, twirling his fire-tipped staff trying to draw all attention away from the mages. He had risked everything to help her and her friends. Now he was the hemies' prisoner.

Eris looked around the Sufani camp. "Where is Leal?"

"Scouting for hemies, I think," Cai replied. "That's about all she's been doing since we arrived."

"No sign of them yet," Marcen added. "But I don't expect our luck to hold. We must be on the move, and soon."

Eris nodded absently and took a careful bite of her bread, little more than warm mush now from being soaked. But she already felt better. She glanced at Adrie again. "You said Leal and her parents quarreled?"

Adrie nodded. "Aderey and Ytel—Leal's father and mother—were not expecting to see their daughter return with nearly a dozen mages. They were under the impression that the Assembly would be taking us on." Her forehead creased. "I still can't believe those heretics have the nerve to turn up their noses at *us*."

"They should be our allies," Marcen added. "None of us have any love for the Circle."

"The Circle is wrong to treat us how they do," Adrie replied as a few others muttered agreement. "But the gods are still real. *All* of them. Not just the One, as the Sufani believe."

"Enough." Eris held up her hand and all talk ceased. "Now is not the time to turn against one another; now is the time for unity. Regardless of what each of us believes, we are all mages. Whether that power was granted by blood, by nature, or," she fought not to roll her eyes, "a god, doesn't matter. We are all the same, inside. Now, why have you all not fled south, like we planned?"

Marcen, Adrie, and the others exchanged startled glances. Cai rolled his eyes. "Why do you think, Eris-the-Crow?"

Heat crept to her cheeks and she took another bite of soupy bread to disguise her shock and embarrassment, though she should not have felt either. Gideon wouldn't have; she could see the gleam of pride in his beautiful dark eyes, hear his wry voice. *They stayed for you, love. Don't let them down.*

"Thank you," she stammered as Adrie took her empty bowl. "But you shouldn't linger. You must leave the province at once."

Adrie studied her. "Why does it sound like you're not coming with us?"

The others broke into startled confusion, but Eris wasn't flustered. "Because I have unfinished business in Whitewater Bastion."

"What do you mean?" Cai asked.

Eris only looked at him.

Marcen caught on first. "You mean to go back for Kali."

"And Drake," Eris said, nodding. "He's one of us, too. And there are others who deserve another chance at freedom."

"You mean the hemie-lovers who refused to leave?" Cai asked. "Why risk our necks for them?"

"Not everyone refused to leave," Eris said. "Because not everyone could be trusted with the offer in the first place."

The others exchanged glances again, faces grim and concerned, but Cai shook his head. "We didn't ask because we could guess that most of the other mages wouldn't have wanted to come with us."

"Kali wanted to," Eris told him. "But the hemies took her away at the last minute." She did not mention Kali's sentinel lover; that shame was Kali's alone, and not Eris' secret to tell. "Besides, Drake is there, too."

"Aye, no doubt shackled with hematite and stuffed in a cell," Adrie said. "How can we get to him?"

"I don't know," Eris admitted. "But we must find a way." She surveyed the others. "You are all free now. None of you need follow me any longer. Especially back to the place we fought to escape."

More nervous glances were exchanged; Eris noted a few who seemed truly frightened, while others—including Cai, Adrie, and Marcen—wore expressions of grim determination.

Out of the corner of her eye, Eris saw someone standing in the shadow of the caravan. Only when the figure pulled down her hood did Eris recognize

Leal. The Sufani woman jerked her chin at Eris in a silent request. "Think about it," Eris said, getting to her feet. "I'll be right back."

She met Leal beside the caravan. The Sufani was tall and lean, and an indigo mask and cowl covered her forehead, nose, and mouth, leaving only her light-green eyes visible. Her appearance was a marked contrast with how she'd looked when Eris had first met her during Heartfire. Then, Leal and Drake had been clad in the guise of fire-dancers: spare leather garments that left little to the imagination.

"I don't have the right words," Eris told her. "'Thank you' seems paltry in light of what you did for us, but I suppose it must do."

Leal shook her head. "Save your thanks. I don't come with good news."

Behind her, Eris could see the other Sufani milling about their camp as they gathered supplies and covered their campfires with dirt. More than a few shot the two women looks Eris couldn't read, but she understood anyway. "You're leaving."

"Aye. It's time to head south, where the weather is not so harsh."

Eris nodded. "I heard of the...trouble we've caused."

"Not just you," Leal replied, grimacing. "Drake's Assembly friends turned against him when they discovered he was a mage, and left him to free you on his own. When he was captured, I had no other choice but to bring you here." She sighed. "My parents are...unhappy."

"They're not alone in that."

"They do not wish your people to remain among us," Leal added.

Eris bit back a swell of anger, for Leal was not at fault. Instead, she surveyed the Sufani again, though her attention was elsewhere. "Could Aderey and Ytel be convinced to let some of my people travel with them? Sirvat is heavy with child, and I fear the coming days will be too treacherous for her."

Leal considered. "I don't know. Perhaps." She snorted. "Da has a soft heart. He might be swayed."

"I know you've done so much for us already, but please ask."

"Very well. How many do you speak of?"

Eris thought of the mages who had seemed reluctant to come with her.

Sirvat was the most pressing, but Gaspar had a bad back and Lyn was so young... "Three, at least."

"Not so many," Leal replied thoughtfully. "But what will the rest of you do?"

A cold wind lifted Eris' matted hair and stole beneath her tunic, but she ignored the chill. Wind was flight's ally, after all. "We're going back to the city."

Leal's eyes widened. "For Drake?"

"Aye, and a friend of mine who couldn't come before." Would Gid have made this choice? She thought so. He'd spoken so highly of Drake, and any friend of Gid's was a friend of hers. Gideon was—had been—the champion of those he had loved. He'd never held a sword, but he had fought every day to make the other mages' lives better.

Her throat went tight as grief stung her eyes again. Both feelings, she pushed down. Later. She could grieve for her husband later. Now, she had work to do.

"Seven mages against a sentinel garrison," Leal said slowly. "Those aren't good odds."

"They've never been." Eris lifted a hand and concentrated until sleek, black feathers bloomed along her fingers. Although she was tired from her days-long ordeal as a crow, the change still came quickly and with relative ease. Another chill wind tickled the pinions with the promise of flight. Eris smiled. "But we're not helpless."

Leal's gaze caught on the new feathers, her eyes wide. But her words were hard as iron. "Once the sentinels get more hematite, you might be singing another song."

"Which means I must act quickly." Eris lowered her hand and urged the feathers to recede. "When will your family leave?"

They both looked toward the Sufani camp. In the few minutes the two women had spoken, the nomads had eliminated all traces of their presence in this copse of trees. A few wagons still needed horses or oxen hitched, but beyond that, Eris thought the Sufani would be ready to leave right away.

Leal squared her shoulders. "Come with me."

She started off before Eris could speak, her long stride quick. Eris followed, threading back through the Sufani wagons, until they reached a bright purple caravan. A slip of a girl leaned against the side, drawing a bow across the strings of a viol. The sound was akin to the screech of a dying cat, but all Eris could think of was Kali learning to play a similar instrument, years ago.

When the girl spotted Leal and Eris, she lowered her bow and said something in Sufa, the nomads' language. Leal replied in kind, gesturing in the direction of Whitewater City, then added in Aredian, "Where are they?"

The girl's eyes flickered to Eris and she replied in Sufa. Unlike Leal, her face was exposed; her features were not as angular as Leal's, but were similar enough to denote a connection by blood. A sister, most likely.

Leal shook her head at the girl's answer. "Dianthe, just tell me where they are."

Dianthe replied with what sounded like scolding in Sufa, and then added, "Mama's inside." She jerked her thumb to the wagon at her back. "Da's helping to fix one of the other caravans." She looked at Eris again. "This was the one you let sleep in your wagon."

Well, that was one mystery solved.

"Observant as ever, I see," Leal replied.

The girl stuck her tongue out at Leal, then studied Eris with interest. "You were a bird."

"Aye. A crow," Eris said.

Dianthe's eyes, green like her sister's, widened. "Can you do that again?"

"Ignore her," Leal replied, stepping forward to rap on the caravan's purple door, speaking again in Sufa.

The door opened to reveal a woman with high cheekbones, dark eyes, and tanned skin. The moment Ytel's gaze fell upon Eris, she swore in Sufa and tugged her crimson hood so it concealed as much of her face as possible. "Why have you brought *her* here, Leal?"

Eris bristled, but Leal's reply was easy as she explained the mages' situation. To Ytel's credit, she listened without interruption, but Eris knew the Sufani woman had already made up her mind. Indeed, when Leal finished, Ytel exhaled hard enough to ruffle her hood. "You know we cannot take outsiders with us. Bad enough we must cover ourselves in their presence."

"That is our choice," Leal replied. "I have gone uncovered among the *kotahi*, and suffered no harm."

"Not yet," Ytel muttered, her gaze still on Eris. "But your life is your own. No, they cannot come with us. And don't even think of asking your father," she added sharply. "You know he'll honor my decision."

Leal nodded, shoulders sinking, but Eris was in no mood to concede. "Thank you for letting my people remain with you while I rested, ser. I know our presence is troubling for your family. But *my* family has been held captive for most of their lives; all we seek now is freedom."

Ytel gestured to the sky. "You have it, thanks to my daughter."

"Not all of us," Eris replied. "Some of my friends were left behind. I intend to rectify that. But not everyone whom your daughter aided is fit for such trials. I humbly ask that you allow them to travel in your company for a few more days, until they are in safer country."

Once they left Whitewater Province, the odds of truly escaping the sentinels increased tenfold. No doubt Talon would have every sentinel garrison on the alert, but it would take a week or more for fleet riders to carry the messages across all of Aredia. Sirvat and the others had time – if only a paltry amount.

"The Circle hates us already," Ytel replied. "Do you know what they'll do to us if they find we're harboring renegade mages? Any excuse to," her gaze flickered to Dianthe, listening raptly, "harm us, they will take. Happily."

"My own grandmother is of the Circle," Eris said. "And hers was the loudest voice that called for me to be sent away to a bastion when I was no older than Dianthe. Yes, ser, I know what the Circle does to those it deems 'heretic,' but they're wrong and I choose to fight back. It's time someone did."

She saw Leal watching her out of the corner of her eye, but her attention was only for Ytel, who met her gaze with granite. At last, though, the older woman nodded once. "Your mage friends can travel with us for three more days, but they must stay inside your caravan as much as possible," she added, looking at Leal. "I'll not have another one contaminated by *kotahi*."

Sweet relief flooded Eris' limbs and she could not help her smile. Seren's light, she had needed a victory. She bowed low, suddenly conscious of her matted hair and disheveled appearance. How wild she must seem, especially given her less-than-conventional entrance to the Sufani camp. Well, mages were part of their precious One god's world. These Sufani had best learn to get used to magic.

Even so, she ensured her reply was warm and genuine. "Thank you, ser."

Ytel harrumphed. "Don't make me regret it."

With that, she slammed the door shut in Eris' face, but Eris was too elated to care. Three of her people would be safe. Now, she had to make sure the others could say the same. She stepped away from the wagon and glanced at Leal. "Thank you, too."

"What will you do now?" Leal asked.

Eris squinted up at the sky. She needed rest. She needed time to plan. Beyond that, she didn't know. "I must speak with the others again."

Leal nodded and they began to walk back to the mages, Dianthe and her viol at their heels. "When will you return to the city?" Leal asked.

"I haven't worked that part out yet," Eris admitted.

"Within a couple of days?"

"Probably not."

"Good." Leal paused beside her caravan, the one Eris had woken up in. "I'll leave this in your keeping, then, until I return."

Both Eris and Dianthe goggled at her. "Return from where?" Eris asked.

Leal's pale green eyes seemed gray in the morning light. "From my own mission."

"You're not coming with us?" Dianthe asked, clutching her viol with white knuckles. "Mama will—"

"As Mama said, my life is my own," Leal broke in. Her voice softened as she knelt to meet the girl's eyes. "You are nearly grown, Dia. Now is not the time for fear. You must be strong, for them and for yourself. Do you understand?"

Dianthe sniffed, but nodded, then murmured something in Sufa. Leal's eyes crinkled with her smile and she embraced the girl, murmuring a reply. Feeling intrusive, Eris looked away, but neither Sufani seemed to mind her presence. When the sisters parted, Dianthe looked at Eris. "Make sure she doesn't die."

Eris tried to summon a genuine smile, but knew it didn't reach her eyes. But Leal scoffed and waved one of her gloved hands in a gesture of dismissal. "I can take care of myself."

After Dianthe slipped back to the other Sufani, Eris looked at Leal. "Where are you going? What mission?"

The Sufani woman lifted her chin. "To improve your odds."

7

SEVEN

Foley awoke, gasping, to pounding thunder and boots outside of his door. It was difficult to catch his breath with the leather collar tight around his neck. In those first heartbeats of wakefulness, he was back in his old quarters in the bastion at Lasath, with Isra by his side and their little girl huddled between them. But no. He was *here* and *now*, in Whitewater Bastion. He was alone. He blinked to reorient mind and memory, and threw back the blankets, getting to his feet just as his door opened and Talon swept into his room.

She stood a few paces inside the doorway, backlit by one of the torches in the corridor. She, too, was alone, with her helmet tucked in the crook of her arm. "I was told you wanted to speak with me."

"Aye," Foley replied, as mildly as he could. "Three days ago, immediately after Heartfire." *Yet you come to me now.*

"I've been busy."

They stood facing each other, neither speaking. Rain drummed outside, as it had all night and the better part of the previous day. Foley studied the sentinel commander as best he could in the restless torchlight. The shadows beneath her eyes were darker than he'd seen in a long time, and she was paler than usual. Her hand trembled upon her dagger grip.

Despite everything else, he still loved her. Foolish old man, indeed. "How long has it been since your last burn?" he asked, stepping toward her.

She did not acknowledge his words other than to slightly incline her head. This close, he could see how her entire body trembled beneath her armor, and how her forehead gleamed with sweat.

"Too long, I think," he added when she did not reply.

"You did not beg an audience with me to ask such a thing."

There was urgency in her voice, but also a more desperate, fearful edge. Against Foley's better judgment, his heart tightened in sympathy, though he kept his own reply cool. "Has the breach been sealed?"

"The masons finished yesterday."

"Good. When will the collars be removed? When will we be allowed to freely walk through the bastion once more?"

"When I can trust you. So perhaps never."

He took a step closer and pitched his voice low, more out of habit than because he thought they'd be overheard. It was too early for anyone else to be awake, and she had come here alone. "You can always trust me."

Her jaw clenched. "Did you know, beforehand?"

No reason to play coy or pretend he did not understand. "No."

Her eyes—dark like her mother's—narrowed. Only in anger did she remind him so much of Isra. "How is that possible? You are the First Mage. You know *everything* that happens here."

Foley tilted his arms as if revealing that he held no weapon; the hook that replaced his right hand gleamed in the torchlight. "Apparently not." When she scoffed, he shook his head. "It is precisely because I am First Mage and steward of the bastion that Eris and," he could not bring himself to say Gideon's name, "her friends did not care for me. They rarely spoke to me unless in anger or derision. I have told you that."

Her lip curled in a sneer. "Even so, you should still have *known* what they were planning. You should have paid more attention. You should have–"

"What's done is done," he broke in. "Eris, Cai, and the others have made their choices. I've no doubt they will be found and dealt with as you see fit. In the meantime," he added more gently, "the mages who made the choice to remain, who showed respect for the gods and your sentinels, should not be punished for the actions of those renegades. Nor should the people

64

of this province be denied magical assistance, particularly in these trying times."

Talon's forehead creased. Much of her earlier hostility had fled from her face, leaving only curiosity. "What do you mean?"

"Kalinda and Sadira described Parsa quite vividly. Kali believes she can cure a thrall, if given the opportunity."

"The sergeant who accompanied them submitted a report with similar speculation. But I have not yet spoken to him. I have...doubts about the truth of his words."

"Is he not trustworthy?"

She did not answer immediately. "He has a history with Mage Halcyon."

Ah. Sergeant Stonewall, then. Kalinda had not mentioned his presence. "You think the two of them are trying to find ways to be together?"

"I don't know what the sergeant's playing at," Talon replied, pinching the bridge of her nose in a rare display of weariness. "Nor the mage. I have other, more pressing matters on my shoulders than the misguided romance between a mage and a sentinel. Stonewall knows the consequences of his actions if he steps out of line again. I have no doubt he'll ultimately make the right choice."

Her tone left no room for discussion, so Foley moved on. "I'm sure, one way or another, you'll get to the heart of this. But in the meantime, it seems the thrall attacks are increasing in number and ferocity. The people will need mages to heal their wounds, regrow their crops, and purify their wells."

Talon had started shaking her head halfway through his speech. "Where magic is concerned, the Circle will decide what the people of Whitewater Province need."

Foley's heart sank at the renewed, rigid set of her shoulders and the iron in her voice. "So we are truly prisoners here," he could not help but say.

Perhaps that reality had never been anything else, but this was the first moment he had felt the truth so keenly.

The sentinel commander regarded him. "You will all be permitted to leave the dormitories," she said at last. "More than that, I cannot allow."

"But the collars—"

"Shall remain in place." She straightened, her gaze turning hard. "You should be grateful."

Grateful. The word struck an old wound within him, unfurling one of those memories he tried so hard to tuck away. His right arm ached with a phantom pain and his own pleas echoed in the back of his mind. He could feel his wife's weight as she lay dying in his arms.

And through it all, a sentinel's voice, hard and cold as hematite. *"You should be grateful I have spared your miserable life."*

"And Gideon?" Foley heard himself ask.

Talon lifted her chin. "That matter has been laid to rest."

Perhaps if she'd phrased her reply differently, he might not have reacted so strongly. Perhaps if she'd shown even the smallest trace of the sweet, shy girl he'd once carried on his shoulders, he might have forgiven her for those cruel words. But she did neither and anger flamed in his heart.

Foley stepped forward again, so that she was within arm's reach. He balled his left hand into a fist. "You disgrace yourself and those under your command. You shame the gods themselves with such a barbaric act. You are a coward."

The words landed with the force of a blow; her eyes widened and she took a step backward. But she banished all traces of surprise, and anger replaced all other emotions as she faced him. "You dare to call *me* a coward, when you watched your own wife die without lifting a hand to save her? When you let your child be ripped from your side, with no argument?"

The anger within him burned everything away but his grief. "As you strive to remind me every day, I had no choice."

"Everything I do, everything I have done, is to protect you..." Her mouth tightened and she caught herself. "I work for the greater good of this province. There must be some of us who will protect those who cannot protect themselves."

The One's ways were mysterious, for Foley could not help his laughter, though it was a bitter, fragmented sound. "Protect? Is that what you think you do?"

"That is what I *know* I do."

He shook his head. "Then you are a foolish girl, Talaséa."

"That girl is dead." She turned to leave.

The flame of anger had extinguished, leaving him cold and dark as an empty hearth. *Alone.* Just as Talon made to cross the threshold, Foley caught her armored elbow. She froze.

"Aye," he said when she did not look at him. "She was killed by a sentinel."

Now the commander turned, pinning him with eyes as black as a crow's wing. "What's done is done. I have made my choice."

And his daughter was gone.

* * *

Word spread quickly through the bastion. Barely an hour after Foley's meeting with his daughter, he stood with the others outside the dormitories, watching the sentinels retreat. The armored figures weren't gone, of course. Squads now patrolled the top of the bastion wall on a regular basis, and the patrols within the bastion itself were more frequent than they'd ever been. Even as one squad left, after having spent all night standing guard outside the mage dormitories, another entered the gates to start their patrol.

After being trapped for three days, most of the mages chose to spend the day outside, despite the intermittent cold rain. Foley was not immune from this desire. He dressed in his warmest cloak, prepared a mug of his favorite tea, and slipped to his garden. Among the quiet sleep of plants bedded down for winter, he found a measure of peace. But he could not remain here forever. He had work to do.

He made his way to the bastion's chicken coop, the one Eris had always tended. Aside from the chickens, the bastion housed a few goats used for milk and the transportation of goods. Most of the bastion's perishables—like meat—were brought in from the city, paid for by the mages' output of valuable glass or healing abilities.

Someone had beaten him to the coop. Foley recognized Kalinda

Halcyon's cloak: indigo that faded to pale blue at the hood. She stood just outside the fence, tossing handfuls of grains and seeds to the rust and white speckled hens that clustered together. As Foley approached, he said her name, but as was her fashion, she seemed lost in her own thoughts. Only when he was beside her did she spot him, and all but jumped out of her cloak in surprise.

"Foley!"

"Good morning, Kalinda," he said, smiling.

Color rose to her cheeks and she smiled back. "'Morning. I can't quite say it's 'good,' though."

He chuckled. "Nor, I suppose, should I." He gestured to the hens, bustling near Kalinda's boots. "They appreciate your efforts, at least."

"I wasn't sure if anyone was feeding them while we were…" She didn't finish the thought.

"That's kind of you," he said. "And it helps me a great deal. Would you mind tending them from now on?"

"Not at all."

"Good. Thank you. With our numbers reduced to nearly half, I'm afraid everyone will have to work a bit harder to keep life going normally."

Kalinda looked back at the chickens as she tossed another handful of feed. "If it ever was normal to begin with."

Out of the corner of his eye, Foley spotted a sentinel squad approaching. If Kalinda noticed, she did not react other than to sprinkle more grain among the hens.

"Not the kitchens," she said suddenly, making him look back at her. At his frown of confusion, she added, "Don't make me work in the kitchens. You'll regret it."

"How so?"

"The cooks back at Starwatch banned me from the kitchen after one too many burned pies. And there may have been an…incident with a week's worth of potatoes that wound up charred…and on the roof."

Foley lifted a brow. "So they banned you with good cause."

"No, I'm just a casualty of circumstance," she replied as the sentinels drew closer.

He chuckled, but could no longer ignore the sentinels' presences. Despite being a mage, the sight of their weapons had never bothered him as much as it did now. The squad passed Gideon's grave; Foley noted how each sentinel glanced at the mound of earth, but no one paused. His stomach turned and the collar felt even tighter around his neck. What he would give for it to be gone!

"I keep thinking about Eris," Kalinda said. All the feed she had brought was scattered on the ground and she clutched the empty sack with white knuckles. "I hope she's alive. You didn't hear anything else, did you?"

"No," he said. "But she's...resourceful. I'm sure she's fine." He knew that bitterness tinged his words, but he didn't care. "More so than we are."

Kalinda looked up at him, though her gaze immediately flickered over his shoulder to follow the sentinels' progress. Her own leather collar moved with her quickened breath. "We're alive," she said. "That's more than some can say."

"There are worse fates than death."

"You sound like Eris."

This stung more than it should have, and he frowned at the girl. "Eris and her friends made their choice and left us to deal with the repercussions."

"Aye, but Eris did what she thought was right," Kalinda said. "I don't blame her."

"Would you have left, too?"

She stared at him, and then looked at the bastion gates. "What are we going to do about Gideon?"

This caught Foley off guard. "What is there to be done?"

"I don't know." She toyed with the collar around her neck. "But he deserves better."

"I'm afraid we have no other choice but to accept Commander Talon's judgment." How he hated to shape the words, but they were truth.

The sound of boots on the hard ground was clearer now that the sentinels were only about ten yards away. The sentinels didn't march, but still strode with grace and precision. Every movement revealed years of training with the weapons they bore. *They are our enemies.* Foley had believed that every day of his life; he believed it now, although he didn't want to. But even his daughter could not erase a lifetime of perception.

Kalinda watched them, hope clear on her face as the squad approached. When they drew closer, however, her shoulders sank. Foley studied her, mindful of his and Talon's conversation that morning, and when Kalinda noticed his attention, her expression shifted to neutrality.

After the sentinels had passed, Foley cleared his throat, drawing her attention. "You still love him, don't you?"

Dark eyes widened, but only briefly before they fixed upon him. "Why would I, after what he did to me?"

Stars and moons, she was a dreadful liar, but Foley played along. "Good. He would have brought you nothing but trouble."

"He already has," she replied, twisting the sack in her hand. "I can hardly believe how foolish I was."

Odd. She sounded quite sure of herself, more so than if she was dissembling. Foley considered questioning her further about the sergeant, but found that he, like his daughter, had more important matters weighing on his mind. *Let it go, for now,* he told himself. So he kept his voice gentle. "We are all foolish, sometimes. The trick is not to let anyone else suffer because of it." When she did not reply other than to nod, he gestured back to the dormitories. "I had an opportunity to organize my books, at least. I found my copy of Artéa Arvad's journal. Did you still want to–"

"Yes," she interjected, nodding eagerly. "I'd love to read it. Thank you." After making the arrangements, she turned out the linen sack to be sure it was empty. "All done. I suppose I'd best find some other way to be useful."

8

EIGHT

A s Talon guided her mount down the road toward Whitewater City's outer gates, her armor weighed on her more than it ever had. The quiet clop of hooves sounded behind her, but none of the sentinels accompanying her had spoken more than a handful of words since they had stopped their search for the night. Even now, more sentinel squads ranged farther afield, scouring the province for any sign of the mages, but Talon held little hope. Five days had passed since Heartfire with not one escaped mage sighted since. If the sentinels had not found the mages by now, chances were they never would. Five days was plenty of time for the magic-users to get a damned good head start.

Gone, too, was the hope of a quick resolution to this dilemma. Thank the One she still had the renegade mage in the garrison's cells. Without him, she did not want to think what Argent would do to those left in the bastion.

The chill had already seeped through Talon's gear and numbed every patch of exposed skin. Longings for a warm bath and a mug of tea vied for attention, but she could allow neither to gain dominance. Whitewater City stood silhouetted in twilight as the last pale hints of the sun eased beneath a veil of inky blue. Waning Seren had set some time ago, but Atal, little more than a curved sliver, brushed the distant mountains as the moon descended to the horizon. A distant rush of water announced the White

71

River, although Talon could not yet see the bridge that spanned it.

"Commander." Talon glanced beside her to see Sergeant Stonewall guiding his dapple-gray mare closer. Rook, his scout, rode on his other side, while the rest of his squad trailed several horse lengths behind them. At Talon's look, both Stonewall and his squad-mate straightened in their saddles, but only the officer spoke again in his lilting, southern accent. "May I have a word with you, ser?"

"You may," she replied.

His horse fell in step with her own mount, a sturdy chestnut mare, and for a few moments, the horses walked side by side while the sergeant seemed to consider his words. Talon rolled her eyes beneath her helmet. "Just spit it out, Sergeant," she said at last. "None of us are getting any younger."

"Have you read my report on Parsa, ser?" he replied.

"I have." Talon cast him a sideways glance. "The Circle sent a contingent of local guards to verify your story."

Light-brown eyes widened beneath his helmet. "What did they find?"

She fought the urge to shudder. "Only the dead remained at Parsa."

Stonewall lowered his head and murmured a quiet prayer, adding, "I feared as much. I hoped otherwise, but…" He trailed off and looked back at her. "Did anyone…recover the bodies of those villagers in the forest?"

"Aye. Everyone who called Parsa home has been sent to their next lives." Talon exhaled a stream of fog. "It was a grim scene, by all accounts."

"It was. But something good came out of it. One of the mages believes–"

"She can cure a thrall," she interrupted. "Yes, I know what you reported."

Stonewall shifted, his saddle creaking. "With respect, ser, I only see one solution. We must allow the mages to try. If they succeed, we could put a stop to this evil taking over our country."

The sentinels approached a curve in the road, the forest closing in on either side, blocking the view of Whitewater City. Once they passed the bend, the trees would recede enough to allow the city to show itself. Soon, they would be home. The knowledge brought little comfort. "A noble desire, Stonewall," Talon said. "But self-serving, too."

They passed the curve in the road and Whitewater City rose into view once more. The river's roar was clearer now and the lanterns on the bridge ahead glowed like yellow stars. Talon kept her gaze forward but still heard the frown in Stonewall's voice. "Ser?"

"The mage who *believes* she can cure the thralls is Kalinda Halcyon. Right?"

He was silent.

Idiot, she wanted to snap. *You think you can keep your heart from me?* But a glance at Rook, who rode in earshot, kept Talon's reply less forceful than she would have liked. "Did you forget our discussion?"

"No," he shot back, with a vehemence that startled her. "I haven't forgotten our *discussion*, Commander. Nor could I if I wanted to."

Rook cleared her throat, and the sergeant's next words were more measured. "My...history with Kalinda—Mage Halcyon—aside, she attempted an act of magic that could save many innocent lives. Add that to the fact that the Cipher we found wore enough hematite to outfit my entire squad, and I don't see how anyone can blame this mess on the mages. We're their custodians; it's our duty to see this through."

Talon stared at him, struck by the defiant set of his jaw and the conviction glinting in his eyes. Both were familiar, but not just because she had seen them in his face before. Another face came to her mind's eye and her heart skidded to a halt when she realized the renegade mage in the garrison had worn that exact same expression when she had questioned him.

The two men were connected somehow, most likely by blood. But did Stonewall know it? He had never mentioned any relatives, so she had assumed he, like many sentinels, was alone in the One's world. Another thought coiled like a snake in her belly. Had Stonewall known about the mage escape? Had he taken part, somehow? Perhaps he'd meant to run away with his mage lover. Perhaps they had meant to flee from Parsa together, but the thralls had changed their plans.

Stonewall was a fool to throw in his lot with a mage, but he was an even bigger one to have returned here. Unless he knew the man in the garrison's hematite cell and was biding his time.

There was only one way to find out.

73

"Commander." He spoke a hair too harshly and gave her that same defiant look as he pulled her from her thoughts. "Will you report our theory to High Commander Argent, ser?"

Our theory? Did he mean his and Halcyon's? Did he dare say such a thing to her face? To hide how her hands shook with fury, she smoothed an errant strand of her horse's chestnut mane. "Get back to your squad," she said to him and Rook, not bothering to answer his question. "And not another word on the subject, unless you want three more months of stable duty."

Stonewall stared at her, his hands tightening around the reins, until Rook murmured his name. His jaw clenched but he nodded once and eased his mount away from Talon's to fall back to his squad. Rook offered a modified salute from her saddle: one hand crossed before her chest, bowing at the waist, then drew her mount back as well. Talon faced forward once more. Another bitter wind blew, and she was glad of the chill that swept through her anger.

* * *

Night had fallen in earnest by the time they reached the outer gates. As the city guards approached, Talon drew her mount up and signaled the others to do the same. Such checkpoints were tiresome, but necessary given the recent mage activity.

"Well met, Lieutenant Faircloth," she said to the officer.

He saluted her, bending sharply at the waist. When he straightened, she bit back a grimace at the bright red slashes around his nose and mouth, along with the hints of burn scars. Gideon Echina had given him those burn scars, and a crow—perhaps Eris Echina—had doled out the scabbing scratches. But Ballard Faircloth had repaid the debt – and then some. "Good evening to you, Commander," he said with a nod. "Any luck, if I may ask?"

Talon shook her head.

Lieutenant Faircloth's mouth thinned as he gestured to the gate guards behind him. "Turns my guts to ice, thinking of those moon-bloods running wild out there, doing Atal knows what."

"Rest assured," Talon said with more conviction than she felt. "We will find them, and soon."

"Of course, serla," the lieutenant replied – without a trace of sarcasm. Talon made to urge her mount forward, past the gates and onto the bridge, when Lieutenant Faircloth called to her once more. When Talon looked down at him, he glanced around as if to ensure he wasn't being overheard. "We got wind of Parsa today. While you and your sentinels were out searching."

Talon resisted the urge to sink back in her saddle. "Aye, it's a dreadful business, but we're–"

"Forgive me, Commander," he broke in, wincing. "But I mean to say that everyone in the city now knows what happened. And most folks' feelings on the matter are...unfavorable."

Talon regarded him. "What are you saying?"

"Take care, serla. Me and my fellows know your sentinels did their best, but the civilians..." Faircloth sighed again. "Well, they're scared. And angry. Lots of folks had kin up in Parsa, you understand. Lots of folks are upset – with *you*. We've busted up more ruthless deals than usual, but three more crop up for every one. Ea only knows where they're getting hematite."

Ruthless. Talon had never cared for the civilian term for hematite; now it seemed particularly crass. "Non-sentinels are likely to die from eating it."

"Some have," Faircloth said. "But some folks will do anything to keep their families safe."

Her stomach flipped but she kept her voice cool. "Why are you telling me this?"

"I've kept faith with the sentinels, Commander. My sister's pregnant with her first child and I fear what sort of world the babe could be born into if mages run free. I know firsthand what vile creatures you guard us all against. But regular folks don't understand. They believe wild mages are creating the thralls."

Talon considered Stonewall's report of the Cipher priestess who'd been dripping with hematite. *Someone* had done magic on the woman, regardless of the dispelling stone's presence. The thought was beyond frightening, but Talon saw no reason to start a panic.

"Wild mages do exist, it's true," she admitted. "And if we weren't so focused on retrieving those who escaped during Heartfire, we'd be looking for those renegades."

"Of course, serla," the guard replied. "But you should know...folks are whispering that your sentinels killed those villagers to hide all traces of renegade mages."

She really shouldn't continue this conversation, but something made her ask, "What possible reason would my sentinels have to kill innocent villagers?"

Lieutenant Faircloth shook his head. "Like I said, serla, folks are scared and searching for answers." He lowered his voice again. "Rumor has it that your sentinels aren't able to control *any* mages any more – that's why so many escaped. People are saying that the escaped mages—either working alone or with renegades—attacked Parsa. Either way, it don't look good."

"That's preposterous," Talon said before she could stop herself.

He raised his gloved hands. "I agree, Commander, and I put a stop to such talk when I hear it, but fear spreads quicker than flames on thatched roofs."

Gods above, this was the *last* thing she needed right now. Although Lieutenant Faircloth seemed earnest, some of his fellow city guards behind him shot suspicious glares towards the sentinels. A few even kept their hands on their sword hilts. Some of the sentinels stirred behind her, but Talon stilled them with a raised hand. "Thank you for the warning, Lieutenant, but we'll be fine."

He dipped into another salute and Talon passed by, her squads following her onto the bridge, which now stretched into darkness over the roaring river. At the end of the bridge, two lights flickered on either side of the inner gates, but they seemed so small and distant, they may as well have been stars. The wind had blown out most of the torches that normally burned at intervals along the bridge, casting the way in shadow. An old, deep fear of the dark touched Talon's heart at the sight, but she ignored the feeling and urged her mount onward.

* * *

"If faces were daggers, we'd all be dead," Flint muttered.

Stonewall tried not to look at the wary, dark expressions of those they passed in the streets. It was late, but a few folks were about, and most regarded the sentinels with barely concealed mistrust. Thank Tor for his helmet shielding his face from their view.

"You heard the gate guard," he replied. "People are frightened and angry by what happened at Parsa."

"But *we* didn't do anything wrong," Milo said as they passed by a group of rowdy young men that had fallen silent the moment the sentinels came into view. "We tried to *help* those poor people."

"Think how the situation looks to someone who wasn't there," Beacon said. "Someone who has no understanding of magic or mages – or thralls."

Rook, still walking her horse beside Stonewall's, shuddered. "I *was* there, and I understand some of those things, and I'm *still* frightened."

She did not add "and angry," but Stonewall heard it in her voice. They passed by the young men, but Stonewall felt their gazes upon his back like a naked blade. "Once we're able to cure thralls, folks will see the truth."

"Do you really think Mage Halcyon can do it?" Rook asked.

Stonewall answered without hesitation. "If anyone can, it's Kali. It's just a matter of time."

"Time." Beacon sighed. "How much do we have, I wonder?"

"Before the next thrall attack?" Milo asked.

The mender's leather gear creaked with his shrug. "That, too."

By the time they reached the garrison, Stonewall was having to work hard to keep from grabbing a weapon to protect himself and his squadmates. No one had offered an overt threat, but the angry looks set every one of his survival instincts on edge. *Danger*, his better sense warned. *Run or fight.*

If only it were that easy.

As Stonewall passed through the garrison gates, Talon said his name. Thankfully, his helmet hid his grimace as he dismounted and led Frost over to her. "Yes, Commander?"

"Leave your horse with one of your squad," she said. "I've something to show you."

Ea's tits and teeth, he thought. *This won't end well.*

He turned, but Beacon had already stepped over to take Frost's reins. The mender gave him an inquiring look, but Stonewall shook his head. Whatever Talon was planning, he would face as best he could. He hoped. Beacon nodded and turned back for the others, Frost's hooves clopping on the courtyard's flagstones. Stonewall watched his squad depart before going to Talon, where she stood near the entrance to the barracks.

"Ser?" he asked.

Her helmet was tucked under her arm, but her expression was blank. His stomach twisted. "Come with me," she said, and slipped through the opening, to the interior door.

The lack of wind, the *silence*, fell upon Stonewall like a crashing wave. Torches flickered down the stone corridor. Talon took one and led him through the hallways, past the men's and women's barracks, past the common room, down a stairwell until they reached the door that led to the garrison's detention area.

Stonewall's head felt light as Talon withdrew a key from a chain on her belt. The need to flee hammered at his brain and body, but why would he run? There was no danger for him here. There was only a renegade mage; surely that was what Talon wanted to show him. *Why* she wanted him to see this mage was anyone's guess. Perhaps another threat aimed at Kali: *This is what will become of the woman you love if you keep to this path.*

Be calm, Stonewall told himself. *The gods are with you.*

Talon pushed open the door, ironwood slats covered with iron bars alloyed with hematite. The detention area stretched before them: a row of cells with stone walls, floors, and ceilings. Hematite was inlaid within the stones to prevent mages from using their powers. The doors—also made of iron alloyed with hematite—were simple bars with room only to pass a hand between them, and a plate or small bowl beneath. It was silent. Light from Talon's torch cast dancing shadows down the cells as they passed by each one: empty. Their steps echoed. Stonewall's heart pounded harder against his ribs until they reached the final cell.

Talon paused and held up the torch, revealing the figure of a large, dark-skinned man seated in one corner, opposite a chamber pot that, judging from the stench, had not been emptied in some time. The renegade mage wore tattered leather pants, and sat with his knees tucked up, his head bowed and hidden in shadow. Stonewall caught the gleam of metal at his wrists and a chain stretching to the wall.

"Mage," Talon said. "Look at me."

The fellow did not move.

Gods above. Stonewall had seen imprisoned mages before, but this sight was somehow worse than his memories. Was this what would happen to Kali before Talon killed her? *We must leave.* The thought was unwelcome as it was strong, but he could not ignore it now, not with reality only a few strides away.

Talon shot Stonewall a glance that was probably meant to be weary, if not for its deliberateness. "He won't even talk to me. I know he's from Indigo-By-the-Sea – I learned that much the one time he did open his mouth. I thought, perhaps, you might have better luck, Stonewall."

The figure's head jerked up and Talon held her torch closer so his features were thrown into stark relief.

Bahar – Drake, as a sentinel.

Stonewall stared at his dead brother's face, shock rolling through him like thunder, like a sudden storm. His mouth opened and he took a step backward, unable to speak, unable to even *think* clearly.

"What is this?" he stammered, looking at Talon. "What's going on?"

"You tell me," she replied calmly.

Stonewall shook his head, his breath caught in his throat. "He's dead. You're dead," he said to the mage wearing his brother's face.

Bahar's dark green eyes—their mother's eyes—were red-rimmed, holding none of the certainty they once had. "I'm so sorry, Elan," he said in a hoarse voice.

"I take it, then," Talon said. "That you know each other?"

* * *

Drake wished Talon had decided to torture him again. Anything would be better than seeing the betrayal on Elan's face and knowing *he* was the cause. He ignored Talon's snide comment and tried to make his voice sound less like shit and more like his own. "Elan, I know this is a shock, but I can–"

"You're dead," Elan said again.

Drake's heart sank at his stricken tone. "Commander, if you've any humanity at all, please let us have a moment alone."

Talon ignored him and looked at Elan. "This *is* your brother?"

Elan blinked hard as if to clear his eyes, then looked back at Drake. "What...? How...?"

He trailed off, clearly unable to put a thought together. Every instinct screamed at Drake to go to his little brother's side and comfort him, as he had so many times when they were children. But when he rose to move forward, the heavy chain that bound him to the wall dragged at his wrists and only let him take a few steps. Even if he'd been walking free, iron and hematite bars separated him from his little brother. Besides, he recognized the way Elan's hands clenched into fists; the kid might very well punch him if he tried to approach. Best let Elan cool off while he explained. But he had no wish to have such a private—and difficult—conversation in front of the sentinel commander who wore the expression of a tabby cat when the fishmonger's back was turned.

So, no privacy, then. Fantastic. Drake managed to get to his feet with minimal grunting; no small accomplishment, given that every muscle screamed in agony. "Elan, I had to make a choice three years ago. I'm so sorry, but it had to be this way."

"A choice?" Elan said. "What kind of choice? What are you talking about? You *died.* Are you..." He went rigid before he took a step back. "Are you a thrall?"

"A thrall?" Drake frowned. "No, *relah*, I'm alive and well. Sort of." He shot Talon a dark look, but she only met his gaze with maddening calm. Damn that–

Drake bit off the thought and focused on his brother. "I tried to be a good sentinel, Elan. Like you. But that life wasn't for me."

"Because you're a mage," Talon said. Her voice was too steady to be genuinely calm.

Elan's eyes widened again. "Is that true?"

"Aye," Drake said, glaring at Talon. "Though I would have liked the big reveal to have gone another way. Yes, Elan. I am a mage. Always was. I just didn't..." He winced. "Didn't tell you."

"Why?"

Drake held his brother's gaze, but his mind was far afield, back home on the bustling streets of Pillau, where everything smelled like the salty sea. "Because it was better not to have magic. The Circle would have separated us: thrown me in a bastion and sent you to the sentinels." Bitter sorrow caught in his throat; he choked out his next words. "I just wanted to keep you safe."

"You lied to me twice," Elan said, dazed. "More than that. My whole life." He ducked his head.

Be calm, Drake scolded himself. *Be strong, for Elan. It's the least you can do.* "I did," he replied slowly, carefully. "But the first time was to protect you, to keep us together."

"And the second?"

Despite Drake's efforts, something hot and fierce burned at his eyes. Now he had to look away. *Tobin. I'm sorry, love*, he thought. *I'm so sorry.* Why did he always hurt the ones he loved most? "I couldn't do it any more, Elan. I couldn't shut away my magic. It's a part of me; I tried to hide from it, or run from it, my whole life, but I couldn't any longer. And only one path became clear. I didn't tell you because I wanted to protect you, in case... In case my plan went sideways, which it did. Tobin and I snuck away from the bastion, but he didn't survive much past that."

"Tobin," Elan said, rubbing his forehead. "Ea's tits, I knew you two were close—more than close—but I had no idea..." He trailed off, shaking his head.

"You see now, Stonewall." Talon's voice startled both men into looking at her. "You see what comes of loving a mage, what comes of lying and sneaking around, what comes of breaking your oath."

Loving a mage? Drake stared at his brother. "What's she talking about?"

Elan glared at him. "None of your business." He looked at the commander. "How did you know about him?"

"I had a hunch." She squared her shoulders. "The question remains: how much do you know of what he did?"

"I don't know a sodding thing about him, apparently," Elan shot back, adding a belated, "Ser."

"So you weren't involved in the missing hematite shipment?" she asked.

Elan swore again and looked at Drake. "That was *you?*"

Drake grimaced. So much for playing stoic.

"What else have you done?" Elan stared at him. "The escaped mages. Eris and the others... That was *your* doing, wasn't it?"

Rather than answer, Drake glared at the commander. "This is cruel, even for you. Let us have a moment alone, and I'll tell you whatever you want."

Talon's smile showed too many teeth. "I have all the information I need." Her smile faded as she turned to fully face Elan. "Until further notice, Sergeant, you are on probation."

Sergeant? Drake thought with a flash of pride. *Good work, brother. Well, except for the probation.*

"For what?" The way Elan said the words, Drake thought he already knew.

She gave him a withering look and began to tick off on her gloved fingers. "Your connection with a renegade mage. Your connection with a *bastion* mage. Your inability to follow a simple order. Your continued, blatant insubordination. Shall I go on?" When Elan did not answer, she stepped closer, her movements fluid as a wild cat. "One more toe out of line, Stonewall, and I'll have you sent to the mines before you can say her name."

Elan stared at his commander. Only because Drake knew his brother so well did he recognize the raw fury laced in Elan's body, running through each vein as thick and hot as magic – or hematite.

Talon regarded him, cool as an early spring morning. "Do you understand?"

At last Elan nodded once, his shoulders sinking. "Yes, ser."

"You're lucky so many sentinels fell at Parsa," she added. "Because we need every pair of daggers right now. Otherwise, you'd already be on your way to Lasath, for Argent to deal with." Before Elan could respond, she turned to leave. "I'll wait outside, if you want a moment alone with your brother."

Elan shook his head. "My brother is dead."

Without another word, he shoved on his helmet and slipped past Talon, his steps carrying him into the shadowed corridor and away from Drake.

9

NINE

"This is unbelievable," Cai said, rubbing his temple. "After all we went through to *leave* that sodding bastion…you want to go *back*."

Eris had not yet recovered fully, so it took more effort than normal to keep the ire from seeping into her voice. "Leal's family is only a day gone, Cai. I'm sure you can catch up with them."

"And miss the fun?" He snorted. "Not on your life, Echina."

"Then stop whining," Adrie replied, stepping out of Leal's caravan with a pot of tea and several mugs.

"I'm saying what we're all thinking." Cai gestured to the others seated around the fire; after Sirvat, Gaspar, and Lyn had gone with the Sufani, only eight mages remained. A few of them nodded in agreement, while others looked skeptical. "And I'm *not* whining," Cai added.

Eris rolled her eyes. Arguing was pointless, but the knowledge didn't make her want to slap her friend any less. "I'll concede that it will be dangerous," she said. "And we don't yet know *how* we'll manage getting in – or out."

"Out of the city or the bastion?" Adrie asked.

Eris looked at the fire, although she did not feel its warmth. "Both."

Silence descended, broken only by the cries of mourning doves.

"I'm sure they've closed off the blood run," Marcen said at last. He paced along the perimeter, plucking his dulcimer. Eris had scouted this patch of woods and was convinced of their safety – for now. They were far from any roads, though not so far from Whitewater City, as the crow flew.

Eris nodded. "No doubt, but I'd like to check, just the same." She studied the rough sketch she'd drawn in the dirt beside their fire. And it was *rough*; she had no parchment or charcoal and besides, Gid had been the artist, not her. *Don't think about that now,* she told herself.

Only when Adrie held a steaming mug of tea in front of her did she look up into her friend's concerned face. Eris tried to smile to show she was fine, but her mouth didn't cooperate and she gave more of a grimace instead.

Adrie took her own mug and sat beside Eris, glancing around. "How much longer should we wait for Leal to return?"

"*If* she returns," Cai muttered.

"She will," Eris said, with more certainty than she felt.

Marcen strummed a few soft notes, his expression relaxed, though his steps were wary as he paced. "Unless she returns with an army or a fire drake, I'm not sure how much she can help. Heartfire's over; there won't be another opportunity like it for months. Should we rely on her so much?"

The tea was sweet and soothing: lavender and honey, warming Eris from the inside-out. Where or how Adrie had gotten it, Eris had no idea. "We'll wait one more day before moving on; I'm not yet back at my full strength, but I don't want to remain in one place for too long. As soon as I'm able, I'll fly to the bastion to try to get a sense of what's going on within before we make any plans."

"But how–"

"I don't *know*, Cai," Eris broke in, glaring at him. "I need more information before I can form a solid plan."

Cai crossed his arms and stared at her across the fire. "This is folly. I'm not sure which would be worse: getting captured or killed."

"You'll be neither, if I have anything to say about it," Leal said, emerging from the tree line. She moved on silent steps and came to stand by Eris. The other mages started, but Eris only felt relief.

Thank the stars, Eris thought as she sipped her tea. But to Leal, she said only, "Well?"

"I've brought...allies," Leal said.

"Other Sufani?"

Leal shook her head, sunlight dappling her indigo hood.

"Friends of yours, then?" Eris asked.

"Not exactly." Leal gestured to someone in the tree line surrounding the caravans. Three figures slipped from the shadows: two women, both ruddy with wind and sun, one with fair hair and the other with crimson; and a lean fellow with fair skin and an auburn beard. The women were armed: one with a bow and arrows, the other with a spear like Drake had used. The man wore no weapons, only a weary, grim expression.

All the mages moved closer to Eris, though no one stood between her and the newcomers. Leal named each one as she pointed them out. "There's Rilla, with the fair hair. Brice has the bow and arrows. That's Ben."

"Who in the void are they?" Cai asked.

Brice leaned on her bow and spoke calmly. "We don't want no trouble, Mage. We just want to help our friend."

"They're from the Assembly," Leal explained. "Friends of Drake's."

"They must be, if they're willing to storm the bastion with us," Adrie murmured.

Marcen was frowning at the newcomers. "What in the stars is the Assembly?"

Rilla raised her fair brows. "You've not heard of us?" Marcen only looked at her, and she sighed, casting her eyes skyward. "After all the Assembly has done across Aredia."

"We're only beginning," Ben said stiffly. He was older than Eris, perhaps in his early thirties, his blue eyes shot with red. He stood a little apart from everyone, watching the mages as if they were wild wolves.

"Gideon often spoke of the Assembly," Eris said. "You're a group of Aredians hoping to abolish the tier system, correct?"

Rilla's smile was thin and dangerous. "That's the idea."

"How's it going?" Cai asked.

Rilla shot him a glower, but Brice nudged her side, muttering, "Love, you promised to behave." When Rilla said nothing else, Brice shifted her bow to her other hand, studying the mages' camp. "This is everyone?"

"For now," Eris said.

"Right." Brice seemed to gather her courage, then stepped closer to Eris and gave a graceful bow. "Seems we have the same goal in mind, Ser Echina."

"And a shared enemy," Rilla added. At the other's looks, she said, "The Circle."

"I don't care about the Circle," Eris replied. "I only want to rescue my friends."

Rilla gave her a withering look. "You should care. The Circle is the reason your people are held captive. They preach the dangers of magic and mages to any who listen."

"The Circle is not wrong," Ben said. "Just…misguided in some ways."

Eris glared at him. "Misguided? Is that how you define imprisoning innocent people, chaining and collaring them like animals?"

"I am not your enemy," Ben shot back. "*I* have pledged my life to gain equality for all Aredians."

"Except those that have magic?" Eris spat upon the ground. "Equality for those you find pleasing?"

"It's better than sowing chaos wherever I go, *Mage*."

He spoke the word like a curse. Before Eris could respond, Brice placed a hand on Ben's shoulder. "Remember what you told me," she murmured. "No more regrets, right?"

Ben's blue eyes narrowed, but his shoulders sank and he looked away from Eris, in the vague direction of Whitewater City. An answering chagrin swept through Eris; Ben was not the only person with regrets. *Keep your goal in mind,* she told herself. *Nothing else matters.*

When Eris was sure she could speak normally, she looked at Leal. "*This* was your mission?"

"You need allies, don't you?"

Eris glanced between the newcomers. "Won't the city guards be looking for you?"

Rilla flashed a pretty smile. "Maybe, but we're awfully good at distracting those sods."

"Aye, and they're strong fighters," Leal added. "Well, Brice and Rilla are. I can't speak for the man, but he–"

"Has some unfinished business with Drake," Brice interrupted. Ben grunted but said nothing.

Eris narrowed her eyes. "You seek revenge? Or something else?"

The Assembly man crossed his arms. "My business with Drake is personal."

"I wouldn't have brought them to you if I thought they meant harm," Leal said.

It was all too vague for comfort, but Eris didn't have the time or inclination to further question the fellow's motives. She and her friends needed all the allies they could get. A glance at Adrie and Marcen showed they were thinking as she was, and although Cai still glowered at the newcomers, he didn't openly object any longer.

Good enough for now.

Eris looked at Leal. "You didn't have to do this. Thank you."

Leal shrugged, crossing her arms before her chest. "Aye, well... At least our chances of getting killed on this foolish errand are a little less now."

Eris started. "'*Our* chances?' Are you not returning to your people?"

All eyes fell upon the Sufani, who shifted beneath their collective scrutiny. Leal's gaze turned to Eris, briefly, before she shook her head. "I'm with you."

"For now," Adrie pressed. "Right?"

Leal's pale-green eyes fixed on Eris with a look Eris did not know how to read. "Until I'm not," the Sufani said.

"That's heartening," Cai muttered, a few of the other mages nodding in dark agreement.

But Eris had no room in her heart for anger with Leal, who had done so much for them, and who—apparently—had reasons of her own for sticking around. So she only dipped her head in an informal bow. "I welcome your aid."

Leal grunted acknowledgement, then came to stand over Eris' scrawled map in the dirt. "So. What's your plan, Mage Echina?"

Everyone looked at Eris; their attention sat upon her like a too-heavy cloak. Cai's words came back to her. Did she really want to go *back* to Whitewater City? Better, smarter, to flee to the south, where mages were treated slightly better, where she and her friends could disappear and get on with their lives. Where she could raise her child in peace.

But if she did that, the weight of Kali and Drake's imprisonment would drag her down every day for the rest of her life.

Eris took a deep breath and knelt beside her makeshift map. "Before we can strike, we must have a better sense of what we'll be up against."

"Well, you'd best hurry," Brice said. At Eris' inquiring look, she jerked her thumb in the vague direction of Whitewater City. "We spotted a sentinel squad in Orieon. Looked like they were bringing another shipment of hematite."

"Took 'em long enough, after the last one went missing," Rilla added with a smug grin.

The mages cast one another curious looks, but Eris was already nodding. "Your doing, I take it?"

Brice offered a short bow. "Ours and Drake's."

"But don't hope for a repeat performance," Rilla warned. "We're in no hurry to face the hemies head-on again."

Ben stroked his beard in thought. "Actually... I may have an idea on that score."

His Assembly friends shot him startled but approving looks, so Eris decided to keep her own reply just as civil as his. "Preventing the sentinels from getting more hematite is vital," she said. "But we still need more information about the bastion and garrison before we proceed."

"You lot used to live there, right?" Rilla asked with a frown.

"We know the compound's layout, yes," Eris replied. "But there's no telling how the sentinels have handled our...disappearance."

"How do you plan on gathering information?" Ben asked.

Slowly, Eris rose from her crouch, assessing her strength. Finding herself able, she concentrated on her particles, and slowly, to ensure the sod could get a good look, she shifted to her crow shape. There was no pain, only a tingle that crept outward from her heart to her limbs, strengthening with each heartbeat. Her vision blurred—usually the process was quick enough to prevent that—and when it normalized, her allies towered above her, gaping down. Eris cawed once and hopped up onto the nearest log, tilting her head to better see the others.

Her fellow mages grinned and nudged each other, while Rilla and Brice simply stared, slack-jawed. Ben's expression was one of revulsion; when her crow-gaze fell upon him, he took a step backward, one hand raised as if to bat her away. Eris cawed again, adding a broad flap of her glossy black wings for good measure, and he flinched.

Leal, though, regarded her with an expression Eris *could* read this time, despite how the Sufani's hood and veil covered most of her face. It was Leal's eyes that gave her away: pale-green, wide and naked with longing.

Strange.

Eris flapped her wings a few more times, assessing her crow body before she began her transformation back to her human form. The urge to fly was strong, but it was wiser to save her energy. She shifted quicker this time and within moments stood as a woman again before her old friends and new allies.

Of course, she was nude, but she was beyond embarrassment at this point. Before slipping back into her clothes, Eris made a show of brushing away a few stray feathers that had not shifted back. "I have my ways."

"Ea's tits and teeth," Brice gasped. She'd dropped her bow to cover her mouth with her hands. "You... You were..."

"A sodding *crow*," Rilla said when her wife trailed off. "Right? Did you see that?" she added to Ben.

He scrubbed his face. "That display was impossible to miss. I suppose you think such an abomination is clever," he said to Eris.

She smiled sweetly as she fastened her cloak. "Don't you?"

"Careful, Ben," Brice said with a snort. "I'd not upset her. You might wake up as a frog one day."

Ben's face went white, and his mouth opened and closed like a fish.

90

"I would never dream of doing anything so...abominable," Eris said. *No matter how much you deserve it,* she added silently. But as irritating as Ben's supposed piety was, the fact remained that she needed all the allies she could get; besides, he could always make good fodder for the sentinels. So she gave him a courteous nod, the kind she'd learned as a girl when her grandmother's second tier friends came to her family home. "You have my word on that, Ser Ben. No transformations of any kind – unless you ask nicely, of course."

It was an empty promise, because her talents had only ever worked on herself. Performing magic on another—aside from something minor, like healing a small wound—was beyond her ability. It was, she supposed, the price she had to pay to fly. Not a bad bargain.

She glanced around again in preparation to continue their discussion, only to find Leal watching her, gaze transfixed and calculating.

* * *

Later, after the talk had turned from planning to speculation and the afternoon had faded into twilight, Eris sat by the fire, trying to untangle her hair while the others chattered.

"I hadn't heard all that about Parsa," Adrie was saying to Ben. "The whole village...lost? Truly?"

Eris looked up in alarm. Kali had gone to Parsa. Her heart began to race. Was her friend even alive?

"That's the talk," Ben replied grimly. "Although I've not been to Parsa in some time. I can't confirm it."

"What happened?" Eris heard herself ask.

"Thralls," Ben said. Eris stared at him, but he offered no more explanation.

But Brice either had no qualms about sharing information, or simply wanted to gossip, for she related the story as she knew it. The rumors were wild, but the gist seemed to be that a group of mages and sentinels had somehow turned the Parsan villagers into thralls.

"There was a fight or something," Brice went on. "Now all the villagers are dead. Folks are blaming the mages."

"Of course they are," Cai muttered.

Eris shared his ire, but tried to keep judgment from her voice. "I know the mages who were there. They wouldn't have harmed a moth, let alone another person."

"Tell that to the dead," Ben replied.

"Tell that to your mother," Cai shot back.

Ben glared at him, but made no reply.

"What happened to the mages?" Eris asked.

Brice shrugged. "No one's sure. Some say the sentinels killed them on the spot." Eris' heart froze in her throat. "Others think they ran off right after. I heard one fellow claim he saw them—and the sentinels—on the road to Whitewater City." She shook her head, crimson hair loose and swaying. "Rubbish, I think. Why would sentinels let mages walk away from that sort of..." She trailed off and hugged Rilla's shoulders. "Well, no one really knows."

Rilla leaned into Brice. "Those poor souls. No wonder folks are scared and angry."

"Perhaps good will someday emerge from this tragedy," Ben said. "The One has a plan for us all."

Eris snorted. The others looked at her, Ben frowning, but Brice cleared her throat. "I suppose there's really no knowing the truth, right now."

"The Circle would say otherwise," Eris said. "And if the Pillars had their way, we'd all be in chains – or worse." She withdrew a black feather from her hair. No doubt she'd be finding remnants of her shifting for days. She let the feather fall to her feet and rubbed her throat; although her collar was long gone, she could still feel its pressure and remember the absence of magic it had wrought.

Ben shook his head. "If nothing else, Parsa has shown how dangerous magic can be."

"Thralls are the bigger threat," Adrie put in. "Not the mages trying to save innocent lives."

Ben continued as if she had not spoken. "And magic is still so new to our world. The Circle is right to show caution."

"Caution?" Cai rose from his seat, hands knotted into fists.

Eris said his name, drawing his attention. At his look, she shook her head. "Don't."

"But–"

"They are our allies now," she said through gritted teeth.

Cai frowned at her beneath his mop of brown hair. "Gideon wouldn't stand for this dreg's kind of talk."

"Gideon isn't here." Tears burned Eris' eyes. "Leave it alone," she said, and focused on the unruly black tangle of her hair. There was so much of it. Gid had loved to run his fingers through the strands, delighting in the way they flowed like silk over his skin.

"Here."

Eris jerked upright. She must have been woolgathering longer than she realized, for the others had stepped away, arranging what would soon become their makeshift headquarters – until they had to be on the move. Only Eris and Leal sat by the fire. The Sufani stood before her, hand outstretched and palm open to offer a small dagger that gleamed in the firelight.

Eris frowned up at the other woman in confusion. "I don't–"

"It's beyond repair," Leal interrupted.

Eris stared at her.

Leal sighed. "Your *hair.* There's so much. You'll never untangle it."

She offered the dagger again. Eris accepted, turning it over to get a better look. The hilt and blade together were barely the length of her palm, with no ornamentation, but the hilt was made of rare, expensive ironwood, judging by how the woodgrain whorls shimmered in the firelight. Eris skimmed her finger along the blade carefully. She'd had little use for weapons in her life before. Perhaps that, too, was about to change.

"I'm not *giving* it to you," Leal said. "Only letting you use it. All those snarls must be painful." She considered, then sat beside Eris and drew back the side of her hood, revealing dark crimson hair cropped close to her skull. So bared, Leal's face looked more angular than Eris had realized; her jaw was square, her cheekbones high and sharp. "I've never looked back. It's so much easier."

"It suits you." Eris could not think of anything else to say.

"I doubt anyone can tell most of the time," Leal said, pulling her hood back into place.

Eris frowned and toyed with the knife. "Why are you so set on helping us?"

Leal shifted like she was about to get up, but remained seated. "I made a promise to my father, and to Drake. And I... I had never seen a bastion before. It's wrong, how your kind are locked away. I couldn't bear it. I don't know how you did."

"Those are nice reasons," Eris said. "But what's the real one?" When Leal glowered, she inclined her head toward Leal's caravan, which would soon host sleeping Assembly folk. "You haven't abandoned your family and agreed to risk your life out of the goodness of your heart. No one's that noble."

The Sufani rubbed her hands together, considering her answer. "You have something I want."

"I have nothing."

Leal reached down, where Eris had dropped the feather. As the Sufani held it up, twirling it in the firelight, Eris' breath caught. "You want to be a crow, too?"

"What? No." Leal frowned but did not drop the feather. "I want to be... different. No, that's not right." She pressed a palm to her forehead. "Never mind. It's foolish. No one can help me."

She made to rise, but Eris' curiosity got the better of her, and she said Leal's name. When Leal paused, Eris pointed to the feather. "Tell me the price for your aid, and I will do what I can."

Leal gripped the feather, her gaze darting everywhere before landing on Eris. "The One gave me the body of a woman, but it's...the wrong body. I'm not a woman." She took a deep breath. "I am a man."

Eris stared at her. "You..."

"No one understands," Leal went on. "My parents try, but they think I'm a little mad – I know they do. And the rest of my family agrees. Da says it's a phase that I'll grow out of, but I'm twenty-two summers and the feeling grows stronger every day. The One is perfect, but was mistaken, with me. I'm no woman. I'm a man. I know it. I feel it, here." One gloved hand pressed over her heart.

"And you want me to…change your body," Eris said slowly.

"Yes. Does that befoul your moral compass?"

"No. It's just…unexpected."

Leal gave a harsh bark of laughter. "What were you expecting? Or do I want to know?"

Despite the severity of the moment, Eris felt a small smile come to her lips. "There's no telling what people want, when magic is involved."

"If the One god has no gender," Leal said, not looking at Eris now. "Why would mine matter? What possible difference does what's between my legs make to anyone but me?"

"It doesn't," Eris replied. "Even my priestess grandmother would agree. I agree, and I don't believe in the gods, like you do. Leal, I think your body is your own, just like your life. You should live the way you want."

Leal glanced over, and her eyes were wet. "Will you help me?"

"I don't…" Denial died in Eris' throat at the beseeching look in Leal's gaze. Could she help this…ally? Eris, who had only ever done magic on herself, found herself staring into a new possibility. "I will try. Everyone deserves to be who they are."

Leal ducked her head. "I don't have the words of gratitude."

"I haven't done anything yet," Eris replied. How in the stars would she manage such a transformation? Could she? She had a sudden, desperate need to speak to Kali. Kali would know; and if she did not, she wouldn't rest until Eris had an answer. "Save your gratitude for when it's deserved," Eris added softly. She hesitated, a new thought coming to her. "Would you like to be addressed as a man, in the meantime?"

The Sufani exhaled. "I don't know right now. But I appreciate the thought."

Nodding, Eris held up the dagger again. "I can't see the back. Will you make sure it's even?"

Leal accepted the dagger and bade Eris to turn her back to the fire. Eris held perfectly still as Leal gathered the long locks in her fist, tugging the hair slightly as they discussed the cut. "You're certain?" Leal asked.

Eris took a deep breath. "Yes. It's time for a change."

10

TEN

Kali's eyelids sagged with exhaustion, but she forced herself to keep reading.

"I felt the tears of the silverwood trees. Each touch brought me knowledge of their deaths, so many giants brought down by sickness. I have spent every night this week sleeping among them; I feel their sorrow and confusion as if it were my own. They are dying, and they do not know why.

Del says I am imagining things, that trees do not feel as we do, but he's wrong. He thinks I'm mad, just as the others say. It was not always so.

Last night I placed my hands upon the tallest tree and gazed up into sparkling leaves; it is the most beautiful sight, one the trees only share with those they trust – or those they are trying to draw closer. The beacon moths love them. But even the strongest trees are sick and dying. I will ask Del again to beg King Solasar to save some. Will he? Can he? Is even a king's power strong enough to withstand this curse?

I have begun collecting acorns. Each one is alive with possibility; I can feel their massive spirits in the tiny pods. Perhaps I am mad. Del is frightened when he looks at me, but I don't care. I must know what is happening to the silverwood trees."

"They all died of sickness," Kali murmured to no one, rubbing her eyes. "But you managed to save some; there's a few left in Lasath, on the royal grounds." Or so her natural history books had told her, but she had never seen the silverwood grove for herself. Would she ever know anything other than a bastion?

The leather and hematite collar felt tighter with each breath, but there was nothing she could do. She had been able to magic Eris' collar off before Heartfire, but that had been before she had a collar of her own. Now, despite how she'd tried, she could barely feel the presence of particles; the world was gray and dull as hematite itself.

A yawn caught her but she fought against it, because she could *not* go to sleep. Every time she slept, every time she dropped her guard, she heard the strange voices in the back of her mind. *Sweet blood. Sweet magic. Give it to us. Now.*

As she had often done in the days since Heartfire, Kali imagined Stonewall was here, listening to her read. She hadn't spoken to him in nearly a week, since they'd returned after Heartfire. She'd tucked his letter away for safekeeping in her viol case, but the lack of his steady presence gnawed at her heart and mind. She fought that feeling, too. She was no simpering girl in a sonnet. She could survive without the man she loved.

"Keep reading," Kali told herself, squinting at Artéa Arvad's journal propped in her lap as she sat upon her sleeping pallet. "Forget everything else."

She had come to the end of one entry, so she turned to the next. This one, like the others, was dated over two hundred years ago, before bastions, before sentinels; only a generation or so after Seren, the second moon, had appeared in the sky. Artéa's writings were…strange, to say the least, but Kali couldn't blame the first mage for her confusion. How frightening it must have been to be aware of particles without knowing what they were.

Sweet blood.

"Shut up," Kali said, and continued reading.

"Del is frightened for me. He says the Pillars want to lock me away, but I think he's being overcautious. The Circle is a friend to all; the Pillars are our guides, our beacons in the chaos. Without them, there is no order in the world. No, I am not afraid of the Circle or the Pillars who steer its counsel.

"I am afraid for the silverwood trees. They spoke to me again last night: stories

of anger and jealousy, and fear. So much fear. And I had the dream again – the one with the great dark cloud that blotted out the stars. So much fear. I asked the trees for answers, but they had only questions. 'Why have they come?'"

Kali's breath caught at the mention of the dark cloud. The same vision had plagued her after Parsa; the same sense of fear. "Why have they come?" she asked aloud. The entry ended there. She turned the page. The next entry was in Zhee, and Kali swore as she tried to puzzle out the language. Stars and moons, why had she not learned more?

A soft knock against her door made her glance up, blinking in the pale light streaming through her window. Morning? Where had the night gone? The knock came again and Kali scrubbed her face, hoping she didn't look as haggard as she felt. "Come in."

The door opened and Sadira paused just over the threshold. As ever, the Zhee mage appeared cool and unruffled, her moonstone-pale hair intricately braided and her expression calm. Sadira still wore her hematite torc, but the leather and hematite collar sat above it. Kali nearly laughed at the sight. Did the sentinels truly think hematite could dispel Sadira's magic? The Zhee mage had healed a room full of Parsan villagers while wearing her torc, and even now, a pleasant warmth billowed from her, filling Kali's small room.

Sadira's pale-blue eyes swept across the piles of books, scrolls, and clothes that littered the space, before coming to rest on Kali. "Are you ill?" Sadira asked.

Kali ran a hand through her hair. Her braid had come undone sometime during the night, and the dark brown strands were tangled. Her eyes itched and she knew they must have shadows beneath them from lack of sleep. Seren's light, she must seem a mess.

She tried to smile up at Sadira as she tapped the journal. "Just got caught up reading. It's Foley's fault, really. He should have known what would happen if he gave me a new book."

"Artéa Arvad's journal?" When Kali nodded, Sadira approached warily, but with that fluid grace she always possessed, stepping around the chaos of Kali's room with ease. "Have you been up all night?"

Kali toyed with the pages. "Can't sleep," she admitted once Sadira sat beside her on the sleeping pallet. "Ever since Heartfire."

"You went through a terrible ordeal."

"We all did."

"Yes, but you nearly died."

Kali's hand stole to her throat. Above the collar, the raised scar was still tender, but otherwise she was fine. Heat pricked her eyes and she rubbed them again. "I'm well. Just... I've had some disturbing dreams."

"What sort of dreams?"

"It's hard to explain. Nothing makes sense. They're mostly strange images and voices speaking a language I don't know and have never heard. There's something about a...huge dark cloud, and an overwhelming sense of fear and loss. And..."

Sweet blood. Sweet magic. Give it to us. Now.

Kali shuddered. "I sound crazy."

Sadira shook her head, her braids swaying with the motion. "You are wary. Weary," she corrected herself. "You must rest."

She made to reach over to close the book, but Kali pulled it away. "I will," Kali said, trying to force her mouth to form a true smile. "What are you doing here, anyway? It's too early for breakfast. Isn't it?"

"Foley wants everyone to gather in the common room," Sadira replied with a glance at the book. "Come. They should not wait for us."

"All right. But first," Kali tapped the page, "can you translate this for me? The only word I could make out was 'magic.'"

"The book will keep."

"Please?" Kali shoved the journal into Sadira's hands. "It's a short passage. I must know what it says. Please, Sadira."

The Zhee mage regarded her again before skimming the cramped writing, her brows knitting as she read. She made a noise of consternation and Kali sat up, looking between her friend and the book. "What is it?"

"Enemy."

"Um...what?"

"Perhaps I have the word wrong," Sadira replied, shaking her head. "But what is written here would make the Circle very angry."

"Then maybe you mean 'heresy,'" Kali said. Her blood beat in her ears. "What does the passage say?"

"It is an old dialog. I'm uncertain how to make you understand."

"Please try."

Sadira exhaled in irritation, but began to read. "I met with the Pillars today. They were curious about me, as I was about them. Del came with me. The Pillars were most interested to hear about the silverwood trees, and my dealings with them. It was pleasant, at first, for I thought they believed me. But as we spoke, I saw something in their eyes: a flash of starlight. It frightened me and I knocked over the tea by accident. Del apologized, but I could see the anger in their faces when they looked at me. And when one of the Pillars touched my arm as we left, I *felt* him. Felt his entire being, his spirit. And it was foreign to me in a way that no one has ever been. It was like a spider crawling up the back of my neck, only more so, somehow.

"I know every particle of Del's being, because he is a man of flesh and blood and bone; the Pillar who touched me wore the body of a man, but he was no man. He was something else.

"Later, Del told me I was imagining things. I think he's reaching the end of his patience with me, although he denies it. But I don't care, not really. I'm so afraid. I can't sleep; I feel that strange presence, even now. And when I close my eyes, I see the Pillars looking at me with starlight in their eyes. Even as I write this, I fear what they will do to me if I am discovered. Thank the stars for Del and his love of old languages; one of the passions we shared. But even he won't understand this. I hardly do, myself. All I know is that I am afraid."

Silence descended like a sword between the two mages. Kali, dumbstruck, only stared at her friend as Sadira traced her fingernail over the small sketch of a tree in the corner of the page; apparently Artéa had a fondness for doodling. At last the Zhee mage looked at Kali. "What was the word you used?"

"Heresy," Kali whispered.

Sadira nodded and closed the journal with an audible *thunk* that made Kali start. "This woman is mad," she said, setting the book aside. "And her Zhee is clumsy. Half of the words are misspelled; I'm not sure I got the transformation right."

"Translation," Kali corrected, though her thoughts were spinning.

Sadira regarded her. "You should remain reading myths and children's tales. This," she waved her terra cotta-colored hands at the journal, "would keep anyone from sleep."

Kali's heart beat furiously against her ribs but somehow, her voice was steady. "What does it all mean? Are the Pillars...thralls?"

"The Pillars are the leaders of the Circle," Sadira said gently. "If they were monsters, someone would have noticed. Besides, everyone in those pages has gone to their next lives by now."

"Maybe." Kali scrubbed her face again. If she could only think straight! A warm hand settled upon her shoulder. "Come on," Sadira said, offering a smile. "We'll see what Foley wants, then get tea. That will bring you to sleep. You'll feel better..."

But Kali didn't hear the rest of her words, for Sadira's touch ignited a thrill of hunger just like she'd felt on Heartfire. Not a desire for her friend's body, but her *magic*.

Yes, sweet blood. Give it to us.

The shock of the urge made Kali gasp and jerk away from Sadira, clambering off her pallet to stumble over the detritus littering her room. Her knee screamed a protest at the sudden movement, but she didn't care.

"Kali?" Sadira came to her. "Are you well? What's wrong?" Her eyes widened and her hand stole to her hematite torc. "Did I...harm you?"

While Kali could not manipulate particles while bound by hematite, she could sense the raw force of Sadira's magic – and the insistent draw of such power. She sucked in a breath, fighting for control, and her collar pressed tighter. She tried to wrench it off, but Captain Cobalt had secured it well, and she only succeeded in scraping her still-healing scar. The pain brought focus, and with focus came the control Kali so desperately needed.

"You didn't harm me," Kali managed, shaking her head. "I just..." *Get a hold of yourself!* "I think I'm more tired than I realized. Perhaps some tea will do me good."

Sadira studied her but nodded slowly. "You need sleep most of all." She pointed to the door. "The others are waiting. Can you walk?"

She could, but it wasn't easy. The sudden scramble to get away from Sadira had twisted her knee, and each step brought a sharp stab of pain, despite the brace. But for once, Kali welcomed the pain as a distraction from a far greater worry. She used the corridor wall to help support her weight and refused Sadira's assistance. Sadira did not question her, but Kali did not miss the concerned glances Sadira shot her way when she thought Kali wasn't looking.

Soon they reached the common room, where fires danced in each hearth and most of the remaining Whitewater mages were already gathered. The room was alive with chatter and speculation, most of which Kali missed in her concentrated effort to not collapse from the pain in her knee. Someone had pulled most of the chairs to the center hearth so that everyone could have a seat. Sadira directed Kali to the nearest padded chair, and Kali sank down, extending her left leg to give her knee some respite. The brace that Gideon had made glinted in the firelight. After a brief hesitation, Sadira slid over a footstool for Kali to prop up her knee, and then settled beside her without touching.

Castor, a slender fellow about ten summers older than Kali, had been pacing just outside the semicircle of chairs. "That's everyone – finally. Foley, *now* will you tell us what this is about?"

Another young man named Jep called, "Are the hemies going to remove the sodding collars?"

Foley, who had been kneeling before the center hearth, straightened and faced the assembled mages. "I've spoken with Commander Talon," he began. "But she has no plans to remove the collars. I'm sorry."

Exclamations of outrage burst out among the assembled mages. "This is horseshit," Castor said. "We've done nothing wrong!"

"Why are *we* being punished for Eris and the others' actions?" Jep kicked a nearby bench. "Should've left with them when I had the chance."

A few other mages grumbled assent.

Hazel, a teenage girl with strawberry blond hair, rubbed her throat. "It's so tight! The lock keeps chafing me. Can't the sentinels at least loosen the buckles?"

"We *stayed*," said Wylie, an older woman. "Surely that makes us...if not Talon's allies, then at least less deserving of such treatment."

Castor nodded. "Aye. And I'll tell you this: I didn't go with Gid and the rest because it seemed too risky, but I'm thinking better of that now. And I sure as shit resent being collared like a sodding dog for *nothing*."

Similar cries filled the room, all aimed at Foley while the First Mage waited for their heated words to ebb. Kali kept her mouth shut. Although she agreed with the others that they should not have been punished for Eris and her friends' actions, she was more curious about why Foley had brought them all here. Sadira, too, sat silently, hands in her lap, gaze fixed on the hearth behind the First Mage.

At last Foley raised his hand—and his hook—and quiet settled over the room. Foley gave a deep, defeated sigh. "I summoned you here to discuss Gideon."

Castor, who had been pacing, stopped in his tracks, his arms tight at his sides. He'd been one of the mages tasked with burying Gid's body. "What about him?" Castor asked, no small amount of bitterness in his voice.

"He deserves better," Foley said, his gaze flickering to Kali.

Heat crept to her face and she ducked her head, though she took no comfort in the fact that he had heeded her words.

"I thought you hated Gideon," Hazel said.

"No, child," Foley replied with a sad smile. "I did not always think highly of him, but hate is a useless emotion I have long since done away with."

Druce, who had also helped bury Gid, leaned back heavily in his chair. "Seren's sodding light... I just want to live in peace and mind my own business. Can't we put all of this other shit behind us?"

A few others murmured similar sentiments, but Foley was already shaking his head. "I can't do that, Druce. Not yet, anyway. Not without showing respect to a good man, even if he was...troublesome at times."

Some of Kali's pain had receded after propping up her knee. The strange, foreign hunger for magic had also faded, so she managed to speak somewhat normally. "Now that we're allowed to leave the dormitories, can we have some sort of...ceremony for Gid?"

What would Eris say to that? Something tightened in Kali's throat that had no connection to the collar. No doubt Eris would just want her husband alive.

Foley gave Kali a warm look. "Aye, something like that."

"But... He's buried in the earth," Hazel said, voice trembling, eyes bright with tears. "His spirit is lost."

Silence fell across the mages, such that Kali could make out the patter of rain outside. A distant rumble shivered through the room and when she twisted around to see out of the windows, she saw only a slate-gray sky beyond the bastion wall. When had the storm sprung up?

"I think, perhaps, that can be rectified." Foley looked at Sadira.

Sadira went still, her lips parting and her hands clenched in her lap. "I cannot," she whispered, so softly that Kali wondered if she'd meant to say the words aloud at all. "Not again."

The others muttered in confusion, but Kali ignored them all and risked a touch to Sadira's sleeve. "This isn't like what happened to your village. You can do some good here."

"There is no such thing as 'good' when magic is involved."

"As someone whose life was recently saved by magic, I'm inclined to disagree."

As Kali had hoped, a faint smile touched Sadira's mouth, but the Zhee mage shook her head. "You don't overstand. This has nothing to do with my...past."

The other mages cast each other curious looks while Kali considered. "Will your fire not work in the rain? You made the one on Heartfire last all night, and on wet wood, no less. I can help if you want–"

"That's not it," Sadira broke in, trembling. "You *don't* overstand."

"Then help me *understand*."

Pale-blue eyes blazing with pain and fury met Kali's. "Gideon is dead,"

Sadira ground out. "Magic cannot return a stolen life."

True enough. Kali was at a loss. What good would it do to cremate Gideon now? If the gods existed, which Kali still could not bring herself to believe, wasn't the damage already done? Gid was dead and buried; surely, if his soul was cursed to wander the void, magic would do no good now.

"There is a pattern to all things that is too big for us to see. After all, we are humble, and the world is vast."

She fought back a swell of emotion at the memory of Stonewall's calm certainty as he'd said those words on their journey to Whitewater City. They'd stopped at a stone structure that he had called a cairn: a place where folks made offerings to the gods. At the time, she had disregarded the notion and his words, but she'd had the lingering thought that it would be good to believe in something greater, something far wiser and stronger than herself. If the truth of reality was that all of them—mages, sentinels, and common folk—were just plummeting through the void... Well, it was terrifying.

But perhaps it doesn't matter if the gods are real, she thought. *Perhaps what matters most is being strong for each other.*

So Kali caught Sadira's eye and gestured to the others, who had been watching the quiet conversation with varying degrees of curiosity and bewilderment. "Yes, Sadira. Your magic cannot save Gid's life. Not now. But perhaps your magic can make others' lives better."

* * *

Half an hour later, Kali stood beside Sadira in the rain and slush, huddled in her cloak and trying to ignore the cold. Even Sadira's presence was not enough to ward off the sleet and biting chill as they stood beside Gideon Echina's grave. All fourteen mages who remained at Whitewater Bastion stood with them. Thick gray clouds had overtaken the sky, casting the world in shadow, but no one held torches. At Foley's request, Castor, Druce, and Oly—the same men who'd buried Gideon after Heartfire—had brought out their pickaxes and shovels once more.

106

As they began to exhume Gid, Hazel glanced towards the gates. "The hemies won't like this."

Kali looked at the gates as well, but only saw indistinct shadows through the sleet.

"Aye, so we must be quick." Foley peered at Sadira from beneath his hooded cloak. "You're certain you can do this with the collar and your torc?"

"I am," Sadira replied, glancing at Kali. The question on her face was clearer than if she'd given it voice: *Will you help me?* But that wasn't possible. Wearing the collar was different than being cuffed; Kali could do no more than feel the presence of particles, and even that was difficult. And even if she could recreate what she'd done with Eris' collar... Sadira was strong on her own. She didn't need anyone's help.

"I can't help you..." Kali said, trailing off as she touched the collar sitting below her scar.

The Zhee mage shook her head. "I don't need your assistance. I just..." Her jaw went tight and she looked at her boots, blinking rapidly.

Understanding washed over Kali like sheets of rain. She debated between compassion and common sense; compassion won. Steeling herself for the onslaught of that strange hunger, Kali laced her pale fingers with Sadira's darker ones. Kali's hand, already damp, felt like ice in the rain and chilly air, but a few seconds in Sadira's grip sent heat spreading from her palm to her arm, warming her from the inside out. The tension in her shoulders eased and she offered Sadira a faint smile of thanks – and encouragement. Sadira didn't reply, only took a breath and faced the now open grave. Rain had soaked through the dark earth and Kali could make out a rumple of cloth, but nothing more. Small mercies.

Sadira closed her eyes and ducked her head. She wore no cloak, only a wool dress now plastered to her body. Despite her hematite torc and the collar, steam rose from her, and Kali could hear the faint hiss of rain evaporating once it struck the Zhee mage. Sadira exhaled and her grip relaxed as she sank further into her trance. Kali tried to follow suite, if only out of solidarity, but focus was difficult through the cold and wet, and the attention of all the other mages. But she had found her focus before, in much more harrowing circumstances, so she fought for it here. She wouldn't let her friend down.

Hematite placed a barrier between mages and the rest of the world, so although Kali could sense Sadira's power building, the collar prevented her from touching that power, herself. The collar rendered her only a spectator. But even so, Kali had felt the touch of Sadira's magic before – many times. She thought she knew what to expect from her observation.

Heat flooded Kali's lungs and face, and prickled at her scalp. Her legs burned as if from hours of running and her toes ached as if she'd stepped into a hot spring after walking barefoot on ice-cold flagstones. Another breath, from herself or from Sadira, it was impossible to say, and the heat within her veins increased, setting each nerve alight and filling her with fire. Sadira's magic burned—even with the collar!—and Kali bit back a cry of pain. Someone gasped. Light flared to life behind her closed eyes; a blooming warmth followed, radiating up from the earth like burning coals beneath charred logs.

Sweet magic.

Hunger sparked in Kali's mind. Before she could react, a sense of possession seized her; an unseen iron grip around her throat, tighter than any collar. A sense of raw, utter *want* crashed over her, consuming, and Kali was only aware of a desperate yearning for the sweet, delicious threads of magic that bound her and Sadira.

"No," Kali gasped, yanking her hand free and stumbling backward, falling to her knees and making her brace creak ominously. The force of the impact sent streaks of hot pain through her left knee, but that was not enough to quell how the cold soaked through her again. But the break of contact also caused the bulk of the strange longing to fade, although she could feel its echo resonating within her body.

Sweet magic. Sweet blood.

"Kali?"

"What's wrong? What's happened to her?"

"Is she all right?"

"Druce, Jep – help her up."

Panting, Kali squeezed her eyes shut, trying to ignore everything but her own breath, trying to shove aside that wild, wholly foreign hunger and find *Kali* again. Someone grabbed her arm but she jerked free. "Stop! Leave me alone!"

Give it to us. Now.

The foreign presence within her laughed; Kali felt rather than heard the sound as if it came from her own lungs, so she clamped her mouth shut and clenched her hands so hard, her nails pierced her skin.

But the laughter came again. *You are ours.*

"No!"

Another hand on Kali's shoulder, warm and reassuring. Sadira. Magic clung to the Zhee mage like the scent of jessamin flowers, and Kali ground her teeth against the urge to fling herself upon Sadira, to wrest magic out of the other woman and take it for herself. Gritting her teeth, Kali shoved away Sadira's hand as hot tears streaked her cheeks, mingling with the icy sleet. Her knee throbbed, so she concentrated on the pain, willing it to drive away all other feelings.

Calm settled over her; not peace, but reprieve. Gradually, the foreign urge dissipated, until Kali could open her eyes and feel like *herself* once more. When she looked around, the other mages were gaping at her. Beyond them, Gideon's grave smoldered, orange embers burning even in the rain. Had the cremation worked? Kali couldn't tell. She could hardly *think*.

"Kali?"

Sadira's voice made Kali jerk her head up to see her friend kneeling beside her, close, but not touching. When Kali looked at her, Sadira made to touch Kali's shoulder again, but Kali shook her head. "Don't. I'm all right." She stood slowly, shakily. "I'm all right. I'm fine."

Perhaps if she said the words enough, they would be true.

Sadira rose as well. "You don't seem–"

"It's just...cramps," Kali interrupted. She glanced between Wylie and Foley; aside from Sadira, only the older mages had come closer, although concern was written on everyone's faces. "They come upon me so suddenly, sometimes," Kali went on. "I should have expected them this week, maybe had some ginger tea, but…"

She trailed off, leaving Sadira and the others to think whatever they liked. Indeed, Wylie offered Kali a sympathetic look. "Mara bless you, child. I used to have dreadful cycles, too." She looked at Foley. "Are we done here? I'm no healer, but Kalinda needs rest and *none* of us should be out in this weather, unless you want the lot of us to catch our deaths."

Foley's gaze shifted from Kali to the grave. Embers still glowed amid a depression in the wet ground where flecks of gray ash mixed with dark mud. "Aye," Foley replied quietly. "We're finished. Are you hungry, Kalinda? I prepared some tea and sweetrolls, earlier."

A few others murmured appreciation, but Kali's stomach twisted at the thought of being near other mages in this state. "No," she said, shaking her head for emphasis. "I'm not hungry. I just want to rest. Alone."

"You are certain?" Sadira asked, expression still troubled.

Kali nodded. Without waiting for a response, she turned to leave. A bitter wind blew, so she pulled her sopping cloak tight as she hurried through the mud, her boots squelching with each step. Perhaps she was imagining this. Perhaps she was overtired, or she'd suffered a blow to the head during the business at Parsa, or this really was the onset of the worst cycle of her life.

But none of those hopes rang true.

Thank the stars, no one pursued. Soon Kali had slipped back inside the dormitories to leave a trail of droplets as she made her way back to her room. She locked the door behind her, and then sank to the floor, heart hammering, soaked in rain and sweat and fear.

Even behind closed doors and far away from Sadira and the others, the strange hunger for magic lingered like a bitter aftertaste to the sweetest wine. Every beat of her heart, every breath, affirmed the truth.

Thrall.

11

ELEVEN

Stonewall tightened his grip on his daggers and lunged at Milo. The younger man hesitated for a fraction of a second before blocking what would have been a killing blow to his heart. He grunted, and then used the leverage of his greater size to knock Stonewall back a few paces.

Although it was midday, the sun had hidden behind a layer of thick gray clouds and only Stonewall's squad was in the garrison courtyard. The other sentinels were either searching the province for renegade mages or patrolling the bastion. Stonewall did not miss how his squad had only been assigned the former in the week since Heartfire.

With the bastion on lockdown and with his squad not authorized to enter, how in the void could he even *get* to Kali? His head swam with the events of the last few days. No doubt she was in much the same state. They needed to see each other again, but he did not think they'd get a chance unless he made one.

"Come on, Mi!" Flint called from where she practiced with Rook and Beacon, the three of them alternating dagger strikes on a wooden practice dummy.

If Milo heard his sister, he didn't show it, only faced Stonewall, lips compressed and body tense. His blue eyes, which should have darted between his opponent's feet and face, looked glazed and red-rimmed behind his helmet. Stonewall made a show of adjusting his grip on the triangular, hiltless daggers that all sentinels carried, but when Milo still looked distracted, he struck again. This time, he went right for Milo's throat.

Only when the younger man was on his back and blinking at the sky did Stonewall speak. "That's the sixth time you'd be dead if this spar was in earnest."

Stonewall sheathed his daggers and offered Milo a hand. Once Milo was on his feet, his chin dropped to his chest. "I know."

Stonewall removed his helmet to better see the younger man. "Are you all right? I know you've had a lot of stalls to muck out."

"That's what happens when people get hurt under your watch."

"You've been...uneasy, since Parsa," Stonewall said. "I don't blame you; the whole thing was...a nightmare. But Milo," he placed a gloved hand on Milo's shoulder, "you must keep your wits about you, now more than ever."

Blue eyes met his. "I know," Milo whispered. "But it's just..." He trailed off, one hand dropping to his sword before jerking away as if the hilt had burnt him. "It's hard."

"Aye, and it's going to get worse, before it gets better, I think," Stonewall said, squeezing Milo's shoulder. "But we're a team. You don't have to fight alone, remember?" He added a half smile, hoping to elicit one from Mi at the callback to words the burnie had spoken to him, not so long ago.

He was rewarded when Milo offered his own faint smile, ducking his head once. "That's good to know."

"Don't forget it." A sudden chill moved through Stonewall's body, making him suck in a breath and glance around for the nearest fire, seeking warmth. His hands trembled and his feet felt like blocks of ice, and the desire for hematite was suddenly a living thing clawing at his mind. He needed a burn – now! Dread pooled in his guts but he forced himself to calm down and ignore the desire. Gradually, the chill abated.

"Done already?" Flint said, bounding up to stand between the two men. "So are we. Rook and Beacon are tired."

Stonewall and Milo looked up in alarm, but Rook shook her head. "It's nothing," she said as she approached. "Just had a rough time falling asleep last night. It's so cold." Her steps lacked their usual lightness and there were dark shadows beneath her eyes.

Beacon, too, moved with heaviness, but his expression was concerned as he removed his helmet to study his squad-mates. "Any other symptoms of withdrawal? Nausea? Pain?"

"No," Rook replied. "I just can't seem to stay warm."

The mender looked at Stonewall, who lifted his palms. "Just chills. If that changes, you'll be the first to know."

"You're all about due for a burn," Beacon replied.

"So are you," Rook pointed out.

The mender shrugged. "I'll manage. Thank Mara none of us are cinders; Slate and Red are about to lose their wits."

"How much longer do we have left before…the urge becomes too much to bear?" Stonewall asked.

"Given the timing of your last burns…" Beacon grimaced. "A couple weeks. Maybe."

Flint's eyes rounded as she looked between the older sentinels. "So soon?"

"Didn't realize you cared," Beacon replied with a smile that didn't reach his eyes.

Flint glared at him, but the expression held no edge. "I'm not worried about *you*. Don't flatter yourself."

"That's right," Rook said, nudging Flint's side. "She only loves me and Mi. You two," she pointed to Stonewall and Beacon, "are on your own."

"Well, the sarge is all right," Flint said. "Sometimes."

The others chuckled, but Stonewall's gaze had slipped to the bastion gates. Two sentinels stood guard on either side within the garrison, and he knew that several squads patrolled the interior and atop the walls.

"Anyway," Flint went on. "I'm tired of sitting around. When are we going to find more thralls? Not to *kill* them," she added at Milo's horrified look. "To try and *cure* them."

Stonewall glanced back at his squad. "The commander didn't believe me."

"No, she didn't," Rook added, frowning. "But the whole situation is difficult to believe."

"Maybe we can sneak Mage Halcyon out," Milo said.

Rook gaped at him. "Sneak out a mage? What's gotten into you?"

"At least it's an idea," Flint replied.

"Sort of," Milo added, beaming at his sister. "But if we *could* manage it..." He sighed, forlorn again. "We just need a little time."

"One of the many things we *don't* have," Beacon muttered.

They all glanced toward the bastion gates now. Stonewall's belly cramped at the mention of time; another enemy he could not hope to defeat. If hematite withdrawal was already creeping upon him...

Even if he and those he cared about could somehow leave this life behind, how would his squad survive without hematite?

Drake will know.

The thought came unbidden and Stonewall fought back a grimace at the realization. He'd spent the last several days trying *not* to think about his supposed-to-be-dead brother; he hadn't even breathed a word of Drake to his squad. The whole situation was too bizarre for him to wrap his mind around. But the gods had a twisted sense of humor and Stonewall didn't think he could avoid this problem any longer.

No matter how much he wanted to.

"There's no sodding way the High Commander will let our garrison go without hematite much longer, especially after Heartfire," Flint was saying.

"Perhaps, but Argent often has his own agenda," Rook said.

"What d'you mean?" Milo asked.

Spots of color crept to the scout's cheeks but her voice was steady. "Nothing. Just that there's no telling what he's got planned." She smiled at the twins. "I'm sure he'll send more, soon. He doesn't want us to be without any more than we do."

Stonewall saw his own doubts mirrored in Beacon's face, but didn't want to worry Flint and Milo any more than necessary. "I know of a sentinel who...stopped taking hematite, and survived."

The others goggled at him. "That's not possible," Beacon said, shaking

114

his head. "Unless she didn't take it very long. The twins here could go without it for the rest of their lives and survive, as they've only had one true dose. But the rest of us…"

Stonewall made a quick mental calculation. "He took it for over ten years."

"How did he manage to go without?" Rook asked, frowning.

"I'm not sure," Stonewall admitted. "I haven't…gotten the details."

"Anyone we know?" Beacon asked, stroking his beard.

Ea's tits and teeth. Stonewall swallowed. "Sort of. He's my brother."

Milo's jaw fell open. "Your brother! You said he was dead."

"I was wrong. I saw him with my own eyes a couple days ago."

More startled glances passed between the squad. Rook stared at him, brown eyes wide as she whispered, "Your brother… He's the mage. The renegade Talon captured during Heartfire."

"A mage?" Flint said, gaping at Stonewall. "*And* a sentinel? How's that possible?"

"Wish I could tell you," Stonewall muttered.

"Sweet Mara's mercy," Beacon exclaimed. The words echoed through the empty courtyard. "Ea's tits, Stonewall. Why didn't you say anything?"

"I thought he was dead," Stonewall replied. "But when I saw otherwise… And given the circumstances of his…reappearance, I just…" He looked at his boots. "I wasn't trying to keep the truth from any of you. I can barely accept it, myself."

A broad hand rested on his forearm. "Drake, right?" Milo asked.

"His birthname is Bahar, but now he goes by Drake."

Milo nodded. "Well, despite whatever else, it's good that Drake is alive, right? I mean… You get another chance to be a family."

A family. Stonewall quelled the bitter laugh that rose in his throat. "Doubtful."

"Aye, given that Drake will probably be shipped off to Argent before too long," Flint said.

Icy dread coursed through Stonewall's veins. "Probably," was all he managed.

Beacon ran a hand through his hair, glancing across the empty courtyard before he looked back at Stonewall. "All other things aside, if your brother has information on how to get by without hematite, I'm eager to learn it. Never hurts to be prepared."

"We'll get more," Milo said, though the words fell flat.

Stonewall met Beacon's gaze and said carefully, "Even if the garrison gets more hematite, I'm not sure I'd want to remain."

Silence fell over the squad. Another cold wind blew, rifling hair and sneaking beneath armor. Just when Stonewall thought he'd made a misjudgment, Beacon exhaled. "Nor am I." The others looked at him, but his gaze had gone distant again. "There are people out there who need help. Help *we* can give them – us and the mages. That's the entire reason I left my family and joined the sentinels: to make the world a better place. If Talon won't listen to you, I'm not sure what other recourse we'll have."

"But we can't just walk away," Rook whispered. "Even if we managed to survive without hematite, Argent *will* find us. He won't rest until we're all Forsworn and dying in the mines of Stonehaven."

"There are worse fates than death," Stonewall said. "And I don't plan on going down without a fight. But this is all speculation, anyway."

"You don't sound convinced," Beacon replied.

Stonewall shrugged. "I'm working on it."

The burnie twins exchanged worried looks before Flint squared her shoulders. "You're all getting nervy for nothing. Argent *will* get us more hematite and Talon *will* let us try to cure thralls – eventually. You're all worse than the sodding cinders," she added in a mutter.

Milo nodded, his expression too bright, too hopeful. "She's right – mostly. Once you get more hematite, you'll feel better."

Beacon gave the lad a grim smile. "I hope so, Mi."

The crunch of boots on gravel drew everyone's attention to the direction of the garrison. Captain Cobalt, flanked by five sentinels, strode towards them. Two cinders, Slate and Redfox, were also close on the captain's heels. Stonewall gave a silent hand signal and his squad immediately formed a neat line behind him, everyone standing at attention as the senior officer approached.

Cobalt's gaze swept over the practice dummy before landing on Stonewall. "Good, you're all kitted up. Come on. There's trouble at the bridge gates."

Stonewall saluted, bowing low. "Certainly, ser. What sort of trouble?"

The captain opened his mouth to reply, but Slate broke in first. "All we know is it involves our sodding hematite shipment. We should already be gone."

Cobalt gave the cinder a dark look. "Mind your tongue. You're supposed to be on bastion patrol, remember? You're staying here."

"He's on edge," Redfox said. "We both are, ser. Let's just go, already. Please."

"You're staying here, too, Red," Cobalt shot back to the older woman. "You're both too much 'on edge' for my liking."

Neither cinder objected, though they cast dark looks in Cobalt's direction. For his part, the captain glanced back at Stonewall, who saw past the helmet to the haggard weariness in the officer's bearing; Cobalt's scar stood out almost white against his gaunt, gray face. Stonewall squared his shoulders. "We're glad to assist, ser. Just point us in the right direction."

* * *

Cobalt stepped onto the bridge first, scanning ahead to get a sense of what he was leading his sentinels into. His heart hammered so hard, no doubt Stonewall could see it pulse beneath his cuirass. But the sergeant only stood at his side, squinting down the bridge toward Whitewater City's outer gates. The overcast sky and mist from the churning river blurred Cobalt's vision, but not enough to obscure the swarm of people on the bridge. Beyond them, he could make out the top of a mage-carriage and a few gray-armored figures. Shouts and cries of anger blended with the White River's rumble.

"Thank Mara, you've arrived." It was Lieutenant Faircloth and a handful of his fellow city guards.

Cobalt jerked his chin toward the mob. "What's going on? The message wasn't clear."

"The dregs won't let the carriage any farther down the bridge," Faircloth replied. "They're all in an uproar about the thralls, and…" He trailed off as several of the other guards shifted uneasily. "We thought it was best that *you* handle the situation, serla."

"You thought right," Cobalt said. *Ea's tits. We should be mounted.* That's what he got for setting off in a rush. He was as dumb as any burnie – or addled from lack of hematite. "Have they been violent?"

"Not yet, Captain, but *I* wouldn't let down my guard."

No kidding. Cobalt nodded thanks to the lieutenant and looked at Stonewall. The other man straightened, entirely business. His squad followed his lead. Thank Tor the burnies at least were still in decent shape; Milo, Flint, and several others were some of the only sentinels not feeling the loss of hematite. Perhaps the new sergeant would use this opportunity to make amends for his past transgressions.

"What in the blazing void are we waiting for?" Slate growled, shoving past the sergeant, one hand reaching for his sword. "Those shits have our hematite and we're sodding standing here with our thumbs up our asses."

Red was at his heels. At least she had the decency to shoot Cobalt a contrite look. "Punish us later, ser. But let us help you now." Both cinders smelled so strongly of *biri* smoke that Cobalt's eyes watered and his stomach twisted with nausea.

"You *need* our help, Captain," Slate added.

Vigil, Cobalt's second-in-command, rounded on the cinder before Cobalt could. "Shut your mouth, Slate, or I'll do it for you."

Slate glared at her, but kept his silence.

A haze of red swam across Cobalt's vision as he stared at the cinders. How sodding *dare* they go against his orders now? Bad enough half the bastion mages had cut loose; bad enough the garrison's forces weakened each day. Now even his most trusted, *loyal* warriors had turned against him.

Stop sniveling, he scolded himself. *They're cinders on their last legs. This has nothing to do with you.* Besides, both Slate and Redfox were skilled. He needed them – and they knew it. Damn them both for knowing him too well.

Still.

"Three months of stable duty for each of you," he said. "And you'd best behave now, or else. We move on my command." He added his most stern glare, the kind that made burnies tremble in their boots, but Slate only shrugged, gaze already shifting to the carriage ahead.

Cobalt ordered Stonewall and the rest of the sentinels to set out across the bridge. Several paces out, the air cooled as mist from the White River coated Cobalt's gear and jaw. The scent of freshwater mingled with the scent of leather and sweat from the sentinels. Ahead, the mob of civilians surrounded the mage-carriage, shouting obscenities at the sentinel escort and making the horses dance in their traces.

"Are we authorized to be...aggressive, ser?" Vigil asked as they walked.

Cobalt placed his hands on his dagger grips but did not draw the weapons free. "Yes, but try not to. Our priority is getting that hematite to the garrison."

"These people are frightened," Stonewall added. "I can't blame any of them for it, after Parsa."

"That's no excuse to threaten *us*," Cobalt replied, frowning. "Cut the chatter, Sergeant, and focus on your duty."

The mob had surrounded the carriage at the middle of the bridge, preventing it from crossing. Cobalt could not see the sentinel escort's horses; perhaps they'd left the creatures outside the main gates. When the sentinels were about halfway to the mob, the folks on the outer edges noticed them and began nudging their companions. Soon all attention had turned to the newcomers and the jeers quieted. Cobalt gave a silent hand signal that Vigil and Stonewall would relay to the others. *Continue with caution.*

When he drew closer, he scanned the sentinels who had escorted the shipment, searching for a familiar face. He caught a flash of silver amidst one set of hematite-embedded armor, and then he spotted Fain's square jaw beneath his helmet. One of Silver Squad, *here*? The High Commander must have taken Talon's message to heart if he'd sent someone from his personal, elite squad.

Fain's gaze fell on Cobalt, too, but the other sentinel did not move. He had drawn no weapons, but none of the civilians had gotten too close anyway. Without shifting his gaze, Fain spoke to the carriage driver, a burly fellow who gripped the reins. The other members of the sentinel escort stuck close to Fain and the carriage, agitation clear in their stances. That did not bode well.

"Oh, look," a woman in the crowd drawled, her crimson hair bright against the gray stone. "*More* hemies."

A blond woman next to her crossed her arms. "They must really be afraid if they're sending reinforcements."

Several others muttered agreement and a few moved closer to the mage carriage. The driver jerked the reins, and one of the horses half-reared. "Back off," the driver snapped. "Or–"

"Or what?" A man with an auburn beard regarded the driver with a mildness that rose Cobalt's hackles. "You'll attack us? We're civilians, you know. Innocents."

"Aye, and victims of *your* stupidity," the blond woman added.

The red-haired woman raised her voice to carry across the crowd. "We demand justice for those slain at Parsa!"

"Justice!" the blond woman echoed.

The crowd took up the cry and began to shove closer to the carriage, much to the driver's ire. But it was Fain who spoke. "As I have said, your anger is understandable. Rest assured, High Commander Argent is working with the Pillars to determine what happened at Parsa, and how to ensure it does not happen again."

"It can't happen again because everyone at Parsa is fucking *dead*," someone from the crowd cried, with others calling agreement. "And *you* sentinels were sodding useless!"

"What good are you if you can't protect us from mages?" the man with the auburn beard added.

A dark murmur rumbled through the civilians. Some reached for the horses, making them jerk their heads up, nearly pulling the reins from the driver's grip. Cobalt met Fain's gaze again. Fain made a rapid, sweeping gesture and Cobalt signaled his understanding. He glanced to either side to ensure that Vigil and Stonewall had done the same. Both nodded to him. *We're ready.*

The silent communication only lasted seconds. Most people in the crowd were fixated on Fain, the sentinel driver and mage-carriage, but a few—the man with the auburn beard, included—noted the exchange. But before they could react, Cobalt and his sentinels shouldered through the center of the crowd, causing folks to step aside enough so that the driver could direct the carriage horses forward. Once the hematite was safe, the sodding guards could make themselves useful and deal with these rabble-rousers as they saw fit.

But the carriage still had to *cross* the bridge. Cobalt signaled Vigil, Stonewall, and the rest, and they turned to lead the carriage back toward the city. Fain called to his companions, who surrounded the vehicle from behind.

Shouts of anger mixed with more jeers and catcalls, but—thank the One—none of the civilians dared try to stop the sentinels' increased numbers. Many folks in the crowd hurled insults like rotten fruit, but nothing more harmful. That was fine. The dregs could moan all they wanted, but the garrison *would* get its hematite. Cobalt would make sure of that. The carriage trundled further onto the bridge and the crowd thinned, with some folks falling back and some darting ahead, though all still shouted obscenities and curses at the sentinels.

Two of the most outspoken, the women with blond and red hair, offered the most virulent swears, while walking in front of the mage-carriage. Cobalt kept an eye on them in case they thought to do more damage than alarming the horses. Neither was armed – that he could see.

Stonewall glanced over at Cobalt. "Should we get them out of the way?"

"Not yet," Cobalt said. Although the drive for hematite beat away at his brain, he forced himself to keep his pace and voice steady. Easy. Careful.

This situation was a tinderbox waiting for a spark. A few more civilians slipped past the sentinels to the bridge ahead of them, slowing their walk to a snail's pace.

Cobalt glared at the burnie twins, whom the civilians had slipped between. "What's the matter with you two?"

Flint scowled at him from beneath her helmet. "Aren't we not supposed to use our weapons?"

"So use *yourselves*. You've armor for a reason, girl. Don't let the dregs shove by. And you, Milo." The boy snapped to attention. "You're the size of a sodding house. No one should get a chance to pass you."

Milo flushed and moved to walk on the outside, right beside the stone bridge's railing, thereby blocking anyone else from coming up behind him. Cobalt shot Stonewall a dark look. "Your burnies are sloppy."

Before the sergeant could reply, Vigil called, "Slate! Get back!"

Cobalt whirled around in time to see the cinder barreling through the civilians in front of the carriage. The sky was gray, but Cobalt still caught the flash of steel from Slate's daggers. His stomach dropped to his knees. "Slate! Stand down!"

But the cinder ignored him, instead shoving aside the mob, including the two women who seemed to be the ringleaders. The man with the auburn beard was in the cinder's path. He raised his hands as if in surrender, but Slate gave a wordless cry and sliced into the fellow's leg.

One of the ringleaders shouted "Ben" as the man cried out and stumbled to the ground, but Slate was already past him, leaping for the carriage.

All this had taken only a second or two. The sentinels tried to rally around the vehicle and the horses, who tugged at their traces, but the brief distraction—and the sight of a civilian's blood—gave the mob the chance they'd been waiting for. Cries of outrage echoed off the bridge, carrying down the river, and the mob surged past the sentinels toward the carriage – and Slate. Cobalt, once surrounded by allies, found himself only with Stonewall, fenced in by angry faces.

Ea's tits! The situation shouldn't have come to this! Cobalt gritted his teeth and drew a dagger. Stonewall followed his lead and the two men stood back-to-back, just ahead of the carriage. The mob had shoved the other sentinels, including Vigil and Fain, either back down the bridge or ahead, but Slate had clambered up into the driver's seat, brandishing his dagger.

"It's ours, you stupid, filthy dregs," he cried. "Go to Nox's void, all of you!"

"You first," the red-haired woman called back.

Cobalt caught a flash of blond as someone ducked in front of the carriage. The next thing he knew, the carriage shuddered as the horses broke free, and someone else grabbed their reins to lead them down the bridge and out of the way.

Out of the way of *what?* Blood hammered through each vein but Cobalt kept his head. He'd faced thralls and lived. He'd faced *mages* and walked away. He could handle some angry dregs. "Get back," he called, lifting his dagger. "Get back at once, or you're all under arrest!"

But his words fell on deaf ears. With the horses free, the mob surged to the carriage, tipping it toward the bridge railing and trapping three sentinels in the process.

Cobalt's heart skidded to a halt. "Fain, Mica, Rook – get out of there!"

Thank the One, they managed to dart out of the way before they got crushed. The driver, too, leaped from his seat and stumbled into the crowd ahead. The civilians let them pass, even going so far as to shove them out of the way.

But Slate remained in the seat, gripping the wooden rail with one hand, his face tight with rage.

"I don't think they're after us," Stonewall said. "They just want our hematite."

"Over my sodding corpse," Cobalt snarled. "Atal curse you, you stupid sod," he called to Slate. "Get down here, now. That's an *order!*"

"Ser, you don't understand," the cinder cried. "I *need* a sodding burn."

Fury and fear rose like bile in Cobalt's throat. "Get down!"

But it was already too late. More civilians swarmed over the carriage, jostling Cobalt and Stonewall out of the way as their combined strength

123

pushed the vehicle up and over the railing. Slate swiped his dagger at anyone who got too close, until he had to release it in favor of hanging onto the carriage sides. The weapon spiraled down into the mist as the crowd pressed forward, pushing the carriage. It hung atop the stone railing for a few seconds, the wheels spinning lazily, before the mob gave a collective heave and the carriage—and Slate—toppled over the side to plummet into the churning waters below.

A cheer rose up from the crowd, but Cobalt ignored it for now. All thoughts went to getting the rest of his brothers and sisters in sacrifice out of the situation. He whirled, searching for Vigil and the rest; thank Mara, they were all safely out of the way and making a beeline for the city. *Stonewall's right,* he realized. *The dregs don't want us. Just our hematite.*

If only the thought brought relief.

Someone grabbed his forearm. Cobalt whirled, dagger raised, but it was only Stonewall. "Come on, ser," the sergeant said, urging Cobalt after the others.

Only when Cobalt was free of the pressing crowd did he take a proper breath. His steps were leaden; his body cold and shaking. His vision swam. Slate was gone. *Nox guide your spirit,* he thought, but couldn't finish the litany even in his mind.

Fain, Vigil, and the rest waited for them down the bridge, stances wary and gazes fixed on the mob, who still celebrated their victory. The moment Cobalt and Stonewall joined the others, Fain jerked his chin and the sentinels hurried back into the city proper. Lieutenant Faircloth and the other city guards scrambled over each other to let the sentinels pass.

"Captain," Faircloth began. "Are you–"

"Break *that* up," Cobalt broke in, pointing down the bridge at the mob. "Do your sodding jobs, for once, without *us* having to intervene."

The city guard blanched. "Yes, ser."

Once they were within the city, Fain fell in step with Cobalt. "That was all the hematite Argent could spare," he said without preamble. "I'll return at once with this...news, but it might be several weeks before we can get more from Stonehaven."

Weeks. Could they survive that long? Cobalt nodded. "Understood. We should…" His breath hitched but he clenched his teeth and continued. "Dredge the river. Try to recover…what we can."

"I'll arrange it, ser," Vigil said.

Like all other sentinels, Fain wore cured leather armor dyed a dark gray and embedded with chips of hematite, but as a member of Silver Squad, he also boasted plates of silver embossed with the sentinels' sigil: twin triangles with the tips intersecting. He paused, causing the rest to halt as well. "Take heart, Captain," he said. "The High Commander *won't* let you down, even if he has to bring a shipment himself."

With that, he signaled to his sentinels, who broke apart from the Whitewater group. Cobalt frowned. "You don't want to come to the garrison?"

"We must leave at once," Fain replied.

Rook had slipped closer. "But the mob…"

Cobalt shot her a dark look for speaking out of turn, but Fain didn't seem to mind. "They don't care about us," he said, echoing Stonewall's observation. "But we'll be careful. You do the same, Rook."

That was odd, but before Cobalt could question either of them, Fain and his squad slipped away, heading back for the bridge. Cobalt considered sending the burnie twins ahead to the garrison to relay the news, but decided against diminishing their numbers. Although the city was quiet here, he didn't want to risk another incident, especially when unfriendly faces watched their progress on all sides.

We're their protectors, he thought, swallowing hard. *We're not the enemy. Why don't they see that?*

As they went, Stonewall fell in step with him. "It wasn't your fault, ser."

Cobalt's stomach twisted, but he only frowned at the other man. "What'd I say about chatter, Sergeant?"

Stonewall shook his head. "It's not insubordination, ser, just the truth. Slate was–"

"An addled cinder whose brain was fried long ago," Cobalt broke in. He spotted Redfox ahead, trudging with slumped shoulders. Mica and Rook walked on either side of her, close, but not touching.

"Maybe." Stonewall was quiet until they reached the garrison's gates. Everyone slipped in, breathing sighs of relief. The others hurried for the barracks, but when Cobalt made to follow, a hand on his shoulder held him fast.

"Captain." It was the sodding sergeant.

Cobalt glared at the other man. "What is it now? Can't you see I have other things to do than talk to you?"

"I know, ser." Stonewall hesitated, and then squared his shoulders. "Let me help you."

"How in the blazing void could *you* help me? And—more to the point—*why* do you want to?"

Stonewall seemed to consider before heaving a great sigh and removing his helmet to better meet Cobalt's gaze. "I've made a lot of mistakes since coming here."

Cobalt snorted. *Understatement of the century.*

"But I want to change that," Stonewall continued. "I want to...be better. Especially now, when there's so much at stake. Will you let me try, ser?"

Interesting. Cobalt studied the other man, searching for any signs of dissembling. But Stonewall held his gaze, unflinching. "What'd you have in mind?" Cobalt asked at last.

"What task do you have the least patience for?"

There were too many, these days, but one stood out. "The daily duty roster," Cobalt replied. "Takes forever and gives me a sodding headache every time."

The sergeant nodded. "I'll gladly take over, if you'll allow it, Captain."

Not unheard of, and in truth, the thought of one less menial task made the knot in Cobalt's gut ease a little bit. But... "Can I trust you, Sergeant?" Cobalt nodded toward the bastion. "Or is this some excuse to make it easier to see your little mage-whore?"

Stonewall's eyes tightened, but his reply was calm. "No, ser. And even if I wanted to do so, I'd expect you—or the commander—to look over anything I draft before it takes effect."

True enough. Cobalt studied the other officer, ostensibly still considering although he had made up his mind. His fury and fear had faded, leaving him numb with exhaustion; he wanted nothing more than to sleep for an entire day. "Very well," he said at last, nodding once. "I'll send you the last couple to use as templates going forward. Bring a fortnight's worth to me. If I find them satisfactory, you can continue."

"You won't regret it, ser."

"Pick another phrase, Sergeant."

Stonewall saluted, bowing deeply. "Thank you."

Cobalt rolled his eyes and turned his back on the other man to make his way for Talon's office. Slate's face lingered in his mind's eye, merging with the cries and jeers of the crowd, and his every step fell like a striking fist.

12

TWELVE

Milo stabbed his pitchfork beneath a pile of dung and dumped it into the waiting wheelbarrow. Blisters stung beneath his gloves and his back ached from the constant bending. All he could smell was shit. The stables were quiet, as most horses were out on province patrol with their riders, but there was plenty of work to do.

"Milo?"

He did not look up at the sound of his name. "I'm not done yet, Rook. Just go on to sparring practice without me."

"What are you mumbling about, burnie?" The other sentinels' voice—feminine and gruff, and definitely *not* Rook's—made Milo glance up to see Redfox standing at the stall door.

Heat rushed to Milo's face. "Sorry, Red. You need something?"

Redfox jerked her head in the general direction of the city. "Talon sent a message. You're to report to her at Mara's temple. Now."

Milo's stomach dropped to his knees and he leaned some of his weight on the pitchfork. "Me?"

"Ea's tits, boy, do you see anyone else here?" Red swore and rubbed her temples. "Sorry, kid. It's not your fault, but I'm about to gnaw through my gear. It's a miracle I'm still standing."

She said the last few words with a note of heavy sorrow, and Milo winced. Three days had passed since the dreadful scene on the bridge.

Milo ducked his head. "I'm sorry about Slate. I know you were friends–"

"Slate made his choices," Red broke in, scowling. But her chin quivered and she crossed her arms before her chest. "Besides, it's not his fault. It's the sodding dregs who tossed him—and *our* hematite—into the river. They'll pay. They must."

"They're scared and angry," Milo said. "And they didn't mean to hurt Slate, I think. He just…" He trailed off at Red's dark look. "Well, thank the One the rest of us were unharmed."

"Aye," the cinder echoed dryly. "Thank the One, for only the One knows when we'll get more hematite." She looked at Milo with interest. "You got any squirreled away, burnie?"

"We were supposed to turn our stores over to Captain Cobalt. You should ask him or one of the menders."

Redfox cast her eyes to the ceiling. "Aye. Good idea. Thanks." She leaned against the stall door frame and eyed the full wheelbarrow. "*That* will keep. But I'd not leave the commander waiting."

Milo hefted the pitchfork, scattering the remaining pieces of dung stuck on the tines before setting it aside. But as he stepped past Red, she wrinkled her nose. "Ea's tits, boy, you stink! Why in Atal's name did you wear your armor to muck out stalls?"

He sniffed his arm and grimaced at the stench, but there was no time to clean his gear. "We're supposed to be armored at all times, remember? We're on high alert. No one's even allowed off-duty time."

"Aye, well, good luck, then," Redfox said as she backed away from him, holding her nose.

"Will you tell Stonewall where I've gone?"

She called the affirmative as she all but ran out of the stables. After grabbing his helmet and weapons that he'd stowed safely away from the dung, Milo was close on her heels.

The moment Milo stepped out into the garrison's courtyard, cold air ambushed him, numbing his nose and cheeks, and making him briefly long for the warmth of the stables – shit or not. Winter had fallen upon the province in earnest. The sun had crept out from behind the clouds to make a brief appearance, but did nothing to warm the world. He hurried through the courtyard, where the sounds of clanging blades echoed. His sword dragged at his side, hitting his leg with every step.

Milo glanced over at his squad, where Red had—thankfully—stopped to speak to Stonewall. The sergeant nodded at Milo, who took heart at the small gesture. Flint, Rook, and Beacon waved; like him, they wore their helmets, so he couldn't make out their expressions, but even the brief sight of his squad—his brothers and sisters in service—was enough to make a little of his anxiety fade.

The feeling didn't last.

Milo trotted briskly to keep himself warm. The gate-guards nodded acknowledgment as he passed through, and soon he was in the Whitewater City proper. Milo hurried past the temple of the One's wide stone steps, past bakeries and pubs, chandleries, butchers, booksellers, and money lenders; more than a few dark gazes fell upon him, but thank the One, no one offered him any trouble. Even so, he circumnavigated the Eye, forgoing the chance to savor the delicious scents from the bustling marketplace in favor of a safer route, and made his way instead to the docks, where the air smelled at once piss-foul and river-clean.

Here was the goddess Mara's home in this city.

An unassuming stone building from the outside, Mara's temple was not nearly as grand as that of the One, but the sanctuary sustained life of all kinds. Behind iron gates held open by a massive ivy, a simple fountain bubbling with clean water rested at the center of a stone courtyard. A woman and her two young children filled ewers as Milo walked up. The woman nodded to him while her children stared at him with wide eyes. Thank the One for his helmet and how it concealed his face, for he didn't feel like smiling back.

There were no doors on Mara's temple, just an archway that separated indoors from outside. Doves, larks, and other birds flitted between beams of sunlight that poured in through the high windows. Potted plants—many of them healing herbs—filled the air with scents of lavender, rosemary, and sweet callia, hopefully also concealing Milo's own odor. Several braziers filled with coals cast warmth throughout the open space. The instant that Milo stepped into the temple proper, a sense of peace settled over him: one of Mara's many blessings. He closed his eyes to relish the feeling.

The main room was empty, but a series of corridors extended from each side. Milo knew he should probably start looking for his commander, but it was just so nice to have a moment all to himself. He cast another look around to make sure he was truly alone, and then approached the statue at the center of the room.

The goddess was carved from a single, massive smoky quartz; Mara's head reached almost to Milo's shoulders. The crystal's inclusions caught sunlight and filled the goddess with tiny rainbows that shifted as Milo came closer. Offerings of herbs, shells, seeds, and other natural items lay at Mara's feet. It was difficult to make out the goddess' expression, but her hair coiled down to her knees and her hands were spread in a gesture of welcome.

Milo knelt before her and his troubles seemed to melt away. Perhaps he ought to come here more often.

"You must be one of Talon's."

Milo jumped to his feet at the unfamiliar voice. The speaker was a man in his late forties, his hair as black as Milo and Flint's, albeit with a few silver strands. His beard was small and neatly trimmed and his eyes were shadowed. He was tall and lean, and his white and black cloak rippled as he walked toward Milo from one of the corridors.

Milo gave a warrior's salute: arms crossed before his chest as he bowed at the waist. "Yes, serla. I'm Milo. Commander Talon summoned me."

The Circle priest nodded, his eyes sharp. "So you were one of those souls sent to Parsa the night of Heartfire?"

"Yes, serla." Milo glanced at the statue and winced. "I was on my way to see the commander, I just wanted to…"

The Circle priest smiled. "No need to explain, my son. All are welcome here, at any time, in any state of body or mind."

Milo's throat was suddenly and inexplicably tight. He nodded, but was unable to speak. The priest placed a hand on his slender chest and his warm voice set Milo at ease. "My name is Iban Vellis. I'll bring you to Talon."

They walked down one of the corridors, emerging into a larger room that reminded Milo of the garrison's common area. The room hummed with activity as Circle folks organized mass quantities of supplies, foods, and medicines. Priests and priestesses called to one another as crates were brought in and disseminated among the tables that filled the room. A few folks glanced at the newcomers, though no one stopped their tasks.

Serla Vellis glanced at Milo. "This place generally serves as a haven for the less fortunate, but as you can see, we put it to other uses when the need arises."

An odd feeling fluttered through Milo's insides; not relief, not guilt, but a mixture of the two. "Do you need help, serla? I can't heal or anything, but I'm pretty strong. I could carry..."

He trailed off as the priest shook his head. "No, Milo, but that is a generous offer. I know your time is valuable. Come," he added, waving Milo forward through the room. "Talon is in my office."

Serla Vellis led Milo through his clergy, offering words of encouragement or direction as he passed. Milo tried his best not to get underfoot, though it was difficult. He was big and bulky enough *without* his gear; all suited up, he may as well have been a lumbering ox. He sure stank like one. He pulled his sword close to keep the scabbard from knocking into anyone and tried not to look as out of place as he felt. Most of the Circle folks only gave him a passing glance, but some studied him curiously. A few wrinkled their noses—he couldn't blame them—and one or two scowled. That, he'd not expected, so he kept his gaze down and tried to make himself invisible.

"What's all this for, serla?" he asked.

"Relief for the poor souls at Parsa."

Milo' stomach twisted. "But...there's no one left at Parsa."

Serla Vellis clasped his hands before him as they walked. "Aye. But although the village itself is...empty, there are several outlying homesteads who have survived. The queen has sent soldiers to search the area and recover any survivors."

"Your people must take care, serla. That Cipher went to help, too, and look what happened to her."

"Her name was Telfair," Serla Vellis said after a pause. "And her loss has hit us hard." He urged Milo onward. They entered another corridor, smaller than the first, and then reached a wooden door, where Vellis ushered Milo in before him. The priest's office was smaller than Talon's, but not by much. A simple desk, covered with scrolls and parchment, rested below a narrow open window, where air and light filtered into the room. Wooden shelves covered two walls, each neatly stacked with books and more scrolls. A locked cabinet filled the third wall.

Talon sat in one of two chairs, back straight, helmet resting on her thigh. Her gaze had been on the cabinet, but when Milo and Vellis entered, she got to her feet, bowing to the priest. When she straightened, Milo could see the shadows beneath her eyes. "Well met, Milo."

Milo saluted her, hoping to conceal his sudden nerves. "Hello, Commander. Red sent me. Is that all right?"

Talon gave Milo a warm, if somewhat strained, smile. "If Serla Vellis has no qualms, then neither do I."

The priest waved a hand. "The boy was at Parsa during Heartfire; that's all I requested." He made to sit, and then gave Milo a rueful look. "I'm afraid we're out of chairs. Do you mind standing, my son?"

"Of course not, serla." After hanging his weapons belt on an obliging hook as Talon had done, Milo tucked his helmet under his arm and stood in parade-rest beside the door.

"I could have a much larger office at the temple of the One," Vellis continued as he slipped around behind his desk to sit. "But I prefer being closer to our citizens in need, who often find their way to Mara's refuge. Besides, have you ever seen the passages beneath the temple? No? Well, the place is a regular rabbit warren. I get lost every time I visit."

As he spoke, another Circle priest came to the doorway, bearing a tray, a steaming pot, and cups. Once everyone had a cup of tea, the new fellow disappeared as quickly as he'd come.

Talon took a single sip of tea and then cleared her throat. "I know you're busy, serla. How may we be of assistance?"

"You can guess what we've called you here to discuss," Vellis said to Milo.

The cup felt too delicate for Milo's hand, as if he'd break it by touch alone. "With respect, didn't Sergeant Stonewall write a report?"

"Indeed, he did," Talon said. "And we have all studied it thoroughly. But Serla Vellis requested to meet one of the sentinels present – one of those tasked with guarding the mages."

Oh, shit. Milo's stomach plummeted to his knees. This was about his negligence in letting Mage Halcyon get harmed, wasn't it? He opened his mouth to say he'd *been* punished, already; he'd been doing his punishment when they'd summoned him, for Tor's sake! The proof stunk up the room.

"Be easy," Talon said, more gently than she'd spoken before. "You're not on trial, Milo. We're simply seeking clarity on a few points."

Milo relaxed a tiny bit and sipped the tea to try and collect himself before answering. When he was a little calmer, he related the mission as best he could.

"After I helped the blacksmith with the door, Flint and I started back for Mage Halcyon. We were talking and..." He winced at the memory, still painfully fresh even after almost a fortnight. "Someone screamed. I think it was Mage Halcyon, but it might've been the woman she was healing. Flint and I ran over as quick as we could, but by the time we got there, more villagers had surrounded them both. That's when we realized the villagers had turned into thralls. We managed to stop one of them from slitting Mage Halcyon's throat, thank Mara, but by then, the woman was... She was dead."

Vellis exhaled. "And the mage?"

"Mage Halcyon was..." Milo's heart hammered beneath his gear and he was, for some reason, loathe to speak the next words. "She was unconscious and wounded. Later, we learned that she had tried to use magic to defend herself against the thralls."

"How?"

Why was it so hard to say this? He wasn't in trouble and he was telling the truth. "I don't know, exactly. I don't understand how magic works.

But she did something to that villager, then the woman…died. Just keeled over." He shuddered at the memory. "We managed to push the thralls back so Sadira could come in. Mage Halcyon was covered in blood. She's lucky Sadira is such a fine healer."

"Sadira." Vellis looked at Talon. "This is the mage who was exiled from Zheem?"

Milo started, for he'd never heard this story. But Talon only nodded. "Aye, but she's docile. She's never given me any trouble."

"Until now, perhaps," Vellis replied. "What happened next, Milo?"

Stomach in knots, Milo recounted the rest of the gruesome story, all the way through the second thrall attack his squad had faced on Heartfire night. He only faltered when he mentioned Stonewall picking up Mage Halcyon to carry her out of the temple. Stonewall's relationship with a mage—whatever it was—wasn't anyone else's business, and besides, Milo still felt guilty for allowing Halcyon to get injured. Vellis seemed calm, only asking a few clarifying questions here and there as he sipped his tea. Talon's tea sat untouched on the desk, the rising steam dissipating.

At last, Milo finished his tale. Silence filled the room until Vellis stirred, adjusting his seat. "Thank you, Milo. That was as your sergeant reported the affair. I must ask, though, did you see any evidence that the mages had something to do with the thralls?"

"No, ser. And I've fought thralls many times before, and the answer is always the same."

Vellis nodded. "So we have gathered."

Milo blinked at him. "So… You don't think the mages started all this? Most folks believe that."

"To *our* detriment," Talon added.

The Circle priest considered. "The Pillars believe that the lack of response from the Canderi to our entreaties for a diplomatic solution to this crisis indicates that the thralls are connected to our northern neighbors. That, and the fact that the attacks seemed to include mostly Canderi warriors, with a few exceptions."

"With respect, serla," Milo said carefully. "The people of Parsa are more than 'a few.'"

"Not in the larger picture," Vellis replied.

How to make the priest understand? Milo thought back over all the thralls he'd seen – or even heard of. "About a month before Heartfire, my squad encountered an Aredian soldier who'd been…changed. And before that, my sergeant says he fought another Aredian-turned-thrall."

Vellis' mouth formed a sad smile, but his gaze was hard and his hands tightened around his cup. "I remember hearing of the soldier, but the matter was investigated and found to be a misunderstanding. Some problem with the poor fellow's armor not fitting properly, and causing marks on his skin. Milo, as someone who's fought the creatures many times, would you not agree that *most* thralls are Canderi.?"

"Err…" Milo bit his tongue to hopefully prevent another flush. "Well, aside from the poor souls at Parsa, I never really counted, serla. I…suppose so, but–"

"Then it is as the Pillars claim," Vellis broke in. "Our esteemed leaders are trying to get Queen Solasar to agree. If—when—that occurs, we will surely be at war with the Canderi, and it's likely that the sentinels will be called upon to an even greater degree."

War. The word was a drum in Milo's chest; the sound too large for his body to contain. He glanced at Talon to gauge her reaction, but she only watched the priest.

"To do what, serla?" Milo asked. "Fight the thralls?"

They'd been doing that for what felt like forever, with no luck. Unless… Had Talon told of Mage Halcyon's hope of curing thralls? He glanced at his commander, but her face remained impassive.

"If the situation comes to war," Vellis said, "mages are our only real asset against our foes. Magic is a tool, and any tool can be a weapon in the right hands. And who controls the mages?" He laced his fingers over his cup of tea. "Ah, I shouldn't speak of such matters. Nothing's set in stone, yet, but options are…under consideration."

"But it may not have to come to war," Milo heard himself say. "Serla, one of the mages at Whitewater Bastion thinks she can cure thralls."

Talon gave him an exasperated look, but Vellis lifted a brow. "An interesting notion, especially since, if mages can *cure* thralls, it stands to reason they can *create* thralls as well."

"I know the mage of whom Milo speaks," Talon added. "She is not to be trusted."

Milo blanched. "She's a healer, ser, like they all are."

The commander gave him another look, one he recognized too well: pity. He could almost hear her thoughts. *Foolish boy, to believe a mage's lies.*

Vellis seemed to feel the same way. "If we had a mage we could trust, it would be an idea worth exploring, but as it stands now, such trust is not possible."

Trust? Milo fought not to point an accusing finger at the priest. Instead, he pictured Stonewall's calm, stoic expression, and tried to school his own demeanor to match. "With the utmost respect, serla, the Pillars are considering using mages as...weapons against the Canderi. Between weapons and healers, I know which seems safer."

The priest's eyes narrowed at Milo, but his voice was cool. "The Pillars feel that mages are a last resort: a resource we should only exploit in times of dire need."

Milo gaped at him, all hope of stoicism forgotten. Was this a joke? Was the slaughter at Parsa not dire enough for the Pillars? Talon's shoulders sank a fraction, but Milo blazed with a fury that would have made Flint proud. "So innocent people should be left to suffer, because the Pillars fear a few more mages will escape their bastions?"

"If that is the One's will," Vellis answered. "Commander, remind your underling of his place in the One's world."

Talon shot Milo a quelling look. "Be still, Milo. Your part here is done."

"Yes, ser," he said as his heart hammered away.

She looked back at the priest. "Of course, we will do whatever we must to help the people of Aredia. But our efforts would be easier if the Circle publicly stated its stance on the mages' non-involvement with the thralls. Our last hematite shipment might not have been lost if the common folk felt differently about sentinels – and mages."

"People will believe what they want," Vellis replied. "But that doesn't make the truth any less—or any more—than what it is."

"Of course, serla," Talon said. "But many of the Parsan victims wore hematite. That alone proves that mages aren't creating the thralls."

"Or that hematite is no longer as effective as it once was," Vellis replied.

Milo thought of Mage Sadira and a blazing campfire, and silently agreed.

"Either way, public knowledge of such a thing would cause bedlam," the priest went on.

Talon's voice rose with impatience. "If the Circle would at least *acknowledge* the fact that mages aren't involved–"

Vellis held up a hand in a call for silence, and Talon snapped her jaw shut. Milo fought back the urge to stare. He'd never seen *anyone* treat her like... like she was a subordinate. As a member of the Circle clergy, Iban Vellis had authority over every sentinel in Whitewater Province. By extension, the Pillars—to whom Vellis must answer—could claim that same authority over every sentinel in Aredia.

The knowledge had never bothered Milo before now.

"Milo," Vellis said. "The commander and I have additional matters to discuss. Please show yourself out."

Milo looked at his commander before moving. Talon nodded to him. "Wait for me by the fountain. We'll walk back together."

He saluted her and Vellis, set his nearly-full teacup down and collected his gear. But when he opened the door, he caught the sound of footsteps pattering down the corridor. Had someone been listening? He considered following, but he'd pushed his luck enough today, so instead he went back to the quartz statue of Mara, thinking to take one last look before he and Talon returned to the garrison.

As he studied the crystal's inclusions, the soft swish of fabric made him turn. A priestess stood about an arm's length away, her white and black robe swaying around her legs. Pale spirals, swirls, and other patterns inked her dark-brown skin, and her eyes were swollen and puffy. "You were at Parsa," she said without preamble.

Milo ducked into a low bow; she was a Cipher, after all. "Aye, serla."

138

She swiped her cheeks. "Did you... You saw Cipher Telfair?"

Understanding swelled in his chest, and his words were suitably gentle, though nothing would make this easier to hear. "Yes, serla. She...was a thrall. But she's at peace, now."

"I know," the Cipher said, sniffing. "I said the rites at her pyre. But she was... She was badly injured. Was she... Did she...?" She took a shuddering breath. "I don't know what I'm asking."

"Have you ever encountered a thrall, serla?"

The Cipher shook her head.

Milo regarded Mara's statue again, focusing on the tiny rainbows caught within the crystal. "I pray you never do." Should he go into more detail? He nearly thought not, then realized how he'd feel if he was searching for answers about Flint, or anyone he cared about. So he related the story of his Heartfire night to the Cipher, who listened in silence. As he had no way of knowing how long it would be before Talon met him, he tried to speak quickly.

"She suffered some," he said at the end. "But not for very long, thank the One."

"Thank the One," the Cipher echoed, though she was weeping again, one hand pressed to her heart. "I'm sure I will, one day."

To give her some semblance of privacy, Milo looked at the floor. "I'm sorry."

"What is your name, Ser Sentinel?"

He gave another salute, bowing deep. "Milo, serla."

"Milo. I'm Natanaree." He guessed her to be in her early twenties. When their eyes met, her gaze upon him softened. "Thank you for telling me," she said. "I have suffered many sleepless nights since they brought my dear friend's body back."

The words escaped Milo before he could stop them. "If I had my way, no one would suffer any longer. Ever."

"A true devotee of Mara," Natanaree said, a trace of wry humor in the words, despite the tears on her cheeks. "You're a credit to your brothers and sisters in service."

Throat suddenly tight, Milo mumbled a goodbye and slipped out of the temple, his sword heavy and awkward again as he trudged to the fountain.

To his consternation, Serla Natanaree followed. "Have I offended you?"

"No, serla," he managed. "I'm sorry. I just..." He glanced around; they were alone out here. "Lately, I've felt like...like I'm not fit to be a sentinel."

"Why?"

Milo hesitated. He'd probably already said more than was wise. But once formed, the thought swelled in his chest like a bubble of air breaching the water's surface. He compromised by withdrawing his sword from its scabbard; not all the way, just enough so that the sunlight caught on the nicks and scratches unique to this weapon, marks that no amount of cleaning would ever scrub away. He had never minded that before Heartfire. Now there were new blemishes: souvenirs of Parsa.

The priestess regarded him before she placed a hand on his sword hilt, pushing it back into the scabbard. "Be patient, Milo. It may not feel like it now, but the One has a plan for you, and for all of us. But we must trust in the One."

He met her gaze. "I will if you will."

A small smile touched her mouth. "I'll try."

They looked at each other for a moment before she took one of his hands in both of hers. Compared to his broad palms and thick fingers, her hands were delicate as teacups; the inked whorls and flowers only added to the imbalance between them. Her skin was warm and soft in the way of one who had never held a sword.

"If you ever need anything," she said quietly. "Send word to me."

Heat coursed through him and he drew his hand back. "Thank you, serla, but I can't write Aredian. Can't even read it."

Sorrow crossed her face, but she pushed it aside and squared her shoulders. "That doesn't matter. Send word however you are able, and I'll give what aid I can manage."

"Tell Serla Iban Vellis to give our mages a chance to cure thralls," he said, adding, "Please."

Her brows knitted. "Cure thralls? Is that possible?"

"I know a mage who thinks so, but Serla Vellis won't hear of it. Mages *aren't* causing thralls," he added quickly. "A lot of the folks who've been turned were wearing hematite, which means mages are innocent. What's more, if anyone can help thralls—like Telfair—it's mages."

He could practically see the gears turning in Natanaree's head as stared at him. "I'll see what I can do," she said at last. "But if I were you, I wouldn't hold on to hope. Iban has no love of mages."

"I'll welcome anything you can do, serla."

She nodded. "Well, in any case, my initial offer stands."

Milo frowned at her. "Why bother with me, serla? I'm sure you have better things to do."

"I do," she said. "But above all, I am a servant of the One, and therefore of all the One's children." When she met his gaze again, her eyes were filled with resolve. "If you need anything I can provide, send word."

Milo still had his doubts, but it was foolish to turn down aid freely offered—especially from a Cipher—so he bowed once. "I will, serla. Thank you."

13

THIRTEEN

Talon silently counted to five after the door closed behind Milo before she looked back at Iban Vellis. "Forgive me, serla. I didn't mean to press you, but our need is very great."

"I'm well aware," Iban said, sipping his tea again. "But what concerns me is that you would have us publicly praise your sentinels' ability to control mages, yet your own subordinate speaks of powerful unauthorized magic."

"Halcyon acted in self-defense when the thrall attacked. Sadira aided her. Would you expect a threatened mage to behave otherwise?" A small part of her found grim amusement in the irony of her defense of Mage Halcyon – the root of only *some* of her recent troubles.

Iban regarded her. "Aye, so they do. I only hope, for all our sakes, that such reliance does not doom us all."

"Rest assured," Talon said. "I will deal with any mages who prove troublesome – as I have always done."

"As you dealt with Eris Echina?"

Heat flooded Talon's face and neck. "What do you mean, serla?"

The Circle priest gave her the chiding look one would give a child caught pilfering sweets before supper. "Don't play innocent, Talon. It doesn't suit you. I know what happened on Heartfire. The gate guards are loyal to the Circle, and they do love their gossip." His features hardened. "And since High Commander Argent is not here to deal with your failure, I can only

142

assume he does not know of it – yet."

This, at least, she could defend against. "He knows, serla. And he has seen fit to let me handle the matter myself." Not exactly true; she'd only sent the letter off a few days ago and had not yet received a reply. But Iban didn't need to know that detail. Determined to maintain her composure, Talon raised her chin. "In the meantime, Eris may be gone, but I have one of her allies: the renegade mage who orchestrated her and the others' escape, *and* who stole our hematite shipment before Heartfire."

This was the card she'd been waiting to play. Sure enough, Iban leaned forward. "Where is this mage?"

"Safe and sound, bound by hematite in one of the garrison cells."

"Along with the rest of your mages, I hope?"

Surely, he wasn't serious. Talon cleared her throat to be certain she could speak normally. "The mages who did not flee Whitewater Bastion are collared. But we don't have enough cells to accommodate all of them."

"The creatures don't need to be comfortable," Iban replied. "Just locked away."

The thought of Foley behind bars made her sick. Bad enough she had to keep her own father shackled like some beast; a better, more gentle man there had never been than Foley Clementa. Talon knew her voice trembled, but for once, she didn't care. "The collars will suffice for now. Only myself and Cobalt carry the keys, and no mage can work magic on hematite."

Iban studied her before shrugging once. "As you say, Commander. Back to the renegade mage; what have you learned from it?"

It. Foley would have winced, but Talon kept her features impassive. There was no time for sentiment, nor time to savor her tiny victory. "Not much," she admitted. "Other than he seems to be kin to one of my sentinels – and is a former sentinel, himself."

Iban went still, his voice dropping to a lower register than Talon had heard before; a distant rumble of thunder. "Kin to whom?" he asked.

"Sergeant Stonewall." Talon's jaw clenched like she'd tasted something sour. First the moron took up with a bastion mage, now he was a renegade's brother. At this point, if the idiot turned out to be a mage himself, she would hardly be surprised.

"The name is familiar…" Iban considered. "Ah, young Milo's officer." His brows drew together. "Did this 'Stonewall' have a part in the Heartfire escape?"

This, at least, she could answer with clarity. "He was in Parsa at the time. Later, I brought him to the renegade mage, and got the impression that neither had seen or spoken to each other in several years. Apparently, Stonewall believed the other man to be dead."

"Assuming he wasn't dissembling." Iban's tone was far too calm for comfort. "I imagine Stonewall is locked in a cell, too?"

"No, serla." Heat swam through her body as the Circle priest's eyes widened.

"Why in Atal's name is he walking free?"

Something seized Talon's heart; fear, perhaps, or anger. Not at the thought of losing Stonewall—he'd caused more trouble than he was worth—but at the idea of stretching the Whitewater garrison's numbers any further. "Because he's *walking*. Unlike most of my cinders, not to mention those under my command whom thralls have murdered. Our numbers are dwindling, serla, and that's not going to change without the Circle's intervention."

Iban gave a genuine laugh. "Your subtlety knows no bounds, Commander. Very well, then. You've followed orders; you've earned compensation."

He withdrew a key from his desk, went to the locked cabinet, and worked the latch. The massive doors swung open to reveal shelves stocked with hematite vials resting in wooden holders. Talon's mouth watered. So much hematite! Iban's supply could stock her garrison for months.

Iban collected some vials into a single pouch and then presented the bundle to Talon. The moment she felt the weight of the vials within the muslin, she could not suppress a shiver of longing. But when she peered inside, her heart sank.

"Can't we have more, serla?" she asked as he settled back at his desk. "The city guards dredged the river, but found no trace of Slate's body – or our hematite. As I have said, our need is–"

"As *I* have said," Iban broke in. "This is all I can give you, now. However, I anticipate more will become available once you carry out your next set of orders." He held up one of the papers on his desk. "The fleet rider brought this before dawn. It comes directly from the Pillars."

Cold swept over Talon like sleet. So here was the heart of his summons. "Orders for us?"

He offered the paper to Talon, but she could only stare without comprehension at the little symbols of Aredian script. "Argent didn't write this," she said. "No sentinel did."

Iban chuckled. "No, Commander."

Blood beat in her ears and her fingers tightened around the paper's edge. Only years of training in self-control allowed her to set it back on his desk, unharmed, although he must have noticed how the paper fluttered as her hand shook.

"What does it say, serla?" she asked.

"What I have already told you," Iban answered. "The Pillars fear that the Assembly will divide our country further. The queen can't have the dregs sowing chaos from within while the barbarians from Cander attack us from without. Thusly, the Pillars have asked every member of the Circle to help stand against this new internal threat while our queen turns her attention to the northern barbarians."

When Talon found her voice, it wavered. "The Assembly haven't been sighted in–"

"A group of known Assembly folk were spotted in Oreion not a week ago," Iban interrupted. "In the company of Sufani nomads."

"The ones who stole our hematite?"

"Perhaps. Until now, the Assembly has only ever been reported in Indigo-By-the-Sea Province, but Haril—my counterpart there—is enmeshed in the troubles of the upper-tiered merchants, and has done little to root out these vermin."

Which left Iban in a position to do more – and to gain favor with the Pillars. Understanding coalesced in Talon's heart. "What must my sentinels do, Serla Vellis?" she asked.

145

He drained his tea and set the cup down with a soft *clink*. "Forget Eris Echina and any other renegade mages. Forget the thralls. As of this moment, your highest priority is rooting out the Assembly, starting with their heretical Sufani allies. Don't look so scandalized, Commander. You will be fulfilling the Pillars' deepest desires." A knowing gleam appeared in his eyes and his next words were hushed. "This is not common knowledge, but it is nearly time for the Pillars' transfer of power to their successors."

The Pillars were older than water, so this was not a complete shock. No wonder Iban wanted to be in the Pillars' good graces; surely every member of the Circle clergy hoped to be selected for the honor. "Have they chosen their successors?" Talon asked.

"Not yet. But completing this task would be a great boon to the current Pillars as well as those who will come after. And need I remind you of your stolen hematite? You should be glad of a chance to settle the score."

"The renegade mage is already captured," she managed. "I'm positive he was working with the Assembly. Is he not enough to satisfy the Pillars?"

"One errant mage?" Iban shook his head. "No doubt, it's better to have that creature behind hematite, but it is not the greater threat our Pillars fear. Dissension, disharmony, chaos…" His expression darkened. "Those are the true enemies of our people. The Assembly is weak now, in its fledgling stages, but its influence is spreading. Several of the wealthier Indigoan merchants have been calling for their governor to pressure Queen Solasar into disbanding the tier system altogether. They claim it's bad for business – among other ridiculous notions."

"I hadn't heard," Talon admitted.

"No, you wouldn't have," Iban replied. "Because your focus is where it should be: the mages. You are always dutiful, Commander, but the scope of the larger story eludes you." He leaned back in his chair to better regard her. "I know that look on your face. You believe I'm in the wrong for not considering the thralls the true threat, but you are small-minded. This is not a slight against your intelligence, but merely a byproduct of your focus. There is balance in all things, after all. We must have peace in the realm if we are to survive. The Pillars realize that sometimes the price of that peace seems unsavory, but they feel—as do I—that the future will confirm the rightness of this decision."

Talon's thoughts chased each other in circles. "Does Argent know of the Pillars'...plans?"

"Argent was informed this morning."

Gods above and beyond, this was *more* information than she'd anticipated. *The future will confirm the rightness of this decision.* How many times had she harbored similar feelings, albeit on a smaller scale? To give herself something to do, she reached for her cup of tea. By now it was cold, but she took a deep drink anyway. "Will there be a war?"

"I dearly hope not. The Pillars are working to avoid such a catastrophe, but we cannot ignore the possibility of war – twice over." He sighed. "Civil or with Cander, if war comes, and if the Queen realizes we will not defeat our enemies without magic, your sentinels may find themselves at the front lines."

She took a shaking breath. War. Politics. All of it more than she ever wanted to think about. "We'll do our best, serla."

"You'll have to." Iban nodded to the muslin pouch, still in Talon's grip. "For now, keep your focus restricted to your orders. The renegade mage and his kin will keep for a while longer. It is curious, though, that a Forsworn sentinel could survive so long without hematite. I suppose magic played a part. How did the creature manage the feat? Did he steal your shipment to sate his craving, or sell hematite to...recreational users?" Iban's face darkened. "We've had more reports of people using ruthless."

"The renegade is reluctant to share any information," Talon said. "But I'm confident that, with time, I can–"

"No need to question the dreg further. Just send it to Lasath once you've carried out your orders and you have the numbers for escort duty. The renegade might know where others of its kind are. The Pillars will want to find the creatures – and I know they will be interested to learn the trick of this traitor's survival. Send Sergeant Stonewall as well. Any connection to a renegade mage—particularly one with such a unique history—must be investigated. And..." A faint frown touched his face. "Send the mage who believes it can 'cure' thralls, too. The one who attacked an innocent in supposed self-defense. I assume she's locked away?"

"Of course, serla," Talon replied. Halcyon *was* locked inside the bastion, after all. "Though it'd be easier to end her life now and be done with the trouble she's caused."

Iban shook his head. "*All* unusual magical activity is to be reported to the Pillars. You know that." He lifted a dark brow. "I'll refrain from asking why you did not do so, sooner, if you comply and send Halcyon to the Pillars as soon as you can spare sentinels to escort her." He exhaled and sat back in his chair, lacing his fingers before him. "But for now, your priority is the Sufani. Bring in as many as you can—and anyone else who you think could be working with the Assembly—and you'll have more hematite than you can handle."

Impossible, Talon thought, but kept her expression neutral as she lifted the bag. "Very well, serla, but this isn't enough to keep us going even for now. We need more."

Iban's smile held no warmth. "Then I suggest you get to work."

* * *

Milo squinted in the sunlight as he watched the passers-by outside Mara's temple. He was close to the fountain; every now and then, droplets landed upon his armor, reminding him of mist from the White River. By now, clouds had overtaken the sky: pure white shaded with pale-gray, blocking the glittering sunlight. His breath fogged in the chill air. Despite the sacred ground beneath his feet, his meeting with the Circle priest had destroyed any peace that lingered in his heart. The dark looks many civilians cast his way didn't help. A few folks even spat in his general direction, albeit not directly on the temple grounds – that would be sacrilege. But he got the hint.

It'd been stupid to come here alone. No wonder the commander wanted them to walk back together.

"Milo."

148

He fell into parade-rest at Talon's voice as she strode up and signaled him to follow. But instead of heading back to the garrison, she wound her way toward the docks on the river's edge. But why?

Thank Mara, he didn't have to wonder long. They reached the docks and Talon's pace slowed as she walked along the river, her gaze distant as she turned her face to the ferries, skiffs, barges, and other boats that cluttered the harbor. No one could travel down the White River's falls, of course, but plenty of trade took place upriver, with Whitewater City often being the final stop on many a merchant's travels. If Milo squinted against the glare of the sky, he could make out the thick hemp net strung across the river, between the city and the far shore, to prevent any unlucky boats from tumbling down the falls. Here, the water's roar was louder than he was used to. If he closed his eyes, the sound drowned out all other thoughts.

The commander's voice broke him out of his trance. Blinking, Milo looked at her. "Sorry, ser?"

A faint smile tugged at one corner of her mouth. "I asked if you were feeling any ill-effects from a lack of hematite?"

"Oh." He shook his head. "Not that I can tell, ser."

"Good. Can your sister say the same?"

"Yes, Commander."

"And how are you, in general?"

He opened his mouth to lie, but couldn't form the words. A group of sailors unloaded a cargo skiff nearby and thankfully did nothing harsher than cast a few glowers at the sentinels. "Not good, ser," Milo said, wincing. "Everyone hates us. And I can't blame them."

Talon's watchful brown eyes flickered to the sailors before resting again on Milo. "People are afraid and angry. With the mages hidden in the bastion, we are the easiest targets for those feelings."

Milo watched the rippling river, uncertain how his words would be met. "We killed those people at Parsa, ser. Yes, it was in defense of the mages. Yes, it was because somehow, those villagers turned into thralls. But still." He put a hand to his armored chest. "I killed civilians in their own village.

In their own *temple.*"

Aye, and the same place he'd fought to protect mere months ago. The man his sister had loved had *died* to keep Parsa safe. Now the village was a skeleton of itself. His eyes pricked with heat at the memories crashing over him: blood and steel; terror and desperation. His sword hung heavily at his side.

"Everything's wrong," he whispered.

"Aye, Parsa was a tragedy, and I'm sorry you had a part in it. But Milo," she rested a hand on his right shoulder, urging him to meet her gaze, "there is a pattern to all things that we cannot see. Sometimes, the only good we can do is serve that pattern, even if its design and purpose are beyond our understanding."

Milo clenched his teeth, for her words had struck true. *Faith.* Perhaps it was a luxury for some, but it was all he had now. "Yes, ser."

She lowered her hand. "Sometimes it's easy to walk this path. Sometimes, our troubles are simple to solve, and it's easy to know that what we do is right and just and good. But most of the time, our path is a difficult one. Do you remember why we carry the weapons we do?"

Milo gripped his daggers. "Two daggers for defense," he recited. "One sword to subdue – but only as a last resort." *Subdue*: a polite way of saying "kill."

"That is what we use our weapons *for*," Talon said. "But do you know *why?*" Milo shook his head and she continued. "Two daggers to represent the dual nature of our role in the One's world. We protect those who cannot protect themselves; we guard against those who could use their power for evil."

Talon's sword slid soundlessly from its scabbard. In the daylight, Milo could see how her weapon, though clean, was nicked and scarred far more than his. "One sword," she said, meeting his gaze. "Because there is one truth we must always bear in mind: we are here to keep balance. The greater good must always come before our own desires, for our duty is, and always will be, to the One."

True words, if ever there were any. Milo nodded and Talon sheathed her sword, and then gestured to the street that had deposited them at the docks. They began to make their way back to the garrison.

Not until they were out of sight of the river did the commander speak again, her voice casual. "How are you faring under Sergeant Stonewall?"

The mention of Stonewall drove away Milo's gathered calm. He kept his gaze on the cobbled streets, lest he crash into anyone. "Very well, ser."

"Did he offer you counsel after Parsa?"

"He did, ser. Good counsel, too. But Parsa was…" He swallowed. "Difficult."

"Sometimes the difficult missions are the ones that strengthen bonds the most." She was silent as they walked and her hand stole to a muslin pouch tied to her belt. "Has the sergeant done or said anything you find unsavory?"

A flush crept up Milo's neck as he recalled the journey back from Parsa. But as Mage Halcyon had said, the connection between her and Stonewall didn't really matter, did it? Milo and Flint had spoken about it all later, and Flint claimed not to care…but then, she wasn't the best barometer of morality. Beacon, too, hadn't opposed to the idea, but Milo thought the mender had his own interests at heart, given how flustered he got around Sadira.

Rook hadn't liked it, but hadn't said anything more after that single conversation the day after Heartfire.

But what do I think? Milo knew nothing of romantic love, but he knew enough about Stonewall to answer Talon.

"The sergeant is…a little closed-off, sometimes," Milo admitted. "I think he's still learning how to work with a team. But otherwise, he's a fair leader and a skilled fighter, and I have no complaints."

They approached the Eye and passed a group of city guards who each nodded to the sentinels. Talon returned the nod, her gaze still ahead. "Has he made any trips to the bastion, alone?"

"Not since Heartfire." Thank the One, it was the truth. If the sergeant had snuck off recently, he'd done so without Milo's knowledge. He risked a glance to see if Talon accepted the answer and found her frowning. His heart began to race again, the feeling of *danger* made stronger by the dark looks some of the market-goers kept shooting at the sentinels.

"He's good for us—all of us—and we all like him a great deal," Milo blurted. "Even Flint, I think, though it's hard to tell with her, sometimes. And–"

"Be still," Talon broke in. Wincing internally, Milo snapped his jaw shut as she glanced his way again. She was still frowning, so he braced for a reprimand, but there was no trace of anger in her next words. "I know the conversation with Serla Vellis was difficult, but I appreciate your honesty – and courage. It takes an iron spine to stand up to the leader of the Whitewater City Circle." A warm smile touched her mouth. "You're growing into a fine sentinel Milo. I look forward to seeing the warrior you will one day become."

The praise caught Milo up short. The only answer he could think to give was a warrior's salute. When he straightened, Talon dug into the muslin pouch and withdrew a single vial, pressing it into Milo's palm. He stared at the full dose of hematite before looking back at her and shaking his head. "I don't need this, ser," he stammered, trying to hand the vial back. "Give it to Redfox, or one of the other cinders–"

But she closed his gloved hand back around the vial. "Keep it. You never know when you'll need more strength. Besides, it brings me comfort to know I can count on you."

With that, she turned her back to him and threaded her way through the Eye, her long, powerful strides causing the market-goers to scramble out of her path. Milo stared at the vial before tucking it safely in his belt-pouch and hurrying after his commander. His head spun. Was the vial a bribe of some kind? But why in Ea's realm would Talon want to bribe a burnie?

As Milo reached the front of the Eye, he spotted a familiar figure heading toward the fleet rider station. He lifted his hand in greeting. "Rook!"

She froze and then waved back. Milo trotted to her and they met in front of the station: an unassuming building with a courtyard and iron gates, open during the day.

"What are you doing out here alone?" Milo asked, shielding his eyes from the sky's white glare.

Rook lifted a brow. "I should ask that of you, burnie."

The tension that had been stringing Milo taut broke at her words. Relief at being with his friend almost made him dizzy, and he grinned at her. "So...what's her name?"

"Whose name?"

Milo nodded to the tight roll of parchment in Rook's grip. "The fair maiden you're writing to."

She flushed, but before she could reply, she grabbed Milo's arm and pulled him to one side just as a girl and her fleet came barreling toward the station. Several bulging sacks bounced upon the saddle with each of the large deer's strides.

"Stay out of the way," the rider called, adding a string of obscenities that made Milo frown.

"Isn't she a little young for that kind of talk?" he asked as the girl and her deer clattered into the courtyard.

Rook watched them go. "Fleet riders grow up fast. Maybe too fast."

"You were one, before you were a sentinel," Milo said. "Right?"

She nodded. "You should get back. Ferro's looking for you."

Milo grimaced. "More stable duty, I guess."

"Aye." She gave him a sympathetic look before nodding to the fleet rider station. "Well, I'd better get a move on."

Despite the reminder of his continuing punishment, despite the strange turn the day had taken, Milo smiled again at his squad-mate. "Aye. Don't want to keep your sweetheart waiting."

He'd expected—and hoped for—a laugh in response, but Rook's face fell and her shoulders slumped. "No, I don't."

"If you're just going to be a minute, I'll wait for you," he offered. "We shouldn't walk about alone, not after what happened with Slate..." He trailed off at her pained expression.

Rook considered, glancing between the parchment and Milo, before nodding once, slowly. "That's kind of you, Mi. Thanks."

He shrugged. "That's what brothers-in-service are for."

14

FOURTEEN

Stonewall took one last look at the bastion. The rest of his squad had already slipped through the gates, heading to the barracks for their midday meal, but something held him back.

Hornfel, one of the burnies on duty at the gates, shifted in place. "Everything all right, Sergeant?"

Stonewall nodded absently, his mind far afield. Something wasn't right. He nearly dismissed the notion as a byproduct of his anxiety, but still stayed behind. Through the gates, Beacon turned to give him a questioning look.

"Not hungry?" Beacon asked.

"I'll be right there," Stonewall replied.

The mender's gaze slid over his shoulder and then back to Stonewall. "You'll be late for the meeting. Don't want to get on Talon's bad side. Again."

"I'll be fine. Just go, Beak."

Beacon nodded and continued with the others.

After they'd gone, Hornfel cleared his throat, drawing Stonewall's attention. "Haven't seen your squad around here lately, ser."

"Cobalt added us to the duty roster," Stonewall replied, still searching the bastion. He half expected to see Kali approaching, and when he spotted a lone figure hurrying up, his heart soared. But she was too tall for Kali, and her pale hair and smooth stride soon formed Sadira.

"Really, ser?" Hornfel sounded bewildered. "But I thought you weren't

154

allowed to..."

Stonewall shot the younger man a look and the burnie grimaced beneath his helmet. "If you have a problem with my presence here," Stonewall said. "Take it up with Captain Cobalt." Yes, he'd added himself and his squad to the bastion patrol, but Cobalt hadn't argued or changed anything. Had they formed a truce after the hematite shipment had been destroyed four days ago? Or did the captain simply have too many other worries to bother with Stonewall?

Either way, Stonewall wasn't about to object.

"Sergeant." Urgency laced Sadira's voice and her dark-blue dress fluttered behind her as she hurried up. "I must speak with you."

Stonewall ignored Hornfel and went to meet her. "What's wrong?"

Pale eyes studied him before darting to Hornfel and the bastion gates. "I must speak with you...privately."

Was Kali in trouble? His heart seized but he tried to keep his apprehension from showing. "My patrol is over, so I'm not allowed to be in the bastion any longer," he said, loud enough for Hornfel to overhear. He gave Sadira a look he prayed she would read. "But the next patrol will be along in–"

Thank Tor, she was quick. "I have information about the Heartfire escape. I know where Eris and the others might have gone."

Stonewall pretended to study her, and then looked at the burnie on gate duty. "Fetch the captain or commander at once. I'll keep an eye on the mage."

Hornfel's eyes widened. "But ser, don't *you* want to–"

"That's an order, burnie," Stonewall snapped. "Move your ass before I do it for you."

The younger man stammered an affirmative before scurrying toward the barracks, leaving Stonewall and Sadira alone. "I am...concerned for Kali," Sadira whispered. "And I did not know who else I could speak to."

Stonewall could not find his voice right away. It'd been too long since he'd seen Kali and longer since they had spoken, but they had agreed that such distance was for the best. He had only just been permitted back into the bastion, and that was probably because so many other sentinels were growing too sick to stand. A few days ago, Talon had managed to get a little bit of hematite, which the menders had added to their dwindling supply. Even so, Beacon said that more and more sentinels came to the infirmary every day.

Stonewall didn't want to think too hard about that, for he, too, felt the chill: the unrelenting urge for that sweet fire in his blood. And although he fell into his bed each night, exhausted, sleep eluded him for all but a few restless hours.

"What's wrong?" Stonewall asked again.

Sadira tilted her head, indicating that he should follow. Without hesitation, Stonewall fell in step beside her as she crossed the bastion courtyard to Gideon Echina's grave. Stonewall shuddered at the mound of dirt marked with a few shining pebbles, dried flowers, and other trinkets. The thought of anyone's soul wandering aimlessly, endlessly, was enough to make his guts roil.

Swallowing his unease, he looked at Sadira, who twisted her hands. "We burned him," she said.

"You...?"

"Kali and I." Sadira took a deep breath, touching the hematite torc around her neck, sitting beneath the collar. Quickly, she related the story of Gideon's cremation, including how Kali had encouraged her to use her powerful magic. There was a softness to Sadira's gaze as she spoke of Kali, and Stonewall took a second to marvel at the trust Sadira placed in him by sharing this information; trust Sadira had probably formed through her friendship with Kali.

"Foley said he had 'words ready' when anyone noticed," Sadira finished, gesturing again to the grave. "But so far, no sentinel has spoken of this."

"Most of the garrison was out hunting for Eris and the others around that time," Stonewall said. "And I suppose the snow covered up any signs of magic. I can't say I'm angry that Gideon got a proper cremation, though officially, I probably should be. But...Kali?"

"Just after we burned the body, Kali began acting strangely. She acted as

156

if in pain, though she bore no wound. She fell and would not allow anyone to help her up."

"Her knee?"

"This was different. She claimed she was ill with women's troubles, but... " Sadira sighed. "She is a poor liar."

"Indeed, she is." Stonewall tried to speak lightly, but his heart was racing faster than before. "Where is she, now?"

"She shut herself in her room and will not come out. She eats only crumbs from the trays I leave, and you can hear her viol all night. I don't know if she sleeps. Foley told me 'let her be,' but something is wrong. And something befell her at Parsa, something that makes me think whatever troubles her is not illness or injury."

Stonewall's head felt light at the mention of the shattered village and he gritted his teeth against the memories. Something *was* wrong with Kali; he knew it, too. Nothing that screamed *danger*, but a muttered warning: Kali's strange behavior the night of Heartfire, after the second thrall attack at their camp. *"Let me go,"* she had snarled at him, and for less than a second her eyes had flashed... He'd told himself the sight was a product of his imagination, and nothing more. But if his brother could come back from the dead, anything was possible.

"I've had similar thoughts about Parsa," he said slowly, forcing away the thoughts of Drake.

The Zhee mage nodded. "Kali and I both sensed a...foreign presence in the villagers. But Kali alone investigated."

Worse and worse. "She...investigated its particles?"

"Yes." Sadira gave him an odd look. "What do you know of such matters?"

"She's told me a little of how magic works." His head swam and his limbs felt weak, as if his body could no longer support his weight. The urge to abandon everything and race to Kali's room beat at him like a hammer. Every muscle, every bone, ached to be at her side. But he could not risk endangering her any more. Not yet. Not until he had a real plan, not just a shadow of an idea.

"I grow fearful," Sadira whispered.

"Me too."

Milo had told the squad of his meeting with Talon and the Circle priest, but the commander hadn't given the garrison any direction – yet. No doubt that's what today's meeting was for. And any moment Hornfel would return with Talon or Cobalt, and Stonewall would be in a world of shit – again. He could not help Kali if he was banned from the bastion a second time. Although he had regained some standing with Cobalt, he was still on probation. He could not risk stepping out of line until he was ready to cross that line forever.

But the woman he loved was in trouble. Sod it all. He'd have to figure something out.

So he ensured his voice held more confidence than he felt. "I'll go to her as soon as I can. I may need your help, though."

Relief swept over Sadira's face and she gave a brief bow. "Thank you." She paused. "Stonewall."

When Cobalt and Hornfel arrived a few minutes later, Stonewall stood by the closed bastion gates, a suitably irritated expression on his face. The moment Cobalt came within earshot, Stonewall made a show of shaking his head and glaring at no one. "False alarm," he said. "She didn't have any information of value. She just wanted to ask after Eris Echina."

Cobalt frowned at him. "That's what you get for being so chummy with mages, Sergeant. They prey on weakness." He jerked his thumb toward the barracks. "Come on. Talon's waiting."

* * *

Shivering, Kali scrubbed the linen towel over her arms and legs. Without magical assistance, her hair would take hours to dry, so for now she had wrapped another towel around her head. The stone floor of the women's bathing room was like ice on the soles of her feet and she thought of her wool socks with longing. But she needed to get dry first.

Hanging lanterns soaked the room in warm light. The scents of rosemary and sunflower oil clung to her prickling skin, and Kali exhaled in relief. Yes, she was freezing, but at least she was clean. As she had hoped, a bath had helped bring a little bit of calm order back to the chaos in her mind. If only she'd been able to use her magic to heat the water. Normally, she'd have asked Sadira to do so—the Zhee mage would not only warm the bathwater, but the entire room as well, including the stone floor—but of course, Kali couldn't be near Sadira now. She couldn't be near any other mage. Not until she had more control over...

Over the Fata that had taken hold of her.

She shivered, but not from cold. *Taken hold*, she reminded herself. *Not taken over*. She still felt the Fata's presence: a wolf prowling through each corner of her mind, searching for weakness. Distraction seemed to keep the creature at bay, so she'd spent hours with her viol, or reading every book in her collection. But in the fortnight since Heartfire, those activities had lost their shine and she felt the Fata within poised and eager to strike.

But did they just want magic? Or was there something else they were after? Had the Fata only tried to possess mages, she might have thought magic was their ultimate desire, but so far only non-magical folk had been turned into thralls. No; something bigger was going on. Kali was sure of it.

Dry enough and ready to be warm, Kali wrapped the towel around her torso so she could tiptoe to her clean clothes, heaped on one of the bathing room's wooden benches.

When Kali had first arrived at Whitewater Bastion, the sheer size of the place and the number of mages living within its walls had left her awestruck. However, that awe had turned to dismay once she'd seen the bathing rooms. Both women's and men's were little more than single dorm rooms with multiple tubs. Back at Starwatch, she had gotten used to the hot springs the bastion had been built over, thus making every bath the height of luxury. Here, it wasn't so bad if Sadira was around—or if Kali could have used her own magic—but the hematite collar prevented her from doing much. Besides, even if she'd been without the collar, she was too exhausted from lack of sleep to try anything magical.

Sweet blood.

Kali clenched her jaw and tried to ignore the Fata's voice inside her head, and instead busied herself with hopping into her socks first – without removing her towel. Not an easy feat, given her knee pain, but her feet were sodding *freezing.* Her antics caused the towel around her hair to come loose and crumple to the floor.

A soft knock sounded at the door. Kali frowned. Everyone should be in the common room, which was why she'd chosen to bathe at supper time. Had Sadira come to check on her again? Or Foley? "Who's there?" she called.

"Someone who loves you," Stonewall replied through the door.

Her mouth fell open in shock. What in the stars was he *thinking*? She limped to the bathing room door, damp hair plastered to her back and one sock in her hand, and wrenched the door open. Sure enough, her sentinel was there, fully armored and glancing down the empty corridor behind him with apprehension.

Kali pulled him inside and shut the door behind them. "What in the blazing void are you doing here?"

He swept a cursory look around the room before resting his gloved hands on her shoulders to study her face. "Are you all right? Sadira said..." He trailed off when she frowned. "We're both concerned," he finished.

His gloves were cold and his armor wouldn't be much better, but the moment he touched her, something inside of her relaxed. Kali pressed against him to better savor his familiar scent; all of him was *familiar* in a way that went deeper than love or lust or any of the emotions they'd shared. *Familiar;* almost kin in a strange sense, although she'd searched his particles before to be certain they shared no blood.

Stonewall wrapped his arms around her and held her close, and they stood in silence. At last, she pulled back to look up at him. "I thought sentinels didn't come inside the mages' private spaces."

Strong hands skimmed down her sides before sliding up to brush aside her damp hair; the light touch made her shiver. "Sentinels aren't supposed to do a lot of things."

"But how did you get in here?"

"That's what doors are for."

Kali rolled her eyes. "Dumb jokes are *my* territory."

A faint smile touched his mouth. "Sadira's with the other mages at dinner; she's to keep any of them from leaving. Nicely," he added with a frown. "Although I'm not sure how."

"She shouldn't risk anything for me," Kali said.

"She wanted to, and besides, I couldn't have gotten in here without her help. Lieutenant Wren's squad was scheduled for bastion patrol tonight, but he *hates* bastion patrol and prefers to be out in the city, which, coincidentally, my squad was scheduled for. Given that the lieutenant had been scheduled for bastion duty *every* day this week, he was eager to trade."

"Convenient," Kali said, one brow lifted. "But something in your eyes tells me none of that was accidental."

"Ah, well. You see, Cobalt's turned the duty roster over to me. And of course, I'll do anything to help the garrison run smoothly in this time of strife."

The formal tone of his voice, coupled with his wry smile, made her stare at him, half stunned, half delighted. "You devious bastard," she said, laughing.

His grin turned boyish. "I have my moments. And most of my squad *is* on patrol, by the way."

"I suppose you can't use your new responsibilities to get this collar off?"

His smile died. His touch against her skin was light as his thumb grazed the collar and her still-tender scar. "Only Talon and Cobalt have the keys, and I couldn't see a way to swipe one without either of them noticing. I'm sorry," he added, softer.

"It's all right." And it was. She leaned into his touch.

"Kali," he said. "What happened to you at Parsa?"

Sweet blood. Sweet magic. Give it to us. Now.

Her cheeks burned. "I don't know what you mean."

"Kali."

Stonewall's voice was quiet, but heavy, and his earnest gaze upon her filled her to the brim. He had risked so much to come here, for her. The moment he learned what was wrong, he'd demand she seek another mage to help her; definitely the wisest option. But she wasn't feeling so wise now.

She leaned her cheek against his cuirass, ignoring the uncomfortable press of hard leather and hematite, and took a deep breath. "I think I'm possessed by the Fata."

His body went rigid until he drew back and urged her to look at him. Worry was plain in his eyes, but she saw his warrior's determination studying her, assessing this new threat from all angles. "Why do you think that?'

"That night—Heartfire—before the thralls attacked, I *heard* them, but only in my mind at first. Somehow, I felt them coming."

"You jumped like you'd been bitten."

"But it's more than feeling emotions that aren't mine. I also want..." Kali struggled to find the right words. "Magic. Not just mine, but other mages'. It's like...a hunger so intense, I can't think of anything else. It started in Parsa, when I healed that woman, the one who..." She trailed off, her fingertips brushing the scar at her throat. Tears stung her eyes. "I sensed something wrong with her particles, something beyond injury or illness, so I investigated." She shivered. "I found the Fata. And they found me."

"Your eyes are...normal."

She swiped away the wetness on her cheeks, working to shore up her own resolve. She was no warrior, but she could fight in her own way. When she looked up at him again, she ensured there was steel in her gaze. "I'm controlling the feelings: the rage and the fear. I've had some...strange dreams, but nothing I can't handle. As to the hunger, it's easier to control myself if I avoid other mages. I can't risk hurting them. But–"

"You *shouldn't* be avoiding them," Stonewall broke in. "You should do the opposite. Maybe Sadira can burn that thing out of you or...something." He strode to her pile of clothes and began collecting them with shaking hands. "Come on. Let's find her and ask."

But Kali stayed in place. "Stonewall... I can't risk it."

162

"It's all right." He held out her tunic. "I won't let you hurt anyone."

She stared at him, but her thoughts had raced ahead. What ifs and maybes whirled through her mind, chasing the *otherness* that she'd come to think of as the Fata within. Whether it was a temporary reprieve or a permanent one, she did not know, but she seized the momentary advantage of a clear head. Her father's words echoed in her memory. *"Magic is a terrifying gift, Kali. The One has entrusted you with great power, so you must always use it wisely, and for the greater good."*

Some of Kali's hard-won calm slipped away and *hunger* prowled on the heels of her agitation. All the power in the world could be hers. She only had to take it. But she shook the thought away at once, focusing on her crystalizing resolve. Yes, this was the reason she'd been possessed: knowledge.

Kali shook her head. "I...need answers."

"Don't we all," he muttered. "Come on. We'll go now. Sod my orders."

"Stonewall, I'm in a unique position to learn more about the thralls – and the Fata."

He stared at her, one hand still outstretched with her tunic. "What are you saying?"

"I *will* seek help," she said. "But not yet. Not until I get some more information."

"What are you talking about? Are you going to..." His hand tightened around the fabric. "Chat with the sodding Fata? You're sick, Kali. You need–"

"I *need* to understand what's going on."

"At what cost?" Stonewall's words echoed through the bathing chamber.

"My life is my own to risk, remember?" she said.

"It's not just your life at stake." He seemed to force the next words out. "If you do...turn into a thrall, completely, you could do so much damage."

"I can handle this," she replied, sharper than she meant to. "For a little while, at least. Stonewall, if I can learn what the Fata want, what they're doing to our people, perhaps I can find a way to help those they've turned to thralls. I might even learn how to stop the Fata, for good."

"This is folly," he whispered, still clutching her shirt. "Kali, you're not thinking clearly."

Anger swelled within her, hot and sudden and strong, and when she spoke, her voice was not her own. "If you don't trust me, then leave me alone."

He stared at her. "I do trust you. But not...the thralls, or Fata, or whatever's...taken hold of you."

She managed a wry smile. "Nor do I. But I'm on my guard. I'll be fine." She held out her hand. "Give me my shirt. I'm freezing."

He passed over the garment, clearly still at a loss. While she dressed, she shot him another look, hoping to change the subject. "Did you really do those duty roster shenanigans out of worry for me?"

Stonewall leaned against the bathing room door, tucked his gloves in his belt and rubbed his forehead. "I've been trying to find a way to see you. A lot's happened since we got back. Talon put me on probation," he added, scowling.

"Can't say I blame her," Kali said as she wriggled into her leggings. "You *are* plowing a mage, after all. That's surely against the sentinel code of conduct."

A low chuckle escaped him and his gaze on her was heavy with longing. "You've asked me twice to run away with you."

Kali's heart stuttered and she looked up at him, her slippers in her hand. "Aye. And twice you've refused."

"Ask me again."

She approached him, her heart beating a wild tattoo against her ribs, the stone floor now only cool beneath her thick socks. "Elan?"

He took her hands in his and pulled her close, and his voice dropped to a whisper. "We must leave."

"How?"

He rested his hand over the collar at her throat, his thumb brushing her scar. "We walk out the front gates."

She scoffed. "And you think *I'm* mad."

"We both are." Stonewall held her cheeks and pressed their foreheads together, speaking with deliberation. "I'll pull some more *shenanigans* with the duty roster. It won't be easy and Talon will likely catch on in short order, so we'll have to be quick. But we have a chance."

She searched his face and found only hard resolve and that earnestness that he put into everything. "You're serious." She gave a weak laugh. "I shouldn't be surprised; you're always serious."

"I was a fool to think we could live here and be together. I see now that's not possible." His breath was warm on her lips. "What do you say?"

If Talon discovered that Kali was possessed, her life would come to a quick end. But in the wide world, away from other mages, she could perhaps learn to control the Fata within her and—even better—help others who had been taken over. Maybe she could learn how to prevent this terror from spreading further.

More than that, though, and perhaps selfishly, Kali could spend all her time with the man she loved, the man who looked at her like she was every star in the sky.

"What about your squad?" she whispered.

He lowered his hands to take hers again. "I believe they're of the same mind as me. I've not officially broached the subject, but none of them are pleased with life in the garrison." He scowled again. "Especially not after Talon's little announcement today."

Kali frowned at him. "What announcement?" As he relayed the garrison's latest set of orders from the Pillars, all other things fell out of her mind and she gaped at him. "You're to capture Sufani? What about the thralls?"

"There was much…discussion on the matter," he said bitterly. "But our esteemed commander was firm in her resolve. Apparently, these orders come from the Pillars themselves."

"And their word is law among sentinels."

"Yes." He frowned again. "Do you remember the Aredian soldier my squad found, the one who'd been turned into a thrall?"

"You said his armor had burned his skin." It was one of the clues that had led her to investigate a connection between the thralls and Fata.

"The Pillars claim they *weren't* burn marks," he said. "But chafing from ill-fitting gear."

A chill swept over Kali as she recalled Arvad's journal, and the Pillars with their glowing eyes. "Stonewall...do you think the Pillars could be connected to all of this, too?"

"The Pillars are *not* glimmers," he replied. "They're mortal men and women. I think someone would know if they were...otherwise."

He faltered and they shared a look. Sadira had said much the same thing, but given Kali's current predicament, she had her doubts. Stonewall evidently did, too.

"But if Fata can somehow wear the skins of men and women," Kali said. "Who would dare question them? Have you ever seen the Pillars in person?"

He shook his head. "But I'm one lowly sentinel. Why would they want to see me? Besides, others have seen them. High Commander Argent, for one, lives in Lasath, where they're stationed, and he often meets with them." He sighed again and squeezed her hands. "None of us were happy with Talon's announcement, but if we want more hematite, we must follow their orders."

"What does that mean?" she asked. "Why wouldn't they give you more..." She trailed off, studying him as best she could in the flickering lantern light. There were shadows beneath his eyes and he looked leaner than she remembered. "You're due for another dose," she murmured.

He lowered his gaze. "Aye."

Fear stirred in her heart – and anger. That sodding hematite. "How much longer do you have?"

"A couple weeks. Maybe."

"Maybe?" She took a deep breath; the collar made even simple breathing difficult and she had to fight the urge to try and claw the thing off. If she could get a sense of his particles, maybe she could ease his suffering, maybe even help him live without the wretched poison his brethren were so eager to ingest.

But the collar remained stubbornly in place, muting her world and her magic.

So her next words were bitter. "The Pillars coerce you into doing their bidding under pain of death."

"We must obey their word, or be Forsworn. And the hematite is for our protection."

Stonewall's voice had taken on a flat, lifeless tone as he recited what had surely been forced into his brain since he was a boy. Stars and moons, she wanted to slap him and cry all at once. Frustration and anger—her own or the Fata's, she could not say—rose like bile in her throat. "How can you possibly believe that?" She grabbed his cheeks, drawing his gaze. "Holy or not, the Pillars control the Circle, who control *you* and your friends. The same Circle who taught you how to swing a sword, but not to read. To obey, but not to *think*. How can you still trust them? They may keep us mages under lock and key, but *you're* their prisoner."

He stared at her, honey-brown eyes wide.

"Kalinda? Who are you talking to?"

Foley's voice outside the bathing room door made her jump. Stonewall reached for his daggers before he checked himself and Kali glanced around the room. She considered grabbing one of the privacy screens for Stonewall to hide behind, but surely the lantern light would create a sentinel-shaped silhouette. Finally, she pointed to the wall behind where the door would open. Stonewall shook his head, but Kali pointed again. This was the best option.

Stonewall grimaced and darted for the wall. But he was bulky with his gear, and should the First Mage enter the room, there was little chance he would miss the armored man.

Foley called out again. "Kalinda, are you decent? I have some ginger tea for you."

"Thank you, but I'm...washing," Kali called, hurrying to the tub to splash the water around. "Just leave it outside."

There was a brief pause, then Foley said, "I'm afraid I must speak with you, Kalinda. I'm going to count to three and then enter. Please cover yourself. One."

She and Stonewall shared wide-eyed looks before he shut his eyes and pressed his back close to the wall.

"Two."

The collar felt tighter with each breath as Kali pushed all her weight against the door and tried to inject vehemence into her voice. "Foley, I'm *washing*. If you're so keen to speak to me, I'll find you when I'm done."

"You haven't yet, though I've left messages outside your door," Foley replied. "I'm sorry, but I must have a word. I'll be quick. Cover yourself. Two-and-a-half."

Kali looked at Stonewall again. He'd ducked his head, like he was trying to make himself as small as possible. She'd have to distract Foley. Perhaps, if Stonewall held still and the door cast a broad enough shadow...

"Three," Foley called.

The door pushed open, making Kali stumble back. The First Mage entered the room, gripping a mug of tea in his hand, with his other forearm flung over his eyes. "Are you decent, Kalinda?"

"Uh... Just a moment." She motioned to Stonewall to slip out, but there wasn't enough room in the small space for him to get past Foley unnoticed. Panic caught in her throat. *Shit!*

Foley exhaled. "Despite all appearances, I *do* have other matters to attend to tonight." He opened his eyes and glanced around the small chamber, his gaze landing on Stonewall...

But Stonewall was gone. Kali gaped at the empty shadow where he'd been. How in the blazing void had he slipped out past her notice?

Foley looked back at her, tilting his head in curiosity. "You're dressed. That was quick." He offered her the steaming mug of tea. "I hope that means your healing sessions with Sadira have made some positive impact on your knee?"

Careful not to touch the other mage, Kali gripped the warm ceramic mug, mentally trying to shake herself out of her shock. Stonewall couldn't have gone far; she had to keep Foley occupied long enough for her sentinel to sneak out of the dormitories. She made a show of rubbing her bum knee and gave Foley what she hoped was a convincing nod. "Yes. Yes, Sadira's done wonders."

"I'm glad to hear that," Foley said. "But is there trouble between you two?

168

She says she hasn't seen you in a few days. No one has, actually."

A flicker behind the door caught her eye. Something stirred in the shadows: the vague shape of a man. An armored man. A sentinel. *What in the stars...?*

Seeing that her attention had slipped, Foley glanced back at the wall, but again, showed no recognition. The older mage looked at Kali again, his brow furrowed, and stepped toward her. "Are you well? You seem... agitated."

Sweet blood. Sweet magic. Give it to us.

Kali swallowed the urge and took a step backward. "I'm just..." The shadow flickered again and Kali bit her tongue to keep herself from looking. "It's just this blazing cycle. It's dreadful this month. Thanks for the tea, though it could have waited a few more minutes." She sipped the warm liquid: the spice of ginger blended with fragrant citrus.

Foley studied her. "I was married, once. Women's troubles are not entirely foreign to me."

"Well, you know... Nature can be cruel." She sipped the tea again. "But I'm quite tired, so I think I'll just finish up here and then head back to my room."

She limped to stand by the door, hoping he'd get the hint. But Foley only regarded her. "You're not...with child, are you?"

Of all the things he could have said, that was the most unexpected. The shadow behind the door stirred. Stunned, Kali only gaped at the other mage. "No!"

"Are you certain?"

"Completely," she shot back. "And even if I were, the...*state* of my womb is none of your business."

"Anything that involves a member of our bastion family concerns me," he replied. "But I admit, I'm glad to hear you're not pregnant. I did wonder, as sentinel men cannot generally father children, but there are exceptions to every rule." He cleared his throat. "And if you were pregnant, you couldn't do anything about it as long as you wore the collar. But I see now that there's no need to fret."

"No, there's not," Kali said as heat swam into her chest and cheeks. "So may I have some privacy, please?"

Foley sighed and made his way to the door. When he was over the threshold he looked back at her, concern etched on his face. Stars and moons, he wore the same expression her father had when he was worried for her safety. Some of Kali's anger softened.

Then Foley placed his only hand over hers. "If you have a problem you cannot solve on your own, please come to me. I shall do everything in my power to help you."

His words barely registered, for the moment he touched her, all Kali knew was *hunger*: for magic, for power, for... *revenge?* She inhaled at the intense, foreign emotion, tried to let it wash over her so she could examine it more closely. *Revenge*; yes, that was rooted with the Fata's anger. *Give it to us. Now.*

"Kalinda?"

"That's...good to hear," she managed, drawing her hand back around her mug. "Thank you, Foley."

He regarded her again before turning to leave. Kali shut the door and leaned against it, heart racing hard enough to make her dizzy. Only when Stonewall plucked the mug from her grip did she remember she still held it.

"What in the blazing void was *that?*" she asked him as he set the mug on the bench.

He looked up, frowning. "What do you mean?"

Kali pointed to the wall where he'd apparently been hiding the entire time. "You're skilled, but you're no shadow. Why didn't he see you? Why didn't *I* see you?"

He harrumphed. "Maybe I'm more skilled than you realize."

She opened her mouth to argue but thought better of it. "Come on, we're too exposed here. Let's go to my room and talk properly. I'll make sure the way is clear...unless you want to play shadow again?"

He frowned at her but made no reply. Thank the stars, the corridor was empty, so they made it to her quarters without incident. Once they were in her room with the door latched, she faced him. "What did you do?"

"I don't know what you're talking about. I didn't *do* anything."

Her heart beat in her throat as she turned over the scene in the bathing room. "I saw you close your eyes, as if you were concentrating..." She sucked in a breath. "Do you...have magic?"

Stonewall's mouth fell open, but he did not deny the possibility, which set every one of Kali's hairs to standing. *Sweet fucking stars...*but if he hadn't had a hematite dose in some time... And it might explain their mad dash through the countryside on their initial journey to Starwatch. At the time, she'd believed she had somehow performed the magical act, for she'd been exhausted in the aftermath. But she had been unable to replicate the magical movement in the time since.

Still, the idea that Stonewall had magic of his own was too much to swallow. "Elan...?" she whispered.

His face went gray as he stumbled through the detritus of her room and collapsed onto her sleeping pallet. "It can't be," he muttered. "It's impossible..."

Kali limped to his side, her knee burning with the simple movement, and flopped down beside him. She pulled his hand to hers and laced their fingers together. Once they were skin-to-skin, she braced herself for the onslaught of hunger—not the kind she normally felt for him, but another sort—but felt only that same, warm familiarity; that sense of coming home. A relief, but it did not solve the dilemma.

"Elan, talk to me," Kali said, squeezing his hand.

He pressed his free hand to his forehead. "My brother's alive. He's here. Talon's got him locked up in one of the garrison's hematite cells...because he's a renegade mage."

Well, this was a far cry from whatever she'd thought he'd say. Kali stared at him. "Drake? I thought he was—"

"So did I." Stonewall's voice dropped to a low, dangerous pitch as he related the strange, sordid story. How his elder brother had kept his abilities a secret their whole lives, even after both had joined the sentinels. How Drake had eventually fled that life with his mage lover who was later killed. How Drake had apparently fallen in with the Assembly and had orchestrated the theft of Whitewater Bastion's last hematite shipment.

The whole tale was astonishing, but the last bit made Kali's blood leap with dread and she temporarily set aside her desire to learn how Stonewall had done magic. "He helped Eris and the others escape?" she said.

"Aye."

Had Eris known Drake was a former sentinel? Likely not, as she probably wouldn't have agreed to work with him. Would Drake know where Eris had gone? "Have you had another chance to speak to him?" Kali asked.

"Once was enough," Stonewall said, scowling. "I'll not give Talon the pleasure of taunting me again."

"Yes, but she doesn't have to know. You could just–"

"He abandoned me, Kali. I mourned him as dead for three fucking years."

"But did he say why?"

Stonewall gripped her hand. "He lied to me. Does it matter why?"

She chose her words with care. "It might. Besides…no one in this room can say they've always been completely truthful." At his look, she gave a wan smile. "I never told you about the others escaping. And *you* tried to make me think you'd grown tired of me. So if you're going to be angry at your brother, you may as well be angry with me – and yourself."

His grip relaxed, but he did not drop her hand, only looked at the floor. "Those lies were different. You never believed I was dead."

"There were moments I wanted to."

This made him look up in alarm, but Kali shook her head. "I was angry, Stone. And afraid. And you were, too. You did something foolish, something you shouldn't have, but we worked through it. Maybe you could try to do the same with Drake."

But Stonewall was already shaking his head. "He died once; he's dead to me now."

Kali stood up as abruptly as she could and tried to quell the hot flush of anger that coursed through her veins. Stonewall rose too and touched her arm, but she shook her head, too furious to speak. Only after a few deep breaths did she collect herself, although she still bit out the words. "Do you have any idea how sodding *lucky* you are?"

"Lucky?"

"I would give..." She was shaking with anger and couldn't think of a clever analogy. "I would give anything—money, magic, my very blood—to see my father again, to speak to him, to just hear his voice. I would give anything to even *see* my mother's face and nothing more."

"This is different. This is—"

"It doesn't *matter*," she broke in, glaring at him. "Stonewall, magic aside, you and your brother have been given a second chance, but you speak as if you don't care. Is your anger so important to you, is being righteous so sodding important to you, that you'll throw this opportunity away? Yes, Stone, your brother lied to you. Yes, he left you alone. Perhaps his reasons for doing so were foolish or beyond your understanding. But if you turn your back on him now, then you're a fool and a horse's ass, and I'm not sure I can ever look at you again."

He'd held still through her tirade, eyes widening with every word, until she stopped and silence hung thick in the air. At last his shoulders slumped. "You may have a point."

Kali rolled her eyes. "So glad to hear it."

"If it'll make you happy, I'll find a way to hear what he has to say, but I can't promise more than that. I can't promise I'll forgive him."

Kali's anger had burned itself out. She rested her hands on his armored waist. "*My* happiness has nothing to do with this...situation. This is about you and your brother – and *your* happiness. Don't you wonder if you turn your back on him now, that you might regret it later?"

He grunted. "Maybe."

Sweet stars, he was always so stubborn! *"Maybe?"*

Stonewall sighed and pulled her close, cupping her cheek and meeting her eyes. "Was I hallucinating, or did Mage Clementa *really* ask if you were with child?"

She ignored his attempt to change the subject. "You can ask Drake if you have magical blood."

"That's not possible," he said again.

173

"How else can you explain what just happened?" She pressed her palm against his hand. "You did magic, Stonewall. Whether you meant to or not, you did it, and you need to figure out *how*."

Rarely had she seen him frightened—truly frightened—but now she read his fear as surely as if it were her own. "I don't know," he whispered. "I don't understand."

"What were you thinking when you tried to hide behind the door?"

His gaze went distant as he considered. "Nothing at all, really. I just saw the shadow and thought, *hide*. That's not magic, right?"

A faint smile tugged at Kali's mouth at the hope in his voice. "It could be. What did it feel like?"

"Nothing. I felt like I was just...hiding, and not very well, at that." He frowned. "What's magic supposed to feel like?"

"Magic feels different for everyone," Kali said slowly. "But generally, it requires lots of concentration and focus." Which her stalwart sentinel had in abundance. Seren's light, could it be true? But she had never seen a crumb of magic from him in all their time together, save for that first, wild escape from the Canderi. But that had been *her* doing, right?

"Do you..." He hesitated. "Do the Fata *want* my magic? Does it feel the same to be near me as it does Sadira?"

Kali stared at him as a strange mixture of joy and apprehension washed over her. "No..." She trailed off as the familiar sense of *home* returned. What in the stars was going on?

"Even when I was a boy," Stonewall said when she did not continue. "I never felt a *hint* of magic – I don't even *know* what it feels like. Four siblings, and none of us showed a trace."

"Other than Drake."

"He never *showed* it. He kept it a secret. I don't know how."

"Nor do I." Magic was as much a part of her as her breath and blood. "Perhaps he wasn't very strong," she ventured. "Or perhaps he started taking hematite so young, his abilities never had much time to manifest. Perhaps that's what happened to you."

Stonewall shrugged. "Drake and I have different fathers. His must've been a mage."

His curt tone indicated that he would tolerate no more discussion on the matter, and for once, Kali chose to let it go as well. Absently she tried to slip her fingers beneath the collar. She could manage, but little more than that, and the increased tightness made the sodding thing that much worse. "Well, I don't blame him for not wanting to live in a bastion."

Stonewall touched her collar, too. "Does it hurt?"

"Sort of. It's a little tight, but that's not the worst bit." She lowered her hand and looked out her window, where moonlight was starting to creep over the bastion wall and into her room. "It...dims the world. Makes everything...less." She laughed weakly. "Perhaps that's not such a bad thing, with the Fata...around."

Around. Stars and moons, she was a fool several times over to stay this course. But she saw no other option.

Warm, calloused hands gripped hers, rooting her in the moment. "I'll help you, Kali," he whispered. "I promise."

She looked up into his honey-brown eyes, still bright, despite the lack of light in her room. "I'll hold you to that, Elan."

15

FIFTEEN

L ife was better on the wing.

The afternoon sky was overcast, the sun hidden by a thick layer of clouds, and the air held a promise of snow. Had Eris been in her human shape, the biting wind would have been far more unpleasant, but now she hardly noticed the cold. Or perhaps she simply cared about discomfort less when the wind's only purpose was to carry her crow-self. She kept a sharp eye out for eagles, hawks, or other raptors, but saw none, and so for a few minutes, she savored the joy of flight.

Eris and her allies—magical and otherwise—had spent the last several days making a careful trek north of Whitewater City to avoid sentinel patrols, travelers, and, perhaps most alarmingly, a contingent of royal soldiers decked in shining plate metal. Leal and Marcen had followed the soldiers for a few hours to discover they were heading north, likely for the Canderi border. War was on its way. Another person might have felt dismay at the news, but Eris' first thought had been one of satisfaction. Perhaps all the dregs would kill each other and leave the mages alone.

She tipped her wings to catch the next updraft and wheeled toward Whitewater City. At this height and distance, the sprawling provincial capital was little more than a smudge next to the river. Mist from the falls cast a veil over one side of the city, and beneath the whistling wind, Eris could hear the constant drum of the falling water. She folded her wings to drop lower, angling for the bastion.

Then she saw the bridge.

A row of city guards stood at both ends, while a sentinel squad—she would know that sodding armor anywhere—waited at the outer gates, at the place where that guard had murdered Gideon. There was a weak flow of traffic into and out of the city, but even from Eris' vantage point, it was clear that the guards were being *very* careful not to let the wrong sort of folks in – or out.

Her little heart seized and she cried out; a pitiful caw that no one would notice. Eris wheeled ungracefully to get as far away from the gates as she could. Each beat of her wings, each cry from her throat, sounded like Gid's name.

It's hopeless. The thought was utterly human. It weighed upon her, forcing her down to the city, for she could not find the strength to move her wings any more. Eris descended and managed to land in a secluded alley near the docks alongside the river. She had no idea that she'd returned to her human form until she felt the cold, hard press of cobblestones against her legs.

Shit, she thought. *Leave it to me to find myself naked in the middle of the sodding city.* But no. When she looked down, she gasped at the sight of her tattered wool cloak clinging to her neck by its brass clasp. Her other clothes were where she'd transformed back in the forest, but the cloak…

She had not even tried to change it with her, but she had done so anyway. Shape-changing in general was getting easier. Was that a sign of her strengthening abilities? A memory of Gid's whisper echoed in her mind: *"I knew you could do it, love."* Eris fingered the rough wool as something like relief coursed through her. At least *one* part of her plan had gone better than expected. She dared not hope for more, but the cloak bolstered her spirits enough to give her the strength to find her bearings. She went to the alley's entrance, ensuring that the shadows concealed her, and surveyed the area.

Dozens of vessels cluttered the harbor: lithe sloops and hulking barges, low and flat to carry cargo to and from upriver. A group of men and women maneuvered a large, sturdy skiff toward the docks, their oars slapping the water in time with their shouts. The scents of water, sweet *biri* smoke, fish, and wet wood clung to the air. People shouted, harbor bells rang, wheels and wagons grated on cobblestones as goods were loaded on and off waiting vessels. There were *so* many people: sailors, merchants, traders, guards, beggars, and countless others Eris couldn't identify.

How many of those dregs hated mages? How many would turn her over to the sentinels without a second thought?

Heart pounding, Eris slunk back into the alley. Even if she could get Kali and Drake out of the bastion—and that was a massive *if*—how could she possibly get them out of the city? The gates were guarded, which left the river, swollen with potential enemies. And there was the little matter of the waterfall churning in the background.

How can we do this? Despair filled her again and she tried to calm herself with deep breaths. She had no choice; she *had* to free Kali and Drake. Then she could put Whitewater City behind her and try to make some sense of this new life without Gideon. *You and me, little one,* she thought, resting a hand on her flat stomach. *We'll get through this, somehow.*

Her resolve hardened. Grief and doubt were distractions she could ill-afford. Eris focused on shifting once more. She had work to do.

* * *

Kali's hands were numb with cold, but she welcomed the sensation as she sprinkled grain for the eager hens. Sometimes numbness was preferable to feeling. She glanced over her shoulder, toward the mage dormitories, but saw only a warm light emanating from the windows and the figures moving within. Good. Everyone was at supper. Something tapped her boot and she smiled at the little white and rust-red speckled hen who peered up at her hand.

"Sorry about that." Kali sprinkled more grain and the hen struck before the feed hit the ground.

Seren had hidden herself already, but Atal rose: a waxing crescent vying for dominance with the shifting clouds. The moon's sharp lines reminded Kali of a blade, and she shivered.

"Kali."

She closed her eyes against the surge of hunger Sadira's presence sparked. *Sweet blood. Sweet magic.* "You should be inside," Kali said. "I'm fine."

"Stonewall came to you, did he not?" Sadira's tread was careful, closing in. A bloom of heat preceded her, making Kali's fingertips prickle back to life. "We had no chance to speak the day he came to see you, but before that, he seemed...discerned."

Kali frowned. "Concerned?" She shook her head. "It doesn't matter. Sadira, you must leave. Please."

"You are my friend."

"Aye, which is why I don't want to hurt you."

"You should know by now," Sadira's voice drew closer; the heat of her brought spring to the air, "that you cannot harm me."

Sweet blood, the Fata growled, coiling within Kali, preparing to strike. *Give it to us. Now.*

Kali's body moved as if to turn, but she dug her heels into the dirt, the opposing forces making her knee cry out in pain. But pain was good; pain shifted her focus. Her trembling hands made the grain scatter atop the waiting hens. "Am I not speaking clearly?" she ground out. "It's not safe for you to be around me. Go. Away. *Now.*"

A pause, then a cool, "Very well."

The spring warmth faded. The air on Kali's wet cheeks was colder than she remembered, and when she swiped her tears away, bits of grain clung to her sweating palms. "I'm sorry," she whispered.

Sweet blood. Sweet magic.

"That doesn't make any sense," she said, glaring at the brushwork behind the chicken coop. "Tell me what you want. With more than those stupid words."

Silence.

She sighed and ran a hand down her unraveling braid. Her efforts to learn about the Fata had been...inconsistent, at best. Most of her energy was spent trying to keep the rage and hunger at bay, and she was starting to think this plan of hers was a bad idea.

Her mouth pulled in a grim smile. No doubt Stonewall would agree.

A crow landed upon the fence post before her, cawing. Kali started back, but the crow only watched her as the wind ruffled the scruff of feathers around its neck. Kali frowned. What in the stars was...?

Her stomach twisted at the realization. "Eris?" she whispered.

Another caw and the crow tilted its head as it regarded her.

"Eris?" Kali asked again, still uncertain if this was some curious, wild creature, or her shape-changing friend. She had never actually *seen* Eris in crow-shape. Even if she had, she wasn't sure if she could have picked out her friend from a true crow. Besides, she sensed no magic emanating from the bird. Surely if it was Eris, the Fata within Kali would have caught the scent of her magic.

The crow tilted its head again and then jumped, landing on Kali's shoulder. Kali yelped in surprise, but before she could do much else, the crow lifted a wing and brushed the tips of its pinions across Kali's nose. The tickling sensation confirmed the crow's identity, and despite everything else that weighed upon her, Kali laughed aloud.

"Stop, stop, Silver Girl," she managed, raising a hand. "I understand."

The crow cawed again, a note of satisfaction in the sound, and hopped from her shoulder, inching down her arm until Kali got the hint. She extended her forearm so Eris could better face her. Even up close, there was no hint of the woman behind the crow's liquid dark eyes, but Kali hardly cared. Eris was *alive.*

"Thank the stars," she whispered, stroking the bird's smooth back. "I feared the worst. Are you...?" She bit back the words, uncertain how to broach the subject, or if she even should.

Eris-the-crow preened beneath her touch, but then cawed again, flapping her wings as if about to take off. Thinking her friend needed room to fly, Kali lifted her arm, but the crow folded her wings and gave Kali an annoyed look that was entirely *Eris.*

"What do you want?" Kali asked. She glanced around, suddenly fearful that Foley or someone else would come upon her talking to a bird when Eris was a known shape-changer. But she and Eris were alone – save the hens.

The crow turned on Kali's arm so that her beak pointed toward the mage dormitories, and bobbed her head. "You want to go to my room?" Kali asked. "So we can talk properly?"

Another caw and another bobbing head motion that Kali took for assent.

But something held Kali in place. Once Eris changed to her human form, would the Fata hunger for her magic? Could Kali even hold a conversation with a dear friend any longer, or had the Fata taken that, too?

And then there was Gideon's grave. Eris probably had no idea what had happened to her husband's body and in truth, Kali was reluctant to share the news of his burial, even though the disgrace had been rectified. Kali sighed. One tragedy at a time. She would tell Eris soon enough. She nodded to the crow. "All right. I'll meet you at my window."

A flurry of dark wings, an absence of weight on Kali's arm, and Eris was aloft. Kali dusted off her hands, pulled her cloak tight around herself, and set off for her room. She tried to hurry without *looking* like she was hurrying, which, ironically, her limp made easy. Once Kali entered the dormitories, she spotted Hazel stepping out of the common room.

"Look at you, out and about," the teenager said with a bright smile. "Are you feeling better?"

"'Better' is subjective," Kali said, clenching her teeth against the Fata's leap of hunger for the other mage's magic.

"Aye, you look…" Hazel pursed her lips. "Well, terrible."

"You should ask Foley if I'm pregnant," Kali muttered, and slipped off before the girl could question her further.

Thank the stars she met no other mages and soon she was safely in her room. Once she latched the door, she rushed to fling open the window and peer out, searching the sky for a distinct black shape. Nothing. Kali squinted up at the bastion wall, when a blur of feathers fell into her vision. She scrambled out of the way as Eris darted into her window and landed between a discarded tunic and her viol case.

Kali latched the window and drew the curtain, but did not turn as she braced herself for the onslaught of Fata emotions once her friend shifted back to her proper shape. Indeed, Kali knew the moment Eris changed, for she could taste her friend's magic in the air; a sweetness that called her name. *You can do this,* Kali told herself, gritting her teeth against the foreign hunger. *You're not a thrall; you just have to control one for a little while.*

When Kali finally turned, Eris-the-woman stood before her, clutching a ragged cloak around her nude body. "What happened to your clothes?" Kali blurted. "And your hair! I've never seen it so short."

"I cut the hair and left the clothes in the forest. It's still difficult to shift them, but apparently I can manage this tattered thing just fine. Still, I'd rather not be naked." Eris glanced around the room, brow furrowed. "Where's that dress Sadira gave you? The one with the embroidery on the collar. That should fit."

They found the dress after some digging, and Kali sat upon her sleeping pallet. Now clothed, Eris made to sit beside her, but Kali held up her hand. "It's best if you keep your distance."

"What does that mean?"

"I'm not sure if you realize it, but crows don't smell…nice. And people who have been crows don't smell much better." Kali tried to keep her voice light and teasing, hoping to deflect Eris' curiosity until the appropriate time, but Eris only stared down at her.

"What's wrong with you?" Eris asked.

"Too much to choose just one thing. You first. What are you doing here?" Kali's throat tightened. "Did you come back for…him?"

Eris' face turned to stone. "My husband is dead. I came back for you."

Kali hugged her sides. "You didn't have to."

"And why not? Seren only knows what sort of trouble you'll get into without me around." Eris lifted a brow. "The hemie took you to Parsa, didn't he?" The bitterness in her voice took Kali by surprise, although it shouldn't have.

"He did," Kali said. "But you were there when I chose to go."

Eris scowled. "You were cuffed and he had the key. You had no 'choice' in the situation. Bastard. Did he force you to...?" She shook her head and began to pace around the room again, searching through the clutter. "Never mind. It doesn't matter now. You'll be gone from here, soon." She found Kali's rucksack and began stuffing it with random clothes, but her movements were jerky and fumbling. "It won't be easy, but I'm working on a plan to get you out of here. But I must find Drake, too. Did the hemies bring in another mage?"

"Yes, but–"

"Good. No doubt Talon threw him in a cell. Getting him out will be tricky, but I must. I owe him a great deal." Eris grabbed a pair of loose trousers and a wooden comb to shove inside the pack. "You'll like freedom. It's harder than life here—that will be an adjustment for you—but it's worth every trouble, I promise. Gid says..."

She trailed off and went still, staring at the sack in her grip, shoulders hunched. Unthinking, Kali rose to her friend's side. Her knee burned, but she focused on that pain and tried to ignore the urge for Eris' magic. She touched Eris' shoulder to draw her attention. When Eris looked up, her green eyes were wet.

"What are you doing, Kali?" she whispered. "We must make plans. There's no time for your woolgathering."

"The sentinels buried his body," Kali said, as gently as she could. "But afterwards, the other mages and I cremated him. We saw Gideon safely to his next life. Eris... I'm so sorry."

Eris was trembling now but nodded stiffly. "Thank you." She seemed to consider something, and then placed a hand upon her stomach. "I'm pregnant."

Kali's mouth opened but no sound came out. Without the magic-dispelling effect of the hematite collars, preventing—or encouraging—pregnancy was simple for a mage, but rarely did bastion mages wish to bring children into their world of high walls and hematite. Life would be hard for the child, no matter on which side of those walls they were forced to live.

"I'm only a few weeks along," Eris continued. "I don't feel any different. Is that normal?"

"I don't know anything about babies or childbirth," Kali managed. "There wasn't much of either back at Starwatch."

Eris' face crumpled. "I can't do this without him."

She dropped the pack and covered her eyes, and shook with the force of her sudden sobs. Kali said nothing. There was no debate within her, although there should have been. She embraced her friend, close enough to feel Eris' frantic heartbeat as tears soaked them both. This close, the Fata's desire for magic hammered at Kali's brain, so she bit her tongue to give herself something else to focus on. At some point, when she thought Eris might collapse with grief, she managed to steer them both back onto her pallet, where she sat awkwardly as Eris continue to weep into her shoulder.

At last, Eris quieted. "Thank you," she murmured.

Kali rubbed her friend's back and tried to keep her own reply light. "Don't mention it. And... We'll learn about babies together, Eris. I'm sure Adrie knows something. Or Sirvat – didn't she go with you? She was rather far along at the solstice. Oh, and I'm sure we can find a midwife somewhere, or perhaps there's a book or scroll I can study. We'll figure it out. Everything will be fine, Silver Girl, you'll see."

She couldn't help but add her old nickname for her friend. At the words, Eris sat up to regard Kali. Her nose was red and swollen; her short hair was plastered to her high cheekbones. But despite all of this, or perhaps because of it, Eris held herself like a queen, and her gaze was steady. Kali smoothed back the matted strands of Eris' hair and gave a soft, sad smile. "It suits you."

"You think?" Eris touched the strands, and then shrugged. "It's far more practical. You should try it."

A memory of Stonewall weaving his fingers through her hair made Kali look away. "Maybe one day."

Eris swiped at her eyes and cheeks, and looked at the unlit lantern by Kali's bed. "They put a collar on you."

"Not just me."

"Because of…" Eris hesitated. "Me and the others?"

"Yes." Kali's hand crept to her throat. There was just enough room to slip two fingertips beneath the leather and hematite. "The sentinels locked us in the dormitories for days. We've only just been allowed outside, but no one can leave for any missions. And there've been so many more patrols than before."

Some of Eris' regal bearing deflated. "That wasn't my intention. I wanted you to come, too."

Kali swallowed. "So did I."

"No, *you* wanted to go to that sodding village," Eris said. "Where everyone's dead now, so I hear. What really happened?"

"It's…a long story." Kali took a deep breath, twisting her hands in her lap to distract herself from the urge to somehow wrest Eris' magic away. "I'd rather hear yours first."

She thought Eris would object, but her friend humored her and shared the tale of the Heartfire escape. Eris' smooth, aristocratic voice remained steady throughout the telling, while horror clutched Kali's heart. Only when Eris related Gideon's death did she falter. Kali could not help herself, and risked a soft touch on Eris' shoulder. The leap of Fata hunger made her head spin, but she tried to ignore the feeling.

When Eris was finished, Kali goggled at her. "You. The other mages, a Sufani, and… The Assembly? All coming here? For me?"

"And Drake," Eris replied firmly. "As soon as I figure out how."

Kali thought back to her and Stonewall's conversation from the previous day. "I might have a way to the cells."

"Well, it's getting *out* of them that worries me." Eris frowned at Kali. "But what do you mean?"

Heat crept up Kali's neck. "I have a…friend who could get down there, unnoticed."

"Your hemie lover?"

"His *name* is Stonewall."

Eris snorted and rose to pace around the room. "This is the one you were weeping over last time we spoke? The one you thought was a 'good man?'"

"He's the kindest and best of men," Kali replied, frustration welling within her. *Yes, sweet blood.* "We made amends. He explained everything–"

"Oh, I'm sure he did," Eris broke in, rolling her eyes. "I'm sure he knew just what to say to convince you to let him back in your bed." She pointed to Kali's collar. "If he's such a good man, why do you still wear *that*?"

"He...couldn't get the key."

Eris crossed her arms. "Forgive me if I don't swoon from the shock of such news. No doubt he'd rather cut off his manhood then let his captive plaything get away. I imagine that's why the sod took you to Parsa when you should have gone with us."

Hatred dripped from each word; an answering anger rose in the back of Kali's throat. What did Eris know of Stonewall? "Aye, and I'm lucky I *did* go with him," Kali shot back. "I can't exactly run with the rest of you. I might've shared Gideon's fate."

Eris' eyes narrowed and she lifted her chin.

Kali flushed. "Eris, I'm sorry. That was–"

"It's fine," Eris said. "You're clearly not feeling well."

"No, I'm not." Kali rubbed the scar at her neck. "But...I would like to leave this place."

Eris lifted a single black brow. "Alone?"

"Well, no. I'd like Sadira to join us..." Kali trailed off at the memory of how she'd treated her friend. *I'm sorry, Sadira. You were right.* She would have to make it up to the Zhee mage – somehow.

"Kali?"

She braced for the incoming argument and tried to rush out the words. "Stonewall wants to come with me. And bring his squad. He says he has a way to simply walk out the gates, and I believe him. He's quite clever, when he pulls his head out of his own..."

She trailed off as Eris threw her head back and laughed, although there was no merriment in the sound. "Walk out the gates with the hemies?" Eris said. "I know you have your own special sort of humor, Kali, but that's ridiculous, even for you."

Sweet blood. Sweet magic. Give it to us.

Kali clenched her jaw against the swell of anger within her heart. Hers, or the Fata's? She could not say. "It's no joke," she managed. "Eris, we need all the allies we can get. *You're* the one working with the Assembly, after all."

"They're friends of Drake's," Eris said, waving a hand. "Fodder for the hemies, as far as I'm concerned. I don't care what happens to them. But you…" She rubbed the bridge of her nose. "Seren's light. 'Walk out the gates.' What other lies has the metal-blooded bastard told you?"

Sweet blood. Give it to us. Now.

"Enough!" Kali rose as quickly as she could—which wasn't very much—and glared at her friend. "You don't know him like I do. You only see the armor, but he's more than that. He loves me, and I love him. I don't care if you don't understand that or don't like him. Your opinion doesn't change a thing."

With each word, Kali's anger bloomed from an ember into a blaze, until she was practically shouting. And beneath it all, the thrum of hunger did not relent, only strengthened. Every muscle clenched tight and her body ached from the tension of trying to keep the Fata's desire at bay.

Eris gave her a pitying look. "You poor, stupid fool. You're his prisoner, too."

Give it to us. Now.

The thread of control Kali had wound within herself snapped and she lunged for her friend. A shriek bounced off the walls of her room, but the voice wasn't her own. It was otherworldly, a high-pitched wail that would have reverberated through Kali's bones had it not come from her own throat. But her body was slow and ungainly, and her knee silently screamed in protest at the sudden motion. Eris ducked out of the way and Kali tumbled into a pile of books at the foot of her bed, sending them clattering to the floor. Her chin struck something solid, making her bite her tongue hard enough to taste copper. For a moment, Kali only stared at the open book: one of the Fata stories she had read with Stonewall. An illustration of a beautiful man with curving horns looked back at her, glowing eyes fixed on hers.

Sweet blood, the Fata snarled in her mind. *Give it to us!*

"No," she whispered, squeezing her eyes shut against the renewed swell of yearning as Eris crouched beside her, reaching for her arm. That hunger beat against Kali's brain like desperate wings against a winter storm; she could hardly think through the force of it.

"Kali. Come on. Get up."

"Go away," Kali cried, jerking away from her friend. She could *not* allow Eris to touch her, not when she was in this state. "Leave!"

"Kali," Eris said, a note of irritation in her voice. Irritation...but also worry. "This is silly. You're acting like a child. You lost your balance, that's all. Here, I'll help you get–"

"Get out of here," Kali interrupted. "Leave me alone, Eris. Just go. *Now.*"

The final word broke with a sob. Eris rose. "I'll return for you in about a week," she said as she stepped away. "If you want to come with me, be ready."

Kali said nothing. If she spoke, if she moved, she would shatter. Tears rolled down her cheeks, making her skin stick to the pages of the open book.

The bed shifted as Eris crept to the window. The curtain whispered, the latch clinked, and then cold air swept into the small room, rifling the paper scrolls scattered about. A rustle of cloth, a flap of wings, and the urge for magic dissipated. When Kali managed to look up, Eris was gone.

But Kali was not alone.

16

SIXTEEN

Despite Drake's best efforts, consciousness ambushed him late one evening, nearly two weeks after Heartfire. At least, he thought it was about two weeks, for it was difficult to mark the passage of time when locked in the garrison's bowels. Only by keeping track of his sentinel guards' routines did he manage even a little.

"Sergeant!" Hornfel exclaimed. He was the burnie who'd been standing guard at the cell door; he jumped to attention as a new sentinel stepped into view. Behind bars and still chained to the sodding wall, Drake couldn't make out the newcomer's face, but it didn't matter. Every sentinel that had stood guard over him viewed him as the enemy. The understanding shouldn't have bothered him as much as it did.

"At ease," the newcomer said.

Elan.

Drake's stomach flipped, whether from joy or fear, he could not say.

"I'm here to relieve you," Elan—Stonewall—added to the burnie, coming to stand before the bars. In the flickering torchlight, Drake could see his little brother was fully armored, helmet and all, and so could not make out his expression. Maybe that was for the best. No one could glare quite like Stonewall.

"Relieve me, ser?" Hornfel's confusion was palpable. "But I've another three hours on my shift…"

"The duty roster says it's my turn." Elan held out his hand. "Give me the key."

The burnie fidgeted, clearly not wanting to argue with an officer, but also devoted to his duty. "I'm sure I've another three hours to go, ser."

"Are you?" Elan asked. When Hornfel nodded, Stonewall jerked his thumb toward the garrison. "Good. Then you won't mind running to check."

"With respect, ser, shouldn't you–"

"*Now*, Hornfel," Elan snapped. "Unless you want to make insubordination a habit."

The kid jumped in his boots, made a hasty salute and all but tossed Stonewall the key before he rushed out, tripping over his feet in his haste. Drake almost felt sorry for him.

"Good work, Sergeant," he said as Elan faced the cell door. "You've taken to the role fairly well. But I imagine he'll be back pretty quick."

Elan withdrew a crumpled piece of parchment, covered with writing. Drake couldn't make out the words from here, but he recognized the format of a duty roster. "Not likely," Elan replied.

"Clever."

Elan studied the key in his grip. "If I come in there, what will you do?"

Drake shifted so that the chains holding him to the wall clinked. "I'm trussed like a ptarmigan," he said, shrugging. "Not much I can do other than talk. Unless," he couldn't help but add, "you came down here to free me?"

His brother was silent. Drake sighed. "Can't blame a man for trying."

"This is foolish." Elan turned to leave.

Drake's heart sank and he scrambled to his feet, tugging the chains for support. However long he'd been down here hadn't give him a chance to do much other than think and let his muscles atrophy. "Don't leave," he called as Stonewall reached the door. "Please, *relah*. Even if it wasn't to free me, you're here for a reason."

Elan froze, one hand on the heavy wooden door outfitted with iron supports, and his shoulders sank. "Don't call me that," he said as he went back to the cell door and began to unlock it. "Don't call me anything other than 'Stonewall.' That's my name, now."

"Never understood why you liked that name so much." Drake tried to make a joke, but the words fell flat as his brother gave him *that* look. *Shit.* He ducked his head in a nod. "Aye. Stonewall."

Stonewall stepped inside the cell and shut the door behind him, and for the first time in well over three years, Drake was with his little brother again. Despite everything, he couldn't help but smile. "An officer, eh? You've done well for yourself."

"You broke my trust."

So no small talk, then. Very well. Drake was silent, his mind racing almost as fast as his heart; as usual when he was in a bind, thoughts of *escape* pummeled him, but of course, he could not run now. At last he managed, "How can I rebuild it?"

"I'm not sure." Stonewall tucked his helmet under his arm and stepped closer, until he was an arm's length away. Backlit by the torches, his eyes looked like shadows. His face was gaunt and his movements lacked their usual fluidity. Drake had heard snatches of the other sentinels' conversations. He knew what Stonewall was feeling.

"How long's it been since your last burn?" he asked.

He thought his brother wouldn't answer, but Stonewall sighed. "Too long."

Drake squeezed his eyes shut. *My fault.* Even if he hadn't been the one to steal the garrison's most recent shipment—and they really should have been resupplied by now—he had been the one who'd set both of them on this path. It had been his decision to allow both orphaned boys to join the sentinels, so long ago. "How long have you got?"

Stonewall shrugged. "A week. Maybe a little more. I'm not too bad, yet. Some are worse off than me. Some are better. Most of the cinders are... fading."

"Why haven't you gotten more?"

His brother ignored the question and instead withdrew something from his belt-pouch, offering it to Drake, who accepted the *biri* with trembling fingers. "You were in a bad way, before," Stonewall said by way of explanation. "I've heard these…help ease the pain."

"I can't light it," Drake managed, too stunned to say more.

Stonewall frowned at him before plucking up the *biri* and slipping out of the cell to light it on one of the torches. He returned and offered Drake the non-burning end. Drake wasn't too proud to take a deep drag, holding in the sweet smoke as long as he could before exhaling it up and away from his brother's face. Oh, it'd been too long. A languid ease crept into his body and suddenly his problems didn't seem quite so daunting. Chains and hematite still bound him, of course, but now he could bear them a while longer.

"Thank you," he said to Stonewall, who watched him closely. But when he offered the *biri*, the younger man scowled and shook his head.

"I'm no cinder."

"Nor am I," Drake said, taking another drag. It wasn't quite as nice as the *biri* Aderey had given him, but he wasn't about to be choosy. He released another stream of smoke and leaned his head against the wall.

"How did you survive without hematite?" Stonewall asked.

Disappointment swelled in Drake's chest, but he fought back the foolish emotion. After what he'd done to Elan, he'd lost the right to be disappointed by his little brother. Besides, given his brother's current state, Drake couldn't blame him for wanting this information.

"That's what you want to know?" Drake replied, feigning mild curiosity. "Out of all the things we could say to one another?"

"This is the most pressing."

"Why? Isn't the garrison getting more hematite?" Despite the warm haze brought by the *biri*, something cold swept through Drake's body at the determined look on his brother's face. "What are you up to, Ela – Stonewall?"

His brother glanced around the detention area, and then crossed his arms before his chest. "Just sodding tell me."

Had they both been free, had Stonewall not been furious with him—with good reason—Drake would have grabbed his younger sibling in a headlock and gotten him to answer the question by force. Ah, brothers. But they were here and the collar pressed tight around Drake's throat, and even the burning end of the *biri* seemed dull.

"I started tapering off about two months before I...ah, left the order."

"Tapering off? So you *planned* to leave?"

Drake tried to keep his voice steady. "Tobin and I wanted to start over somewhere else. I knew that meant I'd have to live without hematite, so I started trying to get used to taking less. It was hard," he added, recalling those first weeks. "Harder than I thought it'd be. I wasn't sure it would even work, but I started stockpiling my allotted doses. I cut back and cut back, until..."

"Until you could use magic again." Stonewall's voice was matter-of-fact and he didn't look at Drake.

"Aye." Drake ran a hand through his hair, long enough now that he usually tied it back with a leather cord. But his hosts here hadn't allowed him that amenity. "Once I stopped completely, my magic returned. And it hasn't left me, since. Well," he amended, tugging at the hematite collar, "not without some help." He took another draw from the *biri;* by now, he'd smoked it almost to nothing. "I'm sorry, Stonewall."

His brother tensed, jaw working as if he were fighting back a string of swears. Drake bit his tongue, trying to allow him time to form his thoughts. If he pushed too hard, Stonewall would walk away, and only the gods knew when they might have another chance like this.

At last, his patience was rewarded. Stonewall looked at him again, and something had softened in his gaze. "When did you first realize you...had magic?"

The *biri* was gone, but Drake rolled the remaining charred bit of paper between his fingertips. "When did you first realize you could breathe? I can't answer that, Stonewall. I don't remember...discovering I had magic. It wasn't like finding a new street in a city you thought you knew by heart. It was always there; always a part of me. A small part," he added wryly, "but present and insistent."

"Did Mama know?"

Doubtful. Their mother had been too busy trying to feed her family to do much for Drake other than give him a name he hated. But he couldn't say that to his brother, so he only shook his head. "It wasn't ever strong enough to get me into trouble." Irony, if ever there was any. "And after she died, I was scared the sentinels would find out and take me away from you."

Stonewall leaned his shoulder against the cell wall, facing Drake, but still out of reach. "You didn't want to end up in a bastion."

"I didn't want to leave you alone," Drake replied, although he winced at the irony of that, too. "And no, Stonewall, I didn't want this," he touched the collar, "to be my new reality."

"I should have realized it," Stonewall said quietly, shaking his head. "Gods above, you were always terrified of sentinels. You went out of your way to avoid them, even the nice ones."

"*Especially* the nice ones. Why do you think they patrolled the worst parts of Pillau, handing out sweetrolls to orphans? They were recruiting."

"They'd come around in pairs, a man and a woman. Usually a little older..." Stonewall's eyes widened. "Like parents."

"A luxury few of us could claim." Drake gave a weary chuckle. "It's brilliant, actually. If I was someone else, I'd be impressed."

Stonewall was quiet, his gaze distant. "If you had magic, why didn't you heal Mama when she got sick? Or Bita, or Omri?"

Drake's stomach twisted at the mention of their dead brother and sister, whose names he had not heard aloud in years. *My fault, too.* His reply was a hoarse whisper. "Wasn't strong enough." Something hot stung his eyes: an old pain that even hematite could never quite burn away. He clenched his hands into fists, disintegrating the *biri* into ashes.

"But you had magic," Stonewall said. "Surely you could have done *something.*"

"I wasn't strong–"

"I don't believe you."

Drake leveled the younger man with his own dark look. "You think I *wanted* Mama and the others to die?"

194

"You just admitted you were scared of winding up in a bastion." Stonewall drew himself upright. He had never been as tall or strong as Drake, but now he seemed as imposing as any statue of Tor. "You're a coward."

Ea's balls, but the truth was a kick in the right place, wasn't it? Drake nodded. "Yes." Stonewall did not immediately respond. *To the void with it all*, Drake thought, and added, "Yes, I'm a coward. I've always been. And I've made a lot of mistakes that I'll never be able to amend. Stonewall, I hated lying to you—hated leaving you—but I couldn't live as a sentinel any longer. I couldn't live a half-life with my magic shuttered away, being told every day that people like me were corruptions in the One's world. I tried. I really did. But the armor was too heavy. It may not seem like it to you, but I was a prisoner back then, more than I am now."

"You were a fine sentinel."

Drake shook his head. "I hated it. Every moment of every day, I hated what I'd become. I stayed for you."

Stonewall bristled. "So this is my fault?"

"This?" Drake shook the chains. "No, *relah*. Sorry: Stonewall. No, *this* was bound to happen, one way or another. But at least I'm here on *my* terms. At least I'm here because I made the right choice. For once, I didn't run."

He didn't realize the truth of the words until he said them, and a warm feeling—better than any *biri*—spread through him at the understanding.

However, his brother was not as pleased to hear this revelation. "Idiot," Stonewall said. "You should have kept running."

"If I had, Eris and her friends would have shared Gideon's fate." Drake's throat tightened at the memory of Gid's body, lying just by the threshold of Whitewater City's outer gates. *If only I'd been a little faster, a little stronger, a lot smarter.*

Was it his imagination, or did Stonewall tense at the mention of Eris? Did his brother know the shape-changing mage? He must have, if he was serving here while she lived in the bastion. This reminded Drake of something Talon had said to Stonewall, back when the commander had so kindly reunited the brothers.

"Are you *really* in love with a mage?" Drake asked.

Stonewall hesitated before nodding once.

And you say I'm *an idiot,* Drake thought. "Talon knows?" Again, Stonewall nodded, and Drake cursed beneath his breath. "Is she – it's a *she,* right?"

Stonewall scowled at him. "Her name is Kali."

"Pretty name. Is Kali still alive?"

Stonewall nodded.

"For now," Drake said. He risked a step toward his brother, who took an answering step back. Drake tried not to let it bother him. "I don't know much about Talon, but I've seen enough. There's something in her eyes; something desperate. Your girl is alive now, but I doubt Talon will let her remain so for too long. If you love Kali, you'll get her the hell away from this shithole and never look back."

"What about you?"

Drake blinked at him, stunned again into silence. "You hate me."

"Blood is blood."

Fury swam through Drake's veins at the words, spoken in monotone, as if by route. He jerked on the chains, the clink and rattle echoing in the cell. "I'm fucked, you fool," he all but spat. "I think Talon means to send me to High Commander Argent. Only the gods know what he'll do with me, and *you* if he gets his hooks into you. So shove your self-righteous attitude up your ass and save your girl – and yourself. Forget about me. I'm dead, remember?"

Well, that last bit was below the belt, but for Tor's sake, sometimes the dolt needed a lesson hammered into his brain before he'd take it to heart. It was this understanding that made Drake add, "I couldn't save the mage I loved, Stonewall. Don't wait for the right moment. Don't make the same mistake I did. Just go."

Stonewall only studied him. From this angle, the torchlight in the corridor now cast his light-brown eyes in gold fire. "Did Mama have magic?" Stonewall asked.

Caught off-guard, Drake answered immediately. "As far as I could tell, I was the only one in our family with magic. Except..." He trailed off, squinting in the shadows as a memory trickled back. "I always thought your father was an odd one."

Stonewall straightened and came closer, enough for Drake to see how he trembled. "He was a mage?"

"No."

"How could you tell?" Stonewall asked.

"I dunno," Drake replied, shrugging. "I just could. Some mages can sense others like them; I can't explain how. It's just…" He trailed off, unable to clarify. How to explain to Stonewall that *feeling* of kinship, of something deeper than blood? Only another mage would understand. Ea's balls, Drake hadn't truly understood until a few years ago, after he'd met Gideon and other renegade mages.

"If my father wasn't a mage," Stonewall said slowly. "How was he 'odd?'"

This, too, was hard to explain. "I was only three summers old when he came around," Drake replied. "I don't remember much, only thoughts and feelings. I was a little afraid of him, but not because I thought he'd hurt me or Mama. He just… He was odd. Different. I remember thinking even when he spoke to me, he was somewhere else. Anyway, he wasn't around long enough for me to think more of him than that. And then later, Mama had you."

Stonewall was silent, absorbing this. "You're sure he wasn't a mage?"

"As sure as I can be about anything." Drake frowned. "Why? You've never asked about him before."

"Well, I'm curious now," Stonewall replied briskly.

Drake saw through the lie, but chose to let it pass. Hornfel would probably be back any moment and he had no wish to start another argument. "You have his eyes," he offered. "Well, mostly. His were brighter than yours – almost gold. And one time, I swear I saw them…" He wriggled his fingers to convey his meaning. "Sparkle. It was right after you were born, right before he went away. I remember how he held you and looked at you. I think he thought he was alone, but the door was open and I saw him. I saw his eyes."

The moment the words left his mouth, Drake snorted. "Gods above and beyond, that sounds stupid. Funny how you remember stuff when you're a kid, huh?"

"Funny," Stonewall echoed, but his voice was weak and he leaned against the cell wall again, this time as if to brace himself.

Drake tried to go to him, but Stonewall had moved out of reach again, and the sodding chains tugged tight at Drake's wrists. "Elan, are you–"

"I'm fine," Stonewall broke in, glaring, once again a sentinel. "I should get going."

A sick feeling twisted in Drake's stomach. "Will I see you again?"

Footsteps sounded down the corridor and Stonewall shoved on his helmet. "I don't know."

"I'd better not," Drake said, causing Stonewall to look at him in surprise. "Take your girl, take what hematite you can. Leave this place and don't look back."

17

SEVENTEEN

Cobalt rapped against the door to the women's barracks, quick and hard enough to disguise how his hand trembled. "Red? Come on, we're about to set out."

The door flew open to reveal Flint's too-blue eyes staring up at him. Armor only covered her lower body and her tunic was rumpled; she was clearly in the middle of suiting up for her squad's patrol. "Red's not here, Captain," the burnie said. "She went to the baths. But that was a while ago."

"How long?"

"Not sure, ser. But Red's not one to dawdle."

"No, she's not." A sinking feeling took hold of Cobalt's gut, aggrandizing the chills and nausea that had plagued him the last week or so since their hematite shipment was destroyed. He inclined his head in the direction of the women's baths. "Come on."

"But we have patrol–"

"*Now*, burnie."

Flint slipped out of the barracks, closing the door behind her. Cobalt strode down the corridor while the girl trotted beside him, hastily tying back her hair. Neither spoke. Cobalt's heart raced faster with each step because he knew, he *knew* he would not like what they were about to find. *Tor, help us.*

The women's baths—like the men's—were small, but functional. A wide stone basin sat set in the center, filled with water from spigots at the sides. The furnace below heated the water nicely, but the sodding thing was constantly breaking down. More often than not, the sentinels had to go without hot water. Today, the furnace must have been working, for the room was pleasant despite the frigid air outside. Even from outside the closed door, Cobalt could feel the warm air brushing his face.

Cobalt knocked. "Red?"

No response.

He tried again; again silence met him. He nodded to Flint, who slipped inside. A beat later, she called for him. Heart in his throat, Cobalt slipped inside and swore. Redfox was lying naked beside the basin, arms curled against her sides, a linen towel draped over her torso—possibly Flint's doing—one of her daggers and her cuirass beside her. The top layer of leather on the chest-piece had been peeled away to reveal the chips of hematite embedded beneath. A few chips lay by Red's slack mouth, beside a pool of bile glinting in the lamplight.

Idiot, was Cobalt's first thought, followed closely by, *Mara, help her.* "Dead?" he asked.

"No." Flint looked up at Cobalt, her eyes wide. "But close."

Cobalt knelt beside the cinder. "Red? Redfox." Her eyelids fluttered but did not open, and he resisted the urge to shake her. "Red, look at me. That's an order."

A soft groan escaped her, and nothing more. Cobalt swallowed his fear and carefully scooped up the older woman; she was light and frail as a pile of bones. She had never seemed frail, before. As he stood, his stomach roiled and dizziness overtook him, but he pushed past the feeling. "Get her gear," he told the burnie.

It had never taken him so long to reach the infirmary, but he couldn't say if his perception was off, or his stride. Each step made Red's weight triple. At one point, Flint shot him a glance before disappearing down the corridor ahead. When she reappeared, Mica was at her heels. Never in Cobalt's life was he so relieved to see Mica's face, or the satchel he carried.

"Set her down," the mender instructed, foregoing the "ser." But Cobalt didn't care about that now. He did as instructed and Mica got to work.

"Flint said she ate raw hematite?" the mender said as he withdrew a vial of dark-green powder from his bag.

"Aye." Cobalt tried to say more, but his mouth wasn't cooperating.

"Do you know how much?"

"Looks like she dug a handful out of her gear," Flint replied. She'd taken to examining Red's cuirass. "But we found some beside her in the baths, so I don't know if she ate all of it. There was some vomit by her, too."

Mica dumped the powder in a flask, closed the stopper, and shook the thing. "And how long it's been since she ate it?"

Cobalt and Flint exchanged glances. "I don't know," Flint admitted. "She went to the baths about a half-hour ago, but she wasn't kitted up."

The mender nodded. "No telling how much she digested. We might be able to get her to purge the rest. Help me prop her upright."

Cobalt knelt and lifted Red's shoulders, while Flint gently tilted her head back at Mica's direction. With a shaking hand, the mender tipped the flask's contents down her throat, murmuring prayers to Mara as he did, but Cobalt hardly heard him. Red coughed, spewing up much of the green-tinted liquid, and groaned.

"Come on, you sodding cinder," Cobalt heard himself say. "Stop complaining and drink that stuff. You're not getting away from me that easily."

Redfox groaned again, her head lolling to one side. Her eyelids fluttered. Mica tried to get her to drink more of the medicine, but she spat it back out. With each moment, the dizziness that had overtaken Cobalt grew stronger; he felt as if he were standing on the edge of a high cliff, looking up at the sky. The acrid scent of the medicine merged with that of Red's bile, making Cobalt's guts roil. Mica urged her to drink, as did Flint, but Cobalt couldn't find the strength to speak. He only gripped Red's shoulders, hoping to offer silent support.

The cinder gasped before she looked into Cobalt's eyes. He saw it then: defeat. "No, Red," he growled, clutching her shoulders. "No you don't. You're staying in this life until I say otherwise."

A faint smile touched her mouth before she took a single breath, then her body went still. The three of them knelt in the corridor outside the infirmary for some time before Mica ducked his head. "Nox bring–"

"Shut up," Cobalt snarled. Heat pricked his eyes but his body was cold as stone. Was he dead, too? He looked at the mender. "What happened? Why didn't that...stuff help her?"

Mica sat back on his heels, rubbing his face. "She ate raw ore out of her gear. Crushed bitterwort sometimes helps to expel the poison, but she must have taken too much."

"She puked up a lot of the hematite," Flint whispered. She still knelt by Red's body, her head bowed.

The mender shook his head. "Not enough."

"Didn't she get some hematite when Talon brought it?" Flint asked.

Mica nodded. "Aye, but I could only give Red a half-dose. It must not have helped her as much as she wanted. It was like that for the others." He looked at Cobalt. "I'm sorry, Captain." There were deep shadows beneath Mica's eyes and his voice was ragged.

Cobalt shook his head. "You did your best."

He sent the burnie to her duties and helped Mica bring Red to the infirmary with the others. Only when Cobalt eased Red's body next to Scoria's did he realize that the entire room was full of bodies. Most of them held living souls, but far too many lay still and silent beneath linen sheets. The room was too warm and smelled of *biri* smoke and thalo; the heat and the scents mingled unpleasantly in Cobalt's belly. He stood back as Mica slid a sheet over Redfox, murmuring the prayer that would send the cinder to her next life.

"How many have...passed on?" Cobalt managed.

Mica's shoulders sagged. "Fourteen, for now. We'll have to cremate them all together – after our next mission, I guess."

Blood beat behind Cobalt's eyes hard enough to make his head throb. His hands tightened into fists and without another word, he strode to the door, weaving through pallets and sick sentinels. None of them groaned or moved; most may as well have been dead. His vision pooled to the exit and each step felt like he was moving through thick sand. At last he slipped into the corridor and could breathe a little easier as he made his way to Talon's office. But just as he turned a corner, she was there, hair neatly braided as usual, expression cool and composed. Cobalt managed to stop before he collided with her, but she still reached out a hand to steady him.

"Captain?"

"Redfox is gone," he ground out. "Our infirmary's filled to the brim. I know we have orders, but we need hematite *now.*"

He didn't bother with "ser." She didn't reprimand him. "Have you brought back any Sufani?"

Cobalt had never had much use for hatred; like love, it was one of those useless emotions that did more harm than good. But as Talon studied him with that cool regard, something hot and fierce churned within his heart. It took every ounce of training and control to speak without punching her. "Not yet, ser."

She frowned. "That must be rectified if we are to get any more hematite from the Circle. Take every squad you can and go find some."

"Have you been to the infirmary, ser? Do you know how many sentinels can still stand?"

She may as well have been one of the bastion walls. "Not many," she said quietly.

"Does the High Commander?"

She was silent.

Anger caught in his throat like bile. "Then how can we possibly–"

"We will follow orders, because we *must.*" Now she drew herself up to her full height and she was nearly tall enough to look him in the eyes. "Because the lives of our brothers and sisters depend on it."

Hatred fled, leaving Cobalt barren and weak. He would crumble if anyone so much as breathed on him. "What of the bastion?" he heard himself ask. "Do the Pillars want more mages to escape while the rest of us are traipsing through the province?"

"Leave one squad behind to watch them, even if it's only from the top of the wall."

"Good thing there aren't many mages left to watch," Cobalt muttered.

The commander gave a humorless laugh. "Aye. The One must have a dark sense of humor; there is balance in all things."

* * *

Stonewall stared at the ring of keys in Cobalt's outstretched hand, uncomprehending. "Just us, ser?"

The captain's stance wavered, but his reply was iron. "Right now, burnies are the only ones we can be sure are resistant to magic. You have two in your group. I've got a few more, but I'll need them with me in the field. Therefore, you're to take over bastion patrol immediately while the rest of us," his lips compressed in a thin line, "search the province for these sodding nomads the Pillars so dearly want."

Stonewall shared the captain's sentiment. "Ser, why aren't the local guards handling this?"

"I don't sodding know," Cobalt snapped, loud enough for the other sentinels in the garrison's courtyard to glance up in alarm. He grimaced and lowered his voice. "And I don't care. If this is what we must do to get more hematite, then so be it."

This time, Stonewall was smart enough not to question the other man. Besides, even the *mention* of more hematite made the persistent chill deep in his bones strengthen; hematite was the only way to burn it out.

Right, and what will you do about that when you leave here? Stonewall tried to ignore the jump of nerves that accompanied the thought and accepted the keys with a salute. "Don't worry, ser."

"Don't cock it up."

Finding no appropriate response, Stonewall simply nodded. Cobalt strode off to where his team waited, along with every mage-carriage in the garrison, while Stonewall turned to make his way back to his squad in the courtyard. Each step made his stomach twist. Bastion patrol, with barely any other sentinels in the garrison for the rest of the day.

Now, he thought, shivering. *We must leave now.*

He hadn't planned on this opportunity, but Cobalt had literally handed it over. Maybe this was all some elaborate ruse to trap him and Kali in an escape attempt, but he shook the thought away as being overly paranoid. The orders from Argent were real—Talon had ensured that every Whitewater sentinel was aware of *that*—and the captain's reasoning was sound enough. Anything else could be attributed to the lack of hematite.

Stonewall's mouth watered. *Stop it*, he scolded himself. *Mind on the mission.* Behind him, Cobalt called a command and the sentinels with him urged their mounts into neat lines, the sound of clattering hooves echoing off the flagstones. The riders made their way to the gates, the carriages creaking at their heels. This morning, the sun hid behind a layer of thick gray clouds, casting the sentinels in a dull light. The scent of snow clawed at the air and cold prodded at Stonewall's gear, biting at every patch of exposed skin. He shivered again and looked at his squad, who stood by their mounts watching him with bewilderment.

"Aren't we going with them?" Milo asked as soon as Stonewall was within earshot.

"Not today." Stonewall took a deep breath and looked at each member of his squad in turn. "We're on bastion patrol."

Beacon's eyebrows shot up. "Just us?"

"Aye," Stonewall said. "But Talon's still here, as are Mica and Ferro. Everyone else is either going with the captain, or..."

He trailed off, eyes pulled toward the garrison.

Flint squared her shoulders. "Are we going to stand here like dolts while the whole world turns into thralls?"

Rook's eyes widened. "We can't leave."

"We haven't really, ah, discussed the particulars," Beacon added.

Flint snorted. "Feels like leaving this place is *all* we've talked about since Heartfire."

Rook began to tremble. "It was just talk."

"It wasn't," Stonewall said, studying her. "Rook, if you don't want to come with us, you don't have to. All I ask is that you don't turn us in."

"Argent will find us," she whispered.

"That's a chance I'm willing to take," Stonewall said. "Especially once we've got a good head start." His heart beat faster with each word and he glanced at the empty gates. They could do this. Right?

"What are we going to do about hematite?" Beacon said.

Stonewall grimaced. "My brother said if we could get more, we could ease off over time."

"You spoke with him?" Milo asked.

Stonewall nodded. "It won't be easy, or enjoyable, but he made it sound manageable."

"But we don't have *any* hematite," Beacon said with a frown.

Milo's eyes lit up and he dug in one of his belt-pouches to produce a small vial. Stonewall's blood quickened at the sight of the dark-gray substance within and he had to check the impulse to snatch it from the young man's grip. Beacon stared at the vial, lips parted, and took a step forward, one hand extended. Rook's breath hitched and she, too, moved toward Milo. Only when Milo stepped back did Stonewall realize that he had moved as well. The three of them had converged on the young sentinel – and the hematite in his grasp.

"Where did you get that?" Beacon whispered, eyes gleaming as if with fever.

Milo shot Flint a nervous look. "Talon gave it to me," he said. "The other day, when we met with that Circle priest."

"You neglected to mention *that*," Beacon said, nodding to the vial.

The burnie flushed. "I'm sorry. I didn't think–"

"Do you have more?" Rook interrupted.

Milo shook his head. Disappointment struck Stonewall with the force of a dagger; Rook and Beacon's faces mirrored the feeling. Flint scowled. "Calm down, you lot. You can split it between you."

Her words brought Stonewall back to himself. He urged Beacon and Rook to back up and give Milo some room. "One dose split three ways won't be enough," he said to the twins. "Drake said it took him months to ease off."

"We're not going to have *months*," Beacon snapped. "At this rate, we'll be lucky if we have a *week*."

Rook wrapped her arms around her middle. "I just want to be warm again. Surely a little bit would help."

"Aye, but it would wear off and then you'd be in worse shape," Beacon said. "I've seen it over and over again since Heartfire. You should know that. You saw what happened to Red."

Anger flashed across Rook's face as she glared up at the mender. "Aye, and what good have you and Mica and the other menders been? How many have you saved?"

"That's enough," Stonewall said. "We're on the same side!"

"I might be able to get more," Milo said suddenly, causing them all to look at him. At their attention, he flushed and gripped the vial. "Serla Natanaree...the Cipher I met at Mara's temple. She said she would help me."

Beacon and Stonewall exchanged dubious glances.

"Even if she does, how long will that take?" Rook asked.

"If we're going to leave, we must do so right away," Stonewall said. "Every moment we delay increases our odds of getting caught."

"I'll be quick," Milo said. "I'll just run over to Mara's temple and ask for her."

"I'll go with you," Flint added.

"What if she's not there?" Rook asked. "Ciphers travel all over the province."

Milo swallowed. "She's the best chance we've got."

"Talon did bring some back with her when she met with that Circle frip," Flint offered.

But Beacon drew himself to his full height. "It's all gone by now. And even if it weren't I refuse to sentence our brothers and sisters to death for my own well-being."

"How noble of you," Flint muttered, but the words lacked their usual sharpness.

"Don't worry, Beak," Milo said. "If Serla Natanaree is there, she'll help us. And if not, I'm sure I can find someone who can. Maybe if I explain that it's an emergency, someone at the temple will give us more."

Stonewall shook his head. "I don't know if we can trust anyone from the Circle. Not when they're holding these orders over our heads. Not when they claim that thralls aren't the real threat right now. Remember what Talon told me about the Pillars claiming that poor soldier we found in Torin *wasn't* burned?"

Beacon frowned, his gaze on Milo's belt-pouch. "Aye, that was odd."

"It's more than 'odd,'" Flint scoffed. "It's fucking idiotic."

"There's more than that," Stonewall added. His breath grew shorter as he considered everything he'd learned. The pieces began to fit together, and the picture was not pretty. "Beacon, it's different for you, but Flint and Milo: didn't you ever wonder why the Circle took us off the street, fed us, sheltered us, trained us, but didn't bother to teach us to read?"

"We don't need to know that," Flint said, brows knitting.

"Reading would come in handy," Stonewall said. "But they never taught us. Instead, we had to learn an entirely different code, and for what?"

Rook was shaking her head. "I think you're making too much of that, Stonewall."

"I'm not wrong," he replied. "But something in this situation is."

Beacon held up a hand. "Conspiracy theories aside, we have a situation of our own to deal with now. Mi, do you really think this Cipher will give you more hematite?"

"She nearly said as much to me the last time we spoke," Milo replied.

"We could use the time to gather supplies," Beacon said to Stonewall.

"Aye, and I need to get Kali," Stonewall replied. "She's been...ill since Parsa."

All eyes turned to him. "Ill?" Beacon asked. "Can she still try to cure thralls?"

How to explain Kali's state to them, when he didn't fully understand it? Stonewall took a deep breath. "Her efforts to cure the thralls...affected her in a bad way. I'm not sure exactly what's going on, but I fear the worst if Talon discovers her state."

The others exchanged glances before Beacon nodded. "Aye, well, another reason to hurry. She's the key to curing the thralls, after all. Her, and probably Sadira." His face fell. "Though, something tells me Sadira won't want to leave."

"Then she's a fool," Flint muttered.

"She has her reasons," Beacon shot back, adding a softer, "Or so I imagine."

Stonewall's hands were shaking, whether from excitement, fear, or something more sinister, he could not say. He gripped the keys like a lifeline and looked at each of his squad-mates in turn. "You all must take care. Talon doesn't need an excuse to lock me up, but the rest of you are still somewhat in her good graces."

"Fuck her good graces," Flint replied. "She's no better than the High Commander. Kissing the Pillars' asses just to get us more poison. For all the good it'll do. Look at you three," she added, waving a hand at Stonewall, Rook, and Beacon. "Not one of you can keep your eyes off of Mi's belt, like any moment, you're going to lunge."

Stonewall hadn't realized it, but she spoke the truth. Shame flooded him and he took a step back, away from Milo. Rook and Beacon followed his lead, albeit with reluctance.

"Besides," Flint went on as if she'd not noticed the older sentinels' actions. "There's a chance for us to *do* something worthwhile in this life, besides chasing Sufani and watching the mages play in their garden."

Beacon gave a weak laugh. "When did you get so dutiful?"

"Shut up, frip."

Milo placed a hand on his sister's arm, quieting her. He looked at Stonewall. "We'll be back soon."

"No, it's too risky to return, and we shouldn't linger in the garrison." Stonewall's mind raced over their options. "Meet us at the inner gates. We'll ride out onto the bridge from there.

"But what if you..." Milo trailed off, unable to finish the thought.

But Flint chimed in. "If anyone runs into any trouble and we can't meet up, what should we do?"

"Take care of each other," Stonewall said. "Do what you must, but be safe."

The twins exchanged worried looks, but they did so in unison. *Tor keep them together, and safe,* Stonewall thought.

"I've been stockpiling some of my medical supplies," Beacon was saying. "Just need to fetch them."

Rook's pulse beat visibly at her throat. "I'll try to get us some rations."

Everyone looked at Stonewall. "I'll get Kali," he said. *Bahar,* his heart urged, but he shoved the thought aside. "And Sadira, if she wants to come."

A faint smile crept to Beacon's mouth, but the mender seemed to banish it at once. "I hope she does. I'd feel a lot better with her firepower at our backs. Literally." He laughed weakly.

"Aye, we know," Flint said, rolling her eyes. "Come on, Mi."

"Be careful," Rook said as the burnies went for their horses.

Beacon started for the garrison with quick steps, but Rook remained in place, her shoulders rising and falling with her breath. Stonewall placed a hand on her upper arm, drawing her attention. Wide brown eyes, wet with tears, looked up at him. "I'm fine," she said before he could ask. She swiped at her eyes. "Just..."

"Me too," he replied when she trailed off. "Rook, I meant what I said. You don't have to–"

"No," she interrupted. "I do. I'm ready." She took a deep breath and patted his hand, smiling wanly. "Thanks, though. You've become a fine leader."

"We're a team," he said, heat creeping to his neck at the praise.

Her smile turned sad. "Aye. A team." With that, she trotted for the garrison, leaving him alone.

Before heading for the bastion, Stonewall glanced up at the upper level of the garrison, searching for Talon or anyone else who might cause trouble. Until now, he could probably explain everything away. But the moment he set foot inside the bastion, alone, he could not go back.

He'd been lucky so far. The lack of hematite in the garrison had been his ally, in an odd way, but his luck would run out soon. If Talon caught him now...

Best not think about that.

Stonewall strode to the bastion, his boots echoing in the chill air. He considered going to his quarters first, but he already carried most of what he needed. He'd probably miss a change of clothes later, but he could do without. There was the river rock Kali had given him; he was sorry to leave it behind, but he did not want to risk too much time in preparation. He and Kali would be together. That was a gift worth risking his paltry possessions.

Drake. The thought of his brother made his steps falter. Could he really leave Drake behind? *He abandoned me,* Stonewall told himself, but the thought lacked its usual bitterness.

No. He could not afford doubt now, nor deviate from their admittedly lackluster plan. *If we had time,* he resolved, *I'd try to free him, too.* Drake had even said as much: Kali and his squad came first.

Even now, he could see her face in his mind's eye: jaw trembling as she clenched her teeth against her constant pain. Her voice reverberated in his mind, clear as if she'd spoken in his ear: *"Stop! Please! Leave me alone. Go away. Please..."*

Surely the clarity of her voice was an echo of his own thoughts and memories. But a sense of panic colored the words, filling his chest and spurring his heart to pick up its pace. The harder he tried to set aside his worry for her and focus on his task, the more insistent her presence became. Thoughts of Kali pounded on the barriers of his mind, howling for entry, while *her* fear beat upon him like waves in a summer storm.

"A foreign presence," Sadira had said. *"Kali alone investigated."* How could he protect her from something she carried within herself?

Stonewall tried to shut out his rising panic and focus only on keeping his steps quick and quiet, but he swore he could hear Kali's ragged gasps. Terror—not his, but hers, he was sure—prickled along his hands and down the small of his back. What in the blazing void was going on?

There was no guard at the gate, only a heavy iron lock laced with hematite. Stonewall slipped inside and closed it behind him without letting the latch fall into place. The creak of iron sounded dull beneath the blood drumming in his veins. This could end so badly. But they had to try. If not now, there might never be another chance.

We leave together, or not at all, he thought, and hurried through the silent bastion.

18

EIGHTEEN

Milo's heart thudded harder than his horse's hooves against the cobblestones. Flint was the more skilled rider, so he followed her lead as she urged her mount through Whitewater City. This late in the afternoon, all tiers could ride through the streets, but only fleet riders—the messengers of Aredia—higher tiers, and sentinels were allowed to keep any pace faster than a trot. But that didn't stop folks from lobbing obscenities at Milo's back after they had to leap out of the way of the sentinels' horses. Milo tried to ignore the curses. *Mind on the mission.*

At last he caught the scent of water and fish, and heard the clanging harbor bells beneath the constant roar of the waterfall. Soon after, Milo called to his sister as he pulled Nutmeg up about a block away from Mara's temple.

Flint leaned back, coaxing Ginger to a stop and glaring at Milo at the same time. "What are you doing? We're nearly there!"

"We can't go barreling up," Milo replied as quietly as he dared. "Remember how Stonewall made us sneak up on those thralls near Torin? He said, 'when you're on the hunt for something, it's best to take an easy approach.'"

Flint pursed her lips. "Makes sense, I guess."

Milo slid from his horse, but Flint didn't move. "You're not coming?" he asked.

She held out her hand for his reins. "I'll watch your back."

The knot in his chest that had been growing since before Heartfire seemed to expand and tighten all at once. "Do you really want to leave?" he asked.

"You saw how they were looking at you, Mi. You saw it in their eyes."

"I trust them with my life," Milo said, frowning. "Don't you?"

"Aye. But that's not what I'm getting at." Flint shuddered, gripping both sets of reins. "I *watched* Redfox die in Cobalt's arms. If we don't get out now, that'll be our fate, too."

Milo went still. "You didn't tell me you...were there, with Red."

Flint looked away from him to survey the streets. "It doesn't matter now. We'll be gone soon. So get a move on, burnie."

Mara's temple teemed with beggars, supplicants, and Circle clergy, and at first, Milo was certain the crowd would spell his downfall. But the advantage to being around so many other people absorbed in their own troubles was that no one paid him much mind. Granted, he got a few curious looks—the armor usually had that effect—but no one questioned him or told him to leave. Small victories.

At first, he merely stood by Mara's quartz statue like a fool, trying to decide how to actually *do* what he'd said he would. Stupidly, he hadn't thought much beyond getting here; had he hoped he'd just bump into the Cipher? Should he ask about her, or just go looking on his own? Even if he did find her, would she remember her promise to aid him? Well, he wasn't going to help his squad-mates by waiting around, so he made his way toward the corridor he'd been to before. The gods were with him, for he met a young man about his age, dressed in the gray robes of an initiate and carrying a stack of scrolls.

Milo flagged him down with a nod and a greeting. When the fellow came over, Milo removed his helmet to better speak to him. "I'm looking for a Cipher Natanaree."

The young man's gaze stuck on Milo's sword, but he managed to pull it away long enough to nod. "Aye, Ser Sentinel. She's at prayer."

Thank Mara! Milo quelled the urge to race off and tried to keep his own advice in mind. *Take it easy.* "Thanks. Where can I find her?"

"Serla Natanaree won't *appreciate* anyone who bothers her during prayer," the initiate replied, brows knitting.

Milo made a show of looking around before he leaned in to pitch his voice to a lower, more conspiratorial register. "I can well imagine. But you see, she told me wouldn't *appreciate* it if *I* was late for our...meeting." He tried to add a look that he hoped came across as knowing, not like he had palsy.

Thank Mara and all the gods, the other fellow seemed to catch on. A sly smile crept to his face and he nodded. "Sounds like her." He flushed and cleared his throat. "Err... I mean, Serla Natanaree is a Cipher of the highest order. Her time is valuable." He jerked his chin down one of the corridors. "Third one down. Good luck."

"Thanks. I'll need it." Milo made to step away, but paused. "Do you know if she's alone?"

The other fellow coughed in his hand. "She should be."

They parted ways and Milo slipped down the stone corridor, his heart hammering again. Each step brought him deeper into the temple, sconces flickering along the walls, casting the way ahead in dancing shadows. Each step brought more doubts. What if the Cipher's promises had been empty? What if he and Flint were late meeting up with the others? What if–

"Milo?"

He jerked to a stop too late, and collided with the Cipher. Luckily, he caught her before she fell, but the result left her in his arms, their faces close. Cheeks hot, Milo released her immediately and stepped out of reach. He bowed. "Serla Natanaree."

She rolled her eyes. "That 'serla' business is tiresome. 'Naree' will do. Why are you here?"

"I need your help." He told her of the destroyed hematite shipment, and of how many other sentinels had died or become too ill to stand because of lack of hematite. The words tumbled out of his mouth, no doubt making him seem even more foolish than he felt, which was saying something. But she only listened, her expression graver with each moment.

When he finished, she took a deep breath. "How much do you need?"

"As much as you can give me."

"Are you…ill, as well?"

"No. But my squad-mates are getting worse and…" He trailed off. He'd not mentioned they were going to leave, and he probably shouldn't. But if she asked, would he lie? Could he lie to a Circle priestess? Wouldn't that be blasphemy or something?

"I heard that Iban gave your commander some," Naree said, brows knitting.

"It wasn't enough. Several sentinels have died since, and apparently, we don't get any more until we bring in Sufani. That's where the others are now."

She muttered something beneath her breath. "Does your commander know you're here?"

He shook his head.

Naree ran a hand over her braids. "I'll meet you by the fountain in a few minutes."

"Thank you," he began, but she shook her head.

"Don't thank me yet."

With those ominous words ringing in his ears, Milo went back to the temple's entrance. He saw no sign of the young man he'd spoken to earlier, but there were even more people about now. A few shot him dark looks, so he eased his way to the street, where he could see the fountain without being on the temple grounds. He waved to Flint, who waited about a block away with their horses. When she spotted him, she led over their mounts.

"She's bringing some," he said when Flint drew close.

She stood on the balls of her feet to see better. "How much?"

"I dunno. Hopefully a lot."

The seconds crawled by, edging into minutes, and then what felt like hours, though Milo knew it wasn't that long. Even so, every moment they delayed seemed like a lifetime. How was their squad faring? Had Talon found them out? Would she really arrest all of them? Again and again, Milo tried to voice these questions to Flint, if only to hear her reassure him that he was worrying for nothing. Again and again, the words stuck in his throat.

At last, thank Mara, Tor, and all the gods, a white-and-black robed figure strode out of the temple's entrance, tattooed hands clasped before her. Those she passed stepped out of her way and bowed in deference, but the Cipher paid them no mind. She reached the waiting sentinels, who both bowed out of long-ingrained habit.

She withdrew several small pouches from beneath her cloak. "It's all I could get."

Flint sucked in a breath and Milo's eyes bulged as he accepted the heavy pouches, although he still wasn't sure it would be enough to sustain his squad-mates. "Thank you, Serl – Naree," he managed to choke out. "This is more than I dared hope for."

"Thanks, serla," Flint echoed.

"I would've gotten more, but I worried that Iban would grow suspicious. But I did learn something useful. Do you know why the Circle wouldn't send you any more hematite?"

"No," Milo said, his stomach knotting. "But something tells me you do?"

The priestess' face twisted into a study in leashed fury. "To make an *example* of the Whitewater City garrison. To show the other sentinels in Aredia the price of failure."

Milo went still, but Flint swore. "Sodding, miserable bunch of..." She trailed off. "Sorry, serla. It's just..."

Naree nodded. "What they're doing is wrong. More than wrong; it's an abomination. Such treatment goes against every edict of the One, and I'm ashamed to..." It was her turn to trail off, her inked hands clenching into fists. "In any case, you have everything I could gather."

"Will you get in trouble?" Milo asked.

"Possibly," Naree replied. "But I don't much care about that, right now."

Milo and Flint exchanged looks; he read his own apprehension in his sister's eyes. "You shouldn't take such a risk for us," Milo began.

But the Circle priestess cut him off. "I shall do exactly as I wish. Besides, Telfair would have wanted me to aid you." When she looked at him again, he only saw the cool Cipher in her eyes. "You're leaving, aren't you?"

Flint shot him a startled look, but Milo nodded. "Aye, Naree. We can't stay in the sentinel order any longer. Not after…everything. Not when there's even the tiniest hope we can cure thralls, even without the Circle's blessing."

"Then you will be Forsworn. The Pillars will hunt you down and send you to the mines at Stonehaven, where you will suffer a slow and painful death. Do you really want to do this?"

"We'll be fine," Milo said with more confidence than he felt. "Don't worry about us."

Naree studied him. A chilly wind rippled her cloak and pulled a few strands of curling, dark hair free from her braids. At last she nodded again; her features shifted and she was a Cipher no longer, but a young woman who looked at him with fear. "Then take care, Milo."

Milo managed to fumble out a farewell, too, but by then, Naree was already heading back to the temple, her cloak swaying in her wake. He stared after her until Flint kicked his shins.

"Come on," she said when he yelped. "We've got a mission, remember?"

"Right," Milo replied, still dazed. He tried to shake off the feeling as he tucked the hematite in his belt and they mounted up.

Flint nodded in the direction of the city gates. "Let's go. The others are counting on us."

* * *

Kali's fingers ached from playing her viol. No, not just her fingers. Her whole sodding *body* was wracked with pain from being held rigid in her attempt to focus, to keep *calm*. Her knee burned; if she'd not known better, she'd have sworn that she'd paced a groove in the floor of her quarters. Movement was good. Focusing on something else, like music, was good. Both helped keep the Fata at bay. But nothing lasted.

Thoughts that were not hers beat ceaselessly upon all corners of her mind. *Sweet blood. Sweet magic. Give it to us. Now.* Again and again and again. Her hopes of seeking information were far away when all she wanted to do was beg for a moment of peace. She wanted to scream. She wanted to cry. She did both. Neither helped. But music… Oh, music was sweet. Where Kali's viol had once been a source of sorrow, now the instrument reminded her of happier times, of love and light and her father's proud smile as she played her first proper song. Now, her viol gave her mind something else to do other than fret and fear, and pulse with a hunger she could not satiate.

She kept playing after the first silver-coated string broke, and the second, setting her bow along the remaining two strings in a teetering wail that echoed in her own heart. But strings were fragile. The third one broke too, leaving Kali in a silence so thick she would surely choke. She tried to play the fourth alone, but was terrified of losing that last connection. She could not leave her room and go for help, lest she endanger another mage, but staying would surely kill her. So she paced, biting her lips and tongue against the pain in her knee, and tried to *focus* on her self-appointed mission, but all she could hear was the litany: *Sweet blood. Sweet magic. Give it to us. Now.*

"No," she whispered, clutching her temples. "Stop. Please. Go away."

Another surge of foreign hunger. *Sweet blood. Sweet magic. Give it to us. Now.*

Fear plucked at Kali's heart. She thought of Neff and the Parsan woman. Was this what their last moments of humanity had been like?

Stop it, she scolded herself. *You're not a thrall, not yet.* She was the only one in the world who could learn what the Fata were doing, so she needed to stop feeling sorry for herself and get to work.

Deep breaths brought a little calm. When she was calmer, it was easier to ignore the terror the Fata brought. *It's all right,* she told herself. *You can do this.*

"Fata?" she said to her cluttered room. "Are you…there?"

No response.

Seren's light, she felt foolish. Her throat was dry but her palms were slick as she clutched her viol, and tried again. "You want magic. Why? Other than the obvious, I suppose."

Any other time, and she'd have felt embarrassment for her silly joke, but now she only knew irritation when she received no response. Not irritation at the Fata—she could not yet quantify her feelings for them—but at herself, for thinking she could learn about them by simply *talking* with whatever wanted to turn her into a monster.

In search of distraction, she went to her window. The bastion wall cast her room in shadow, and the darkness reflected her own face back to her in the glass: shadowed eyes, lips bruised and bleeding from where she'd bitten them. Her hair blended with the wall outside, casting her face moon-white.

Give it to us.

"If you're not going to cooperate," she said. "Go away."

But the voice was not hers; it was rough as boots on wet gravel. The woman in the reflection was a stranger.

Now.

She had to be anywhere but here. If she stayed in her room one more second, she would suffocate. No doubt it was cold as Nox's tits outside, but Kali didn't care. Cold could cut through all other things and bring clarity. She set her viol down and rushed out of her room, silently praying—*praying? To whom?*—that she wouldn't see anyone else. A tingle ran through her palm when she shoved open her iron door handle, but she ignored the discomfort. Only when the door closed behind her did she think of going out the window.

If there were gods, then they were merciful. Kali met Druce and Wylie in the corridor, but neither stopped her, even when she ignored their questions and exclamations of concern. But she could sense magic hanging in the air around them, like the scent of jessamin blossoms, and could not allow herself to stop. She hurried as best she could, for her knee throbbed and she had not abandoned the desire for magic back in her room. Again and again, she fought the urge to stop at Sadira's room, or Hazel's, or Foley's, or *anyone's*, and try to wrest their power from them like a sodding leech. So it was a victory of the highest order when she emerged from the dormitories and into the chilled air.

Kali took a deep breath, savoring the clean scent of snow, and looked into the gray-white sky. When a blast of wind hit her, she realized she'd forgotten her cloak, but she refused to go back to her room, and instead made her way to the farthest corner of the bastion. The garden. She would go to the garden and rest her back and aching body against the high wall. Like her viol, the garden held both bitter and happy memories, the latter of which she sorely needed.

She limped toward the back wall. By now, she knew the way by heart, so she squeezed her eyes shut against the pain in her knee and the foreign, violent urges. Each step burned, but she would not stop until she was–

"Kali." Strong hands gripped her shoulders. She looked up into Stonewall's almost-golden eyes, wide with concern. He was armored, his helmet clipped to his belt, and his cheeks were dark from the wind. "It's time. We must leave."

Leave? She pressed a hand to her forehead, trying to recall their plan. "How?"

"Most of the other sentinels are gone, but not for long. Talon's still here. We don't have much time. We must go now." He held out his gloved hand. "Please, Kali. Come with me."

Kali nodded and swiped at her runny nose with her sleeve. Another gust of wind cut right through her, reminding her how foolish she'd been to come outside in just a tunic and leggings. It was just as stupid to think she could face the Fata, or any force beyond her control. Eris was right. A snarl of anger built in the back of Kali's throat. She clenched her teeth against it, shut her eyes against it, and wrapped her arms around her torso to keep from trembling. The anger did not dissipate, but turned inward, burning her eyes with more sodding tears. Of course, she wept when she most needed to be strong. Stars and moons, she was so tired!

Stonewall took her arm to help support her weight. He began to thread through the bare trees and dead grass of the garden, his steps moderated to keep pace with her. Even so, Kali had to lean upon him so she wouldn't stumble. But when she realized he was heading for the dormitories, she froze. "What are you doing?"

Stonewall frowned down at her. "You at least need a cloak. And don't you want to see if Sadira can come? And get your viol?"

"You said we had to hurry."

His brows knit, but he nodded and began to walk again. "Aye. Well, let's get Sadira then, and–"

"I can't be near her, now," Kali said. "I can't be near any other mage. It's gotten worse. The...Fata's desire for power. I can't risk hurting anyone else."

"You would leave your friend behind?"

"It's for her own safety. Besides," Kali closed her eyes, "she wouldn't want to leave."

Stonewall exhaled in a fog of breath that the wind swept away. "We don't have time to argue."

He withdrew a ring of keys from his belt and reached for her collar, his thumb tracing the scar on her throat before he brushed her messy braid aside. A faint pressure at her neck, a snap of release; the bite of cold air against her skin where the collar had lain. So, too, did color and life rush back into her world. Only with her senses' true return did she remember—again—the void that hematite created. Would she ever get used to the feeling?

With the collar gone, Kali braced herself for an onslaught of Fata emotions, but she felt nothing new. Odd. So hematite had no effect on their magic? If that was the case, then the Fata's magic was truly different than that of the mages.

Stonewall's touch at her arm was firm, no doubt meant to be reassuring. "Don't be afraid," he said. "I'll keep you safe."

"Safe?" Her voice was a stranger's. "You can't protect me from myself. The harm is done." Another bitter wind blew, tossing a few snow flurries between them. Something wet and cold crept down the sides of her nose. "Just leave me," she told him. "I was stupid. I was wrong. I can't do this. I can't fight it. It hurts..."

Sod it all, she couldn't stop crying even when her tears turned to ice on her cheeks. But Stonewall only pulled her to his armored chest, which offered no warmth, no real shelter. Even so, the moment his arms wrapped around her, she knew she was home. "It's all right, Kali," he said in her ear. "You don't have to fight alone. I'm here."

Something broke within her and Kali surrendered. She pressed her cheek against him and wept hard enough to steal her breath. She wept into his solid chest, where his heart beat so strong. Somehow, he pulled her closer; the movement jostled something from his belt and sent it to the ground with a faint *clink*. His whispers were part of her own mind rather than spoken aloud; the only words that dampened the Fata's relentless litany. *It's all right. You're not alone. You're safe with me.*

The Fata within her started, and then roiled with a keen interest in the sentinel. A new sensation overtook her awareness, unfurling within her chest as warm recognition; reconnection with a lost comrade. She knew, somehow, that Stonewall *belonged* to the Fata, that he was tied to their innumerable voices.

Kin, the voices murmured, all focus now on the sentinel. *Old blood. Ours.*

The Fata's anger began to fade. A sense of calm crept over Kali, flowing into her battered mind and heart with each breath. Her head cleared and she allowed herself to enjoy the feeling of being close to this man.

Sweet blood, the Fata replied, traces of annoyance seeping through what remained of their anger. *Give it to us. Now.*

"Shut up," Kali whispered. Stonewall tensed, but she looked up at him, managing a wan smile. "Not you."

"The Fata?"

She nodded.

He muttered something she did not catch, took her hand and guided her behind the dormitories, where they could hopefully slip to the gates unseen. As they passed by the window of her room, a thought struck her. "How did you know where to find me? Did you come to the garden first?"

He stopped in his tracks, his gaze distant. "No. I just... I knew where you were. I could," his cheeks darkened, "feel you, here." He pressed his fingertips to his temple. "I sound crazy."

Old blood, the Fata within her murmured. *Ours.*

"The Fata," Kali said. "They seem to...recognize you. Like they *know* you

223

somehow."

He blanched. "Me? Unless the sodding things know how many of their thralls I've killed, I doubt..." He trailed off as she grimaced. The mild amusement of the Fata vanished at his words, replaced with that same driving fury, this time directed at Stonewall.

"Old blood, traitor," the Fata hissed, but the words came from Kali's throat. "Traitor blood, tainted with human flesh."

All color drained from his face. She knew this not because of the sunlight that struggled through the cloud cover, but because another light shone from a place she could not see. It was only a brief flash, but even that was enough. His eyes widened, and he released her arm to take a step back. "Sweet Mara's mercy," he whispered. "Your eyes..."

It was so *hard* to make her voice work! Kali tried to say his name, but no human sound emerged. Instead, there was a shrill cry that sent arrows of fear through her heart. She snapped her mouth shut, for she'd heard that sound before. *No!*

She had to leave, and she had to do so alone. His presence was only making the Fata more angry. Even now, magic swam through her veins, eager to drown him, to consume him in the roil and fury. Hematite did not shelter him from the Fata's hunger; they *wanted* him just as they wanted magic. She could not be near Stonewall, either. She could not be near anyone. But maybe if she could be alone, if she could focus...

Kali was no warrior, but she was not defenseless. She just needed to *think*. "Leave me," she managed to choke out – in her *own* voice, thank the stars! "Leave me alone."

Stonewall stared at her and she knew he was collecting his nerve, shoring up his calm. A fighter to the last. Damn him. He came forward again, arm outstretched. "I made that mistake once. I won't do it again. We leave together, or not at all."

If he touched her, she would shatter. If he touched her, the magic building within her body would drain his life away. Kali took a step back and stumbled when her knee faltered. She fell against the dormitory wall and slid to the cold ground. "Go away," she sobbed. "*Now.*"

He came closer, wariness and determination radiating off him like ripples of heat. "Kali, there's no time. We must–"

"What's going on here?" The new voice snapped Kali's focus, making her look over to see Foley standing a few paces away, a mug of tea in his hand.

Stonewall straightened. "Mage Clementa. Kali is–"

"She is ill, Ser Sentinel," Foley replied in a cold voice. "As everyone in the bastion knows. Except you, it seems." Without waiting for a response, he strode to Kali and held out his hook. "Here, child," he said gently. "Come inside. I'll not let him trouble you any longer."

Kali stared at the hook, her heart pounding. She could not touch him. She could not stay on the ground forever. Slowly, she reached for Foley, bracing herself against the forthcoming onslaught of *hunger* for his magic. She wrapped her fingers around the cold, smooth metal – and shrieked at the burning sensation that erupted from the point of contact. That same eerie light filled her vision. No; it came *from* her eyes. Thrall's eyes. Kali cried out again.

Both men said her name, but she barely heard either. She dropped the hook and fell back to the ground, staring at her own palm. There was no sign of burn or blisters, just irritation from playing her viol too much. But the burning sensation lingered.

In every corner of her mind, the Fata recoiled, hissing. *Poison.*

"Sweet fucking stars," she whispered.

Foley rounded on Stonewall. "What have you done to her? Or, rather, what has she done to you, to deserve such treatment? What have any of us *ever* done to your kind?"

Stonewall ignored him and dropped to Kali's side, reaching for her shoulder. "Kali, look at me."

Sweet blood. Sweet magic. Give it to us.

"Leave me alone," Kali choked. "Please."

But the First Mage stepped between them before Stonewall could touch her. "Leave us. Go back to the garrison, where your kind belong."

Stonewall replied with some invective Kali did not hear. She was deep in the Fata's power now, with that same litany circling each thought,

225

delighting in her chaotic heart. *Sweet blood. Sweet magic. Give it to us.*

Then she was in Stonewall's arms. As before, his touch, even through his gear, was soothing, and some of the turmoil within her eased. He lifted her, brushed past Foley, and strode for the gates.

"Talon will hear of this," the First Mage called.

"No doubt," Stonewall replied. "Just stay out of our way in the meantime." They reached the gates within moments; he shoved them open and left them so after passing through. They were really on their way out. Kali tried to find joy that she was finally free of the bastion, but she knew that she was still a prisoner.

19

NINETEEN

Foley's steps echoed in the garrison's corridor. Every muscle was tense, for he expected a host of sentinels to discover him at any moment, but he met no one as he slipped through the barracks. Aside from Talon's office, he had never been inside the sentinels' private spaces before, so it was unsettling to see how the bastion and garrison's layouts mirrored each other. There were differences, though. Rather than the individual rooms of the mage dormitories, there were two sets of barracks for men and women. There were a few individual rooms as well, closer to Talon's quarters, possibly for the other officers. None of the sentinel's private spaces made him think the occupants were meant to live there for very long.

The barracks were empty. So, too, were his daughter's office and bedchamber. Foley was at a loss. Was she even in the garrison? He'd watched a host of sentinels ride away earlier, but had not spotted their commander among them. Despite the press of time—and his own indignation at the sergeant's words—he lingered in his daughter's quarters, smiling at the neatly made sleeping pallet. Talaséa had *never* wanted to make her bed as a girl. His smile faded, though, when he wondered if she'd even slept inside it lately. A single lamp rested on a small table, along with an ewer and bowl. A chest, no doubt filled with her additional clothes and gear, sat across the little room from where she slept.

Otherwise, there were no decorations, no indication that his daughter lived here. It was the room of a sentinel commander, nothing more. Disappointment swelled in his chest. Foolish. He should not have expected anything else.

An unlocked door divided Talon's bedchamber from her office. A stack of scrolls rested on her desk amid sheets of parchment littering the surface. More scrolls and bound papers sat on shelves across from her desk. He thumbed through one of the volumes, thinking it was a book, but frowned at the sentinel script. He'd often asked her to teach him their peculiar code, but she had always refused. *"Ignorance is safer for you,"* she had said every time. *"This is for the best."*

Foley turned to leave, but noticed one of the desk drawers was slightly open. He hesitated; he really needed to find her, or someone, to tell them what was going on, but he so rarely got a glimpse into his daughter's life. He heard no footsteps approaching, so he went to the desk and pulled open the drawer. Within was more parchment, inks and quills and drying powder, sticks of charcoal and wax, and a seal with the sentinel sigil. Nothing of interest.

He made to close the drawer, but noticed something gleaming beneath the parchment. When he lifted the paper, he frowned at the sight of three hematite vials nestled against one another, wrapped in a linen cloth that had come undone at the motion of the drawer.

Hematite. The dispelling stone, indeed, for it muted magic and leeched away life, and his child had been regularly poisoning herself with the stuff for...gods above, nearly twenty years now. Hematite would claim his daughter's life one day soon, if her duties did not.

Foley's jaw tightened against the anger that flooded his heart. He slammed the drawer shut and slipped out of the office, fury and bitterness warring for his full attention. He considered going back to bed, because what did any of this matter? So Sergeant Stonewall wanted to run away with Kalinda. Let them. They were doomed, anyway. Talon would find them, or High Commander Argent, or the thralls, or regular folks with violence in their hearts. They would no longer be anyone's problem but each other's, and perhaps his daughter would know some peace.

He began to make his way back to the bastion, but a wrong turn brought him to a large open room, much the same as the mages' common area. An unfamiliar man murmured from within, so Foley made to slip past. Then he heard Talon.

"Nox bring your spirit safely over the river. Tor guide your steps into the next life. The One keep you in all your days."

Foley knew her well enough to hear the despair in her voice. All other thoughts fled his mind, save one: his child was hurting. He stepped into the large room.

At first glance, it was an infirmary, for every available surface held a sentinel. Only some of them were moving upon the tables and sleeping pallets that cluttered the space. Talon and a slender, dark-skinned mender stood over one of the tables, where a male sentinel lay still and silent. Talon's back was to Foley as she drew a cloth over the dead man's body, but the mender looked up, and his eyes widened.

Talon glanced at the mender, and then turned. When her gaze fell upon Foley, her lips parted in shock before her eyes narrowed into dagger points. "What are you doing here?"

He stared at the shadows beneath the commander's eyes, at the way her hands trembled, at the waxy skin that covered her face. Where was his daughter? Where was the little girl who had crawled into bed with him and Isra when she'd had a nightmare?

Gone, you old fool, his better sense told him. *She was gone the moment she was born, for she has no magic. She was never yours.*

The truth had always lived in his heart but he'd never wanted to acknowledge it.

"I asked you a question," Talon snapped, now barely an arm's length away.

Foley blinked in surprise. He hadn't noticed she'd moved. "Sergeant Stonewall and Kalinda are gone," he managed. "I encountered them as they were leaving the bastion. I thought you'd want to know."

She stared at him. "When? Just now?"

"I'm not sure," he admitted, for he didn't know how long he'd been

229

wandering through the garrison. "But I don't believe they are long gone. You can probably still–"

"What good are you?" she broke in, clenching her hands. "Did you stop them? Did you even *try*?"

"He's a sentinel." Foley was not without his own mettle, so he brandished his hook. "I'm in no hurry to lose the other."

"Stonewall is a soft-hearted imbecile. Like you. He wouldn't have harmed you."

"Love makes people commit all manner of foolish acts," Foley replied, narrowing his eyes.

Talon scoffed and looked back at the mender, who grimaced beneath her gaze. "I'll be back as soon as I can. Mica, you're in charge."

Mica looked around the room filled with dead and the barely alive, and his shoulders slumped. "Yes, ser."

"And you." Talon grabbed Foley's arm and began to force him down the hallway and out into the garrison courtyard. "Get back to the sodding bastion, where you'll be safe."

But Foley held his place. His daughter was strong, and she came by such strength honestly. "No," he said, digging in his heels.

"What?"

"No." He placed his remaining hand on her cheek. "Perhaps they have the right idea. Let's go. Now."

"You're mad," she whispered, her voice hoarse and shaking.

"There's nothing standing in our way, Talaséa. We can be free, together."

She stared at him with eyes the color of dark tea. His wife's eyes. "I can't leave, Da," she whispered at last. "You know I can't."

"Why not?" He gestured to the empty garrison around them. "No one will know. No one will care."

"Da–"

"You've wasted your life on me," he broke in. "But there's still time to change that. We can both live the lives we were meant to."

His daughter looked at the gates, and then back at him. Her eyes were wet. "If we run, Argent will find us. I'll be too weak to save you – weak or dead. And no one will be left to keep you safe."

Foley's heart swelled. "Oh, child. Is that what you truly believe?"

A tear slipped down her nose, but she swiped it away. When she met his gaze again, she was pure *Commander.* "I can still salvage this mess. Wait in your room. I'll tell Argent... Well, I'll think of something." She released him and turned for the stables, and ignored how her name—her birthname—echoed on the garrison walls.

Only when she was out of sight did Foley return to the bastion. The gates to the city still beckoned, but he would not leave his daughter alone.

* * *

All is not lost, Talon told herself as she readied her mount. *I can fix this.*

Possibilities raced through her mind as she guided her horse out of the garrison stables. Cobalt and the others couldn't have left more than an hour ago. If Stonewall and his allies had left immediately after, they might already have reached the gates. If so, her failure as a commander would be complete, and Argent would purge the bastion of every remaining mage. But if Stonewall had lingered for any reason, there was still a chance to catch him.

Hooves clattered on the cobblestones as Talon urged her horse out of the garrison's gates. The sound was not enough to drown out her thudding heart, so she focused on maneuvering through the crowded streets as quickly as possible. The sky was dull and gray and the wind blustered harder with each moment. It was still morning, but midday drew closer, and the city-dwellers out and about would only grow more numerous. When Talon reached one of the main roads, a convoy of massive wagons pulled by equally massive oxen took up most of the way, so she was forced to pull her horse to a stop and wait for them to pass.

She gnashed her teeth at the delay. Was nothing in her control any longer? Perhaps it had never been. Gamber had just passed into his next life, and he was not the first she'd seen to Nox's care since she had risen before dawn. The feelings of withdrawal were getting worse. Despite the cold air, despite how her insides felt like ice, sweat rolled down her back. Her hands shook, so she rested them on the pommel of her saddle to keep them still.

The last of the oxen passed and Talon dug her heels into her horse's sides, urging the creature into a canter. Passers-by shouted obscenities. Something whistled past her head and she caught the scent of rotting fruit, but she ignored everything. Her vision darkened on the edges, for all that mattered lay directly ahead.

She reached the inner gates in less than an hour but did not relish the victory. The city guards on duty swarmed to her horse, and her stomach dropped at the panic on their faces. "Have any other sentinels passed through the gates?" she demanded of the nearest guard.

The young woman saluted. "Aye, Commander." Talon's heart froze, but the guard added, "A host of them, hours ago, led by Captain Cobalt."

"No others?"

The guards exchanged glances before the first shook her head. "No, serla."

The gods were merciful. Talon offered a quick, silent thanks to Llyr, the god of luck, and dismounted, handing off her horse to the young guard. "Where are the other officers on duty? I have a mission for you all."

* * *

A little later, Talon concealed herself just behind the outer gates. A squad of city guards stood by her side; another waited outside. All of them held perfectly still, as she'd ordered. She knew that Lieutenant Faircloth and his guards waited in a similar position behind the inner gates, out of sight of any passers-by. Only four city guards remained on either end of the bridge, ostensibly guarding it as normal. A few guards had gone down the road that led into the city, to delay any approaching travelers.

The city guards were not her sentinels, but Talon was in no position to be choosy. Besides, the guards felt no ill-effects from lack of hematite, for the metal had never run hot and fierce through their veins. Talon prayed that wouldn't spell anyone's doom, but she had warned them of a potential mage threat.

One of the guards, the young woman Talon had met before, leaned over to peer through the gates. She drew back and rested a hand on her crossbow. "They're coming, serla."

"Have they stepped onto the bridge?"

"Aye, serla. Three sentinels and a dark-haired woman."

Only three sentinels? Talon risked a glance and could not suppress a swell of satisfaction. Her hasty plan had worked: the burnie twins had remained loyal to her. They were the only ones. Rook had taken point; Beacon drew up the rear. Stonewall rode his dapple-gray mare at the center, Mage Halcyon seated behind him with her arms wrapped around his waist. The driving wind had pulled her hair free to ripple like a dark banner around her head.

Talon frowned. Only one mage? Where was Stonewall's renegade brother? Had Stonewall left the fellow to rot in the garrison, or had he been unable to free the bastard? She glanced around, expecting the renegade mage to leap out of the void, but saw no one. Perhaps Stonewall had left his own blood behind. A traitor of another kind, then.

Stonewall's squad had just ridden onto the bridge, having only encountered the barest of questions from the guards at the inner gates. Talon had ordered the guards not to detain the group, thus luring them into a false sense of security. Lieutenant Faircloth had been happy to comply.

The squad's horses went at a brisk trot, the sound of their hooves lost beneath the White River's roar. No doubt Stonewall planned to gallop once they reached the outer gates. Talon and the guards would have to be quick. The squad was in the center of the bridge. It was time.

Talon stepped out first, weapons still sheathed. The city guards at her back formed a wall of arms and armor before the outer gates. Their swords and crossbows came out, the metal dull against the blustery gray sky. They would kill if she gave the command. Someone else—again, at her order—pulled the inner gates closed and dropped the iron lock in place. The errant squad pulled their mounts up, looking wildly around, but

Faircloth and his guards had done the same to the inner gates. Stonewall was trapped.

"Traitors," Talon called as she approached the squad. "You are all under arrest."

The three of them drew close together, keeping the mage between them. Stonewall glared at Talon from beneath his helmet. "Call us whatever you want, ser, but at least we'll be able to live with ourselves."

Self-righteous moron! Talon drew her sword. "Dismount, all of you. Turn over the mage and your weapons, and no one will be harmed."

Rook and Beacon both looked at Stonewall, whose hands tightened on his reins. "We're taking this mage to cure thralls," he called over the wind and river. "We mean to leave in peace."

"Dismount," Talon said again. "Comply, or else."

"Or else, what?"

It was not Stonewall, but the little mage behind him. Halcyon peeked around his armored form to look at Talon. The wind whipped her cloak, but Talon swore she caught a flash of starlight. But when she blinked and looked again, only the mage's dark eyes met hers in a challenge.

"What will you do?" the mage said again, her voice light, almost merry. But there was an eerie, otherworldly resonance to her words that sent a chill up Talon's spine. "What *can* you do to us?"

"Kali, be still," Stonewall hissed. His helmet concealed most of his features, but no armor could hide the fear in his voice.

The mage ignored him and glanced at the assembled guards. "Who among you will be the first to fall?"

Some of the city guards shifted, muttering in consternation, but a word from their officers silenced them. Beacon said something to Stonewall, while Rook held still, her gaze darting over the guards. None had reached for their weapons. No doubt Stonewall would not want to harm anyone unless absolutely necessary. Rook and Beacon were soft in that way, too. Talon caught Lieutenant Faircloth's gaze across the bridge and lifted her sword.

A renewed blast of wind. A shouted order to surround. Bedlam overtook the bridge as the city guards drove forward, pressing at the front and rear of the errant squad. The sentinels' mounts, too well-trained to balk at the ambush, still danced nervously as the guards swarmed. Stonewall drew his daggers, the others following his lead, but there were too many guards and he was a sodding fool. He should never have stopped. He should have plunged through the guards and gates, and ridden to freedom. If he truly loved Mage Halcyon, nothing should have stopped him from keeping her safe.

The city guards pulled him and the mage from the dapple-gray mare; Beacon and Rook met the same treatment. The sentinels struggled, even got a few good strikes in, but Talon saw no blood drawn. Soft fools, all of them. Had Talon not been so wrung dry, she might have lamented the ease of their capture.

Movement by the inner gates caught her eye. The burnie twins and stepped onto the bridge, faces pale beneath their helmets. Their weapons were drawn. Talon allowed herself a flare of satisfaction and motioned them over. They both stared at her, and then began to lead their mounts forward.

Two guards had grabbed the dark-haired mage. Now that Halcyon was free of her sentinel lover, her bare throat made Talon's breath catch, more out of reflex than surprise. Of course, Stonewall had released *her*, even if he'd left his own kin behind.

Talon faced the sergeant. "You are a shadow of what a proper sentinel should be. You break your oaths to the gods while your brothers and sisters in sacrifice suffer and die." She allowed the full force of her anger to add venom to her words. "You are Forsworn–"

One of the guards who held Halcyon screamed and jerked away from the mage as if she'd been stung. But Halcyon only grabbed the young guard's wrist and pulled the other woman closer. The guard twisted, her helmet clattering to the stone bridge as she cried out again. But the sound trickled into a gurgle as she clutched at her heart. All life drained from her face, leaving her cheeks hollow and her eyes dull. The other guard also tried to wrest himself free of the mage's sudden, unnatural strength, but within seconds his cries faded into nothing. Both guards crumpled to the bridge, unmoving, as a few flecks of snow drifted to their gear. Halcyon looked at Talon with eyes that shone like stars, and smiled.

"Thrall!" The cry rose on all sides, reaching above the White River's roar.

Stonewall, who had stood frozen with the rest, came alive and struggled in the grips of the guards. He broke free, but two more guards lunged for him. "Kali," he shouted as he ducked to avoid them. "Kali!"

The mage glanced at him, but looked back at Talon, eyes still blazing. Everything seemed darker, as if Halcyon had pulled what little light remained into her own gaze, turning it back upon the world in a perversion of the natural order. Talon's heart hammered and she took a step backward. Then she caught herself and whirled to the guards behind her, "Take her down!"

One of the younger guards stood about ten paces from the mage, and answered the call. She fired a shot straight for the mage's heart. The guard's aim was true; her crossbow's bolt flew through the wind and snow…

And landed with a dull *thwack* in Stonewall's side. He'd broken free of the guards to reach his little mage-whore—the sodding *thrall*—and grunted with the bolt's impact into his thick leather cuirass. He collapsed at the mage's feet and did not move. Had the bolt cut through his gear and into his skin? Talon could not tell. Armor could only protect a sentinel from so much. Mage Halcyon dropped to his side. Beacon, too, jerked free of the guards who held him and darted to his sergeant. The city guards, unnerved, looked at Talon for instructions.

Only a few seconds had passed since she'd called the order. Talon's stomach roiled but she ignored the feeling and strode forward to the sergeant and the mage. The burnie twins had reached the pair first, sheathing their weapons as they knelt beside the mender.

"Take her," Talon ordered them, nodding to Halcyon.

Flint and Milo exchanged glances. From behind them, Rook said their names, softly. Milo tensed, but Flint nodded and reached for the mage.

"You're with *us*, now," she muttered.

All trace of threat had fled the little mage. She sagged against Flint, tears streaming down her face as she looked down at the sergeant. "Elan?" she whispered as Milo took her other arm. "Beacon, is he–"

The sentinel mender shook off the guards who reached for him. "He's alive," he said. "But only just. Your magic must have–"

"You're all under arrest," Talon broke in. She signaled to the city guards. Lieutenant Faircloth called a command and the guards pressed forward again. They hauled Beacon off the sergeant, bound him and Rook, and began to push them back to the city. The burnie twins, after a glance at Talon, urged the dark-haired mage to follow. But Halcyon ignored them and twisted around to see Stonewall, who still lay upon the flagstones, flecks of snow falling upon his face and gear. His chest rose and fell – slowly. Something dark and gleaming spread from his side, staining the new snow bright crimson. Talon gestured to the city guards. "Take him back, too."

Two guards grabbed him, pulled him upright. He did not object until the crossbow bolt sticking out of his side got caught on one of the guard's gear, then he cried out in pain. Talon ignored him and turned to the guards who knelt beside the two that Mage Halcyon had laid to waste.

"They're dead, serla," the young guard said, clutching her crossbow.

No surprise, but Talon ducked her head. "They are on their way to their next lives now," she said, loud enough for all the remaining guards to hear. "But I promise you: their lives *here* will be avenged."

20

TWENTY

As far as Eris was concerned, strong winds were only good for flight. A freezing gust tore through her cloak, ripping off her hood, so she pulled the wool fabric tighter to her body and re-covered her short hair. She glanced at Rilla, who walked beside her between the teeming stalls of the Eye, Whitewater City's marketplace. The blond woman moved with ease, stopping to ostensibly browse a merchant's furs. They had taken a risk coming here, but Rilla and Brice were convinced that this was the best way to learn about the state of the city and the garrison.

The furrier, a stout, fourth tier woman with rosy cheeks, stood at the front of her stall, chatting with a pair of customers. "Midwinter's come and gone, but the dark days are just beginning, you mark my words."

The first customer, an older fellow with a lilting southern accent, exhaled deeply. "Consider them marked."

The other ran a hand through his graying beard and studied the furrier. "What makes you say that?"

The furrier glanced around. Eris watched her out of the corner of her eye and pretended to be engrossed with a pelt of blue-gray fox fur, holding it up to her neck and chest. Another wind blew, rippling the furs stacked on crates and tables, and hanging from wooden stands. Other market-goers drew their cloaks and coats tighter, but otherwise ignored the chilling wind.

Satisfied no one was listening, the furrier dropped her voice to a near-whisper. "Word is, the hemies caught a whole bunch of Sufani, not a day ago."

Eris bit her tongue to stifle her gasp. Leal would be heartbroken – and furious. Why would the hemies bother with Sufani?

The second man made a noise of disbelief and echoed Eris' thoughts. "What do the sentinels want with those dregs?"

"The nomads have been harboring those Assembly folks, haven't they?" the first man replied, a frown in his voice. "No wonder the queen's after them."

"These dregs were sheltering *mages*," the furrier said, sounding pleased.

Eris' fingers tightened over the fur and she gritted her teeth, lest she exclaim in shock. Sirvat and her other friends, back in the bastion after all they had gone through to escape! And it was *Eris'* fault.

"Did the sentinels know the Sufani had their mages?" the first man asked.

"No telling," the furrier replied. "Word is, the sentinels let a whole bunch of the moon-bloods slip off during Heartfire, and haven't been able to track them down. The garrison commander had all but given up the search."

Eris swallowed tightly and set the fox fur down, moving to another: a thick, gray pelt brindled with white, large enough for a cape. Her heart thudded and the urge to fly beat at her brain, but she forced herself to remain calm.

She risked a glance at Rilla. The other woman's mouth was pressed into a thin line. She caught Eris' eye and tilted her head toward the front of the stall, to the corridor between the rows of stalls. Time to leave, already? Eris frowned and gave a tiny shake of her head. This furrier was well-informed and prone to gossip. Why leave now?

But Rilla brushed past the furs, toward Eris. She said nothing, only gave Eris a determined look, and then kept going. Eris lingered, running her hands over the nearest stack of pelts, but the furrier had stopped talking. The hairs on the back of Eris' neck prickled, so she slipped off after Rilla. The two women wove through the other market-goers, pausing every so often at a stall to blend in with the other idle shoppers.

"We spent all morning here," Eris said as they went. "And we barely heard anything useful until just now. I could have learned much more if I'd infiltrated the city guard barracks."

"Aye, but you said you wanted to conserve your strength," Rilla countered as they reached a stall filled with crates of produce. "Or did I imagine that conversation you and Leal had before we set out?"

Frowning, Eris squeezed a few drupes, as if checking for ripeness. The small, purple fruits were hard as rocks, no doubt imported from Indigo-By-the-Sea. Rilla was right. By now, Eris had recovered from her Heartfire ordeal, but she was wary of spending her magical strength too much before she had a more solid plan in place. Getting into the city today to gather information was one of the few times in the past several days she had allowed herself to shift.

"Do you think that the furrier was telling the truth?" Eris asked as they moved past the produce stall.

Rilla skimmed her fingertips over a table stacked with wood carvings: toys, boxes of all sizes, and trillim game boards. "Could just be rumor, but..." She trailed off. "If the hemies did find mages with Sufani, it's Leal's family. I'll let you be the one to tell her."

"If it's true, it's going to make our task that much harder."

"We've come this far," Rilla replied, shrugging. "And I've faced worse odds. We'll manage." Despite her confident tone, something in her voice wavered.

Another shiver crept across Eris' skin, and she fought back a swell of despair. This entire plan, mission, task, *whatever*, was foolish. *Fly*, her good sense urged. *Get away from this wretched city. Keep your child safe. Survival is all that matters.*

But in her mind's eye, she could see the pain and terror in Kali's face, and the collar around her friend's neck. Clearly *something* had happened at Parsa that had changed Kali so radically – that or the sentinel had addled Kali's wits. In any case, Kali's judgment could not be trusted. And Drake... Was he still the hemies' prisoner? Was he even alive?

Eris squinted at the sky. The cloud cover was dense and pale, but she

240

estimated that it was about midday. "We should get to the fountain. Brice and Ben will be there soon."

Rilla nodded. She changed course, ducking through the stalls and around preoccupied shoppers, making a meandering line for the fountain of Llyr, the god of luck and commerce that rested in the center of the Eye. Eris, who had never been to the Whitewater City marketplace, struggled to keep up with Rilla through the bustling crowd. When they had first arrived, Eris had been overwhelmed at the number of people, but by now she felt nothing but contempt for all of them. A young man gave her a winning smile, but Eris ignored him. No doubt he wouldn't be so flirtatious if he knew the secret inked upon her wrist. No doubt all these dregs would be happy to see *this* moon-blood buried alive.

About a quarter of an hour later, Eris and Rilla reached the fountain, where their allies already waited. Ben sat upon the fountain's edge, rubbing his upper thigh, while Brice paced before him. When she spotted Rilla, a relieved smile came to her face and she bounded over to embrace her wife. "Thank the One! We were starting to think you got lost."

Rilla gave her a quick, fierce kiss, and laughed. "If anyone's going to get lost here, love, it's you."

"That was *one* time," Brice chided. She glanced over her shoulder at Ben, and then spoke so only Rilla and Eris could hear. "We've been waiting far longer than I reckoned, because *someone's* wound is still bothering him."

Indeed, the auburn-haired man wore a pained expression as he sat alone by the fountain.

"The wound he got during your most recent…adventure on the bridge?" Eris asked. "He said it wasn't that bad."

Brice rolled her eyes. "Ben says many things, but I know better. Ea's tits, I bandaged him myself."

"But the wound shouldn't still be hurting," Rilla said.

"Can you help him?" Brice asked Eris.

Eris looked at Ben again who frowned back, no doubt aware that he was the subject of their conversation. "He doesn't want my help," Eris said. "He made that clear when you all returned that evening."

Besides, her magic had only ever worked on herself. Eris winced internally; she had promised to *try* to help Leal, but she feared even "try" would turn out to be an empty promise.

"He's an idiot sometimes," Brice said, nodding. "But–"

"If he wants help from a filthy moon-blood," Eris interrupted. "He can sodding well ask. Otherwise, we have work to do." She turned from the two women and made her way back to Ben so the four of them could speak together. Ben straightened and gave a prim nod, although his gaze upon the other two women was softer.

"We weren't recognized," he said by way of greeting.

Brice slid beside him onto the fountain's smooth stone edge. "Aye, all anyone can talk about is whatever's going on at the bastion."

Eris and Rilla exchanged grim looks. "We heard," Eris replied. "But it doesn't change anything except the number of people we need to rescue. And…" Her mind raced as an idea sprang to life. "Ytel and the other Sufani are as fierce as Leal. They could aid us once we release them from the garrison."

"Fighting from the inside out," Rilla mused, nodding. "I like it."

"I do, too," Brice said. "But it's risky."

Ben cleared his throat. "Yes, and there's still the matter of how to get all of these people *out* of the city." He gestured in the direction of the gates. "We made it through without trouble, thank the One, but we can't possibly bring mages *and* Sufani out with us next time." He gave Eris a knowing look. "There's no festival any time soon. Unless the rest of your people have your particular *gifts*…"

She lifted her chin. "We'll find another way."

"There *is* no other way," Ben replied. "It's the gates or…" His gaze crept across the Eye, toward the White River. Despite the scramble of the marketplace, Eris could still hear the river's constant thrum.

A memory of bobbing boats came to mind and her breath caught. "The river," she whispered.

"What was that?" Rilla asked.

Eris swallowed her excitement and tried to look composed. "Forget the gates. We have the river."

"Can you change into a boat?" Ben asked.

Eris glared at him. "No, but I can steal one. Or help steal one," she amended. "I've never been on a ship, but I'm a fast learner."

Ben and Rilla scoffed; Brice toyed with her chin, her expression thoughtful. "It won't be easy to find a vessel large enough. How many people will need to use it?"

Eris did a quick mental calculation. "All four of us, Leal, Kali, Drake, Sirvat and the others, and anyone else we pick up..."

"And Leal's family," Rilla said. "Ea's tits. We're going to need a sodding barge."

"Which will be slow, and difficult to steer upriver," Brice added with a frown.

"What other options do we have?" Eris asked.

No one had an answer. At last, Ben took a deep breath and sat up, although he did not rise. "Brice and I learned something else from our contact. The sentinels have not yet received more hematite."

"Seems like the garrison's fallen on hard times," Brice added. "One of the sentinel officers was caught trying to escape with part of his squad...and a mage."

Dread settled over Eris, as if a flock of buzzards had landed on her shoulders. "Any names or descriptions?"

"None that we heard," Brice said. "Why? Think it's a friend of yours? Or is the whole place jumping ship?"

"It could be Kali. But I told her when I'd come back for her."

"She must've taken matters into her own hands," Rilla replied. "And convinced one of the hemies to join her."

I've failed her, too. Eris clenched her jaw against the sting in her eyes.

Ben's hand stole to his thigh again, rubbing while he considered. "In any case, if the hematite situation is true, we might not face much opposition in the garrison itself. But that doesn't solve the problem of getting out of the city."

"I like the boat idea," Rilla said. "Even if we have to steal a couple of 'em,

I think the plan could work in our favor, especially when some among us have," she eyed Eris, "*advantages.*"

Ben frowned, but Eris could not stop her smile. "Let's speak with Adrie and the others before we get too excited."

"Right." Brice rose from the fountain's edge and nodded to the market. "Rill and I still have to pick up some supplies. Will you two be able to wait here without killing each other?"

Her voice was honey-sweet, but there was genuine concern in her gaze. A flush of chagrin crept up Eris' neck as she and Ben exchanged glances; his face mirrored her feelings. "I'll be on my best behavior," Ben said to Brice. "You have my word."

Brice looked at Eris, who nodded. "Me too. Go on. We'll wait here."

"Unless something happens," Ben added. "In which case, we'll meet at our secondary location."

The couple slipped back into the crowd, instantly lost in the tumult of the Eye. Another wind whipped Eris' hood and cloak, and her skin tingled with the promise of flight. A deep inhale brought the clean scent of snow. It had snowed yesterday; no doubt it would again, and soon.

Ben cleared his throat. Eris tensed, expecting another quip at her expense, but the Assembly fellow only looked uncertain. "How well do you know Drake?"

Eris blinked at him, taken aback by the question. "Not very. He and Gideon were close before Gid came to the bastion, but I only spent a few hours in Drake's company."

Ben's gaze flickered toward the bastion. Even from here, Eris could make out the stone walls surrounding the wretched place. "He's stubborn and reckless, but has a good heart." His voice dropped to a whisper. "A kind heart."

"When we first met," Eris ventured, "what did Brice mean about no more regrets?"

Ben looked at his hands, twining in his lap. "Drake did not tell me of his plans to help free your friends. When I found out, I was," he winced, "less than kind."

"Because we didn't deserve his aid?"

"In part." Ben ignored Eris' glare and looked toward the bastion again. "But I regret my harsh words, and my anger. Drake was only trying to help his people, as I have tried to help mine. He kept his magic a secret from me, you see," he added with a glance back toward Eris. "Never breathed a word of it. So I was...shocked, to say the least. I reacted poorly." He sighed, his breath fogging the air. "I regret how I behaved."

Aye, now that his mage lover was chained and imprisoned, or worse. Bile rose in Eris' throat at the thought. "You only wish to free him so you can make amends."

"One reason of many."

"If it were me, I'd not feel charitable towards the one who abandoned me in my darkest hour."

"Drake isn't you," Ben said. "And I don't care if he forgives me." He exhaled again and rubbed his thigh. "Well, it doesn't matter. I simply want to see him free. Whatever happens after that is the One god's will."

The One god's will. Eris wrinkled her nose and readjusted her cloak, which the wind had pulled akimbo. "I should think Drake has a say in such a thing more than the One."

"Perhaps." Ben shot her a glance. "You do realize that Drake believes in the One god. Not all mages share your conviction – or lack thereof."

She hadn't realized that about Drake, but it wasn't a surprise. Ben was right; there were mages who believed in the gods. Just not that many. Eris shrugged. "Well, no one's perfect."

To her surprise, the Assembly man chuckled and ducked his head in acknowledgement, though he grimaced and his hand crept to his thigh again. Eris took pains to keep her voice neutral. "How has it healed?"

"I'm fit for this mission, if that's what you're asking."

She stood up from the fountain's edge and gestured to the hubbub around them. "Come on. We shouldn't linger in one place for too long."

Ben hesitated. "We're fine for now."

"You were worried we'd see wanted posters with our faces. We haven't, but that doesn't mean someone won't remember you from your," she smirked, "various *adventures.*"

"You mean foolhardy errands," he grumbled. "On *your* behalf, I might add."

"On Drake's as well."

Ben's shoulders sank. "Aye. Drake."

Neither spoke. Eris studied the slender, auburn-haired man seated before her. The wound pained him; she could see it in his eyes, in the way he held his body. Memories of Kali trickled back. Kali, too, hated to let others see how often her knee bothered her. Eris had long since grown used to Kali's preferences, but in her heart of hearts, she wished she could have helped her friend, even a little bit. She wished Kali could have come to Whitewater Bastion for *her* help, not Sadira's. The thought of Kali imprisoned made her throat tight and her hands shake with fury, so she forced the images away to regain control of herself. Nothing had changed. She was doing everything in her power to help her friend.

What would Kali do now? she wondered as she studied Ben.

The answer was simple, and Eris didn't like it.

She plunked back down beside him, closer this time. "All right. Let's see it."

Ben froze. "See what?"

"Your wound."

"I don't... You can't... Not here!"

Eris rolled her eyes. "It won't hurt. It probably won't even work, but I ought to try. Don't be a child. Let me see."

Ben's head whipped around as he searched the plaza. "I can't strip down right here. Besides, if anyone guesses what you're doing..."

"Under no circumstances are you to strip down." Eris shuddered at the thought. "Besides, my actions won't *look* odd to anyone else. If anything, others will think only that you and I are..." She grimaced. "Well, all it will look like is me putting my hand on your trousers."

"But I thought..." Ben scrubbed his beard. "Drake healed me once. My arm. He had to touch my skin. And I've heard that's how *it* works with... others."

Neither one spoke loudly, but both still talked around the word 'magic'. That was for the best, although the necessity grated Eris. She tried to keep her voice suitably conversational, so no passers-by would think anything was amiss. "Touching you would be easier," she admitted. "But I don't wish to. And besides, I'm not sure I can do anything for you at all. I simply want to find out."

"I thought you needed to conserve your strength."

"If you don't want me to bother with healing," Eris snapped. "I can certainly try my hand at changing you into a more agreeable form. Perhaps a mountain goat? It would suit your," she pulled air around her chin as if stroking a beard, "particular features."

She was not above satisfaction when Ben scowled at her. "That won't be necessary." He considered, and then leaned back and placed his palms around a spot on his upper thigh. "The arrow went in here. Brice treated it, but it still pains me."

"Obviously." Eris rested her right hand over the place his hands circled. Ben tensed, but seemed to be making an effort not to grimace, so Eris returned the favor as she concentrated on his particles.

First her attention dove down into the fabric of his trousers, where the sturdy cloth's particles clung together like a group of people standing with arms laced in preparation of a running assault. With more concentration, Eris delved deeper, until she found the particles of his skin, muscles, and bones. Ben's particles here shifted and shivered like a group of bees whose hive had been rocked by the wind. In her mind's eye, she saw them as bright crimson specks, writhing around each other in their injured state. Cool yellow particles made up the exterior of the wound—evidence of Brice's medicines and whatever healing Ben's body had done so far—but the center still pulsed red with agitation. Eris recalled the healing lessons she and Kali had undergone as girls. If Ben's particles remained untreated, infection would set in soon,.

"I don't feel anything," Ben whispered. "Is it working?"

Eris shushed him and returned her focus. An assessment like this took no skill and only the most rudimentary understanding of particles. Healing would be more difficult – if not impossible for her. But she should at least *try*. Kali would want her to. So would Drake, if only so he could kick this fellow's arse fairly.

Besides, this attempt would be a good benchmark of how she could help Leal – if indeed she could at all.

"Hold still," Eris murmured, and got to work.

For Eris, healing was difficult. Focus was not an issue—it had never been—but healing like this made her realize how *weak* she was, magically. Eris could see and sense Ben's particles and knew, logically, what needed to be done. But soothing the agitated particles was like smoothing out sand churned by the tide's relentless assault. Every time she focused on one area, another seemed to get worse. By comparison, turning herself into a bird and taking flight was child's play.

At last, *at last,* she managed to repair the worst of the damage, although she knew any other mage could have done leagues better in a fraction of the time. But as she sat back, wiping her damp forehead, an overwhelming sense of pride and wonder filled her, because she *had* done magic on another. True magic, not just an examination. Gideon would have been proud. Befuddled as well, because no doubt he'd have disliked Ben even more than she did, but proud of her, nonetheless. That alone made her smile.

"Eris?"

She looked up, blinking in the harsh white glare of the clouds. "How do you feel?"

Ben had been studying her, but now he glanced down at his leg, his brows knitting. "It's better. Less painful." He flexed his leg and looked at her again. "You–"

"It's not healed completely," she broke in, glancing around to be sure no one had noticed. "But the risk of infection is gone. You were foolish not to have one of us look at it sooner. Adrie and Mar are fine healers; one of them would have been glad to help you." Well, *glad* was probably an overstatement.

The Assembly man ducked his head. "Thank you."

248

She shrugged and looked around again, this time assessing her own strength. Despite the difficulty of healing, her magic remained strong. She could change shape and leave this city whenever she needed, but she ought not to attempt to heal anyone again for a while. Perhaps the two types of magic were different, or drew from different energies within her. Kali would probably know.

Brice and Rilla emerged from the crowd, several full packs in tow, and Eris nodded to them as she got to her feet. "Come on," she said to Ben. "It's time to leave."

Ben rose as well, his movements smoother than before. As they began to walk to meet Brice and Rilla, he shot a glance at Eris. "Drake *likes* the beard."

Eris rolled her eyes. "As I said: no one's perfect."

21

TWENTY-ONE

Drake leaned his head against the cell wall. He'd done this so often since his arrival to the garrison, he should have made a divot in the stonework by now. "I'm so sorry, Aderey."

The Sufani man's voice resonated throughout the detention area. "For all the good that does us."

The other Sufani now imprisoned here muttered in what Drake assumed was agreement. He only knew a few words of their language, but he understood anger in any tongue. His throat was dry, his head ached, and the hematite collar pressed tighter with each ragged breath.

"Did *any* of your people escape?" Drake managed.

Aderey was silent. Ytel, his wife, was not. "Only one of my children walks free, and I don't know how much longer that will be, given that she's in the company of your–"

"Ytel." Aderey's voice was sharp. He added a few words in Sufa that Drake did not catch. His wife responded with equal bitterness.

"Stop it, both of you," a new voice said. A young girl – Drake vaguely remembered Leal talking about a younger sister.

"Hush, Dianthe," Ytel scolded.

But the girl was not cowed. "You could have turned the mages away, but you didn't. You made the right choice."

Aderey and Ytel both shushed their daughter, and this time, she fell silent.

Indeed, all the Sufani were silent. Near the back of the detention area, a baby began to cry. Drake winced at the piercing wail that echoed off the stone walls, but no one complained. A woman began to hum to the babe, and it quieted within a few moments.

"I'm sorry," the woman whispered.

Ytel sighed. "You cannot help when the One sends you into labor, Sirvat."

Drake scrubbed a hand through his matted hair. What a sodding mess he'd made of things. And it was only going to get worse. If he'd understood his sentinel guards' chatter, these people were all going to be sent to Lasath, to stand trial for harboring illegal mages and Assembly dissidents. He didn't want to think what would happen to the mages who'd been recaptured.

Creaking wood and iron made him look toward the detention area's entrance, where the heavy door was opening. Two sentinels stepped inside, ushering a third figure: a petite woman with dark, tangled hair, and a collar around her neck. Another mage?

The sentinels stood at the threshold and peered down the row of cells.

"Where are we supposed to put her, Haste?" asked the first, a young woman. "The cells are all full."

The second, a man, glanced at Drake's cell. "That one's alone."

While the female sentinel held the mage, Haste went to Drake's door. His chest puffed out and his voice was carefully schooled to sound threatening. A burnie, if ever there was one. "No tricks now, Mage."

Drake spread his hands so that the chain between his cuffs rattled. "None left."

Haste shot Drake a skeptical look from beneath his helmet, but motioned to his partner. "Bring her in, Stout."

The female sentinel shoved the mage forward, sending the collared woman stumbling into the cell. She glanced off the wall and collapsed onto the stone floor, whimpering and clutching her left knee with bound wrists. Stout ignored her and studied Drake, eyes narrowing. "Are there no other wall mounts for her chains?"

"I don't think the crippled moon-blood is going anywhere," Haste replied with a laugh.

251

Stout regarded the woman at her feet, her mouth twisted with disgust. "No, I guess not. But she's still dangerous. Word is she's a thrall, and she killed those guards while we were out with the captain."

"We should get going. The commander told us to be quick."

"The commander *also* told us to secure the mage," Stout shot back. Her voice was high-pitched and young; was she a burnie, too?

Both sentinels glared at each other before Haste drew himself up. He was taller and broader than Stout, who had to look up to meet his gaze. "The mage is collared, cuffed, and locked in a cell. That's about as secure as we can get her without freeing *that*," he jabbed a thumb at Drake, "and risking his escape, too. No point in unchaining him just to tie up the crippled one. Come on. Let's get back." His teeth flashed white as he grinned. "I don't want to miss the fun."

Stout's hands balled into fists. "You think any of this is *fun*? Those guards are *dead*, our brothers and sisters aren't far behind, and traitors spring up from our midst with each moment."

Haste blew out an impatient breath. "Ea's balls, it was a figure of speech. Come on, let's get moving. The commander wants our help with a few more things before we bring these dregs back out."

Back out where? Drake thought, alarm pulsing through each vein.

Stout glared at her brother-in-service. "Don't you understand the sodding shitstorm we're in right now?"

Haste crossed his arms before his chest. "If you want to argue, maybe I can fetch the captain. I'm sure he can clear up any orders you find confusing."

"You're such an ass," Stout replied, but she stepped over the mage, back to the cell door, closing it with a *clang* that reverberated through the entire area. The burnies slipped out, still bickering as they passed through the outer door and locked it behind them.

Only when Drake was certain they were gone did he scramble forward, trying to get close to the newcomer. Thank Tor, they had not dropped her out of his limited reach. "Ser?" he whispered as he knelt beside her. "Are you all right? What's your name?"

He had to tug his chains to reach her side, but even then, he barely got close enough to touch her. She was a young woman, probably quite lovely when she was clean and healthy, but she looked like she'd not slept nor bathed in weeks. Her breathing was harsh and uneven, and her pulse beat too quickly.

"Can you hear me?" Drake asked. "Open your eyes if you can hear me."

"What's going on?" Aderey asked from his cell. "Who is she?"

"That's what I'm trying to find out." Gently, Drake tried to pull the young mage closer to him so he could reposition her, as the sentinel had tossed her to the ground with no regard for her comfort. But when Drake touched her, dark eyes flew open and she gasped, making his heart leap for his ribs.

"Seren's light," he said as she sat up. "I nearly soiled myself. Nearly," he added a little louder. "Though I doubt I'd smell much different at this point." When she did not reply, he pressed a cuffed hand to his chest. "I'm Drake. Who are you?"

Something in her eyes was...off. Distant, unfocused, like she was not entirely in this place and time. Her voice was hoarse. "Bahar?"

Drake's jaw fell open. "How did you...?" Ah, Stonewall's mage-girl. What had Elan called her? Drake struggled to dredge up the memory. Name recollection had never been his strength. "Callie?"

"Kali," Aderey said, his voice faint. The Sufani man stretched out the "a" sound in her name, and the mage looked around wildly.

"Aderey?" she whispered.

He gave a weary chuckle that echoed off the stones. "I had a feeling we'd meet again, Kali. I rather wish I'd been wrong."

"Small world," Drake managed. "Kali, then. You know me too, I take it?"

Dark eyes met his. In the flickering torchlight of the corridor, tears gleamed on her cheeks. "I know of you."

"Well, only the good bits are true," he replied grimly.

To his surprise, she gave a sharp bark of a laugh, but then began to weep again. "I'm so stupid. I thought..." She trailed off, too overcome to speak further. Until, "He's going to die, Bahar."

Drake's stomach plummeted to his knees as she recounted her and Stonewall's escape attempt. When she'd finished, he couldn't find the right words, so he only jerked the chains that bound him to the sodding cell. Helpless. The Sufani and other mages began to murmur among themselves, but Drake didn't pay attention to their chatter, nor to Kali's weeping, nor to the stink of blood, waste, and iron. All he knew was the feel of his heart breaking deep within his chest.

Then the outer door opened again and four sentinels stepped inside.

* * *

Stonewall awoke to burning pain in his side. Candlelight danced at the edges of his vision, although it was dark in front of him. Even so, he could still see Kali's eyes blazing like stars. His throat went dry. "Kali?"

"Be still." It was Beacon, kneeling beside him, one cool hand on his forehead. "She's not here, though you'd be dead without her magic. Roll over so I can get a look at you."

Stonewall obliged, though the renewed flare of pain made him grimace. Beacon lifted his tunic away—where was his gear?—and Stonewall shivered at the sudden brush of chilled air.

As Beacon began to prod at him, Stonewall blinked into the flickering shadows, his brain slowly making sense of his surroundings. He was on his sleeping pallet in his own quarters, back in the sentinel garrison. If he extended his legs, his toes brushed the wooden chest that held his spare clothes. About an arm's length away, the river stone that Kali had given him rested on the floor beside his pallet.

"Why am I here?" he asked.

"You mean, why are you *not* in a cell?" Beacon's voice was wry. "Because Talon, in all her wisdom, has ordered that you stand trial for your crimes before you're brought to the Pillars for their final judgment. It's protocol, after all." He sighed and sat back, rubbing his forehead. "Thankfully, she conceded to allow me to patch you up first."

Stonewall turned back to his mender. Beacon was fully armored, but his weapons were gone and his face was haggard in the light of the single lamp he'd brought. Stonewall swallowed hard. "Trial?"

"Aye. Turn back over." Beacon reached for his mender's kit.

Stonewall did as instructed, but his heart was racing. "When?"

"As soon as I'm done." Rustling sounds came from Beacon's direction, and then the mender exhaled. "I'm afraid this is going to hurt. Be thankful you were already unconscious when I pulled out the bolt."

"Just get on with it," Stonewall said, gritting his teeth. The astringent poultice stung, but that was only the beginning. To distract himself, he tried to get Beacon to speak more. "Why aren't you behind bars? And Rook? Is she–" A needle-sharp pain dug into his side and he sucked in a breath.

"She's...alive and free," Beacon said quietly. "Since we're both able-bodied, Talon has granted us mercy – for now. The burnie twins are better than all of us. It seems Talon mistook their late arrival at the bridge for loyalty – to her. Kalinda is fine," he said before Stonewall could ask. "She's in a cell with the renegade mage. Your brother, right?"

More pain, strong enough to make Stonewall dizzy and his vision blur. Gods above, he needed hematite now, more than ever. "Right," he managed to choke out. "Drake." Thank Tor. If Kali was with Drake, then she might be safe, at least for a little while. But the news brought no real relief. "What does Talon have planned for her?"

"I'm not sure. Probably not a tea party. Hold still. I'm not done. This wound is deep."

"I *am* holding still."

Beacon exhaled again. "You're bleeding a lot. You need hematite."

"Think Talon will spare some once she gets more?" Stonewall tried to keep his voice light, but the words came out as a croak.

The mender chuckled. "Certainly. Just flash her that pretty smile."

More pain. Stonewall hissed through clenched teeth and burning eyes. His jaw was starting to ache and shadows kept trying to creep into his vision. "You... You're..." He sucked in a breath, forcing his voice to work. "You're all right?"

"With all due respect, *ser*," Beacon said. "Shut. Up. You can debrief me when I'm done – if there's time. But now I must concentrate."

Stonewall managed a nod and looked back at the river stone, calculating. If he moved slowly, carefully, he might be able to...

"Sodding hold still, I swear to Mara..."

"Sorry, Beak." But Stonewall's fingers closed around the stone and he pulled it close, savoring the small weight and cool, smooth surface.

Beacon was quiet as he worked, leaving Stonewall to his thoughts, which was rarely a good thing. Kali's glittering eyes... He would remember that sight for as long as he lived, which wouldn't be much longer, if his current state was any indication. She'd seemed so certain she could handle the Fata possession, and he'd believed her – like a fool. Now she'd be lucky to outlive him by days rather than years. He clutched the stone she'd given him as a peace-offering and stared into the shadows of his room, the weight on his chest crushing out all breath, all hope. They'd gambled and lost. But what else had he expected? That they could have ridden off into the wild, to live happily ever after, like in all the stories?

Another lance of pain made his breath catch. "Sorry," Beacon muttered. "I'm trying to hurry. She told me I only had a few minutes before she sent Cobalt in after me."

"Has the captain returned?"

"Aye, about an hour ago."

Stonewall frowned. "How long have I been here?"

"Most of the day. It's evening now. Be ready, this will be unpleasant." Another sharp pain, made worse by the already-tender skin of Stonewall's side. Beacon cleared his throat. "Their mission was a rousing success. A bunch of Sufani are now guests in our detention cells. Poor bastards. But among them were *three* of our missing mages. I hope Talon's happy."

"I thought they'd have all fled south by now."

"One of them had just given birth. I think the only pregnant mage here was Sirvat Amaris?" Beacon sighed. "Anyway, they're all in our cells. Including the babe. Talon even ordered a collar on the little thing. Can you imagine?"

The disgust in Beacon's voice was plain, and Stonewall found he shared the sentiment. "Talon's a coward."

"No argument here."

Stonewall's memories of their escape attempt were clear, although he wished he could forget. "What happened to the city guards?" he asked. "The two that Kali..."

He couldn't finish the thought.

Beacon sighed and sat back, the sound of cloth against his hands grating in the small room. "Dead."

Stonewall closed his eyes, letting the pain wash over him. Pain was the body's way of telling him something was wrong, that the balance was off. *Message received,* he thought. "You and Rook... What will Talon do to you?"

Something cold and wet pressed against Stonewall's side, and the familiar, sweet scent of thalo gel cut through the stink of sweat and blood. The worst of the burning began to fade to a dull throb, and he sighed in relief.

"Apparently Rook and I will be spared from your fate if we 'renounce' you, and pledge our loyalty to our dear commander," Beacon said as he smoothed the healing gel over Stonewall's wound.

Carefully, Stonewall twisted around to see the mender. "Will you?"

Beacon frowned at him. "What do you think?"

"I think you should do whatever it takes to avoid my fate."

A faint smile tugged the corner of Beacon's mouth as he set the jar of thalo away, wiped off his hands again, and reached for a bandage. "Ah, so falling in love with a mage is off the table."

"If you're wise." Stonewall shifted to let Beacon wrap the clean linen around his torso. "But some things can't be helped."

"I suppose not."

"And even if I could," Stonewall added, rubbing the stone with his thumb. "I wouldn't change anything."

Now Beacon went still, his gaze resting on his open satchel. "Nothing?"

"Well...I'd not get caught."

Beacon chuckled again and began to pack his bag. "Smart man."

"If I was, I wouldn't be here." Moving still hurt, but not as much, thanks to the thalo, as Stonewall twisted around to face Beacon properly. "I'm serious, though, Beak. You and Rook...do whatever you must to survive.

257

Mi and Flint, as well. Will you tell them for me?"

Beacon toyed with the bandage roll before stuffing it in the bag with the other supplies. "I will. But…" He sighed and looked at Stonewall again. "Rook's in a bad way. She's tougher than all of us, but I think she's been hiding how sick she really is. I should have noticed," he muttered, scraping a hand through his mussed, coppery hair. "But I was distracted."

"And sick, yourself," Stonewall added. Now that the worst of the pain had subsided, he felt the gnawing desire for *more* hematite along with an unrelenting chill. No doubt it would only grow worse as time passed, until his body couldn't handle the *want* any longer. Despite the sweat that coated his skin and dampened his tunic, he shivered.

"Aye." Beacon stared at his trembling hands and Stonewall winced, thinking of the needle those hands had wielded only minutes ago. No wonder the stitching had hurt.

When Beacon looked at him again, his eyes were hard. "What's the point of all this? Innocent people are suffering *needlessly*. Why aren't the thralls everyone's priority? Why won't the Pillars let us work *with* the mages, rather than against them?"

Stonewall opened his mouth, but he had no answer. He shook his head.

Beacon gathered the lantern and his mender's satchel, and began to rise. He had to brace himself against the wall for support. "Well, perhaps now that the Pillars have their Sufani, they'll send more hematite."

Stonewall's heart sank. "Milo and Flint couldn't get any?"

"Hard to say. I haven't spoken to either one. Talon's got them either running errands or stuck to her side like shingles on tar. It's the same with Hornfel and the other burnies." Beacon set his bag over his shoulder and looked down at Stonewall. "The Circle's pulled out the garrison staff, as well."

"What for?"

Beacon grimaced. "After that incident with Slate, the Circle fears for their safety. A few of the most loyal folks have remained, but the rest are gone; reassigned or who knows what." He sighed. "We could use their help, now more than ever."

Worse and worse. Stonewall made to ask another question, but a quick knock came from the door's other side. "Beacon? Have you finished?"

"Nearly, Captain," Beacon called.

"Everyone's assembled. Commander Talon wants to get started right away."

"I'm sure she does," Beacon muttered.

"What was that?"

"One moment, ser." Beacon rolled his eyes, then looked at Stonewall and mouthed, *I'm sorry.*

Stonewall held out his hand. When Beacon reached down, Stonewall grabbed the mender's forearm and whispered, "Thank you, brother-in-service."

"Well, ser, you're about as patched up as I can manage," Beacon said, much louder than before. He rose shakily and nodded to Stonewall before going for the door. "I'm coming out, Captain."

With that, he stepped out. Stonewall caught a glimpse of candlelight flickering in the corridor before the door closed and his world went dark.

22

TWENTY-TWO

Milo trailed after Commander Talon out of the garrison and
into the courtyard, Flint at his side. Torches snapped in the
chilling wind, their lights too weak to do more than press
against the encroaching darkness. His scabbard slapped against his leg as he
walked, creating a jarring jangle in the freezing air. The commander's brisk
strides carried her toward the center, where the other sentinels and the
remaining handful of garrison staff had already gathered. Where Stonewall
waited too, kneeling upon the flagstones between Captain Cobalt and Vigil.

The moment Milo caught sight of his sergeant's—*former* sergeant's—bare
head and hands bound behind his back, his stomach churned and his body
went cold. A group of mages huddled behind the bastion gates, watching
the sentinels through the iron and hematite bars. Beacon and Rook were
nowhere to be seen. Beacon's hushed words, spoken in haste, rang through
Milo's mind: *Do what you must to survive.*

Talon's long strides soon brought them to the others. Milo's heart sank at
the dismal number of waiting sentinels: the infirmary was full to bursting
with sick or worse, and the common room was not much better. Eighty-
odd sentinels normally called the Whitewater garrison home. By Milo's
reckoning, only a few dozen had assembled on this cold nightfall.

He couldn't decide if fewer sentinels around was a good thing or not.
These were men and women Stonewall had fought besides, bled for, shared

ale and laughter and stories with. But these were the same sentinels who shot looks of disgust at Stonewall, who only stared at the garrison wall before him. Even some of the kitchen staff who had come out glared at the former sergeant.

Commander Talon swept past the neat rows of sentinels and went to stand about ten paces in front of Stonewall, the garrison wall at her back. She made a subtle gesture, and Milo and Flint flanked her. Milo could feel Flint's impatience radiating off her like heat from a fire. He shared the sentiment, but was too nervous to look anywhere but straight ahead, toward the garrison's main entrance.

At last, Talon lifted her voice. "Bring him to me."

Cobalt and Vigil hauled their prisoner to his feet. They brought him forward and shoved him back to his knees, barely a sword's length from Talon. Stonewall wore his off-duty soft clothes: a plain wool tunic, breeches, and his boots. A fringe of stubble covered his jaw, and his face contorted with pain at each step.

"We all live in the shadow of magic," Talon began. "Such that it is easy to forget how dangerous those who wield it truly are. Recent events have confirmed what the Circle has always taught us: that mages cannot be trusted to act in the best interest of others. It is," she hesitated, "an unfortunate truth, but an inescapable one. At the end of all things, our duty is our oath: honor, service, sacrifice. We uphold the tenets of the One; we serve the good people of Aredia. Often, we do these things at the cost of our personal happiness, because such sacrifice is necessary to protect innocents from those who would do them harm."

She pointed to Stonewall. "One of our own has broken his oath and shattered the bonds of trust that bind us all."

An uneasy murmur rippled through the audience. Stonewall stiffened at the commander's words but did not look surprised. And why would he be? He must have known this was coming.

"Stonewall," Talon said. "You are accused of unethical fraternization with mages: both the renegade and one of our own bastion mages. Do you deny this?"

261

"In part, ser."

The other sentinels shifted in confusion and Talon frowned. "In part?"

Stonewall met Talon's gaze. "Love can be inconvenient, but it's not wrong."

Flint exhaled through her nose, a sound Milo recognized as his sister's approval – and amusement. Commander Talon, however, did not share the sentiment, for her mouth pressed into a thin line. "Then you are a bigger fool than I realized. But," she added, her words ringing off the walls, "you have performed great services for the people of Aredia. Your prowess in battle is proven and you are a godly man. Therefore, I shall give you a chance to redeem yourself and reaffirm your oath – as much as you can."

Startled mutters swept over the assembled group. Milo could not help but glance at Flint in shock, and found his twin frowning deeper than ever. His heart hammered beneath his cuirass and he started at the sound of boot steps. Everyone looked over at the garrison, but Milo saw only shadows. Then, like some specter from a nightmare, four sentinels came into view: Hornfel, Stout, Haste, and Shard. All but Shard were burnies, although Shard was not long past her burnie days. Hornfel and Haste were burly fellows, but the man they led outmatched them in size and muscle.

Drake's skin was darker than Stonewall's, but the planes of his face echoed his brother's. A hematite collar rested around his neck and hematite cuffs clinked at his wrists. But even bound and weakened from his time in the garrison's cell, he moved with the confidence of a warrior. As Drake drew closer, his gaze flickered across the sentinels, Talon, the gates, everything, assessing the situation as best he could. When his eyes fell upon Stonewall, they widened. Drake halted, only to have Haste prod him forward.

Stonewall's features remained impassive, but when he spotted the next mage prisoner, he tried to jerk upright, only to have Cobalt shove him back into place as Stout and Shard brought Mage Halcyon out. Both women were strong in their own right—Shard had bested Milo many times in sparring sessions—but neither one seemed to want to touch the mage more than necessary. Halcyon, like Drake, was cuffed and collared, which seemed like overkill as she limped along. Her gaze was on the sky, where no stars nor moon shone through the thick cloud cover.

Milo searched for signs of possession, but the mage's dark eyes looked normal. Even so, Milo shuddered at the memory of the bridge—was it only this morning?—and the eerie light he'd seen flash in Mage Halcyon's eyes. Was she a thrall? Was that the illness Stonewall had tried to warn them about?

Milo risked another glance at Flint. Her expression remained hard and cold as a blade. He gathered his own resolve, schooled his features to match Flint's, and readied himself for whatever was about to pass.

The other burnies brought the mages before Stonewall, whose gaze darted between the magic-users before he glared at Talon. "What would you have me do to *redeem* myself?"

Drake shot Talon an incredulous look. Mage Halcyon, however, held still, not even seeming to breathe.

There was a smile in Talon's voice. "Surely you can guess." When Stonewall did not reply, she gave a deep, long-suffering sigh. "Very well. I shall spell it out for you." She placed one hand on Drake's shoulder, making him tense. "This man stands accused of theft of our hematite, aiding bastion mages in an escape, and felonious uses of magic. He has confessed to his crimes; the Pillars plan to judge him accordingly."

Talon then gestured to Mage Halcyon, but did not touch the dark-haired woman. "By now, all of you have heard of how this mage murdered two city guards in cold blood. In fact, she–"

"Kali acted in self-defense," Stonewall broke in.

"That may be so," Talon agreed, to Milo's shock. Judging by the astonished glances that passed between some of the others, he was not alone in the feeling. Talon, however, remained cool as ever. "But her behavior on the bridge proves her to be a thrall."

Silence swept over the group as if propelled by the same winds that tugged at hair and nipped at every piece of exposed flesh. Silence, save Stonewall's protests. "Nothing is certain, Commander. And if indeed Kali is…ill, she believes that magic can cure–"

"Mage Halcyon is a thrall," Talon broke in, somehow calmer than before.

"But you are right, Stonewall." Again, the audience shifted with uncertainty. Flint even shot Milo a wide-eyed *what in Ea's balls is going on* look.

Talon turned to glance at Halcyon, and Milo caught the tiniest half-smile on the commander's lips as she spoke again. "Nothing is certain. And it may be that Mage Halcyon has a role to play in the One's world. It's not for me to decide." She withdrew her sword and offered it to Stonewall, hilt-first. "So I shall let you."

She nodded to Cobalt, who, after a brief pause, released the former sergeant's wrists, swaying a bit as he did. Stonewall accepted the sword and leaned on it to stand. His voice was quiet. "What game are you playing, Talon?"

The commander stepped out of sword's reach and spread her gloved hands to indicate the two mages. "Pick one. The two of you will immediately be released from my custody; no questions asked, no one following. You have my word on that, Stonewall."

He watched her, his light-brown eyes cast in shadows. "What of the other?"

Talon nodded to the sword. "You will send the other to their next life."

None of the sentinels moved, but the mages muttered in alarm and confused murmurs rippled through the remaining garrison staff. This was...unorthodox, to say the very least, but cruel as well. Maybe Talon hoped to later claim she gave the former sergeant a chance to repent. It didn't really matter right now. Milo was afraid to move, afraid to breathe too loud, lest Talon realize the true allegiance within his and his sister's hearts. Despite how he could see his breath, sweat pricked beneath his gloves and trickled down the small of his back.

Stonewall clutched Talon's sword as he stared her down. Flint shifted, no doubt thinking he should stab the commander and be done with the whole mess, but Milo knew their former sergeant too well. Stonewall was a warrior but he was not made of his namesake. He was no stone-hearted killer. Besides, even if he knew that Milo and Flint would not raise arms against him—and he would be right—Cobalt, Vigil, and the rest of their squad remained within sword's reach, along with Hornfel and the other burnies.

No, Stonewall was not a murderer. And even if he was, he was not a suicidal one. Probably.

But would he really kill one of these mages? Milo's heart stuck in his throat as he watched the former sergeant glance between his lover and his brother. Kalinda's head drooped, her hair falling into her face like a dark curtain, but Drake remained unbent.

"Of all the shit I've encountered here," the renegade mage said. "This stinks the worst. Elan. Don't be stupid." He jerked his chin to Kalinda. "Take your girl and leave this sodding place. We both know I'm not worth the trouble."

Stonewall studied him briefly, and then nodded, straightening. He hefted Talon's sword in his bare hand. Milo's blood went cold as if all the hematite in his body had burned out at once. Torchlight gleamed upon the sword hilt; a few stray snowflakes dusted the blade. Stonewall took a deep breath, raised the sword, and flung the weapon at Talon's boots, where it clattered upon the flagstones.

"I swore an oath to the gods," Stonewall said. "Not to the Pillars. Not to the Circle. Not to you." He lifted his chin, his eyes blazing with defiance. "And we both know your word is worthless."

No one breathed. Milo didn't even blink when something icy touched his nose: more scattered snowflakes had begun to fall.

Talon stared at the former sergeant, but there was no surprise in her voice. There was nothing at all. "Then you are Forsworn." She nodded to Cobalt, who grabbed Stonewall once again. "You will be sent to Lasath to face the Pillars and their judgment. In the meantime, you'll be locked back in your quarters."

Cobalt and Vigil began to drag Stonewall away, but he dug his heels in and twisted to look back at Mage Halcyon – and Drake. The renegade mage took a single, tiny step toward his brother. Stonewall looked at Milo and Flint, then, his desperation plain. *Help her, if you can.* Milo nodded; briefly, and hopefully unnoticed. The former sergeant's shoulders slumped and he allowed himself to be led back into the garrison.

Talon did not watch him go, only turned to the burnies again. "Lock the mages back up," she said briskly. "Take every precaution. Milo, Flint." She began to walk toward the garrison as well. "You're with me."

Milo shot his twin an incredulous look, but Flint only shook her head once, her expression clear. *Play along, for now.* She stepped after the commander without hesitation. After a moment, Milo followed.

* * *

The moment Eris returned to her human shape, a swell of nausea overtook her, strong enough to bring her to her knees in the forest clearing where she'd landed. She retched in the dirt and dried leaves, her eyes pricking with tears as convulsions racked her body. Only when nothing was left in her stomach did she realize she was not alone. She looked up in alarm, but it was only Leal, watching her calmly through the twilight.

Heat crept to Eris' cheeks but she bit back her embarrassment and began to get to her feet. But she was exhausted and lightheaded, more so than she had ever been after changing. A byproduct of her pregnancy, or was something wrong? Leal came forward to offer a hand, but Eris shook the Sufani away. Once Eris was upright, she swiped at her mouth and eyes, sniffing.

"Morning sickness?" Leal asked. Despite being on more friendly terms with the mages than before, she still wore her indigo hood and veil, which left only her eyes visible.

"If so, it's poorly named, seeing as it's dusk. Strange; I felt nothing as a crow."

"Perhaps birds don't suffer as humans do when they bear young." Leal shuddered. "My mother was ill the entire time she carried Dia. It was dreadful."

"I feel better now," Eris replied, glancing around the clearing. No sign of anyone else. "Did you come alone?"

Leal nodded. "We weren't sure when you would return from the city. Your mage friends have been productive while you lot were gone. Did you learn anything useful in the marketplace? Where are the others?"

"Not far behind. I wanted to return quickly, because…" Eris trailed off and ran a hand through her hair. When her fingers hit empty air so quickly, she couldn't help a flare of surprise.

She forced herself to meet Leal's confused green eyes. "I hoped to find you alone," Eris began. When Leal's brows knitted, Eris took a deep breath. "The sentinels have taken a group of Sufani nomads prisoner. There were mages among them."

Leal sagged her weight against her spear.

"But this changes nothing for us," Eris went on. "We'll still storm the bastion, only now we have a few more to rescue from the clutches of those metal-licking fools."

Pale-green eyes met Eris' until Leal straightened. "Your new allies are coming."

Sure enough, Brice, Rilla, and Ben stepped into the clearing, glancing around. Brice had her bow and arrow ready, but when she spotted Eris, she tucked the weapons away. "Thank the One," she said as they came forward. "I always worry you won't be able to change back."

Eris gave the blond woman a thin smile. "Let's go. We have much to discuss with the others."

The three Assembly folk exchanged nervous glances before Rilla said, "Did you tell Leal about…?"

"Aye," Leal snapped. "But it changes nothing."

With that, she stalked down the game trail that led to their camp. Eris watched her go before nodding to the others. They followed Leal, whose steps were silent; not even a leaf trembled after the Sufani's progress. Brice was nearly as adept, while Rilla, Ben, and Eris could not conceal the traces of their passage. At least Ben wasn't limping any longer, which Eris noted with smug satisfaction. He did not look at her, nor at anyone else, only kept his gaze on the trail ahead.

Night had nearly fallen by the time they reached the camp. The Sufani wagon sat dark and silent beneath a spreading oak tree. The other mages were already standing around what must have been a roaring fire at one time; now the embers glowed bright orange, with no smoke, and a pot of stew cooking above. Adrie and Cai met Eris first, both grinning broadly.

"Look what I did," Cai exclaimed, shoving his bare forearm under Eris' nose.

She pulled back, frowning at him. "Seren's light, Cai, what's gotten into–"

"*Look*," Adrie interrupted.

Even in the dim light of the embers, Eris could see the fourth tier mark upon Cai's wrist. A tier mark – and nothing else. No twin crescent moons marred his skin. Eris gaped. "How...?"

He waggled his brows. "How do you think?"

"Magic?"

"How else? I was thinking, how could we all get into the sodding city if we're marked as mages? Then I got this crazy notion..." His smile faded and his hands dropped to his sides. "It was the sort of thing Gid would have come up with."

It was, and the realization made her grief swell all over again. "Aye," she whispered, blinking back tears.

Cai turned away, swiping at his eyes, and then nodded to Adrie and Marcen. "Not only me. All of us. We *all* were able to get rid of our mage marks."

"Though those of us who had tier marks, kept them," Adrie said. She had knelt by the stew, ladle and bowl in hand. She handed the full bowl to Marcen, who brought it, and a piece of hard bread, to Eris.

But the moment Eris caught the scent of broth, onions, and mushrooms, her stomach flipped. "I'm not hungry," she said, passing the bowl and bread to Ben, who accepted warily.

Adrie frowned at her, but Eris ignored the other woman and took a seat by the glowing embers, which cast little light but created enough heat to chase away the wintery chill. The others gathered their supper and settled around her. Except Leal, who hovered on the outskirts of the fire's warmth, sharpening one of her blades. After Eris related what they had learned in the city, no one spoke for a few seconds, but all eyes turned to Leal. The Sufani did not look at anyone, only skimmed her whetstone over one of

268

her daggers, sending sparks into the darkness.

"After this news, we'll need a bigger boat," Cai said, gaze distant. "Or several. And strong arms to paddle upriver."

"Unless you can magic the waterfall," Brice said hopefully. "Then we could just float with the current all the way to Indigo-By-the-Sea."

Eris laughed. "No mage in the world is strong enough to control a waterfall."

"Upriver is our only real option," Adrie said. "But even if the hemies have less hematite now, I'm sure they could rally enough strength to pursue."

"Aye," Eris agreed. "We'd have to abandon the boats not long after stealing them. Probably take to the opposite shore in the loneliest spot we can find, and then backtrack south."

Rilla blew out a breath. "Talk about going through your ass to get to your ear."

"If you have a better idea," Eris said. "I'd love to hear it."

Rilla shrugged. By now, the other mages were stirring, speaking in hushed, excited tones. Eris caught their excitement and for the first time in far too long, felt the first stirrings of true, real *hope.* Perhaps this plan wasn't doomed to failure.

Eris pulled down her sleeve and studied her right wrist. The intricate, eight-pointed star that marked her as a second tier had faded with time. She couldn't remember getting the mark; she had only been a babe. But her mage-mark—twin crescent moons, back to back, resting about a palm's length down from her wrist—*that* pain she remembered all too well. The sting of the needle; the bite of ink into soft skin. She'd been all knees and elbows at eleven summers, but even so, it had taken three sentinels to hold her still so the Cipher could mark her. Only then, as Eris had screamed and struggled in the hemies' grips, did she understand that her family had cast her aside.

Eris glanced at Cai, who sat beside her. "How did you do it?"

He'd been staring at the fire, allowing the others to plan, but at her words, he turned her way. "It wasn't easy," he said slowly. "Not at first. But once I really concentrated, it got easier. We couldn't figure out how or why, until

Mar pointed out that there's no hematite anywhere nearby."

"I didn't think the presence of it in the bastion walls had any real effect on us," Eris said. "I thought it was just a show of power. The collars and cuffs were always the true danger."

Cai shrugged. "I thought that too, but maybe we were just accustomed to being," he waved a hand, "*less* than we ought to be."

Perhaps it was true. Eris watched Ben, whose limp had left him after their healing session earlier that day. Now he spoke as eagerly with the mages around him as he did with his Assembly allies. Leal was gone, no doubt patrolling the area. Eris flushed; why hadn't she thought of setting someone on patrol?

Because she was still new to this life, this *freedom.*

"In all the planning Gid and I did to get here," she murmured. "I never really understood what would happen once we did."

Cai nodded. "Because you never truly believed we would."

Eris looked at her mage-mark again, and concentrated. She had done this before, many times, but had only ever been able to sense the particles of ink that clung to her skin like grease to the bottom of a pan.

"How?" she whispered to Cai.

He blew out a soft breath; an echo of the wind that rustled the sheltering trees. "Scatter them. Make them disappear."

Eris closed her eyes, and concentrated. The ink's particles appeared in her mind's eye as tiny black specks, stiff and resolute amid vibrant skin and muscle. Eris focused on the particles of ink. She imagined them scattering into her blood, like the grain she'd once tossed to her hens, to be purified by her body's natural processes. *Go away.*

Before Eris could open her eyes, Cai gave a low whistle. "Nice work."

When Eris looked at her wrist again, only her tier-mark remained. The crescent moons were gone. She stared at the unblemished skin. She'd have to check again in the sunlight to ensure no trace remained, but she was finally free of the bastion.

Just in time to return. But even that thought was fleeting and distant; smoke swept away by an eager wind.

"Gid would be proud," Cai said.

Eris managed a faint smile at her friend. "Aye. He would."

23

TWENTY-THREE

Stonewall placed a trembling hand against the door to his quarters. Per Talon's orders, it was barred and locked from the outside, but the wood was smooth with age, and comforting in its own way. More comforting, at least, than the cold, unyielding stone walls that surrounded him. He allowed himself a grim smile at the irony.

The expression fled with a renewed flare of pain from his side and an accompanying wave of nausea. He'd been standing too long. But instead of lying down, he ducked his head and pressed both palms against the door, bracing for the onslaught, counting the seconds until the nausea passed. It didn't. He gave up and retched, his injured side screaming, but nothing came up. There was nothing left, but he heaved anyway, as he had for the last two...or was it three days, now? His thoughts were sand churned by pounding waves.

The time immediately after his "trial" was a blur. His clearest memory was...strange. Fear, but not just his own, although he had enough. Fear: his own and Kali's. He knew it was hers; he'd seen it in her eyes as Talon had tried to force his hand, and he'd felt the answering knot in his own chest. But he couldn't help her then. Now would be no different. He only prayed the gods would keep her safe after he had failed so completely.

Cobalt and Vigil had not left a lantern, and his room had no windows, but light from the corridor crept in beneath the door. By now, Stonewall's eyes had adjusted to the shadows. The stink of sweat, bile, and his chamber pot filled each breath. If he closed his eyes, he could imagine himself back in the alleys of Pillau, the city of his birth. If he concentrated, he could smell the salt tang of the sea too, but that was purely his imagination.

Stonewall flexed his hands, fighting the trembling, but after two—or three?—days with only the barest food and water, plagued by his wound and the desire for hematite, he was starting to think the tremors would never cease. Would he be able to hold a weapon again? He snorted. He probably wouldn't live to *see* a weapon again, let alone wield one.

He turned and leaned his back against the door, resting his head against the smooth woodgrain. The walls of his quarters held no heat and he shivered in his tunic and breeches. With only traces of hematite in his blood, the cold pressed upon him like so much dirt over a grave. By the One, he needed a burn.

But there would not be any hematite ever again, and the loss would kill him. Well, he'd long since accepted that hematite would kill him, one way or another. Like so many other sentinels, he'd hoped to fall in combat before the desire for hematite took him down. Before he'd met Kali, he had certainly never anticipated *this* fate.

Forsworn.

Stonewall shook away the thought and glanced at his sleeping pallet. Beacon would tell him to conserve his strength, and indeed, the thought of lying down called to him like nothing else. When he slept, he didn't think or feel; he only dreamed. But despite his injury and weakness, his stomach protested worse when he was prone. Standing was better, but not by much. Walking was probably foolish, but manageable, although he'd grown weary of pacing the tiny room.

Another deep breath made the stitches in his side burn, except this time he caught the stink of infection. His stomach twisted again and he surrendered to his body's desire. Two steps brought him to his pallet where he collapsed, grimacing at the flare of pain from his wound and the renewed swell of nausea. The crack of light beneath his door glowed brilliant gold but cast the rest of his meager quarters in deeper shadows by contrast. Stonewall groped out until his fingertips brushed the river rock that Kali had given him. It felt like a block of ice after resting on the floor, but he didn't care. He held the stone close, tugged the blanket over himself, curled on his non-injured side, and prayed for sleep.

Fear touched his mind again, though he had none for himself. *He* was lost. Drake wasn't, though he probably would be soon. Thoughts of his older brother merged with bittersweet memories of their lives together: shared, stolen sweetrolls dissolving on his tongue; two skinny bodies pressed close while rain and wind hammered their flimsy shelter; the coppery tang in the air and his brother's gentle murmurs as he mopped the blood off Stonewall's cheek after an ill-fated run-in with the older orphans.

But no, the fear wasn't entirely for Drake, or *from* him. Drake would never have wasted energy being afraid, and would have told Stonewall not to do so, either. Stonewall rubbed his thumb across the river rock's smooth surface, and turned his thoughts—again—to Kali. If the gods were kind, he'd see her again in his dreams.

* * *

When Stonewall could bear his solitude no more, he threw off his blanket and slipped out of his room. Each step was fluid and free of pain. The door opened and closed soundlessly, allowing him into the sleeping shadows of the garrison. Moments later, he stood in the courtyard. Winter air slapped him, but he ignored the chill and hurried to the bastion gates. If magic was at work, Kali would know. He could find out what was hurting her, and put a stop to it. If he could.

If he could not...

The garrison was silent, empty. Stonewall's boots made no sound against the gravel in the courtyard as he crossed over to the bastion. Atal and Seren both hung high and full amid the inky sky and the glittering stars. But the mage moon was huge, bigger than Stonewall had ever seen; so vast, he could make out each pockmarked scar on Seren's misshapen, shining face.

There was no guard at the bastion gates and the heavy, iron lock laced with hematite lay upon the flagstones, cast silver by the moons. The gates swung open, soundless, with a single push. Once inside the bastion, Stonewall closed his eyes and took a deep breath, inhaling the crisp air. *Kali,* he thought. *Kali, where are you?*

When the sweet scent of jessamin filled his awareness, he realized she was in the garden. On the heels of this strange knowledge came her fear again, clinging to her like mist on cold iron, like the taste of blood in the back of his mouth. The force of her emotions was strong enough to sting his eyes. Everything else fell away as he hurried through the silent bastion, intent on his mission, unarmed, and alone.

Not three heartbeats after Stonewall had the thought, he found himself in the mage's garden, pacing through trees in full blossom despite the frost that clung to each flower, fruit, and leaf. The press of cold was nothing more than an errant breeze. Kali was not in sight, but the scent of jessamin was stronger than ever, so he went to the bastion wall where he had found her what felt like a lifetime ago.

The wall rose high, high above his head, taller than any mountain, and jessamin vines blanketed every inch of stone and mortar. Stonewall allowed himself a moment of gaping, head-tilting awe until the yellow flowers stirred, snapping him out of his trance. Heart racing, he slid into a ready-position, just in case, and listened, but he heard only his own blood pounding in his ears. The jessamin rustled again and this time he caught Kali's whimper of pain. Stonewall did not hesitate; he plunged both arms into the vines, searching for her.

Kali? Kali? His voice wouldn't work; he could only think her name. Stonewall gritted his teeth and rummaged through the vines until his fingers brushed the wall. But Kali was not there. He stepped back, frowning.

A single, slender hand burst from the leaves, grasping for his, and he heard her voice in his mind, answering in that same silent speech. *Elan?*

Stonewall grabbed for her hand, but it slipped out of his grip and disappeared back into the vines and flowers. *I'm here,* he tried to shout, but again he could only think the words as he groped for her in the jessamin again. *Kali, hang on! I'm coming.*

It hurts, she called back, but her voice was fainter.

Panic seized his heart but he tried to ignore it, instead yanking the vines free of the wall and tossing them over his shoulder, furiously trying to get to her. Spade-shaped leaves and tiny yellow flowers cascaded down upon him, but he ignored the gentle fall. At last, at *last* he spotted her bare shoulder, and then curve of her jaw, and then, thank Tor and all the gods, her face. Kali's dark eyes were closed. The vines had coiled around her naked body, holding her upright and tight against the bastion wall, her skin streaked with red and pink where they gripped. Handfuls of jessamin blossoms, bleached to bone by moonlight, clung to her dark hair.

Was she breathing? Stonewall gripped her shoulders. *Kali, look at me. Kali, can you hear me?*

Her eyes flew open and the world turned to starlight. Blinded, Stonewall staggered back and lost his grip on Kali. No! When he looked again, twin stars burned in the darkness, as if they'd sucked out all light from the world. Stonewall reached for her once more, but pain flared in his side, sending him reeling, and when he righted himself, the vines had crept over Kali again, slithering around her body, coiling between each limb and finger, lacing through her hair and over her face. But her eyes still burned with starlight.

* * *

Stonewall gasped and sat upright in his pallet. His stitches burned again, but he didn't care. Surely, he was delirious, for even though he was awake now, he could still *feel* her in the back of his mind, as if she stood at his side without speaking. Kali teetered between panic and dread; the latter held a strange curiosity that he did not understand, nor trust. How much of that curiosity was *Kali* and how much was the Fata? She was always inquisitive, but now? In this state? His gut roiled again and he clenched his jaw against the urge to retch.

Perhaps he was a lost cause, but Kali was alive, which meant he could still help her. Or try to, at least. He saw her face in his mind's eye, pale with fear, jaw trembling as she clenched her teeth against some phantom pain. Her voice reverberated in his mind; a silent speech. *Stop! Please! Leave me alone...*

Stonewall tried to ignore his own discomfort and focus only on his breath, but all he heard were Kali's ragged gasps. Her terror prickled along his palms and down the small of his back. As much as he wanted to believe the feelings were a hallucination, he knew they were real. She had said the Fata had *recognized* him, but what did he have that the Fata would recognize? He was just a man, and not a noteworthy one at that.

Unless what Drake had told him of his father was true. Did he really have Fata blood?

If so, maybe he could use it to his advantage. If not...well, only the shadows would hear him speak.

"Kali," he whispered to the empty air. "Kali, can you hear me?"

As he spoke, he tried to reach out to her, picturing her face and focusing on the residual emotions from his dream. He likened the action to grasping for a fishing line sunk beneath murky waters. *Kali? Are you there?*

No response, although he could somehow still feel her emotions. Was she truly lost, or was he worse off than he realized?

Stonewall's stomach churned and he sat up, shuddering, unable to fight the urge to retch this time, and leaned away from his sleeping pallet. When he was finished, he collapsed back down, head swimming, each limb leaden. His lips were dry and cracking, his muscles burned. He did not think he would rise again. He tried to calculate how much longer this life might last, and grimaced.

Think of something else.

He clutched the river-rock—it had never left his grip—and tried to reach for her yet again. *Kali?*

No response. Again. Anguish filled him but he had no water left to weep. She was gone. Everyone he had ever loved was gone.

Hopeless. Stonewall lay in the darkness, alone, and the river rock slid from his hand.

Then, like a flicker of candlelight around a corner, he recognized Kali's answering plea. Not directed at him—was she even aware of him, as he was of her?—but far reaching and aimless, a dark mirror of his own despair.

Tor, help me.

* * *

Sweet blood. Sweet magic. Give it to us. Now.

Kali clenched her jaw against the urge to scream. Screaming would make no difference to the Fata, whose voices trilled in constant cacophony. When she opened her eyes, the stone walls of the garrison cell were illuminated too well. She had no desire to see the dark stains upon the stones, nor the fear in her cellmate's face, so she kept her eyes closed and tried to think of something else if only to calm herself.

Her efforts were in vain, for she could still feel the city guards' iron grips; one had smelled oddly of lavender, while the faint scent of *biri* smoke had clung to the other. She could still see the whites of their eyes rolling back as she stole their lives to help her friends.

For all the good it had done.

As much as Kali wanted to believe the *Fata* had killed those two guards, she knew the truth. *She* was a murderer – several times over now. First Neff, then Shada, and now these poor souls who had been unlucky enough to cross her path. It didn't matter that she had slain them in self-defense, nor that she had used their energy to save the man she loved. No doubt each guard had family and friends who would mourn their passing and foster a new hatred of mages.

Tears crept to her eyes again. She swiped at them, the metallic cuff scraping her cheek. No. She could not lose herself to the Fata. She could not give in to despair. She had to keep fighting. For despite how she was jailed, despite how both her and Stonewall's lives—not to mention Beacon and Rook's—were probably forfeit now, she still had a mission. She had to learn more about the Fata. She *had* to find a way to stop them.

A male voice said her name. His accent reminded her of Stonewall's, but she could not spare the attention to reply, or even nod in acknowledgment. She only curled closer to the cell wall, shackled hands pressed against her midsection. A pity that hematite did nothing to dull the Fata's persistent, silent mind-speech.

Kali's palm still stung where she'd grabbed Foley's hook, but she wasn't sure if the pain was real or a memory from the Fata that prowled the edges of her mind.

"Poison," the Fata growled, but the sound emerged from Kali's own throat as a rasp.

"What now?" Drake asked.

But Kali barely heard the other mage's voice, so lost was she to her efforts to withstand the Fata possession. She snapped her jaw shut and counted each deliberate breath. She was still *Kali*. She was not a thrall yet.

There will be more thralls, as you call them, the Fata whispered in her mind; no single voice, but a chorus. *Until we take back what is ours.*

Did the Fata understand *her* thoughts? If she could understand their silent speech and feel their emotions, it made sense that the connection went both ways. The notion sent chills down her spine.

"Please look at me, at least." Drake sounded closer, but Kali did not open her eyes.

Instead, she tried to think calmly and clearly, and directed her thoughts to the Fata. *What are you talking about? What will you take back?*

It was beyond strange to communicate in this way, but her gambit was rewarded with the Fata's bewilderment. The foreign presence started, giving Kali the impression of a sleeping person jerking upright after being tapped on the shoulder. Perhaps this confusion was the reason for the Fata's reply. *This world is ours. It has always been ours. Your kind are invaders – a plague upon our home. We destroyed you once. We will do it again.*

So much to glean from the words! Kali's thoughts spun in a hundred different directions, but she seized on the most logical question that came to mind after all her research. *Invaders? Do you mean the strange storm cloud? What happened? What did they do to your people?*

With the silent speech she tried to pass on the image from her dream

279

and from Artéa Arvad's journal: the massive, dark cloud that blotted out the sky.

The Fata recoiled from the image and threads of anger and fear snaked around Kali's heart, tighter and stronger than before. She gasped aloud. Drake said her name again, but again, she could not spare even a second to reply. Within her mind, the Fata seethed in fury. *You came from the sky, from another world. You stole our sky, our world, our way of life. You brought disease and death, and drove us to this shadow of existence.* The Fata's hatred pulsed from every word and their vengeance resonated through Kali's bones. *This world is ours. We will take it back again – for the last time. We have already begun.*

Perhaps they spoke of one of the most common myths of how humans came to exist: that the One created them from the stars. A fantasy, of course, but why would the Fata believe such a story? Kali's thoughts spun, but she tried to focus on what she deemed the most immediate threat. *What exactly did we steal from you?* she replied. *And how? Or–*

Her silent speech died as the Fata seized her, snarling a reply in a voice that was not Kali's, though the words came from her throat. "We will take back what is *ours*, sweet blood."

"Ea's balls," Drake gasped. "You really are a thrall, aren't you?"

"What's going on?" another man called, his voice vaguely familiar.

Kali, struck with horror, did not hear Drake's reply, as she clapped her hands over her mouth. Her heart pounded but her body was cold, as if the Fata had leeched all warmth away, but she fought to gain control over herself. Such control was almost impossible to come by when she had to act as both audience and speaker. But her persistence had paid off: the Fata were really *talking* to her now, not just spouting that same litany. This might be her only chance to gain information before *she* was lost.

And what then? She was locked in a cell, deep in the bowels of the garrison. Who would she tell? What good were her efforts?

A memory of Stonewall's voice reverberated through her mind. *You're not alone.*

Perhaps Kali didn't need to speak *and* listen to the Fata all on her own.

Perhaps her cellmate could help.

Kali took more deep breaths until she was certain she could speak normally, and then she risked opening her eyes to look at Drake.

Thank the stars, her eyes did not cast any light now, so they regarded each other only through the dim lamplight. She'd expected him to be pressed against the far corner of the cell, as far from her as he could be in the small space. But instead he sat within arm's reach and watched her with a serious expression that reminded her so much of Stonewall, her heart ached.

"Drake?" she whispered.

"I'm here," he replied, although he did not move. "Are you?"

"For now."

"Glad to hear it. Are you all right?" He exhaled sharply. "Sorry. That's a stupid question."

"It is," she said. "But I don't care. No, Drake, I'm not well. I need your help."

He held up his wrists, bound together and attached to the wall by a long chain. "I'll do what I can, but I'm afraid it won't be much."

"I only need you to listen." Kali glanced around the rest of the detention area, suddenly aware of the full cells.

Drake cleared his throat. "I'm not sure how much you, ah, remember, but the sentinels have brought in some new guests."

Of course. Kali called out to the other mages, then to Aderey and Ytel.

Relief was plain in the Sufani man's reply. "We're here, Kali. In one piece. More or less."

Tears pricked Kali's eyes; she thought they were from joy at his familiar voice, although she should not be happy that Aderey and his family were imprisoned. But they knew her; they trusted her. Perhaps her mad plan had a chance to succeed.

"Now's not the time for your jokes," Ytel said to her husband. To Kali, she said, "Drake has told us you're..." She hesitated. "A thrall. What can we possibly do to help you?"

"We can't use magic," Sirvat added tearfully.

"Just listen," Kali said. "Listen well, and be prepared to share what you learn to whoever will hear you later."

She dared not say more, for if the Fata could sense her thoughts, they might sense her motives and stop talking to her. Instead, she looked at Drake again, gathering her courage. He seemed to understand, for he moved closer after only a brief hesitation and began to wrap one strong arm around her shoulders.

But Kali shoved him away. "Keep back. Other mages aren't safe around me when I'm...like this. The Fata want your magic."

Drake held up his bound wrists. "Even without these, I don't have much magic to speak of."

"I can't risk hurting you."

"You won't." Drake offered one dark hand. His voice was gentle. "Trust me."

Fear clawed at Kali's throat, at her heart and mind, seeking victory over her whole self. Would she let that fear win? Besides, Drake was much stronger than her; perhaps if the Fata within her tried to harm him, he'd be strong enough to slip out of her grasp. Kali stared at his calloused palm, torn between seeking comfort and the fear she would attack him, too. Even if Stonewall was still angry with Drake, he would never forgive her for hurting his brother.

"I know I'm not him," Drake murmured. "But I'm here."

Kali surrendered. She moved closer to him, allowing him to pull her close, though he had to drape the chain between his cuffs across them both to do so. Warmth spread through her body and she relaxed against his side. "Aye, and you're better than nothing," she whispered back, letting her head fall upon his shoulder.

She felt rather than heard his low chuckle of amusement. "My greatest aspiration in life."

Kali allowed herself a smile in return, took a deep breath, and concentrated on the foreign presence within. The Fata were still there, lying in wait, but Kali sensed their bewilderment at her sudden calm – and their interest in Drake. She bit back her alarm; would they seek his magic?

Would they sense his Fata blood? If he was Stonewall's brother, and Stonewall had Fata blood, Drake might well share it. But Stonewall had told her that he and Drake had different fathers, so perhaps the Fata wouldn't recognize Drake as kin.

Even so, Drake was a mage. Kali readied herself for the onslaught of desire for magic, but it did not come. Instead, she felt the Fata's attention skim this new presence and then discard it as unimportant. She could not help but smile in relief.

"Are you smiling because you're about to kill me?" Drake asked.

"They don't want you."

"Familiar story," he said wryly, hugging her closer. "Very well, then, Kali. Do what you must. We'll listen."

She nodded and fell back into concentration. But this time, she spoke aloud and did not try to sear the responses into her memory. "Where did my people come from?"

The Fata's surprise flooded her, and perhaps it was this feeling that spurred their reply. "Your kind dared set foot upon this world—our world—dared to cross our borders and press barbarian hands upon our skin. You are a plague; an infection to be burned away."

Surprise faded into familiar fury, blended with a hate that made Kali's eyes sting. She whispered, "When?"

"Not so long ago, for us," came the growling reply. Before Kali could respond, the Fata added, "Enough of this. Your history is your own."

The foreign presence in her mind did not fade, but she got the impression of someone turning their back to her. No! She had to keep them talking; had to learn everything she could, even if it made so little sense to her right now. She'd sort through the information later – assuming she *had* a later. But if not her, then hopefully someone else in this wretched place would remember these words.

Hoping to goad the Fata back into conversation, Kali forced her voice into Eris' imperious tone "How can you hope to defeat us? We have strong armies. Besides, we fought you once. We'll do it again."

The Fata's fury broke over her anew, strong enough to make her head

283

spin, and she was grateful for Drake's solid presence. A sense of satisfaction colored the Fata's next words, although they were still laced with fury. "We walk between worlds, where your kind cannot follow. Our shadow selves dwell everywhere, within and without you, but you are blind, deaf, and dumb, and even if you scour the veins of the earth, you will never find us."

An answering chill moved through Kali, but she tried to keep her dread at bay. She had the Fata talking now; she needed to keep up the momentum and learn what she could. "What do you mean, 'walk between worlds?'" she said in her own voice. "There is only one world."

"For you, perhaps," the Fata replied, and Kali's throat burned with their laughter. "Not for *us*. Yet," the voice turned considering, "you *are* strong in your own way. But we are stronger now than when your kind came. Even with your sweet blood, we will defeat you this time."

"If there's one thing my people are good at," Drake said suddenly. "It's killing dregs like you."

Kali started at the vehemence in Drake's voice, but she was lost to the Fata now, and could not form a reply of her own. Was he trying to goad the Fata as well?

It must have worked, for the Fata spoke through her again, sneering. "Barbarian cur. We have weapons you cannot imagine; we have our shadow selves. We have *your* own foolish minds and molded memories. We have poisoned your weak bodies. You are ours, already. We need only take the final steps to defeat you."

"We have weapons, too, and magic," Drake said, snorting. "What do you have? A bunch of mindless thralls who can't even hold a sword."

Anger burst through Kali's heart, strong enough to make her gasp aloud. But she couldn't speak, could hardly move, for she was a prisoner in her own skin. "We do not need weapons to destroy you."

"What are you talking about?" Ytel called out, adding a few choice words of Sufa that Kali could not have deciphered even if she were in her right mind.

But the Fata did not answer with speech, silent or otherwise. Instead, their mocking laughter prickled Kali's skin, made the hairs on her neck stand upright, and sent a shiver of dread through her entire body. Instinct screamed at her to run, but there was nowhere to go. And although she was among allies, she was still alone.

Suddenly, her body seized, her limbs going rigid against Drake as if pinned in place by invisible hands. Beneath her back, Drake's arm smashed to the wall with a sickening *thud*, and he cried out in pain and surprise. Something closed around Kali's throat, but she saw no one else but Drake, and it was not his hand at her neck. Panic threatened to overwhelm her as she struggled beneath the unseen grip.

"We will take back what is ours," the Fata snarled in Kali's voice. With each word, the pressure on her throat increased. "And this time, we will take more. We will take the blood of the second moon; that sweet magic that first came to the trees. We have only grown stronger, and we will take everything from you."

Abruptly, the pressure released and Kali fell forward, gasping and coughing. She managed to catch herself with her palms, scraping them roughly against the stone floor, but her knee struck the floor as well, making it throb. As she tried to right herself, her heart raced and sweat prickled across her whole body.

"Drake? Your arm–"

"It's not broken," he ground out. "Just fucking felt like it. Shit, fuck, Ea's sodding balls!"

"Please keep talking to them," she gasped. "We need more information."

Drake cursed again, clutching his forearm, but managed to collect himself. "Blood of the second moon. You mean mages' blood? You want our magic?"

At first the Fata did not answer, and Kali thought she had botched the pseudo-interrogation. But then she felt the Fata's attention shift, as if they had heard a distant call.

"Sweet magic," the Fata said at last, in Kali's voice. "New magic. Brought by the usurper moon, first to the trees, then to your people. We laid the trees to waste, but your magic spread. But we are patient and our lives are long." The Fata's attention shifted again, centering on Kali this time. "This one's blood is the sweetest of all."

Kali's mouth fell open, but it was Drake who replied. "Kali's blood? What do you want with her?"

The Fata did not answer immediately, once more giving Kali the impression that they were listening to something she could not hear. This time, she strained to listen as well; she thought she caught a faint echo of her own name, but she couldn't be sure.

"Answer me," Drake barked. "Or are you full of lies and posturing? Who's the fool, now?"

Again, no response came, and the silence was worse. Because even though Kali was not near temptation now, she remembered the desire for Sadira's magic, and Eris', and the magic of all her mage friends. What would happen if the Fata controlled her completely? No other mage would be safe. She thought of Neff, Shada, and the two city guards she'd killed. No one would be safe, mage or otherwise. Kali leaned back against the wall and shuddered.

"You take what you want to make yourself stronger," the Fata said suddenly, and Kali's throat ached with each sharp word. "We heard the song of your magic; our own blood awakened and answered."

Although her eyes were closed, she could hear the frown in Drake's reply. "What does that mean?"

But the Fata had apparently grown tired of the conversation, for Kali felt their presence recede. In their place, a roaring hunger overtook her, coming on so suddenly that she cried out in surprise. *Sweet magic. Sweet blood.* This was an urge unlike anything she'd ever known; a lust so deep and strong, it would surely never be sated. The desire filled her mind and body to its shattering point. An otherworldly thrall-shriek built in her throat, but this time she bit her tongue to keep the sound at bay. No! She would *not* let these monsters take over her mind; she would not be used as a weapon against innocents. She was human. She was *Kali*.

Someone called her name. Kali's eyes snapped open, illuminating the entire cell as if by a lightning strike. The cell was bare, save for a chamber pot and cup of water, and silent, save for her and Drake's panting breaths. She closed her eyes again and tasted copper. *Sweet blood. Sweet magic.*

Give it to us.

Drake said her name again, but Kali could not reply, for she could not think. She could hardly breathe. She clenched her fists, pressed her back to the stone wall, and prayed. *Tor, help me.*

24

TWENTY-FOUR

Three days after Sergeant Stonewall's arrest—and Kalinda's imprisonment in the sentinel garrison—Foley stepped out of the mage dormitories and into a world turned white. A light dusting of snow covered the dormitory roof, the chicken coop, workshops, and the high walls surrounding the bastion. Although no flurries fell, Foley could smell snow on the wind and see its promise in the thick cloud cover.

His boots crunched over the frosted ground as he went to his garden, thinking to ensure that the hardy trees and other plants were still alive, but his focus soon shifted to the garrison. None of what had passed that day should have startled him in the least, but he could still hear the clatter of the sergeant's sword as the sentinel tossed the weapon to the flagstones. No doubt Talon would send Stonewall to Lasath too, unless she killed him first. Well, it was her right, and Foley had played his own role in Stonewall's misfortune, but a part of him regretted that the situation had come to this grisly end.

The path turned and Foley got his first full view of the garden since the snowfall. He halted, gaping. Each bare branch should have been covered in white, but there was no trace of snow in the garden and the air was almost warm.

Foley glanced around the shrubs until he spotted a familiar figure, clad in a dress the color of a summer sky. "This is your doing, I take it?" he said as he approached Sadira.

The Zhee mage stood beside a pear tree, one hand on its scaly bark. She still wore the hematite collar, but her torc was gone. "I did not think you wanted your plants to die," she said without looking at him.

"They're not just *my* plants," Foley replied. "But all of ours. And you shouldn't flaunt your magic. You'll make the sentinels uneasy."

Sadira kept her hand splayed upon the bark and tilted her head up to the branches. The air around them grew even warmer and sweat prickled at the small of Foley's back, beneath the layers of wool and fleece which had seemed so sensible only minutes ago. "Will they unrest me as well?" She frowned. "Arrest?"

"They might. I know you're angry about Kalinda," Foley added quietly. "But she brought her fate on herself the moment she took that sentinel to her bed."

"You believe this?"

"Such truths are the way of our world. I shall tell you what I keep telling Hazel, Druce, and all the others: Kalinda put the rest of us in danger with her careless actions." He exhaled and could not see his breath. "She *and* Eris. Both have no regard for those left behind."

"Do the other mages feel as you do?" she asked.

"They should."

"Many now speak of leaving."

"Aye, and they're fools for it." Foley tapped a gloved hand against his own collar. "You, of all people, should know how dangerous we can be."

"Dangerous," Sadira repeated, looking back up at the pear tree's bare branches.

"Keep your head down," Foley said. "Keep your voice low and keep your eyes on your own path. That is the only way for a mage to survive in the One's world."

A gust of wind picked up, scattering snow at Sadira's feet, although it melted before it touched the ground. "Perhaps that is how it used to be."

When she said nothing else, Foley could not help his impatience. "Where is your torc? The sentinels won't like seeing you without it."

Sadira's pale-blue eyes met his as she withdrew the heavy necklace from a pocket in her dress. As she did, the air around Foley swam with heat so sudden and strong, sweat beaded at his forehead. But the heat faded immediately and the next cold wind made him shiver. Sadira's bare hands closed over the torc before she tucked it out of sight.

"Wear it," Foley said, although the words fell flat.

"No, Mage Clementa. Never again."

She began to walk away from him, toward the chicken coops. Frozen with shock, Foley could only call after her. "They'll arrest you, too!"

"They will try," was Sadira's calm reply.

When she was out of sight, Foley leaned against the pear tree, scrubbing his face and beard. This place, these mages, would drive him to madness! Why did none of them understand the danger that Kalinda had put them all in? After Kalinda's arrest, the others had plagued him with questions about why the sentinels had arrested her, as if it wasn't obvious, as if Kalinda hadn't blithely thrown the natural order of their world into disarray.

Magic was too dangerous for hearts drawn to chaos.

He exhaled again, frowning at the stream of fogging breath. With Sadira gone, the chill in the air had returned in full force, biting his nose and cheeks, so he turned back for the dormitories. However, a flash of metal on the ground caught his eye. He knelt and brushed aside a few fallen leaves to reveal a set of keys on a circular ring. Foley's heart froze and his hand stole to his collar. But why the keys to the mages' collars *and* the bastion gates were lying in the garden was beyond his understanding.

Take them and run. The iron pieces were without decoration, but delicately wrought; beautiful in their simplicity. Although he could not see the hematite that had been mixed with the iron, he could feel the void left by the ore. Foley's hand closed around the ring and he glanced in the direction of the bastion gates, where the burnie twins stood guard. His heart began to race. The twins were kind, but naïve, and could be easily distracted or misled. But there would be no need for verbal trickery if he could remove his collar, if he could once more touch the place within him where his magic lived.

Run.

Foley scowled at the iron keys. What was he thinking? He could not abandon his daughter to her fate any more than he could abandon the other mages here. Thank the One *he* had found the keys, and not Sadira, for only the One knew what sort of commotion their discovery would have caused.

He pocketed the keys and made his way toward the bastion gates. Once he left the perimeter of the garden, the sound of his boots crunching on snow startled him, but he should have known better.

* * *

Talon's gloved hand closed around the keys, which felt heavier than she remembered. She looked at Cobalt, who squared his shoulders. "These are yours."

"Yes, Commander," he said. "I gave them to Stonewall prior to leading the others out for Argent's," he grimaced, "mission. The sod must have dropped them when he went to fetch Mage Halcyon."

Talon looked back at Foley, standing opposite her and Cobalt, inside the bastion gates. "Are you certain no one else has seen these?"

"Quite," he said, nodding. "I found them in the garden, out of sight."

"So they were hidden deliberately?" Cobalt asked.

"Not deliberately, no. Just...misplaced." Foley added a knowing look at the captain, who scowled, and then glanced back at Talon. "I knew you would be missing them, Commander."

She caught her father's meaning at once, and her heart swelled with love for him. "Your loyalty is noted and appreciated, Mage Clementa."

"I don't like this," Cobalt muttered. He shifted again, resting trembling hands on his daggers. "Ser, something's not right. Clementa's lying. I know it."

Foley drew himself up, his brown eyes narrowed, his hook gleaming in the morning light. "You know no such thing, Captain."

"You'll speak when you're given leave, Mage," Cobalt shot back.

Talon held up her hand to quell any further bickering and looked at the burnie twins, who'd been waiting beside her. "I want you two to check that the others are still collared, but I believe the First Mage is telling the truth."

Cobalt stared at her. "Ser, he's one of *them*."

One of them. The vitriol was plain in Cobalt's voice, and Foley flushed even as he looked at his own boots. Talon's fist closed over the keys and she forced her voice to be calm. "If you won't take even a little hematite, you should rest, Captain."

All eyes crept to Cobalt, whose jaw clenched as he seemed to stand even straighter. "I'm fine, ser. Just a little tired. Save what we have for those who truly need it." He nodded to the burnies. "You heard your commander. Get to work."

Milo and Flint both looked at Talon, who smiled at the young sentinels as she handed Milo the keys. "Keep them, for now," Talon said.

Cobalt made a noise of frustration while the burnies exchanged incredulous glances. "Ser," Cobalt said. "I see no reason for–"

"You don't have to," Talon interrupted. "But I do." She nodded to the twins, who both stared at her with huge, blue eyes. Gods above and beyond, some burnies seemed to be in a perpetual state of shock. Had she ever been so young? She made a shooing motion. "Go on."

Foley stepped back so the twins could enter the bastion. "Shall I accompany them?"

Talon nodded. Foley's presence would soothe the other mages and make the burnies' task easier. Under normal circumstances, she wouldn't have concerned herself with such a thing, and she was loathe to send only two sentinels into the bastion in such stressful times. But it couldn't be helped.

As Foley followed the burnies to the dormitories, Cobalt glanced at Talon. "With respect, Commander, you place a great deal of trust where it might not be warranted."

"The burnies might be some of the only ones left standing, soon," she replied. "Along with Hornfel and a few others."

"I wasn't speaking of the burnies."

"Clementa is loyal," was all she said, and nodded back to the garrison.

292

Cobalt's steps were halting, almost staggering at first, but with effort, he seemed to right his pace. "I'll divide the essential garrison duties between the burnies. Have you heard from the Circle? Will we get more hematite?"

"Yes. Soon." She glanced over her shoulder, but she couldn't see the burnie twins or Foley through the gates any longer. "I hope."

"You hope, ser?"

She frowned in thought. She had sent a message to Serla Iban as soon as Cobalt and the others had returned with their Sufani and mage prisoners. But her message had been answered by one of the senior priest's underlings: Cipher Natanaree. The Cipher had assured the commander that once the Circle confirmed that the Pillar's orders had been carried out, more hematite would be sent immediately. No time frame had been given, but Serla Natanaree had seemed unusually sympathetic to the sentinels' plight.

But before she could say any of that to Cobalt, the captain stumbled and dropped to the gravel, catching himself with both hands. He waved away Talon's aid and rose with great effort on shaking legs. "I'm fine," he managed as she knelt beside him.

"You're not," she said, rising as well. Her head swam with the simple movement, and something sharp stabbed at her guts. "Go to the infirmary," she added.

"It's full. I'm fine, ser. Really. I just need a second to get my bearings."

Clattering hooves drew their attention to the garrison's main gates, where a fleet rider pulled up her mount. "Anyone here?" the rider called. Like all the fleet riders, she was petite and slender; the massive deer she rode dwarfed her. "I've got a message for Commander Talon."

Talon went to the gates. "I'm the commander."

"Where's Rowen?" the rider asked. "She usually meets me."

"We're...short on staff at the moment," Talon said, holding out her hand.

The rider passed a scroll through the bars, and then frowned over Talon's shoulder. "What's wrong with him?"

Talon did not reply at first, for she spotted Argent's seal and her heart began to race. "What? Oh." She looked back at Cobalt, who stood hunched over, hands braced against his knees. "He's...not feeling well," she said to the girl. "Thank you. Stay safe on your travels. The One keep you."

"Aye, you too," the rider replied. She frowned at Cobalt again before turning her mount back toward the street, disappearing in a clatter of hooves and a flurry of snow.

Talon ripped open the seal and scanned Argent's neat, fluid script.

Commander Talon,

By the Pillars' request, every remaining mage in Whitewater Bastion must be destroyed. The Pillars believe them to be unstable, corrupt, and treacherous, and wish Aredia cleansed of their poison. It is the will of the One.

By the time you read this letter, Silver Squad and I will be but a few days from your garrison to carry out this task and return to Lasath with your renegade mage. Additionally, we will bring ample hematite to be distributed among your sentinels.

Your loyalty thus far has been commendable, although I cannot say the same for your competence, which the Pillars have questioned at length. We will discuss the matter further upon my arrival.

Honor. Service. Sacrifice.

High Commander Argent

Silverwood Garrison, City of Lasath, Province of Silverwood

"Commander?"

Talon's vision had gone white. Although the sun hid behind a thick layer of clouds, the sky was painfully bright and the glare cut through her head. The letter trembled in her hands. She blinked and the world came into focus again; more snow drifted down to cover the garrison courtyard, creating a peaceful winter scene.

It is the will of the One.

"Da," she whispered as dread coursed through her veins. It wasn't fair. She had done everything right, everything according to protocol, but the situation had spiraled out of her control. Her father's fate was sealed. She could not catch her breath and had to bite back the urge to retch.

No. She refused to accept the Pillars' judgment. There must be something she could do to prove her competence and save Foley's life.

"Commander Talon?"

She looked beside her, where Cobalt was scanning the letter over her shoulder. Talon crumpled the parchment and shoved it in her belt. Chastened, he briefly lowered his gaze, but soon met hers again. Ea's balls... he looked worse than she felt. His cheeks were gaunt and the smudges beneath his eyes had only grown more prominent.

"Go lie down," she began, but he cut her off.

"Argent's bringing more hematite? Did I read that correctly, ser?"

"That letter was not meant for you."

The captain's next words were too measured. "Ser, given what happened the last time a hematite shipment came to us, the High Commander might have trouble getting the supply *to* the garrison. How well does he know the streets?"

"Argent and Silver Squad can look after themselves."

His pale-blue eyes bored into hers; his scar seemed pink against his parchment skin. His voice was hoarse, almost a whisper. "Does he know the extent of our situation?"

She glared at him. "Argent knows enough. And we still have work to do. We have a mage to execute."

Only when she said the words did she realize their truth. Halcyon's death was the only solution she could see. Foley and the other mages had proved their loyalty. Cobalt and the burnies could attest to that. Argent could be reasoned with. It would be folly to kill all the mages in Whitewater Province, particularly with war pounding on their front door. Surely the Pillars realized this. If Argent took the renegade mage back with him, and if Kalinda was executed, perhaps the rest of the remaining bastion mages would be spared.

Resolve crystallized within her heart and she felt the gods smiling upon her. Yes, this was the way. "We must set an example to the others, and to the Pillars," she said.

Cobalt considered. "But Gideon Echina *was* killed..."

"Not by a sentinel. The mages must understand who is in control. Halcyon has proven to be more than enough trouble for us. Her death will solidify our hold upon the bastion."

Cobalt frowned again, but nodded, his face contorted with pain. "When shall we perform the execution?"

Talon thought of the three vials of hematite tucked away in her desk. "Halcyon is secure for now. Get some rest. At dawn, gather who you can and meet me at her cell. We'll bring her to the bastion gates. The other mages can watch from within."

No doubt Foley would call this plan cruel, but it was the best way to send her message. Even so, she fought the gnawing despair that had burrowed into the furthest corners of her heart. *It won't matter. Argent will come, anyway. Foley will die, anyway.*

Not if she could help it.

Talon did not hear Cobalt take his leave, nor did she realize she had returned to her office until her hand brushed the door. How long had she been lost in her thoughts? She slipped inside her quarters, locked the door behind her, and went to her desk drawer. She pulled out the three vials of hematite that she had kept back. Her legs trembled as she slipped from her office to her living quarters, ensuring that this door was locked as well. The fire in her hearth was little more than embers, but she had no wood nor the strength to fetch more. An ewer of water and a single mug sat on a small table beside her bed. Carefully, she removed her armor, placing it upon the wooden stand made for this purpose, slid her chamber-pot to her bedside, and sat shivering upon the feather and straw mattress.

Three vials, each filled with chips of purified hematite ore. Heart hammering, Talon tipped the contents of all three into her palm and studied them in the faint light cast by the glowing embers in her hearth. There was a chance this would kill her, but it was a small chance compared to that of her father's execution. She would need every ounce of strength, speed, and ruthlessness she could muster if she wanted to save Foley's life. If, by some miracle, Argent did not destroy the other mages here... Well, she would deal with the aftermath, later.

Sacrifice, she thought, and swallowed all three doses at once.

25

TWENTY-FIVE

A crow's call split the silence. Milo saw no trace of black against the white sky beyond the bastion walls, but even so, his heart beat faster with the memories evoked by that sound. The wind that crept beneath his armor seemed too cold and each step made his leather gear creak too loudly. Out of habit, he kept one hand on a dagger grip as he and Flint followed Mage Clementa through the bastion.

"You will find I have spoken truly," Mage Clementa was saying. "All of us still wear our collars."

Flint rolled her eyes, no doubt at the mage's eager tone. But Milo did not share his twin's annoyance – at least, not with Mage Clementa.

"I'm sure they are, ser," Milo said to the older man. "But you know we have our orders."

The First Mage ducked his head in acknowledgment, his boots crunching on the snow. "Aye. So you do."

"At least this won't take too long," Flint muttered to Milo as Mage Clementa walked ahead. "I want to find Rook and Beacon."

It was a testament to Flint's nerves that she'd not spoken of the squad's mender with her usual sharpness. Milo wished he could offer his sister some comfort, but his stomach had been in knots since well before Stonewall had been arrested.

"Me too," he said. "But we must take care. We must follow the commander's orders."

He said the last bit gravely, maybe a little too much so, but Flint nodded and replied, a little louder, "Thank the One we're not in the infirmary with the rest of those sodding traitors."

Milo grimaced internally, but the lie was necessary to keep up their ruse. He shot a glance at the mage ahead, but could not tell if Clementa paid them any mind.

The crow called again. Flint squared her shoulders, but her hand tightened upon her sword hilt at the sound. Was it closer than before? Milo squinted again, but could make out nothing but high walls and clouds.

Calm down, he told himself. *Nothing within these walls can harm you.* The knowledge was easy to believe when surrounded by his sentinel brothers and sisters. Now, though, with just him, Flint, and Mage Clementa, even the sound of his own footfalls set him on edge.

They reached the mage dormitories. Mage Clementa slipped inside first, Flint followed. Milo stood at the threshold for a moment, peering around in awe. He'd never set foot in here before. A woven mat and several pairs of shoes in all different sizes rested on the stones outside the wooden door. Milo wiped off his boots, and then entered after his sister.

Warmth enveloped him and he sighed in relief. He hadn't realized just how cold it was outside until he was inside where several hearths burned merrily. What mages remained at Whitewater Bastion had gathered in the room, sipping tea or wine, playing cards, or speaking in low tones. At the twins' entrance, however, each went still, their eyes fixed on the sentinels. Someone dropped a mug and the resulting shatter echoed through the otherwise silent room.

Mage Clementa held up his only hand. "Be easy, friends. They have only come to ensure the collars remain in place."

The mages exchanged nervous glances, but the First Mage's words seemed to go over well enough. Milo and Flint moved among the assembled mages, checking each collar. No one spoke; some barely seemed to breathe. The only movement aside from the sentinels came from the nervous glances that darted from the sentinels' swords to their daggers. Sweet Mara's mercy... Milo could practically taste their fear – of *him*. Hot shame flooded him at the understanding.

When they'd finished, Flint frowned over the lot. "Has anyone seen Mage Sadira?"

The others shook their heads. Mage Clementa stroked his beard in thought. "She was in the garden earlier, but I believe she went back to her quarters... Ah, there she is." He nodded to the common room's entrance, where the white-haired mage stood staring at the twins.

Milo thanked the First Mage and went to Mage Sadira, Flint on his heels. "We're here to check your..." He trailed off when he caught sight of her neck. Her collar was in place, but she wasn't wearing her hematite torc. Was something amiss?

"I found something in Kalinda's room," the Zhee mage said without preamble. "Come. I must show you at once."

"'Something,'" Clementa repeated. "What in Atal's name do you mean?"

But she shook her head. "It is for the sentinels' eyes, and no one else's."

"I'm the First Mage of this bastion. You will show me, too."

Sadira shot Milo and Flint a beseeching look. Flint caught on first. *"You'll stay here,"* she growled to Clementa. "And remember your place in the One's world."

The First Mage regarded her, his only hand clenching and unclenching. He glanced around at the other mages, who all stared at the unfolding scene before them. At last, he gave a half-bow.

Flint scoffed and looked back at Sadira. "Show us."

The Zhee mage slipped into the stone corridor without another word, and Milo and Flint hurried after. The moment the common room door closed behind them, Flint grinned. "Always wanted to tell that one-handed bastard off."

"He's only trying to do his job," Milo replied. When Flint glowered at him, he chuckled and elbowed her cuirass. "Ah, I'm kidding. He deserved it."

"Ass," she muttered, before looking at Mage Sadira. "What's going on? Where are we..."

She trailed off as Sadira stopped in front of an unremarkable door. The Zhee mage glanced around, and then met each sentinels' eyes in turn, her voice low and serious. "Do you know where Kali is?"

"Locked away in the garrison's detention area," Flint replied grimly. "We made sure she's got food and water, but Talon's had us too busy to do more."

Milo nodded. "Aye. And we haven't been able to check on Stonewall..." *That* had been a direct order from Captain Cobalt, who had placed Hornfel on guard duty at the former sergeant's door. The thought of Stonewall, injured and probably dying, made Milo's stomach sink. His hand stole to the hematite vials tucked in his belt. If he could have one minute alone with Stonewall, he could save the other man. It wasn't fair!

One step at a time. They'd been quick in the bastion; perhaps after this, he and Flint could sneak hematite to their squad-mates, and maybe, somehow get some to Stonewall, too.

Mage Sadira's voice brought Milo out of his dark thoughts. "Is...is Beacon...?"

Her cheeks darkened and she trailed off.

Milo frowned at her. "Is he...what? Alive?"

"He's alive," Flint said. "Though I can't say for how much longer. We must get him, Rook, and Stonewall away from the garrison, Forsworn or not." She glanced at Milo. "Same goes for you and me."

Milo nodded. The knot in his chest relaxed a tiny bit at her words. Getting away from the garrison, from this life... It would be a relief, to say the least.

"If we're going to continue our chat," Flint added. "We should take cover."

The Zhee mage opened the door and ushered the sentinels inside. After she entered, Milo heard the lock click behind his back, but he didn't turn around, for Eris Echina stood in the clutter, green eyes narrowed like arrowheads.

"Shit," Flint swore and dropped her hands to her daggers, though she did not pull them free of their scabbards. Milo's blood leaped at the sight of the renegade mage's murderous glare, but he, too, did not draw his weapons.

Thank Mara for the hematite running hot through his veins.

"What are *they* doing here?" Echina said to Mage Sadira. "You told me you would fetch some of Kali's friends!"

"And so I have." Sadira picked her way through piles of books, scrolls, and clothes to stand between Echina and the sentinels. "You are all on the same side."

"*They* are monsters," Echina shot back. "And *you* are an even bigger fool than I reckoned, if you think I'll place any trust in them."

"We're *not* monsters," Milo replied. "We're trying to help others."

Flint lifted her chin. "Aye, and what have you done, Echina? Other than make life harder for everyone you left behind?" She pointed at Mage Sadira's collar. "Or do you think that's just the latest fashion trend?"

Echina's eyes widened but Flint's words seemed to strike a chord, for some of the anger left her face. Some, not all. "*You* accuse *me* of making mages' lives harder? Metal-licking sods."

"Coward," Flint replied.

"Stop it," Milo and Mage Sadira both said at once. They exchanged wry looks before the Zhee mage cleared her throat. "Eris, they wish to leave the garrison," she said. "And they have the means to do so."

She shot Milo a meaningful look. At first, he only stared at her, then he remembered the keys he'd shoved into his belt pouch. With some fumbling, he brought them out and held them up so the mages could see.

Echina's gaze caught on the iron pieces before she looked back at Sadira. "As I said when we met before, I only came back for Kali and Drake. If you think to taunt me with these," she wrinkled her nose at Milo, "metal-blooded idiots, then I shall take my leave."

She began to back toward the open window, where the curtains rippled in the breeze. But Mage Sadira stepped toward the other mage, saying her name. "They are allies of Kalinda," she said, gesturing to the twins. "And of Stonewall."

The shape-changing mage glared. "That dreg has caused enough trouble."

"He's dying as we speak," Milo said, heat stinging his eyes.

"He's not the only one," Flint added. "Until we get more hematite, we're royally fucked."

A thin smile curved Echina's mouth. "Good."

Fury swept through Milo's veins and he stepped forward before he could stop himself, Flint at his side. "Stonewall is an honorable man who loves your friend," Milo said. "He risked everything to save her."

"For all the good it did him," Flint added darkly. She looked at Mage Sadira. "I hate to agree with Echina, but why in the blazing void did you bring us all here?"

"Because you must set aside your..." She grimaced in frustration. "Your... quills if you are to survive."

"Quills?" Echina said, brows knitted. "What in the stars are you talking about?'

"Quarrels?" Milo offered.

Mage Sadira shot him a grateful look and nodded. "You all have the same goals, do you not? To free your allies from this prison and leave in peace."

"She's right," Milo replied. "Mage Echina, we could use your help. We don't have a way to get out of the city, but I'm guessing you do?" She must have, if she'd come back here to free Mage Halcyon and Drake. Unless she planned to turn the other mages into birds, too...

Echina regarded him coolly. "I might."

"You *might*?" Flint said. "Have you seen the city guards at the gates? Do you know how difficult it'll be to get past them?"

"Don't speak to me of those guards when my husband's blood still stains the threshold into this miserable city," Echina spat.

As she spoke, her eyes brightened with tears, and she turned away. Flint murmured something about keeping watch and slipped to stand by the door, but Milo risked another step toward the mage, carefully avoiding a viol case. "I'm really sorry about your husband," he said quietly. "He didn't deserve that fate. He just wanted to be free. I understand that, now."

Echina glanced at him. "Pretty words, Sentinel. But they won't bring Gideon back to me."

"No, they won't," Milo admitted. "And no doubt he'd tell you not to trust a couple of metal-blooded morons like us."

"Milo!"

He ignored his sister and instead held the keys in front of Echina. "If you want our help rescuing the others, including Kali and Stonewall's brother, you have to trust us a little bit."

She frowned. "Stonewall's brother? Another sentinel?"

So she didn't know. Milo winced. "Ah…I mean Drake."

"Drake is related to Kalinda's…" Echina grimaced. "Sentinel lover?"

Milo nodded. "But he's a mage, through and through. It's why he's imprisoned, after all." Best to keep Drake's life as a former sentinel a secret for now.

The shape-changing mage seemed to consider, though some of the anger had left her expression. "If there is truly a One god," she said at last, sighing. "They must have a grim sense of humor."

"I think so, too," Milo replied.

Echina crossed her arms and lifted her chin. "I shall accept your aid – until we are free of this place. After that, you and your hemie friends are on your own."

"How kind of you," Flint drawled.

Milo ignored her. "Trust goes both ways," he said, bowing once. "We accept your help, too."

He thought the mage would scoff at him, but she merely shrugged, as if his words were a foregone conclusion. He glanced at the keys, and then began to pry the iron ring apart so that he could pull two free. "Here," he said as he handed them to Mage Sadira. "The smaller one's for your collars. The bigger one's for the bastion gates."

She accepted both. "What of Kali? Can you free her?"

Milo glanced at his sister, who gave a single, small nod. "Aye, we'll free her and Drake."

"And the mages and Sufani imprisoned with them," Echina said, startling the sentinels.

"What do you know of that?" Flint asked.

Echina only stared at her. Milo held up one hand. "We'll free all of them, too." How, he didn't know. They couldn't exactly stroll down there,

303

unlock the cells, and let everyone out. Talon would have every able-bodied sentinel waiting for them. Milo wasn't sure which was worse: the fact that so few sentinels were fit to fight, or that he was even considering fighting *any* of his fellow brothers and sisters in service. "But the rest will be up to you," he added.

Echina nodded. "We have a plan."

"How are you going to get in?" Flint asked. "Unless your friends can turn into birds, too?"

Some of Echina's haughty expression faded into uncertainty. "We have a plan...*and* magic."

"The city guards have crossbows," Flint countered.

"Perhaps, but they *don't* have hematite." The mage's smile held no warmth.

Milo's blood ran cold at the thought of yet more bloodshed on the Whitewater City bridge. "There must be a way to get by them with magic, *without* hurting anyone."

"I shall do what I must," Echina replied. "And if I were you, Sentinel, I'd keep my focus where it belongs: here."

They discussed a few more details, but no one wanted to linger. Flint had kept watch at the door to guard against any would-be eavesdroppers, but surely any moment, Foley would come by and demand to know what they were doing.

At last, Echina exhaled deeply and looked between Milo, Flint, and Mage Sadira. "Until later, then."

Flint nodded. Milo offered a warrior's salute. The mage rolled her eyes, and then, as quick as a breath, melted into the shape of a black crow. Milo stumbled backward in shock, tripping over the viol case; he would have fallen had Flint not caught his elbow. By the time he righted himself, Eris Echina was gone.

"Ea's balls," Flint breathed.

"Aye," Milo replied, gaping at the open window. He couldn't help a chuckle. When Flint looked at him, one brow raised, he smiled. "At least we know she really did turn into a bird that night we chased her down. I was afraid we might have imagined the whole thing."

"I wish we had."

A gust of wind swept through the room and Milo shivered. "Me too." He looked at Mage Sadira, who rubbed the keys between her fingers. "Thank you."

The Zhee mage's fist closed around the keys. "You are well met," she said. "But we still have much to overcome."

26

TWENTY-SIX

Eris' head spun as she cast her crow-body on the wind. Help from the hemies? Surely she was going mad. But she couldn't deny that the young sentinels' aid would be useful while their misplaced conviction remained strong. The boy spoke with courage, but no doubt he'd sing another song once the reality of his words came back to haunt him.

As Eris knew too well, liberty had a price.

By early afternoon, after some additional scouting along the main road, she reached her allies' hiding place: a secluded patch of woods not far from the main gates of Whitewater City. The moment she shifted back to her human form, a wave of nausea overtook her again and the others descended upon her, a question on every tongue.

"Did you find Kalinda?"

"How about Drake?"

"Does anyone else want to leave?'

"How is the garrison? Are they still suffering from lack of hematite?"

Groaning, Eris held up one hand to silence them until she could find her voice. "No, Mar, I didn't see Kali, but I know where she is." She related what she'd learned, but when she reached the part about the hemie twins, Cai swore.

"And you trusted them?" he growled.

Eris leveled him with her coolest look. "I had little choice."

"They're our enemies. Or have you forgotten?"

This time she embraced her fury; too long had it been collared in favor of pragmatism. "Do you think I *like* the idea of working with sentinels? Do you think it pleases me to set aside all notions of decency and safety, and encourage those metal-blooded shits? Well? Answer me, Cai."

His cheeks darkened and he dropped his gaze. "No."

"Sentinels are monsters and murderers. And if I had my way, every one of them would suffer a slow and painful death for lack of their precious hematite. But right now, we have few options. Besides," she added, taking a breath to calm her roiling stomach. "The younger ones are stupid and easy to rile, which may prove to be useful during our escape. You know how deluded they all are. You've all heard their insipid oath of service and *sacrifice*. What better end than defending one's allies?"

Cai stared at her with wide eyes, but it was Adrie who spoke. "You mean to use the burnies as...fodder?"

Eris forced herself not to look at Ben or the two Assembly women. "I mean to keep my options open."

"Ea's tits, woman," Rilla said, shaking her head. "You may look like a frip, but you've a heart of stone."

"If you don't like my methods, you're free to leave."

Rilla blanched and Brice held up her palms. "Settle down. No one's leaving, yet. We're on the same side. We all want the same thing. Right?"

Murmurs of assent ran through the others. For her part, Eris smoothed out her hair to distract herself, and then looked back at Cai. "In any case, we have a plan to remove the collars and get into and out of the bastion, which we didn't before, so I'd say we're better off than we were this morning."

Marcen coughed into his hand. "Kali can do magic on hematite."

"Kali has been imprisoned for days," Eris replied, calmer now. "No doubt she'll be too weak to manage any magic at all. Remember how tired she was after removing my collar?"

Adrie offered Eris a plate of rabbit and roasted vegetables. "Brice's doing," she said, nodding to the meat. "And don't tell me you're not hungry. You must keep up your strength."

Eris *had* been about to protest the meal, for the scent of cooked onions made her stomach twist again, but Adrie was right. She could not afford weakness. Eris thanked the other mage and took a seat upon the steps of the Sufani wagon while her friends gathered around her. Except for Leal, who hung on the fringe of their group, scanning the forest.

"The garrison was nearly empty, eh?" Rilla was saying. "Good news for us."

"The sentinels are in a bad way," Eris said between bites of wild mushroom. "Many of them are sick or dead, and they have not yet received more hematite. But the burnies were convinced that the Circle would provide more, and soon."

"Why hasn't the Circle done so before now?" Ben asked.

"Who cares?" Cai replied. "What matters is that the hemies are weak."

Eris picked at a piece of rabbit with her bare hands. "The Circle might be withholding hematite until—"

"*Withholding* hematite?" Cai interrupted, incredulous.

The others exchanged similar dubious glances. "Seems a bit counter-productive," Brice said.

Back when Eris had been a girl living at her family home, her grand-mother, one of the leading priestesses in Silverwood Province, had made certain proud insinuations. At the time, Eris had been too young to comprehend their meaning, but now she understood fully. And her bitter heart was *glad* of the hemies' suffering.

"It's more like blackmail," Eris replied. "Don't let anyone tell you the Circle is merciful."

The rumbling of the White River was more noticeable this close to the city, and seemed especially loud in this moment. Leal stabbed the butt of her spear into the ground. "Well, the Circle has their prisoners now. We must not delay. While you've been in the city, I tried to find the rest of my people. Surely not all of them were captured."

"Any luck?" Eris asked.

Leal's grim expression was answer enough.

Brice nodded toward the other mages. "Davet and Izell have some experience with boats and ferries."

Both mages squared their shoulders as they looked at Eris. "Don't worry about the river," Davet said. "We'll sort it out. Izell's from Pillau, and my Da used to run, ah, *cargo* between Whitewater City and Saskah, right on the border with Cander; I can handle a barge with the best of 'em."

"Aye, but can you steal several?" Eris asked. "We'll at least need something quite large."

Izell and Davet exchanged looks. "We'll have to," Izell replied. "Won't we?"

Leal looked directly at Eris. "Did you find another way into the city?"

"Not exactly." By now the nausea had relented, thank the stars. Eris swallowed the rabbit, savoring the smoky taste from the cooking fire, and the tang of whatever spices Adrie had used. "But I did get an idea."

* * *

"You're mad," Leal muttered from where she crouched with Eris behind a snow-dusted log beside the road. "Raving, frothing mad."

Eris squinted into the falling dusk. "Yet here you are, anyway."

The coach-and-four trundled down the road, still several minutes away from Eris and her friends' hiding places. The renegades had chosen the site of their ambush well. The trees were thick here and the terrain was hilly, so that even with no leaves on any branches, they could remain hidden. Furthermore, the road curved around a bend ahead, so the main gates of Whitewater City, about three miles away, were well out of sight.

Leal plucked a single, black feather from Eris' hair. "I had little choice."

Some of Eris' anticipation fled as she met the Sufani's eyes. "You think I wouldn't aid you if you didn't join us?"

"That was our agreement, was it not?"

Heat crept to Eris' cheeks and she looked back at the coach. In the dusk, the silver trim of the driver's livery shone like moonlight. Eris swallowed hard. "I suppose. But you're no prisoner, Leal. You are free to do as you wish."

"You're wrong about the first," Leal replied, scanning up and down the narrow road. At Eris' look she pressed a hand to her chest. "I am a prisoner in my flesh. Or so it feels that way, sometimes." She frowned and shook her head. "They're nearly upon us."

The coach trundled closer. Along with a driver and four matching chestnut horses, two guards rode at the coach's rear, and another rider sat postilion upon the left rear horse to offer further guidance to the team. Each member of the party wore the same livery: dark blue with silver trim, with a silver star and scrolls embroidered upon their chests. A thin layer of snow covered the coach, and mud splattered the wheels and lower half. The horses' steps were heavy and slow, and even the guards sat with slumped shoulders. Evidently, it had been a long journey. Dark curtains covered the coach's windows, but Eris guessed at least one or two servants would be inside, along with whoever this noble was.

Across the road, a mourning dove cooed into the twilight; although Eris could not make out Brice, Rilla, or the other mages, she recognized the call from their plans. Leal glanced at Eris, a question in her eyes. Eris nodded once. Leal lifted her own voice in a similar, answering cry, and then slipped out from behind the fallen log and onto the road. The others followed, with Eris coming last. Brice kept her bow ready while Leal and Rilla hefted their spears. No mage carried a weapon.

The postilion rider spotted them first, swearing and pulling up her mount. The coachman followed, withdrawing a short club as he shouted to the guards, who jerked upright and drew their weapons. "Nox's frozen tits," the coachman snarled. "Get out of our way."

Eris stood between Leal and Rilla and spoke clearly into the dusk. "Who does this coach belong to?"

"None of your business, dreg," one of the guards hissed, urging her mount forward, mace raised. Her chainmail glinted in the sun's final rays and Eris noted the braided sash around her waist, marking her as the leader of this outfit. "You heard him: get out of our way."

"Yes, I did hear your subordinate," Eris said mildly. "But I asked a question first. Did you not hear *me?*"

One of the curtains drew back and the window slid to the side, revealing a young, wide-eyed girl who looked at the lead guard. "Captain, the mistress wants to know what's going on."

The guard captain shook her head. "Looks like some bandits. Not to worry: we'll handle them." The girl drew the curtain closed and the guard lifted her hand. "We don't have time for this. Serla wanted to reach the city by nightfall. Take them out!"

"Now," Leal called, lifting her spear. She jabbed at the lead guard's horse without striking it, forcing the frightened creature backward. Rilla, Cai, and Marcen flung handfuls of cloud dust at the coach's driver and the postilion rider, sending plumes of vivid yellow and purple powder into the air. The wind carried much of it away instantly, but the initial moment of confusion was successful. Both the coachman and the postilion driver coughed and swore, and the team of horses snorted and shifted in alarm. Leal and Rilla rushed forth, spears ready, while Cai and Marcen stood out of the guards' reach. Both men's eyes were closed in concentration, and the chill faded from the air as flames bloomed upon the branches they held – another distraction. Brice released an arrow at the driver, sending it into the wooden seat beside him with a *thunk* while the clatter of spears rose through the air.

With the retinue struggling to fight back and to regain control of their frightened mounts, Eris lifted her voice. "For Seren!"

The last four mages sprang from their hiding place and leaped for the dirt road about twenty paces ahead of the coach, slamming bare palms against the bare ground. Seconds passed, and then the road beneath them began to quake, until a great cracking sound rent the air. The earth crumbled down and away from the mages' touch, revealing a chasm about as deep as the coach was tall, and wide enough to stretch across the entire road.

The coach horses scrambled backward in their traces while their drivers fought to control them. The guards' horses—probably trained for chaotic situations—fared a little better, but their riders lost precious seconds to distraction. Leal and the others seized their opportunity and forced the guards from their mounts. When the wind dissipated the remaining cloud dust, Eris' allies had the guards and drivers bound, kneeling, and surrounded.

The guard captain glared at Leal. "What do you want, moon-blooded scum?"

Leal looked at Eris, who nodded to the coach, where a pale face peeped out through the curtains. "What's your mistress' name?"

"What do you care?"

Leal shoved the tip of her spear point against the captain's throat, which her armor had left exposed. Ben cleared his throat and said, "Please, answer the question."

The guard captain swallowed. "Serla Kerenza Vellis."

Vellis. Eris smiled at the familiar surname. The Vellis family were prominent second-tiers, with close ties to the upper echelons of the Circle. The Vellis name was almost as distinguished as Eris' own. Her grandmother had been close friends with this woman's mother. "Kindly fetch Serla Vellis," Eris said to Cai. "I'd very much like to make her acquaintance."

The bound guards cast nervous looks between Eris, the coach, and their leader, who now watched Eris with a mixture of curiosity and dread. "Who are you?" the captain asked again as Cai opened the coach door.

Eris ignored the guard as Cai poked his head into the coach. "All right, now," Cai said. "No tricks, unless you've a burning desire to be a pile of cinders."

Brice snorted a laugh. "Good one." At Rilla's look, she shrugged. "What? It was."

A refined female voice shouted in reply. "This is outrageous! How dare you?"

Eris signaled to Davet, who went to help Cai bring out the passengers. Moments later, a terrified handmaid and a lady of middle years dressed in silk and wool traveling clothes tumbled out of the coach. The lady was spitting like a wet cat. "What business do you have stopping my retinue, dreg? We must reach the gates before nightfall…"

She froze when she saw her bound guards – and Eris. As Eris approached,

Serla Vellis' eyes narrowed and her gaze turned calculating. "I know your face."

Eris smiled at the upper-tiered lady, who blanched. "Do you not remember me, serla? Think carefully. It's been many years since we were last in each other's company in Silverwood Province."

Serla Vellis gaped at her, still uncomprehending. Sighing, Eris offered a slight bow at the waist; an approximation of a greeting from a higher tiered person to a lower tiered individual. "I suppose my grandmother, Inniss Nassor, would send her regards to you, but I have not seen or spoken to that woman in well over a decade."

Vellis' dark skin went ashen. "Eris Nassor. The mage."

When was the last time she'd heard her full birthname spoken aloud? The closest she'd come recently was Kali's nickname for her: Silver Girl. "I go by another name now, but you have the rest right."

"What in Atal's name do you want with me?"

Eris swept her hands over the coach-and-four. "Nothing. We have everything we need."

The captain shifted in her bonds, but Adrie and Marcen lifted their hands and the guard flinched, looking away. Serla Vellis glared at her guard captain. "Why did you not dispatch them?"

"They're mages, serla," the guard cried.

"All the more reason to send them to their next lives," Vellis shot back.

The captain shuddered. "But serla, look... The road!"

"Aye," Leal said. "And you'll be in worse shape if you resist."

Serla Vellis stared at Eris with wide eyes. "You mean to kill us?"

Everyone looked at Eris, but she ignored all of them in favor of holding this second tier's gaze as memory welled within her. She'd been so young when her parents had sent her away to live at Starwatch Bastion – at her grandmother's insistence. How many other young mages had suffered the same fate? This woman and the Circle she so closely clung to were the root of so much evil in the world. How sweet it would be to end this dreg's life.

"Secure them," Eris said to Leal. "And ensure they cannot call for help. Do not fear, Kerenza. Someone will be along to fetch you soon."

Or so she imagined. Eris didn't care what happened to this dreg and her retinue, as long as they complied. Leal and the others began to bind the guards' hands, but Ben shot Eris a beseeching look. "We can't just leave them here."

"We can't take them with us," Eris replied.

"What if they get away?" Cai said. "What if they run to the guards? Eris, we cannot let them live."

"The city guards are expecting us," Serla Vellis cried as Rilla bound her hands behind her back. "My brother is the leader of the Circle in Whitewater City. When we don't reach the gates, they'll come looking."

Eris smiled at her. "Then I'll send your regards."

* * *

It was a tricky, time-consuming business to steal what clothes, weapons, and armor Eris and her allies would need to continue her plan, and get the coach past the magic-torn ground. But by the time Atal hung high in the sky, Eris sat upon one of the coach's padded seats, watching the world trundle outside the window. The coach's lanterns cast a faint light ahead, but unless she pressed herself against the thick, cold glass, all she could see was her own reflection. The glass was smooth, but if she looked closely, she could make out the faint swirls and spirals within, which marked it as mage-made. How readily dregs relied upon magic and all it could do for them, yet they'd just as soon imprison every mage in the world for that self-same magic.

Ben, who sat opposite her, cleared his throat. "I wish you had not left them in the forest."

"Would you rather I killed them?"

"You may as well have. They'll die from exposure before anyone finds them."

"They're bound together," Adrie said from next to Eris. "They'll keep each other warm. Besides, I reckon that guard captain will have them all freed before too long."

314

Marcen sat next to Ben, hands resting in his lap. Like the others, he wore some of the fine clothes the group had found in Serla Vellis' luggage; perhaps gifts for her brother. They looked out of place on his lanky frame. "I dunno. Leal's knots were strong."

Ben sighed. "A sister to a Circle priest. Is her death worth the lives of your friends?"

Still not looking at him, Eris tapped the coach door. "You're free to leave any time, Ben. I'm sure Serla Vellis would appreciate you coming to her rescue."

Ben was silent. Eris smirked to herself and continued watching outside. She caught muffled snatches of Brice and Rilla's conversation in the driver's seat, with a few of Cai's enthusiastic comments sprinkled in from where he rode postilion. She could not make out Leal or the other mages through the window, but knew the Sufani rode the captain's mount, and had taken some of the guard's armor.

A call came from outside. Rilla and Brice's conversation halted and the coach jerked to a stop. Eris sat up, listening to the muffled cries that followed, and then the shouts and clang of steel.

"We're being attacked," Marcen whispered, hands clenched, skin glowing as he prepared his magic. Adrie did the same and the air within the coach thickened with heat. Eris held up her hand in a plea for silence. A few more shouts, and this time, Eris recognized one of the male voices as Cai's. Light flashed somewhere in front of the coach, and the vehicle shuddered. Only a few seconds passed before silence descended. Heart pounding, Eris clenched her own fist, willing her magic to create heat and fire as Adrie and Marcen could, but nothing happened. Just as she was about to peer outside, the coach door opened, revealing Cai's narrowed brown eyes.

"You need to see this," he said, nodding toward the road.

Eris slipped out and sucked in a breath from the shock of the cold, which struck her anew after being within the magic-warmed coach. She clutched Serla Vellis' velvet cloak around her shoulders, thankful for the fur lining, and followed Cai past the horses, with Mar, Adrie, and Ben on her heels.

Leal, Brice, Rilla, and the other mages stood around a pair of Whitewater

315

City guards kneeling in the road. Auda held their mounts a few paces away. Eris stopped before both guards, whose heads were ducked. "So Kerenza was telling the truth," she murmured.

Cai shook his head. "Aye, but that's not what I…" He made a noise of frustration and knelt beside the larger of the two guards, whose helmet lay on the ground beside him. "Look up, you miserable shit. Show her your ugly face."

"Don't touch me, you filthy moon-blood," the guard spat. But he did look into Eris' eyes and her heart froze at the sight of the burn marks and scratches that marred his already bruised face. Her fingers itched with the memory of raking her crow-talons into his skin the night this guard—this *monster*—had murdered her husband.

The guard stared back at her, blinking, until a crooked smile came to his face. "Come back for another round with Ballard Faircloth, moon-blood? Come back for revenge?" He spat again, and drops of blood pattered to the snow. "Do what you like to me, but your friend is rotting in the ground. Nothing you do will change that."

"Eris," Ben said quietly.

But she ignored him, too overcome to speak, or even move, until Cai touched her arm and nodded to the guard. "He–"

"I know," Eris said.

"Please," Cai growled. "Please let me."

Those who did not hold either guard in place stood in a ring around the prisoners, and at this, they shifted in place. Adrie cleared her throat. "We could at least use their gear."

"We will." Eris ignored the second guard and took a step closer to Faircloth, who met her gaze without flinching. Something hard rose in her throat; fury coiled in her belly and danced through every vein. "Murderer," she whispered.

"Aye, and I'd do it again." Faircloth grinned at her with bloody teeth. "If you kill me, mage, you won't be no different."

"Eris…"

But she had no thought for any of the others. They didn't matter, not

316

right now. Only Gideon mattered. The dreg was right; nothing she did now would bring her husband back.

But this moment was not for Gideon.

She grabbed the fellow's thick neck, making his eyes bulge in surprise, and stared at him as magic swarmed within her body, seeking a release. As she had tried to do with Talon what felt like a lifetime ago, Eris focused on the tender, exposed whites of his eyes, and forced her magic upon him. Her fingertips prickled and he gasped aloud, his eyes rounding again, his mouth opening in shock. He shrieked and tried to wrench out of her grip, but the others held him firm. Eris stared into his watery, red-rimmed eyes and willed them to melt away like candle wax. The guard shrieked again, twisting and writhing, but his movements were erratic now; no struggle for freedom but the helpless thrashing of a trout on dry land. Magic swam through Eris, burning hot, fueling her rage and grief.

"Enough." Leal shoved Eris aside, hard enough to break the contact with the guard, but not so hard that Eris stumbled to the ground.

Veins still thrumming with magic, Eris whirled on the Sufani. "What are you doing?"

Leal stared at her, breathing hard. "You said you wanted to save your strength for later."

"This...*thing* must die," Eris replied, glaring down at Faircloth, who had collapsed at her feet, whimpering.

"You've made your point," Leal said. "Now let's tie them up like the others and be on our way."

"No." Cai stepped over, the silver braid on his stolen livery shining in Atal's light. "I made a promise," he said to Eris. "To you, and to Gid. Let me fulfill it."

Eris stared at her fellow mage, who had been Gideon's closest friend. The desire to take the dreg's life still gnawed at her, but revenge was costly and she could feel her strength flagging. Leal was right.

She glanced at the other mages, but none offered any objection, though Marcen looked as if he was about to be sick. Brice and Rilla, too, remained silent. She didn't care about Ben.

"Finish him," Eris said to Cai.

Faircloth whimpered again, though whether it was because he heard their words or because he was lost to his own pain, Eris did not know, nor care. Cai, grinning in the darkness, knelt beside Faircloth, took the fellow's chin in his hands and forced his bloodied face up. "That's right, dreg," he whispered as the guard moaned. "Know that you breathe your last. And know that your fate will be the same as Gideon's."

A choked scream filled the air, then a gurgle, and then Faircloth fell to the snow and did not move again. No one spoke at first until Brice cleared her throat and pointed at the other guard, a young man whom Eris had hardly noticed until now.

"What about that one?" Brice said quietly.

The remaining guard looked up at Eris. "Please, I don't have anything against mages. Lieutenant Faircloth just asked me to come along at the last moment. Please, don't kill me. Please show mercy."

"We'll need his gear, too," Eris said. "The other guards back at the city will be expecting two to return."

"Please," the guard cried again.

"Leave him, Eris," Marcen said. "He's not our enemy."

Brice and Rilla chorused an agreement, but Eris was already nodding to Leal. "Take care of it, would you?"

Leal stared at her. "It is against the One's edict to kill without just cause. This man is innocent." The Sufani's shoulders squared. "And I am *not* yours to command."

"He's a fucking murderer, like they all are," Cai snapped.

Eris ground her teeth and glared at Leal. "Aye, and you've had no qualms until now."

"There is a difference between seeking justice and slaying an innocent," Leal shot back. "This man had no part in your husband's death."

Cai rolled his eyes and grabbed the guard's throat. "Well, if you won't, I will."

Before anyone could stop him, Cai's hands glowed with heat once more. The second guard cried out as he burned from within, but he fell to the snow before the sound had finished echoing off the trees.

Cai dusted off his palms and nodded to Eris.

"Do you feel better?" Ben hissed. "Now that you have 'justice?'"

Cai didn't answer the Assembly man, but as the others began to strip the fallen guards of their gear, Eris looked within her own heart for the answer. She found only a void.

* * *

A few hours later, Serla Vellis and her retinue arrived at Whitewater City gates, escorted by two city guards. The company passed into the city without incident.

27

TWENTY-SEVEN

Dusk had fallen by the time Flint and Milo emerged from the bastion. Milo fastened the lock over the gate but did not secure the catch even though he had given Mage Sadira the key. The lack of sound from the secured lock seemed to echo in the gathering dark, and he shot a nervous glance at Flint. "There's no going back now, is there?"

"There never was, Mi."

"Right." He made one final check of the bastion gates to ensure they at least *looked* secure before the twins began to head back for the garrison. Snow fluttered down around them, carried by a steady wind. He had no feeling in his cheeks, nose, and chin, and the cold had long since seeped through his gear, despite the additional layer of underclothes he wore.

"We should find Talon," Milo said as their boots crunched over the snow. "Make sure she doesn't expect us to run any more errands for her. Then we can see to Stonewall and the others."

Flint's voice was hard as her namesake. "What if she *does* have a task for us? Won't it be more suspicious if we check in with her and then take off? Why not just help our squad now?"

"But if she *is* looking for us," Milo countered, "she'll find us. Better to keep her thinking we're on her side. Right?"

His twin exhaled a scattering plume of breath. "I guess. I hate this," she added, kicking at a stray stone that poked through the snow. "Planning.

Waiting." She gripped her sword hilt. "I want action."

"I'm sure we'll find some soon..." Milo trailed off as a horse and rider trotted out of the stables. It was difficult to make out the rider through the snowfall, but he recognized the horse at once. "Who's riding Frost?"

"Not the sarge, that's for sure."

They exchanged a brief, worried glance before hurrying in the direction of the horse and rider, heading for the main gates that led into the garrison. When they drew closer, Milo sucked in a breath. "Captain Cobalt!"

"What in Nox's frozen tits is he doing out here?" Flint muttered. "Sod was half-dead last time we saw him."

"He might know if Talon wants us," Milo ventured. Checking in with the captain was almost as good as checking in with the commander. They could fulfill their duty and help their squad-mates that much sooner.

Flint nodded. "Let's ask."

They hurried to meet the officer and his mount. But Cobalt didn't pay the twins any mind until they were right in front of him, waving and calling his name. Only then did the captain pull Frost to a halt.

"Out of the way, burnies." Although he was fully armored, weapons and all, the pale eyes that looked down at the twins did not seem to see them, and Cobalt's hands trembled as he gripped the reins.

Milo spoke before he could stop himself. "Ser, you're not well. You should go to the infirmary."

Cobalt glared down at him, his scar an angry red against the parchment backdrop of his jaw. "That was an order. Back off."

"We're just looking for Talon, ser," Milo said, raising his hands.

The captain snorted. "Good luck." He considered, and then nodded to the gates. "Open them for me and secure them once I'm through."

Milo goggled at the older sentinel. "You're really going out *now*?"

"A storm's coming," Flint said, gesturing at the increasing snowfall around them. "If our roles were reversed, you'd tell us to get inside. Ser."

Frost danced beneath the captain's seat, as if eager to be underway. Cobalt slipped in the saddle, but righted himself before he fell. "Argent will fix this," he muttered. "Argent will bring back order when she can't be trusted."

"Ser?" Milo said.

"One more word," Cobalt snarled, "and I'll throw you both in a cell with that Sufani rabble. Now, open those gates."

Milo exchanged another glance with Flint. Should they comply? "He's not well," Milo said softly. "He could die out there."

"We tried to stop him," Flint replied. "Better to let him leave now. One less person to get in our way."

It was a cold truth, but it resonated. Besides, if the captain was right and High Commander Argent really was on his way here, that would make the twins' task infinitely harder. Milo's stomach began to creep to his throat.

"Burnies!"

Milo jumped to attention out of habit and they both rushed to the gates, where Milo opened the lock with trembling fingers to allow horse and rider to pass through. With a clatter of hooves and a flurry of snow, Cobalt and Frost darted into the city and the night.

The twins watched him go for a few seconds, and then looked at each other. "We must hurry," Milo whispered.

Flint nodded, her face tight. "Aye. Stonewall first, or Beacon and Rook?"

Milo frowned at the keys in his hand. "The sarge'd want us to help the others first."

"Stonewall could be dead by now," Flint countered, but she shook her head. "Ah, you're right. Come on."

As with the bastion gates, they closed the garrison gates but did not fasten the latch. What did it matter if the gates were locked? They wouldn't be here to be punished for the infraction, and even if they were, who was left standing to do so?

* * *

Tor, help me.

Cobalt leaned his weight against his mount's dappled-gray neck as he urged the horse down the road from Whitewater City in the encroaching dusk. He had only fragile memories of winding through the city streets, crossing the bridge, and leaving the main gates, although if he listened, he could hear the waterfall calling his name.

His armor was stone. *He* was stone, too, for he allowed himself to feel nothing; not cold, nor fear, nor weariness. He was beyond all discomfort. He only existed for *right now.* He had to get to the High Commander. Argent would bring order back to the garrison. Only then would Cobalt allow himself to *feel* again.

A thick layer of clouds hid the rising moon and earliest stars, casting the road ahead into darkness. Although it was not snowing now, hoarfrost blanketed the ground on either side of the road, while slush and mud made the going treacherous. At one point, Cobalt passed a coach-and-four, but he did not spare the vehicle more than a passing glance.

Cobalt's breath fled in streams of fog and his horse was already steaming. Frost was a good mare, hardy, strong, and steadfast, but he would ride her to death if it would bring him to Argent even a minute sooner. He nudged her sides again, urging her *faster.* No time to worry about the footing. No time to worry about anything but his mission.

So focused was he that Cobalt almost ran down the sentinel scout who'd stopped in the middle of the road. Frost noticed the other horse before he did and whickered once in soft greeting even as she shimmied out of the way.

A woman's voice called, "Well met, brother in sacrifice. Are you from Whitewater garrison?"

She held no torch and it took Cobalt a moment to make out a flash of silver in her armor. But the familiar greeting was enough to set him somewhat at ease. He opened his mouth to reply, but his words wouldn't come. Weakness overtook him, making his vision swim, making him aware—again—of just how exhausted he was. He slumped in his saddle and prayed he wouldn't retch on his fellow sentinel as her horse came closer.

"Ser?" she said, alarmed. "Are you ill? What's your name?"

But Cobalt heard nothing else and saw only darkness.

* * *

Cobalt awoke to the sound of his name. Not his rank, which was clear by the insignia on his armored shoulder, but his *name,* spoken by an unfamiliar male voice, smooth and polished as glass.

"Ah, he's conscious," the man said. "Give me the mixture."

Someone pressed a cup to Cobalt's mouth and he took several deep swallows of water before he noted the metallic tang: hematite powder mixed in. *Thank you, Tor. Thank you, sweet, merciful Mara.* He drank greedily and allowed himself a moment of pure pleasure as that familiar, delicious heat swam through his veins, setting him on fire from the inside out. Bliss, that's what it was: slipping into a hot spring after a cold, exhausting day; fresh-baked bread slathered with melting butter; a lover's knowing caress. He hardly noticed the urge to retch for the sheer joy of hematite.

At last, Cobalt's head cleared enough so that he thought he could speak. He met the cool gray eyes of a man about his age, mid-thirties, with neat blond hair and noble, aquiline features. When Cobalt noted the insignia on the man's armored shoulder—a circle with two lines crossed at its center—he jerked to attention.

"High Commander," he said, ducking his head in the best warrior's salute he could manage while seated. "Ser, forgive me, I did not see–"

"No need for formalities now, Cobalt," Argent said, a faint smile touching his lips. "I'm just glad to see the famed Whitewater garrison captain recovered so quickly. After Harper found you, we feared you were halfway to your next life. Whatever were you doing on the road in your condition?"

Cobalt flexed his gloved hands. Was he going to be reprimanded? "Ser, I came for *you.* We've had trouble getting hematite to the garrison, and I thought I could help–"

"You are in no state to help anyone," Argent broke in, lifting a palm. "If you speak of the civilian's attack on your last shipment, you need not have worried."

Fain, who stood behind the High Commander, shifted in place. "We're prepared to handle any of those dregs."

When Cobalt looked around him, he realized that Argent had indeed come with plenty of reinforcements. Besides Fain and the rest of Silver Squad, another two sentinel squads waited on the road nearby, watching the way ahead and behind them. There was no mage-carriage in sight, but each sentinel's saddlebags bulged with what Cobalt hoped was hematite.

Heat crept to Cobalt's cheeks. "Ser, I meant no disrespect."

"I know," Argent said. "It is unfortunate that the situation in Whitewater City has deteriorated to the point where brave sentinels like you are driven to desperation on such a night."

"It's...been difficult," Cobalt managed. But hope stirred within him at the certainty in the High Commander's voice. "How much do you know, ser?"

Argent's mouth was a thin line. "Enough. The Heartfire incident alone was cause for my intervention, although I was occupied with matters in Lasath. But your commander's mishandling of the mages' escape was... sloppy, to say the very least."

"Ser...about Talon." Cobalt took a shaking breath. "I think she's hiding *something* with the First Mage, Foley Clementa."

"Something like what?" Argent frowned. "Another romance?"

"No, ser," Cobalt replied, though he wondered how much Argent knew of Stonewall's history. "But she...trusts him, and I cannot fathom why, after what's happened in the bastion this past year."

The High Commander regarded him a long moment before he said, "Promoting Talon was a mistake I'll not make again."

There it was. Cobalt could not find sympathy for his commanding officer, only relief. His blood sang with energy and strength, and the High Commander's words stirred a renewed conviction in his heart. He had made the right choice. He ducked his head again in a deep salute. "As you say, ser."

Argent glanced over his shoulder, where a female sentinel with a mender's bag waited. "Nelse, we need to move out. You only gave the good captain a half-dose, yes?"

325

"Aye, ser," the mender replied. "He'll be fine for the next day or so. A proper dose after that should set him to rights." She nodded to Cobalt. "A full dose now would be too great a shock to your system. It's best to ease back into hematite once you've not had any for some time."

"There." Argent smiled at Cobalt again, and more of Cobalt's tension eased. "You see? Everything is under control. Now, then." He got to his feet in one fluid motion. Cobalt did the same. Argent was taller and broader than him, and his armor gleamed silver in the first hints of starlight.

The High Commander indicated the road to Whitewater City. "Silver Squad, move out. We have brothers and sisters to save."

* * *

Milo stepped into the infirmary first, squinting in the shadows. The few staff who remained were clearly stretched thin in their efforts both to keep the garrison running and tend to the sick sentinels. The lanterns here were either burned to nothing or had never been lit. The hearth was dark, though embers smoldered beneath a thick layer of ash. Milo could see his breath in the torch that Flint had grabbed as they'd raced through the corridors.

He found a mortar and pestle on one of the tables, next to a slow-breathing Gray. "Where are they?" he said to Flint.

"Beacon's here," she replied from across the room, holding up her torch. "Shit, Mi. I think... I think we're too late."

"No!" Milo slipped between beds and stepped over pallets—every one full—and knelt beside his twin as he dug a hematite vial from his belt pouch. Beacon had not risen from where he'd slumped against one of the infirmary walls. The mender's face was ashen and his mouth was slack; even his coppery hair seemed dull in the torchlight. But his chest rose and fell—weakly—and his eyes flickered behind closed lids.

"Thank Mara," Milo murmured. He willed his hands to be steady as he poured half the vial's contents into the mortar. Tiny hematite chips fell into the stone bowl with a soft *clink*. Thank Tor, he didn't spill any. He handed the vial to Flint, who stuck the cork back inside and secured it in her belt.

"I'll find Rook," she said.

Milo gripped the pestle, and for a few moments, the only sound was the low grinding of granite against hematite and Flint's soft footfalls as she searched the room. Gods above and beyond, for a room so packed with sentinels, it was quiet. If Milo concentrated, he could make out intermittent, labored breathing. So many sentinels. He didn't have enough hematite to save them all. The scent of sick and body odor clung to his nostrils, and his stomach twisted. Would anyone burn those that died, or would they just rot away here? Where was the honor in this kind of sacrifice?

His gut lurched again and he didn't dare look up from his task until the hematite was ground into powder. When he reached for his waterskin, he found nothing, and silently swore.

"Flint," he said, not looking around. "I need water. You got any?"

"Aye." She was at his side in a moment, passing him both her waterskin and a ceramic mug she must have found nearby. "Rook's in the common room," she added. "Alive, but barely."

"She's next." Carefully, Milo tipped the powder into the cup, and then poured in a few splashes of water. He swirled the cup to blend the two, and then offered the mixture to Flint. "I'll lift him if you pour."

Milo knelt beside Beacon and hefted the other man upright, trying not to notice how frail and cold the mender felt. Once Beacon was secure, Milo tapped his cheek to rouse him, wishing for once he was snoring. "Beak," he murmured when the other man did not stir. "Beacon, wake up. Look at me, Beacon."

No response.

Still holding the cup with the hematite mixture, Flint pulled off one of her gloves with her teeth, and slapped the mender's cheek. "Wake up you stupid, sodding frip! Wake up, or I'll kick your arse back to Redfern, where you belong."

Beacon groaned. His eyes fluttered and blinked, and then focused on

Flint. "What'd you call me, burnie?" he mumbled.

Thank you, Mara. Milo shifted to ensure that Beacon's head was upright, and then nodded to his sister, who held the cup to the mender's lips.

"Here," she said. "It's just a half-dose, but it should…"

She trailed off as the mender took a single swallow, closed his eyes again, and then gulped the rest of the mixture down. The effect was immediate. Beacon's head lolled back as he sucked in great breaths of air; he groaned, but the sound was not entirely painful. Spots of color bloomed on his pale cheeks and his hands opened and closed.

At last he regarded Flint with a dazed grin. "Knew it," he croaked. "I knew you loved me."

Flint scoffed and set the cup aside. "You sodding wish."

Beacon chuckled weakly and twisted around to look at Milo. "Help me up?"

Despite his bulky gear, Milo rose fluidly and pulled the mender to his feet. Beacon swayed a little, but already his color was returning to normal. He glanced around the infirmary with a grim expression and then looked back at the twins. "How much do you have?"

"I haven't heard a 'thank you,' yet," Flint replied.

Milo hurried to answer before they could start bickering again. "Enough for now, and a little for the future. Not much more."

Nodding, Beacon scrubbed his face and hair. "We knew it might come to this," he murmured. "You gave me a half-dose, right?"

"Aye, and we've another for Rook," Flint said, pointing toward the infirmary door.

"And Stonewall," Milo added. "We have to hurry."

Beacon gave Milo a look he recognized too-well and spoke with his mender's *I've-got-bad-news-for-you* voice. "Stonewall's probably gone by now. You should prepare yourselves."

"Fine," Flint snapped as she grabbed the cup, mortar, and pestle. "But for now, we have to help Rook. Come *on.*"

They hustled down the corridor, boots clattering on the floor, and rushed into the common room, where they found Mica on the floor beside one of the pallets. At the others' entrance, the mender jerked awake, blinking. "Beak?"

"Be still," Beacon replied as he passed his fellow mender. "I'll be right back."

But Mica only watched the three of them slip past and make a beeline for Rook, curled upon one of the pallets in the back. "What're you doing?" Mica asked.

"Hush," Beacon said, his mouth a thin line.

Beacon shot Milo a questioning glance, and Milo nodded. "After Rook and Stonewall."

Flint was already at Rook's side, kneeling to better prop her upright. Milo knelt beside them both, holding out an arm in a silent offer. Flint hesitated, but nodded and allowed him to take Rook in his arms. Sweet Mara's mercy, she was so little and frail, like a porcelain teacup. He held her as gently as he could lest he shatter her bones. Beacon ground the hematite with deft, sure movements. Once the mixture was ready, the mender glanced up at Flint. "Help me."

"Right." She had not left Rook's side.

Together, Flint and Beacon carefully opened Rook's mouth, tilted her head back, and tipped the cup's contents down her throat. She coughed at first, and then drank deeply, gasping once she'd finished. When her eyes opened, they darted wildly around before resting on Flint's face. She smiled. "You're all a sight for weary eyes."

Flint smiled as well, no small amount of relief in the expression. "Well, *you* look like shit."

"But I'm alive," Rook murmured. She frowned at Beacon. "Right?"

"We all are," he said, rising as he began to mix another half-dose of hematite.

While he went to Mica, Milo helped Rook to her feet. She swayed a bit at first, but soon found her footing, pressing a hand to her head, face contorted as if with effort. Before Milo could ask what was wrong, her eyes widened and she looked between the twins. "Argent's coming," she whispered. "If we're going to survive, we must leave before he arrives."

Flint and Milo exchanged glances. "Aye, he's coming to bring more hematite," Milo said, frowning. "At least, that's the rumor I heard."

"How do *you* know?" Flint asked Rook, one brow raised. "Not like there's much gossip down here."

Rook frowned at her. "I heard the same rumor."

There was little time to investigate. Milo glanced up at Beacon, who was helping Mica to his feet. "Beak."

"I know." The mender rubbed Mica's back, murmuring whatever it was that healers said to their patients to set them at ease. Milo only caught snatches, but he made out the High Commander's name. Hearing this, Mica's face fell as he nodded, and he gave Beacon a look filled with sorrow.

"Brother in service," Mica said quietly.

Beacon embraced the other mender. "Brother in sacrifice."

With that, he rejoined the twins and Rook, and the four of them hurried out of the common room, toward the officers' quarters. They passed no one on their way.

They came to Stonewall's door, but found it locked. The keys jingled in Milo's trembling hands, but none of them fit into the brass lock. Flint swore and kicked at the door, and Rook cleared her throat. "I can try to pick it..."

Heart hammering, Milo looked at the door, assessing its height and construction, measuring its strength against his own. "No time." He stepped backward and braced himself. "We'll have to make our own way."

28

TWENTY-EIGHT

Stonewall was only aware of two things: the darkness that filled his vision, and the cold that had seeped into his bones; a chill so deep it could never be banished. At least his pain had all but disappeared. He did not know if it was nighttime or if his eyes had failed him at last. He tried to recall sun-warmed, sugar-soft sand between his toes, but the conjured memory was little more than a whisper in the empty chamber of his mind. He tried to remember the sun itself, but saw only shadows.

He tried to picture Kali's face, but she, too, had faded from his mind, although he could not say if she was truly gone or *he* was. Either way, he'd failed. Her bright spirit would be lost to the Fata that had taken hold of her heart. And he was so cold.

Tor, he formed the thought with effort, *help her.*

His squad's faces swam before his mind's eye. Were they any better off than he was, right now? *Tor, protect them.* His eyes stung, but he had no more tears to give. *Tor, please help me too, if you can.*

All sense of time had vanished, like mist upon ocean waves burned away by the sun. Stonewall's next moment of awareness brought the feeling of warm breath upon his forehead. The sensation was so strange and so sudden, his body jerked involuntarily, sending him off the edge of his pallet and onto the floor. He should have at least tried to get up, but he did not have the strength to do more than turn his head to press his cheek against the icy flagstones. He blinked, trying to clear the shadows from his eyes, but the darkness did not recede. Another exhale feathered against his ear.

Stonewall's breath caught and he curled his hands around his midsection to shield himself. The voice that left his throat was not his own: rasping and hoarse. "Who's there?"

Do not fear, my son. The speaker was male, with an accent Stonewall could not place. That hardly mattered, though, for the words echoed within his mind in that same silent speech from his dream of Kali. A sensation of calm slipped over him, as if some loving hand had laid a soft blanket across his body.

Wrong. This feeling was strange and foreign, and thus surely dangerous. Stonewall's heart began to race again and he tried to push himself upright, but his arms buckled and dropped him jaw-first to the stone floor.

"What's going on?" he managed as his chin throbbed.

Be still.

Exhaustion darkened his vision, but he marked the movement of something in the shadows, something close, something at least the size of a man, that came silently across the stone floor to stand beside his pallet. When Stonewall caught sight of two gold, glowing eyes, he gasped aloud. A thrall! Here? But how? He had probably been in and out of consciousness for a while. Had the monster slipped into the room while he slept? Did that mean that the garrison had fallen to the demons? Or the city? Sweet Mara's mercy... Had the whole province been conquered?

Stonewall gritted his teeth and tried to get up again. If he was going to die, he'd do so standing. But his weak, aching body betrayed him, and he could manage no more than to roll back onto his side.

As he struggled, the thrall watched him with gold, unblinking eyes. They glowed, not quite as bright as other thralls', but the sight was enough to set Stonewall further on edge. What was the monster doing just *watching* him? Stonewall shot the thrall the best glare he could manage. "Either kill me or leave, demon."

The soft-blanket feeling descended again, but Stonewall pushed it away. He would find his own calm. Heart pounding, he focused his energy on another attempt to rise. *Don't talk to it,* he told himself as he groped for the chest at the foot of his sleeping pallet. *Don't engage. Just try to get up.*

There it was again, that strange voice in his mind. *I am no demon, my son. I am here because of you.*

Despite his assertations, Stonewall said, "Me?"

You summoned me.

This froze Stonewall in place, leaning on his side, body propped upon his elbow. Summoned? Too confused for caution, he said, "What are you talking about? Who are you?"

The golden eyes did not waver. *You know who I am, Elan.*

And all at once, he did, although surely the understanding was akin to madness. That, or he was dead. *That must be it,* Stonewall thought. He'd stepped from one life and now hovered between it and the next. "Where is the river?" he heard himself ask, like a fool, like a child.

A low chuckle filtered through Stonewall's mind as Tor replied in that sacred, silent speech. *You will cross – in the fullness of time.*

So he *was* dead. He thought of Kali and his eyes burned. He would never see her again in this life. Would the gods allow a mage to pass into another life? He opened his mouth to ask, but before he could, the golden eyes shifted their gaze to the door. A few seconds later, Stonewall caught the sound of footsteps and muffled voices, and the harried, desperate shape of his own name.

The god's golden eyes met his again and came closer. *Come, my son,* Tor said. *You hurt too much. It's time I took you home.*

But Stonewall was only listening with part of his mind, for now he recognized the voices just outside.

"I can try to pick it…"

"No time."

These voices were no ghostly echoes in his mind. These voices were real and accompanied by pounding against the wooden door to Stonewall's quarters. His stomach knotted. He tried to call out to his brothers and sisters in service, but couldn't manage more than a groan.

What were they doing here? Beacon and Rook were supposed to be dead, while the twins should have been long gone. Why had they not left?

Come Elan, Tor said again, more urgently. *Come home. Come now.*

"We'll have to make our own way."

Moments later, a massive thud shook the door, making even the stone floor tremble. Another thud, and another; the wooden door creaked and groaned.

Was it truly his squad, or a trick of his weary, weakened mind? Stonewall squeezed his eyes shut; if only he could *think* clearly!

My son.

Stonewall looked into the golden eyes, which were starting to fade. His throat was tight, his eyes burned, but all of that was impossible for a dead man. Right?

Come with me, Tor said.

"Hang on, Stonewall," Milo cried from behind the door. "We'll be right..." His words trailed off into another thud, sending splinters drifting to the floor.

"Wait," Stonewall said to his patron god. "I have to know..." If his friends were truly here, perhaps they could all cross the river together, maybe even step into their next lives together.

But the golden-eyed god faded into the shadows and the warm-blanket feeling slipped away, leaving Stonewall cold and empty as his namesake. The door flew open and Beacon and Milo stumbled into the room, light pouring in behind them, Flint and Rook on their heels. Stonewall twisted his head up—he could not find the strength to do more—and watched his squad mates kneel beside him.

"Stonewall," Beacon said, pressing a calloused palm to his cheek. "Look at me."

"He's breathing," said Flint, who knelt by Stonewall's feet. "Here."

"Thanks." Beacon accepted something from the younger woman.

Rook's voice drifted from the door. "Someone's coming."

"Shit." Flint leaped up and joined Rook, and the shadows descended upon the room once more.

Milo dropped to Stonewall's side and grabbed his hand. "Hang on. It's all right."

"I saw him," Stonewall whispered. "I saw Tor. He spoke to me. He called me by my birthname. We can go with him, *relah*. We can go home."

Milo squeezed Stonewall's hand harder. "Beacon? What's he talking about?"

"He's delirious." Beacon lifted a cup to Stonewall's lips. "Drink up, sarge. You're not going anywhere just yet."

* * *

Raw power surged through Talon's body. The feeling would have shattered a lesser woman, but she was iron and stone; she would not bend. She would keep her father safe and she would show Argent that she was a force to be reckoned with.

She did not remember waking from her burn, nor the worst parts of hematite ingestion. She did not remember putting on her armor, gathering her weapons, or leaving her quarters. After, she made her way through the quiet barracks and past the infirmary, heading towards the detention area, alone but for the furious lash of her heart. A pause by each room to listen confirmed her worst fears: although many still lived, she was the only sentinel fit for duty. Even the stalwart Captain Cobalt was nowhere to be found. Guilt tore through her heart at the thought of the three doses she'd consumed; that hematite could have saved lives. Talon clenched her jaw. Her brothers' and sisters' sacrifices would not be in vain. She withdrew her sword, relishing its heft, and continued.

Silence blanketed the garrison like a snowstorm, muting Talon's steps and quickened breath. Only a few torches were lit. Their shadows danced at the edges of her vision, but she ignored them as a byproduct of so much hematite. In great amounts, hematite was known to toy with a sentinel's mind; to turn harmless shadows into enemies waiting to ambush. There was no danger for her now, but there would be soon. Talon descended the stairs that led to the detention area.

All the torches had gone out here, so she met only darkness. No matter;

she didn't need light to find the mage who had poisoned her bastion. The fire burning through her veins heightened every sense and sensation. Each breath brought salty sweat mingling with the acrid tang of fear. Halcyon's frantic heartbeat seemed to reverberate through Talon's body as she mentally calculated the distance to the mage's cell, which she'd crossed so many times. Every stone of this garrison was ingrained in her mind like the lines around Foley's eyes. This was their home. Argent would not take it from her. Halcyon had to die.

As her eyes adjusted, harried voices reached her; frightened men and women speaking in Sufa.

Save one man.

"I don't know," Drake was saying. "She's not responding."

Another man spoke in a thick Sufani accent. "You're sure her heart still beats?"

"Aye," the mage replied grimly. "But–"

A Sufani woman interrupted, hissing a command in her native tongue, and the others fell silent. The only sounds were soft, hiccupping sobs trickling from Halcyon's cell. At last, the renegade mage said, "Who's there?"

Talon ignored him as she came to the cell door, unlocked it, and pushed it open. By now her eyes had adjusted, so she spotted the two mages huddled together in the corner. Once the renegade realized who she was, he shifted so that his bulky frame formed a barrier between Talon and Halcyon.

"What do you want now?" he growled.

"Get away from Halcyon. She'll be Nox's problem, soon."

Drake staggered to his feet and into a sloppy fighting stance "Over my dead body."

Talon could not help herself and laughed aloud. "Certainly, if you wish."

"Go fuck yourself, hemie bitch," the first Sufani woman called. A chorus of similar insults followed, in both Sufa and Aredian, but Talon paid them little mind. Even the infant's wail and the clinking chains and fists pounding the stone walls did not distract her as she entered the cell sword-first. Even cuffed and collared, mages were still dangerous creatures.

Halcyon curled against the wall behind the renegade, face hidden by her dark hair, murmuring too softly for Talon to hear.

Hematite made her reckless and curiosity took over. "What was that, Halcyon?"

"Let us go," Halcyon snarled, but the voice was not one Talon had heard before. It had a deeper, ethereal resonance, as if the words came from many throats and from far away. The otherworldly speech sent a thrill of terror through Talon's veins; a harsh sound that rolled through her like the first crack of thunder. Suddenly she was a child again, trembling beneath her bed during a summer storm.

No. She was strong, she was right, and the gods were with her. Talon swallowed her fear. Faster than a breath, she struck the renegade mage's temple with her sword pommel, knocking him breathless to the floor. Talon seized the advantage and grabbed the binders around Halcyon's wrists so she could jerk the other woman to her feet. The little mage cried out and stumbled, but came along as Talon dragged her out of the cell.

"No," Drake shouted as he scrambled upright.

His chains rattled as he lunged for Talon, but she and Halcyon were beyond his reach. Talon threw Halcyon to the stone floor and pressed a booted foot upon her chest to hold her down. But Halcyon did not go quietly. She clawed at Talon's leg, twisting and struggling beneath her, and glared up at the sentinel commander with eyes that shone like stars. A spine-tingling shriek resonated off the walls.

"You will never kill us." That thunder-voice rolled again, making the hairs on Talon's neck stand upright. The air felt heavy and thick, and it was difficult to take a proper breath.

Then Halcyon shook her head, her entire body shifting with the movement; her voice was frail and human now, barely a whisper. "Please, let me go."

Talon ignored the sound as if it were no more than a crow's caw and pressed her foot down harder to hold the writhing mage in place. Halcyon was a little thing, after all, and Talon had undergone years of physical training. She gripped her sword hilt and angled the blade at those star-bright eyes.

By the One's will, with Tor's aid, she would extinguish this demon light. She would bring order back to her world.

* * *

The fire started in Stonewall's heart and bloomed out, lashing each vein and muscle, squeezing his lungs so he could not catch his breath. Waves of nausea swept through him, stronger than he'd ever known. He had nothing to purge but heaved anyway and almost fell back to the floor.

Almost.

A pair of strong arms caught him, held him upright. "Easy, easy," a man's voice said. Dimly, Stonewall recognized the speaker, but his thoughts swam with hematite. Someone pressed a flask to his lips and he greedily sucked down the rest of the cool, faintly metallic water that trickled down his throat and into his empty belly.

As he drank, the arms that held him eased him back, propping him against the wall. Gradually, the insidious chill that had seeped into his bones began to recede. His head cleared and he was able to get his bearings. He was still in his quarters, but now his squad-mates all knelt around him; sheltering him while he came back to himself.

Stonewall scrubbed a hand over his face; his eyes were crusted and he dearly needed to shave. "I'm not dead," he managed. "Right?"

Flint snorted. "You should be." Milo shot her a chiding look and she sighed, adding, "We all thought you'd be ashes by now."

"Welcome back," Beacon said wryly, although his gaze was assessing.

Stonewall swallowed, and for once the action didn't feel like he had gravel stuck in his throat. "Glad to be here."

"How do you feel?"

"Better. Thank you for..." The words died on his tongue as a cold wave of terror crashed over him. Mortal fear; the sort that pinned a body in place and stole one's breath. But it was not his own fear. It was Kali's. He hadn't reached out to her; the feeling had come to him on its own.

"Stonewall?"

He looked up into his squad-mates faces. "Kali's in trouble," he said without thinking how it would sound to them. "I must help her at once."

Flint frowned. "How do you know that?"

"Talon's had it out for her," Rook replied from her place near the door. "Not too much of a stretch to think she'll act now."

Milo rose. "Then we still have work to do."

He and Beacon helped Stonewall to his feet. Stonewall's head swam at the movement, his limbs tingling as his body adjusted to being upright, but the feelings faded quickly. Once standing, he glanced around for his gear, but none of his armor or weapons were in his room; he'd been quite literally stripped of all his sentinel trappings before being tossed in here to rot. Seeing his dismay, Milo unbuckled his sword belt and handed it over. He looked older than Stonewall remembered. "Don't worry," Milo said. "I've still got my daggers."

Stonewall ducked his head and murmured his thanks. But as his fingers closed around the weapon, doubt needled at his heart. Would he be useless against this foe?

"We're with you, Stonewall," Milo said softly.

With that, Stonewall rushed for the door, his squad-mates on his heels. They tore through the corridors until they reached the winding staircase that led down to the bowels of the garrison A faint light shone from the open door at the bottom, and a thrall's shriek split the air.

"Ea's tits," Rook swore as they descended.

Stonewall's gut lurched. Were they too late? He all but flew down the stairs to the open door. He shoved through just in time to see Talon, sword in hand, pressing one boot to Kali's chest. Kali's dark eyes intermittently flashed like stars as she tried to struggle out of the sentinel commander's control. The detention area was dark except for that ghastly light gleaming on the clean length of the commander's blade.

"Stop her," Stonewall cried, and launched himself at Talon.

With a curse, Talon swung her sword his way, but Stonewall blocked the blow. The force of it made his arm ache. That and the fevered gleam in the commander's eyes gave away her secret: hematite. How much had she taken? Stonewall had no time to think beyond that as the commander lunged at him again. He parried the thrust and got in one of his own as Milo tossed Rook a set of keys before he and Flint joined Stonewall, hemming Talon in on all sides as best they could in the limited space. Moments later, Beacon, Rook, and a freed Drake surrounded the commander while Talon glared between them, her dark gaze landing on Stonewall.

He hovered his sword over her throat. "You're done, Commander."

Talon spat at his feet. "Traitor."

"You'd know better than most." Stonewall risked a glanced at Kali. She still lay on the floor, eyes closed, and he couldn't make out her face in the darkness. Rook lit a nearby torch with a few strikes from her tinderbox. Now Stonewall could see that Kali was pale as bone; only the rise and fall of her chest and her pulsing, frantic fear told him she was alive.

It took the entire squad and Drake to wrest Talon's weapons away and hold her in place. "We've got her," Milo said, although the words came out as a grunt as Talon struggled to free herself. "Help Mage Halcyon."

Heart in his throat, Stonewall sheathed Milo's sword and knelt beside Kali. Flickering torchlight revealed how the pulse at her neck beat too quickly and how her face contorted with pain. Tears streaked through the dirt on her face. When he touched her, she shrieked again in that unholy way, and tried to twist away from him. The thrall's voice sent chills across his skin.

No. Kali was *not* lost. Not if he could help it. Stonewall forced himself to think through his fear. He had stood at the edge of Nox's river, but he had not crossed. He had spoken with a god, but had come back to this life, nonetheless. Why else if not for love or destiny?

In Tor's name, he had to get her out of here, had to get her away from Talon, away from this sodding prison, but that same thundering wave of fear overtook him again when he brushed her cheek with a trembling hand. "Kali? Are you–"

His words faltered as Kali's opened and he stared into starlight.

29

TWENTY-NINE

S *weet blood. Sweet magic. Give it to us. Now.*

"Let me go!" Kali's voice was not her own; the words escaped as a thrall's shriek. A dull pain throbbed through her skull, tailbone, and shoulder blades, but the memory of the sentinel commander slinging her to the floor was distant. Something pressed upon her chest, hard and unyielding as stone. It was dark all around and she was alone, but for the Fata.

Her unseen captors clutched her with invisible, searching hands as they murmured into her mind. *Sweet blood. Sweet magic. Give it to us. Now.* Kali tried to wrench away from them, but there were too many and she was too weak. At last she sagged in their grip.

"Please, stop," she whispered. The weight on her chest increased and pushed the air from her lungs. The shadows swam and her head seemed to disconnect from her body.

The Fata did not stop their litany, but once Kali surrendered, she caught more voices, more words, spoken somehow alongside those she had already come to know too well. Before, the Fata's voices had been like single notes, but now, Kali heard an entire orchestra. Kali could not begin to estimate the Fata's numbers, but their song filled every bone, vein, and particle of her being, merging with her own thoughts and memories. The Fata's song was too vast to contain. It was like standing atop a mountain and craning her head back to see every star, with the whole sky rushing down to meet her. Their song would destroy everything.

A shadow blots the sky, obscuring our sun, binding our world with shadows and a deep, strange roaring sound. A thunderhead? But this storm is like none we have ever seen. This storm will destroy us. We seek shelter beneath the surface, where the black water flows, where nothing can find us. But the shadow draws closer to our world, to the very ground we cower beneath. So we flee again, deeper, farther. Into the void.

They spoke to me again last night: stories of greed and jealousy, and fear. So much fear. I asked the trees for answers, but they had only questions. "Why have they come?"

We destroyed you once; we will do so again.

"No," she whispered as hot tears streaked down her cheeks. She stared into shining starlight. *Kali* was fading, leaving only the thrall behind, and she couldn't fight any longer. There were so many Fata and she was so tired; she was ready to surrender.

Then the weight upon her chest lifted and Kali gasped, sucking in musty air.

"Kali?"

The shape of her name was distant, surely a byproduct of her exhaustion and fear. But before she could react, the Fata's anger swelled, sharpening upon this new presence. Kali tried to force her eyes closed—anything to drown that demon light—but the Fata's emotions overtook her again, blinding her with their anger, their vengeance, their hunger for magic. That hunger burned; was this what hematite felt like? Fire in her blood and a need so great she thought she would shatter.

"Kali." It was a man's voice, familiar. As with the Fata, she felt the tremors of his terror through his own words. "Kali, look at me."

Was it some Fata trick? She couldn't think, could hardly breathe. The weight was gone, but the Fata had stormed the barriers of her whole self. All that was *Kali* was slipping away like grains of sand held in a hurricane.

"Kali," the man said again. "Kali, look at me! Kali, come back!"

Back? Back to what? There was no one here but herself and the Fata.

Had there ever been anyone else? Kali tried to put a face to the voice, but the instant her focus slipped away from the Fata, their words returned in full force: *Sweet blood. Sweet magic. Give it to us.*

Now.

Someone lifted her upright. Someone wrapped her within something solid and warm. The Fata? It must be, for she was their prisoner in body, mind, and spirit. A renewed flare of hopeless terror filled her and she struggled again, desperate to get out of their grip, even if only for a moment.

The man spoke again, his voice now in her ear. "Kali, you're strong. You can fight that bastard. Kali, you can do this. Come on. *Fight!*"

The last word echoed in her mind. At first it blended with the Fata's ceaseless litany, but gradually, it built strength until it overwhelmed their words. *Fight.* Along with this came emotions that were not hers, but not the Fata's. Determination filled her, although it was tinged with a despair and a fear that she recognized. The breach in her mind widened, allowing other things to pour inside: hope, joy, safety. *Love.* That solid warmth surrounded her, both a part of and shielding her from the ghostly, searching fingers. So, too, did the Fata's words recede, giving her respite and a determination all her own. *Fight.*

No, she would not die this way. She would not let these incorporeal monsters wrest away her soul, her humanity, her *life.*

Fight. It became her new litany, her new act of magic.

Kali clenched her jaw and concentrated on that warmth, and on the determination that was not entirely hers, but not quite foreign. With her reclaimed calm came focus, and with focus came comprehension. The knowledge she'd gleaned from Artéa Arvad's journal and her own conversations with the Fata coalesced.

Even the strongest trees are sick and dying. We have poisoned your weak bodies. We laid the trees to waste, but your magic spread. You brought disease and death, and drove us to this shadow of existence.

Understanding shot through her like lightning. The Fata's control was a poison, a sickness. Magic might burn it out, just as it could cure an infection.

Kali's awareness dove into her own particles, seeking the foreign presence that had infested her body, mind, and spirit. She found the Fata buried deep within her heart and laced within every drop of her blood, but she was past all doubt. Only intention remained. Kali gathered her strength and focused on the foreign presence; an infection to burn away. Heat swam through her veins and rolled down her back, but she did not relent. Screaming, unfettered fury filled her mind before the Fata's words faded to a whisper, then a dull hum, and then nothing at all. In those first few seconds of sweet silence, all she knew was a racing heartbeat, although it was not her own. It belonged to the man who held her close, the man who still murmured her name in entreaty.

"Kali," he whispered. "Kali, you're strong. You can do this."

"Elan?" she managed.

His breath hitched and he shifted so there was a space between them. Cold air rushed in; she tried to lean close to him again, but he held her cheeks so he could look into her eyes. No starlight shone upon his bruised, tear-streaked face; only naked hope stared back.

"Kali?"

"I'm here," she replied. Was it true? Had she cured herself from the Fata possession? She sifted through her own particles, searching for traces of the Fata, but found only *Kali*. Bruised, battered, but wholly herself. Tears slid down her cheeks but she didn't wipe them away. "I'm right here."

Stonewall searched her face before he gave a laugh that was more of a choked sob. "There you are," he agreed hoarsely.

"I cured myself..." She trailed off, too overcome to say more.

But he only smiled at her; one of his true smiles that lit her from within. "I knew you could."

Her heart swelled with love and joy and gratitude, so she threw her arms around his neck and buried her face in his shoulder. In turn, he wrapped his arms around her and held her close, his breath coming in short, trembling gasps. Relief poured off him, though it might have been her own. In that moment, she could not tell where *Kali* ended and *Elan* began. And she didn't care.

"What's happened?" It took Kali a second to recall Drake's name. The fear in his voice made Kali pull back enough to look at him, kneeling beside her and Stonewall. The rest of Stonewall's squad stood nearby, a stunned Talon in their grip.

The moment Kali met Drake's eyes, he smiled. "You're...you?"

"I think so." She looked at Stonewall, who still held her. "I feel...more like myself."

He brushed his thumb along her jaw and she leaned into his touch. She felt rather than heard his words in a kind of silent speech. *Kali, I was afraid you were lost.*

I think I was, she replied, belatedly realizing she'd not used her voice, either. They stared at each other in shared shock.

"Now that *that's* settled," Flint said. "Can we leave this shithole already?"

30

THIRTY

F oley's stump ached with a phantom pain as he looked from one face to another, searching for someone he could reason with. He'd known many of these mages for years; by the One, he'd known Hazel since the sentinels had brought her to the bastion as a babe. How many hours had he spent in the garden with Druce and Wylie, coaxing their crops from seedlings?

He saw only strangers now.

Every hearth in the mages' common room blazed, mirroring the fires in the hearts of these fools. More than any other mage, Sadira had come alive, busying herself with unlocking collars and gathering what supplies they would need in the wide-open world. Every so often, she'd pause to glance in the direction of the sentinel garrison, worry plain on her face.

"You'll never make it out of the gates," Foley heard himself say. "The sentinels will kill you. They won't even bother to bury your corpses – they'll just fling you over the falls."

Hazel rubbed her bare neck, her collar at her feet. "I don't care. I can't stay here a moment longer."

"Nor can I," Wylie said as Sadira began to work her collar. "If I'm going to die, I want to die as a free woman."

Druce tossed his collar into the nearest hearth. The leather caught almost immediately, the hematite sending up red flames. "Besides, have you seen any sentinels around, lately? Just a few burnies are left standing. The odds are in our favor – for once."

Anger flushed through Foley's body, making his missing hand ache further. "I thought you had no wish to leave."

"That was before things got so bad," Druce said. "Sadira, I'll need a few minutes to get my belongings."

"Us too." Castor, Oly, Fellan, and Jep stood nearby, collars already gone. They were the only young men left in the bastion. Good boys, all of them. Foley's heart sank at the gleam in their eyes. By now, eleven mages had gathered in the common room, some already with knapsacks and traveling packs, eager to meet their deaths outside the bastion gates. The sight pierced Foley's heart. What good had he done as First Mage? They were all going to die.

Along with his daughter. For if these mages fled, if the bastion truly succumbed to chaos, there was no way in Ea's realm that High Commander Argent would allow Talon to keep her position – let alone her head.

Foley's eyes stung and he clenched his hand into a fist. "Freedom is worth your lives?"

Several of the others exchanged glances, but it was Hazel who spoke. "I don't know, but I'd like to find out."

"Prisoners or prey: we're fucked no matter what we do," Druce added, kicking the hearth logs to send the remains of his collar into crimson flames. "May as well do what we want."

Sadira nodded, but her gaze was distant. "Eris' people should be at the docks. You must leave."

"You're not coming with us?" Druce asked.

"Not yet. I must gather some items and find Kali."

Wylie frowned. "Aye, about that... You said she'll be bringing some sentinels with her?"

"Eris won't be pleased," Hazel added.

"We must all work as one to survive," Sadira replied.

Druce gave a snorting laugh. "Have you *met* Eris?"

The others began to file out of the common room to gather the last of their belongings. No one gave Foley more than a second glance, each wholly absorbed with romantic notions of freedom. Foley's heart sank with their steps.

Sadira came last and held up the key, gleaming in the hearthlight. The air around her was too warm and Foley could not take a proper breath. "This may be your final chance," she said quietly as she pressed the key into his palm.

Foley shoved the iron piece back to her hand. "My last chance passed a long time ago."

With that, he slipped into the night. The cold struck him like a sword in the heart and his missing hand ached fiercely, but he ignored the pain. Nothing mattered but Talaséa. He had let his child go once; he would not leave her side again. Snow fell in silent sheets across the bastion courtyard, thick enough to mute all sound and cut his line of sight; thick enough to blot the footsteps of the mages who rushed toward the outside world. Foley followed them as far as the bastion gates, but while they made a bid for freedom, he went back to the sentinel garrison, back to his daughter's side.

* * *

Had Talon not watched the transformation with her own eyes, she'd not have believed that the thrall who had taken over Mage Halcyon could have been defeated. But the proof was in Stonewall's arms, sobbing into his shoulder while he held her close, as if the ragged little mage was someone precious, someone worth saving.

Someone he loved – *openly.* Bitterness caught in her throat and she tasted bile.

The sound of footsteps and creaking iron meant that Rook was freeing the Sufani and the captive mages; soon Talon would be even more outnumbered. She cast quick, careful glances to the sentinels who held her. Flint, Milo, and Beacon were all engrossed in the tableau, frozen with shock. This was her moment.

348

But not everyone was distracted. Fierce green eyes met hers as the renegade mage held himself in a ready stance between Talon and the ill-fated lovers, Stonewall's dropped sword in his grip. "Give me a reason not to kill you," he muttered to Talon.

The Sufani and freed mages joined the others now, all of them closing around Talon, eyes upon her like daggers. She was alone, captured, with enemies on all sides. Her heart beat wildly against her breast and despair stung her eyes.

"You've lost, Commander," Stonewall said quietly as he helped Halcyon to her feet. "But no one else has to get hurt. Surrender, and we'll leave in peace."

"Speak for yourself," one of the Sufani women snapped.

Faint footsteps sounded. At any other time, Talon would have missed them completely, but so much hematite in her system made every sense alight and attuned. She knew the tread, and for the first time this night, true fear swelled in her chest. *No. Not him. Not now.*

"You'll not leave at all," she said, hoping to distract the traitors, but it was too late. Foley entered the detention area, causing the others to glance over, startled.

"Foley?" Halcyon said weakly. She leaned against Stonewall, who had one arm wrapped around her waist.

But Talon's father ignored his fellow mage and instead gave Talon a pleading look as if they were the only two people here. "We must leave. Now."

Her heart stuck to her throat. Her mouth opened, but her tongue was clumsy and useless. "Argent is on his way. It's too late."

"No, Talaséa." Foley stepped forward, brushing past the sentinels as if they were plants in his beloved garden. "Where there is life, there is hope. There is no other path for us now."

Every sense screamed to go to his side, but even had she not been held prisoner, she could not have allowed herself that weakness. Her body burned, her vision swam, her heart sped so fast she could not catch her breath. The litany rolled through her mind, over and over. *Too late. I've failed.* Fear clawed her throat but she stifled a scream. "I can fix this," she said to him. "Father, I can still make it right."

Soft gasps erupted, but she ignored them as she would a fluttering moth. Only one thing mattered, and he was shaking his head. "Oh, child," he whispered. "If only that were true."

She clenched her jaw. "You must get back to the bastion, or–"

"Or what?" He spread his hand and hook. "Let them go, Talaséa. They don't matter."

"What should we do?" Milo whispered. Of them all, he stood closest to Talon, just within reach.

Flint scoffed. "Leave them to their family troubles and put this sodding place behind us."

"Aye," Stonewall murmured. Out of the corner of her eye, Talon watched him take Halcyon's hand, saw them exchange one of those wordless looks that only passed between lovers, friends…and family.

Hematite flowed through her veins; her vision swam crimson with the burn. Rage filled her heart, pure and sweet, and it washed her clean. In one fluid movement she shoved Flint to the floor, where the girl yelped in surprise before scrambling to her feet. The others lunged for Talon, but fear and hematite spurred her movements to unnatural quickness. She knocked back Beacon and Rook, freed one of Flint's daggers, and buried it into Milo's heart. The burnie cried out and staggered backward while his twin drove herself against Talon, blue eyes blazing with fury.

"You miserable bitch," Flint shrieked. "I'll kill you where you stand!"

Talon had reared back to defend herself, but Foley was not without his own mettle. He grabbed Flint's hair, snatching the loose tail and yanking her head back, his hook raised as if to spear her throat. But the girl slammed her shoulder into Foley's nose, and he fell back, ducking his head as blood streamed between his fingers.

Strong hands grabbed Talon as the Sufani ripped away her keys and shoved her into the cell where Mage Halcyon had been only moments ago. It had all happened so fast. The lock shut with a clang that bounced off the walls.

"Mi?" Flint knelt beside her brother, who lay whimpering in a rapidly expanding pool of blood. "Mi! Look at me! Beacon...?"

The mender was at the lad's side, along with Halcyon. Beacon's hands were steady as he tore off a piece of Milo's shirt and began stuffing it beneath the boy's cuirass to steady the dagger.

"Take the fucking thing out!" Flint's voice was high and thin.

"Not yet, might make the bleeding worse," Beacon muttered, and then looked at the mage beside him. "He's got a few minutes, but this is beyond my skill. Can you...?"

Halcyon bit her bruised lip. "No, but Sadira could."

"But the hematite," Rook began.

"Won't be a problem for Sadira," Halcyon interrupted. "We must find her."

No sooner had the words escaped her lips did the others carefully lift Milo's form to carry him out of the detention area. "Flint, talk to him," Beacon said as they went. "Keep him conscious."

"You'd better not fucking die on me, you stupid oaf," Flint replied, her fierce words marred by sobs. "Otherwise, I'll make you regret it..."

Their words trailed off as the group ascended the stairs. Several of the Sufani cast dark looks at Talon, but a command from their leader made them continue, helping the additional mages as well. Only Rook remained, watching Talon and Foley as the others slipped out.

"Release me," Talon said to her. "That's an order."

Rook shook her head. "Mage Clementa is right. Argent's coming. It's too late." With that, she backed out of the detention area and followed her companions.

The lack of bodies and sound made the space heavy. Talon looked at her father through the hematite and iron bars. By now, he'd staunched the blood flow from his nose with his sleeve, and her heart tightened at the red stain on his left cuff. He came closer to the cell and gripped the bars with his only hand as he lowered himself to sit before the door. He pressed his fingertips to his nose, grimaced, and closed his eyes in concentration.

"What are you doing?"

"Never been much of a healer even without hematite around," he replied wryly. "But I must try to do something for this broken nose."

Talon scowled. "That's not what I meant."

"I'm not leaving you alone."

She knelt before the bars, gripping them with white knuckles. "You must! Argent will kill you if he finds you here."

"I have remained while all the rest have fled," Foley said. "Doesn't that count for anything?"

Her blood raced, but with ice; she no longer felt the burn. "It won't. Argent's coming to kill you all. Da, you must leave. Please!"

But her father only gave her a sad smile and reached through the bars to touch her cheek with his remaining fingers. "Never again, child. Never again."

* * *

The coach-and-four pulled up to the garrison gates unhindered. When Eris opened the door, a gust of cold air swept inside, making her shiver.

"No guards?" she asked Leal as she clambered out. Seren's light, the cold stole her breath! The instant she stepped into the open air, she both regretted the action and thanked the stars for Serla Vellis' fine, fur-lined cloak. She hefted one of the traveling cases, filled with warm clothing for the mages they had come to rescue.

Brice, Rilla, and the others had already dismounted. Leal turned her back to Eris and went to the gates, where there were no sentinels in sight. Eris tried to set aside her irritation at Leal's non-answer, and instead glanced over at Auda, Izell, Gow, and Davet. "As we planned: you'll go to the docks and secure a boat – or two. Leave the carriage."

The four mages turned their horses away, trotting through sheets of snow and empty city streets. Only Auda and Izell knew how to ride, but the other two had gotten a hasty lesson on the road to the city. Their mounts' footfalls made no sound against the snow. There was no sound at all, actually, save for the faint drum of Eris' heart. She pulled the cloak closer and gestured to the gates. "The coach-and-four will be fine for a few minutes. Shall we?"

"Time to see if your little alliance will pay off," Cai muttered as they approached the gates.

Eris could not help a sigh of relief when she pushed open the unlocked gates and stepped through. Sadira and the burnie twins had made good on their word – at least for now. The garrison courtyard was empty and silent, the only movement from the falling snow. As the group crossed the open space, Rilla cast a dubious look at the sky and tugged her cloak tighter.

Ben scrubbed his beard. "The sooner we find our friends, the sooner we can leave."

Brice shot him a knowing look. "Fear it might freeze off, eh?"

"Stranger things have happened," he replied wryly, and Brice and Rilla chuckled.

Leal hissed a command and they fell silent. She pointed her spear across the courtyard, in the general direction of the bastion. "I can hardly see through this mess. That's our destination, yes?"

Eris frowned as she glanced around. "Kali and Drake will likely be in the garrison's detention area, but…"

She'd been here before, many times, but never at night, during such a heavy snowfall, and without the company of sentinels who knew their way around. The last time she had been to the garrison's detention area, she'd been fuming and had not paid the place as much mind as she ought to have.

"But…?" Leal prompted.

"I'm not sure how to find it," Eris admitted. "The garrison's like a rabbit warren if you don't know your way around."

The Sufani did not reply, but Marcen pointed toward the bastion. "Who's that?"

The group came to a stop, weapons raised and magic ready. Energy teemed within Eris' veins and she tensed, squinting through the snowfall. Frozen flakes stuck to her lashes, further obscuring her vision, but eventually she spotted a familiar flash of strawberry blond hair.

"Hazel," she said, and rushed forward. "It's other mages," she added, calling over her shoulder. Her friends followed, and soon the two groups met just outside the bastion gates. All the bastion mages carried traveling packs and wore multiple layers of clothing, along with nervous expressions.

"What in the sodding stars are you lot doing out here?" Cai asked, glancing between Druce and Jep.

"Leaving this place, for good." Druce grinned at them; his dark brows were already speckled with frost. "Sadira told us to meet you at the docks, but I'm not complaining to find you here."

"Where are the sentinels?" Eris asked.

Hazel jerked her head in the direction of the garrison. "Sick or dead, I guess. All we know is they don't have as much hematite as they want."

"Aye, so this looked to be our best chance for freedom," Druce added.

Eris and Adrie exchanged looks. Saving all the remaining bastion mages was *not* in the plan. But now that the others were here, Eris couldn't very well deny them the chance to flee. But nor could she divide her forces any more than she already had. She glanced between her allies and realized that they were all waiting for her cue – even the non-mages. Even Leal, though the Sufani's gaze never strayed too long from the garrison around them.

"Auda, Izell, and a few others just left for the docks," Eris said, pointing toward the garrison's main gates. "There's a carriage waiting outside. Take it. You should still be able to catch them if you hurry."

"How in the void did you get a coach and horses?" Druce asked.

"Long story," Cai said.

"Right. I hope we'll get to hear it." Druce glanced at his companions, and then back to Cai, one brow raised. "You lot need any help?"

Cai looked at Eris. "Dunno. Do we?"

All eyes, including Leal's, fell upon Eris again. No doubt Gideon would have urged her to keep them around, if only to fortify her allies' numbers. More mages meant more power... but also more potential for someone to get hurt. Despite Druce's assured expression, Eris read the fear in his eyes and the tension in his stance, and he was not alone in those feelings.

These mages were not yet the fierce, rebellious allies she'd come to trust with her life; these were soft bastion folk, spurred to escape only through desperation. Perhaps they could be more one day, as she had, but not right now. Besides, Izell and the others would no doubt have a difficult time at the docks; more magical aid would probably benefit them.

So she pointed toward the garrison's main gates. "We'll be fine. Go, and be safe."

As the bastion mages rushed off, Eris caught Leal's gaze. The Sufani gave her a single nod, as if in approval, and then turned to head toward the garrison itself. The others followed, leaving Eris to scowl over her relief at Leal's nod. What did it matter if Leal approved of her actions? Leal was only here because she had a personal stake in the success of this mission.

An icy blast of wind prompted Eris to hurry after the others. As she drew closer, she spotted a group of folks emerging from the garrison: sentinels. Eris sucked in a breath of freezing air that hit her lungs like a punch as she called a warning to her allies. But there was nowhere to run, nor time. Eris' heart beat in her throat as the others raised their own weapons.

Leal squinted through the falling snow, and then darted forward, calling out in Sufa. An answering shout rose from the other group and several of them peeled away from their allies to race toward Leal. Only when the four Sufani were embracing in the garrison courtyard did Eris realize that she and her friends had stumbled upon Leal's family, whom the sentinels had thrown into their prison.

Which meant...

Huddling in her cloak, Eris hurried past the Sufani toward a group of sentinels carrying a prone form. Kali limped after them.

Eris couldn't suppress a thrill of relief at seeing her friend alive and moving. "Kali!"

The snowfall muted Eris' voice, but Kali jerked upright, her dark eyes falling on Eris a beat later. Seren's light, Kali looked dreadful: her hair was matted, smears of dirt and blood marred her cheeks and forehead, and the shadows beneath her eyes were darker than ever. But she was alive, thank the stars! Several other mages came behind Kali and the sentinels; Eris recognized the other bastion mages she'd sent with the Sufani, including Sirvat, no longer pregnant, who clutched a small bundle to her chest.

Kali smiled, but the expression faded almost at once as she turned her attention back to the sentinels'—and Drake's—burden: Milo.

Frowning, Eris hurried to her friends, the other mages and her Assembly allies on her heels. Eris grabbed her Kali's arm. "Come on. We've got to get out of here."

"Not yet." Kali twisted out of Eris' grasp and continued with the sentinels and Drake. Spots of blood dotted the snow behind them. Drake glanced up once, noted his Assembly friends, and looked back down at Milo, his face stony as the group hurried along. Leal and the other Sufani spoke in their native tongue, Leal gesticulating to the gates while Aderey pointed toward the bastion.

Eris trotted after Kali, who was clearly struggling to keep the others' pace. "What are you doing? We must leave. Now!"

Kali didn't look at her. "We will – after we see to Milo. Is Sadira in the bastion?"

"I don't know. I imagine." Eris reached for Kali's arm again. "She can catch up. Kali you must–"

"I *must* help Milo," Kali broke in, ignoring Eris' reach and limping after the hemies.

Eris stared at her friend. It was as if Kali spoke another language. Kali's inexplicable love for the sod Stonewall was one thing, but why bother with the burnie? The effort of weeks of speculation and planning seemed to press upon Eris' chest, making her breath come in short foggy gasps. She had cooperated with dregs who hated her kind. She had waited and watched and listened before storming this place. She had worked *with* sentinels to return to this prison! All to free her best friend in the world, who now behaved like a stranger.

How dare she? Eris clenched her fists and her next words came out as a snarl. "Forget the sodding hemie! Or are you fucking this one, too?"

Kali whirled around faster than Eris had ever seen, dark eyes wet and red-rimmed, and filled with her own fury. "He's going to die without help,

Eris. Stay or go; do what serves *you* best. As usual. But leave me alone."

With that, she turned to limp after the sentinels. One of the hemies fell back to offer her shoulder in support. Kali accepted the sentinel's aid and the two women hurried after their allies.

Their allies. Eris stood in place, buffeted by a wind she no longer felt.

"Eris." It was Adrie, supporting Sirvat and her baby. "We must get to the bastion. Now."

"I'm not going back there," Eris replied, hefting her bag. "We brought you some clothes and can probably still catch up to the carriage."

Sirvat had bundled her baby beneath her own tunic and cloak, so they were skin-to-skin, and clutched the newborn close. "I can't run around out there with him, Eris! It's too cold and he's so little. I must get him warm before I can think of leaving!"

Adrie nodded. "Come on, Eris; let's regroup. Maybe pick up some more warm things while we're at it. Even Vellis didn't have enough cloaks for everyone."

"The sentinels–"

"Won't be an issue," Leal said as she returned to Eris' side. "Da says they're all as useless as wet yarn, and the commander's locked up in the garrison. We have a little time."

"No," Cai replied, shaking his head. "We don't. We must leave now. Who knows what tricks that bitch of a commander tucked away in her armor?"

Sirvat rubbed the bundle in her arms. "I'm going back to the bastion, just for a few minutes. Just to get him warm."

Eris gritted her teeth, and glanced back at Kali and the hemies, who had reached the bastion gates. Her hands stole to her own stomach, where her and Gideon's child grew.

The past was a lost cause; Eris had to protect the future. "Fine, but be quick; we're leaving soon – forever."

31

THIRTY-ONE

S tonewall stepped inside the mages' common room, careful not to jostle poor Milo overmuch, and glanced at Kali for direction. She pointed to the nearest table, and he, Drake, and Beacon eased forward to lay Milo atop the polished woodgrain. Beacon carefully removed the dagger and they began to strip off Mi's gear. The sentinels' part would be done soon, although Stonewall hated the idea of standing around while others did all the work. It was Parsa all over again.

Kali pulled back Milo's undertunic and studied the wound while Flint hovered. "You think Sadira can really help him?" she asked Kali.

"She'll try."

"Try?" Flint's voice broke on the word.

Kali met Stonewall's gaze; he felt rather than heard the tenor of her request, so he said Flint's name. "You know how this works," he said when the young woman looked at him. "Give her space."

Tears shone in Flint's eyes, although her face was still tight with rage. "Go fuck yourself."

"Flint," Kali said calmly. "Go find Sadira."

"No need." A familiar, white-haired woman entered the room, a knapsack and Kali's viol case in her grip. Warmth bloomed out around her, making Stonewall's fingers and toes ache with relief.

"Kali!" Sadira set down her burdens and hurried to her friend, but stopped just short of embracing the dark-haired mage and instead looked at Milo.

"He needs need your help," Kali said. "*Our* help. I'll do what I can."

Sadira's collar and hematite torc were gone; she pulled a key from her pocket and removed Kali's collar, letting it fall to the floor. Kali rubbed her neck, but kept her focus on Milo and the bright, angry wound above his heart.

Sadira glanced between Stonewall and Beacon. "This will be painful. Hold him."

Flint sucked in a breath but Stonewall urged her to be still as he and Beacon took positions at Milo's chest and legs. "Talk to him," Stonewall said to Flint as the mages got to work. "Let him know you're here."

Flint swiped her nose and bent to Milo's right ear, squeezing his hand as she began whispering. Kali and Sadira closed their eyes and pressed their hands over Milo's wound. Nothing happened at first, until Milo tensed and cried out, twisting against the table as if trying to escape.

"Shut up, you big baby," Flint said hoarsely. "You're going to be fine. But if you die on me, I'll hunt you down in Nox's void and kick your sorry ass right into your next life, do you hear?"

Milo cried out again and his body spasmed, thudding against the table. Stonewall braced his palms against Milo's hips, holding the younger man firmly. Beacon and Drake did the same at Milo's feet; Drake shot Stonewall a look that clearly said, *Will this work?*

Stonewall ignored him and focused on Milo. The squad had rallied around their fallen brother-in-service, helping in any way they could. The knowledge made Stonewall's heart swell.

Please keep Milo here a while longer, he prayed silently, thinking of Tor's golden, glowing eyes. *He can't be done with this life yet.*

Kali and Sadira's faces contorted with effort, and gradually, as Stonewall and the others watched in muted amazement, the wound in Milo's chest began to knit. Skin wove over blood and muscle as if on a loom of flesh. Stonewall's heart began to race – not just from his recent hematite dose. Milo was going to pull through!

But the knitting ceased. The skin ripped as if Mi had been stabbed all over again, and blood pulsed anew from the wound. Sadira sucked in a breath but did not lift her trembling hands.

"No," Kali muttered. Gods above, her face was pale and her cheeks had sunken against her bones, giving her a gaunt, starved look. Her eyes looked huge and black, but there was no trace of starlight within them.

Renewed fear tugged at Stonewall. "What's wrong?"

"I need..." Kali's eyes closed as she grimaced in pain. Then he heard her voice in his mind, in that silent speech. *We need more help than I anticipated.*

He tried and failed to reply in kind, and instead spoke his words aloud. "What can I do?"

Flint looked between them, panic rising in her voice. "What's going on?"

Kali's dark eyes flew open and landed on Stonewall. *Remember Neff?*

Tor help him, he did. His guts twisted at the memory of the Aredian hunter who'd been turned into a thrall; the man whose life Kali had stolen when he had attacked her. She had saved herself, but in doing so had killed Neff, and somehow taken his energy to use later.

"You need...strength?" he managed. Kali nodded.

"What in the blazing void are you talking about?" Flint asked.

Beacon and several of the others echoed the sentiment, although Eris was oddly silent. Kali had closed her eyes and returned her focus to Milo's wound, which had not gotten any worse – for now.

"Kali can pull strength from one place and send it to another," Sadira said. "Like a river flows from the mountains to the sea."

"Is that...safe?" Rook asked. Startled, Stonewall glanced over his shoulder at his squad-mate, who brushed snow off of her shoulders with one hand, the other clutching a bulging sack. A familiar weapons belt, sword, and two daggers were tucked beneath her arm.

More startling, though, was the woman beside her who shook snow off a white and black hooded cloak. From Milo's description, it could only have been Serla Natanaree who took in the scene with wide eyes.

Rook motioned in the direction of the bastion gates. "Found her outside."

"You can do magic upon hematite?" Serla Natanaree asked Kali, breathless.

Color rose in Kali's cheeks but it was Sadira who answered. "Stand aside and let us work. And hematite is not the pollution you believe it to be."

"Solution," Kali murmured. "I think."

The Cipher ducked her head and did as instructed. Stonewall searched her for signs of anger, fear, or distrust, but he found only confusion. Out of habit, he glanced over at Drake, who also studied the Cipher; Drake gave Stonewall a familiar look. *I'll be on my guard, too.*

Relief swept over Stonewall at the notion, although he tried to ignore the feeling – and his lying brother. No doubt he'd have to deal with Drake later, but not now.

Flint shook her head and glared at Kali. "Can you help my brother or not?"

"I can," Kali replied. "I just need..." She faltered. "I'm not strong enough on my own."

Sadira held out her hand. "I can–"

"*No,*" Kali broke in. She was trembling now, beads of sweat appearing on her forehead. "No," she said more gently. "You're helping enough. I can't—won't—take anything from you."

Pain emanated from her: at once an old wound that had never properly healed; and a newer, sharper pang akin to desire, laced with guilt. Had Stonewall not been so attuned to her, he would have missed the feelings, or perhaps mistaken them for his own.

But none of that mattered to him as much as the one truth he'd come to realize, which washed away his own doubts and fears and granted him the strength to meet her gaze unflinching. *I love you.* "You are strong," he added aloud. "Kali, you've fought thralls, from within and without. Surely you can–"

"Fight the Laughing God, too?" Kali broke in. Tears trickled down the sides of her nose and his heart twisted at the fear in her voice. "No, Stone. There isn't enough magic in the world to do that."

Flint made a noise of exasperation. "You need strength? Here." She thrust out her free hand, the one not clutching Milo's. "Take whatever you need. Just..." Her voice broke. "Just save my brother."

Beacon had been following the exchange with furrowed brows, but now he shook his head. "I don't think that's—"

"I've never given two shits what you think, frip," Flint snapped. "I'm not going to start now."

"You don't have to do this," Stonewall began. "I can—"

But the burnie silenced him with a cutting glare. "He's *my* brother. Besides, Milo would do this for me in a heartbeat. You know that." She ripped off her glove and offered Kali her hand again, trembling like an autumn leaf. "Let me help him, for once."

Kali had already made her decision. Her resolve poured over Stonewall like a sheet of falling rain; any lingering hesitation was likely due to the presence of so many witnesses.

Well, he would make it easier for her. "It's all right," he said to Serla Natanaree and Rook, who still looked uncertain. "You can trust Kali."

Kali accepted Flint's hand and squeezed. "I don't know if this will hurt, but I'll stop before I kill you."

The Cipher sucked in a breath; Beacon's face was set with a mender's grim determination. Rook's eyes went round and she shot Stonewall a look that was part terror, part disbelief. Stonewall tried to make his expression calm and reassuring, despite the thrum of anxiety in his heart. "Go on," he said to Kali.

He also tried to send her some measure of his love, but she'd shut herself away again, wholly lost in her concentration. Nothing happened at first, but then Kali's brow furrowed as more sweat gleamed upon her skin. Flint went rigid, clenching her jaw as she had done the last time Beacon had stitched her up. Sadira gave a soft gasp, and then ducked her head and pressed her hand to Mi's wound again – harder. Milo cried wordlessly, arching up from the table and struggling in the men's grips. His cries turned into whimpers and his breath hitched and hiccupped.

The wound started to knit again, as before, but with each moment, the knitting went faster. Kali's breath came in shallow pants and Stonewall could not pull his eyes from her, not even to watch Milo or Flint. The others would look after the twins; right now his attention was for the woman he loved, whom he had almost lost. Her face turned gray and ashen and her hands, covered in Milo's blood, trembled harder. As Stonewall had seen before, Kali's life drained away as she tried to save another.

Now Stonewall risked a glance at Flint, only to see that she too looked as if she stood at the void's edge. She bore it silently, gaze latched on her brother.

At last Milo went quiet, his head lolling to one side as his breathing evened out and his body relaxed. The wound had scabbed over, leaving only an angry, crimson mark. Flint and Sadira both exhaled, while Kali dropped Flint's hand and leaned her weight against the table, her arms shaking.

Before Stonewall could go to her, Eris was at her side, touching her shoulder. "Kali?"

"I'm fine." Kali managed a weak smile first at her friend, and then at Stonewall. His heart lifted at the sight even though he could not convince his face to return the expression. Blinking hard, Kali looked at Flint. "Are you...?"

Flint was gaping between her hand and Milo's wound. "I'm...I'm fine. And he's..." She choked back a sob as Milo let out a long, peaceful sigh. "Ea's balls. You fixed him. You *saved* him!"

But at what cost? Stonewall thought.

While the mages got cleaned up, Beacon dug around Milo's belt and prepared a dose of hematite. "But...how?" the mender asked Sadira, notes of wonder in his voice.

"Magic," Flint said, rolling her eyes, but her expression softened as she touched Milo's cheek.

Beacon carefully gave the younger man the hematite mixture. "Yes, but *how?*"

Kali clutched the rag she'd used to clean her hands. "I think my magic is...changing, or growing. I never used to be able to do magic on hematite, until..." She flushed and met Stonewall's gaze. "On our journey here. Do you remember when we escaped the Canderi?"

"Which time?" he asked wryly.

She smiled. "The first time. I think that escape...awoke something in my magic. Something new."

"What makes you think that?" Drake asked.

Kali shook her head, her tangled hair swaying. "Something I learned recently, when the Fata..." She trailed off and looked at the table, waves of sorrow and bitterness sweeping from her.

Stonewall left his place by Milo and went to her, stepping around Eris so that he could stand at Kali's other side. He put an arm around her shoulders and tried not to grimace at how insubstantial she felt. "A story for another time. We must move out as soon as we can."

Eris had followed his progress with narrowed eyes, but at his words, she nodded once. "Yes, the rest of us *mages*," she emphasized the word, "should be on our way. Anyone who wishes to stop us can jump off the waterfall."

"Charming, as ever," Aderey muttered. The Sufani and Assembly folk had wisely kept out of the way during the healing, but now the group had reconvened. Stonewall recognized one of the women as his squad's "captive" before Heartfire, but had not the time nor inclination to speak to her. Besides, she probably wanted nothing to do with *him*, either.

Eris shot the Sufani man a warning look, but Leal—Stonewall recognized her with a start—returned the look in kind. "Will you come with us, then?" she said to Stonewall. "You and your squad?"

"If you'll have us," he replied.

"We must hurry," Rook said. "Talon's locked away but Argent is coming. We *must* be gone before he arrives."

Was it Stonewall's imagination, or was there a trace of guilt in her voice? She stood hunched as if trying to make herself smaller.

"How *do* you know Argent's coming?" he asked.

Before Rook could answer, Drake grabbed Stonewall's arm. His green eyes—their mother's eyes—were wide. "If the High Commander finds us, everyone here is as good as dead."

Stonewall jerked out of Drake's grasp, though the stricken look that crossed his brother's face made him wince. *No,* he told himself. *He's not my brother anymore. My brother is dead.*

"There are too many of us for the boats," Leal said to Eris.

Kali frowned. "What boats?"

Eris ignored her. "Well, then I suppose the hemies will have to swim."

"Did you not see the sodding blizzard out there?" Flint growled. "How in Tor's name is Milo supposed to make it through that?"

Beacon nodded. "We won't last an hour without the right gear."

Rook pointed to the sack she'd brought. "I found some cold weather gear, and your armor," she said to Stonewall. "But it's not enough for everyone."

Cai held up his hands. "Are you hemies deaf as well as stupid? You're *not* coming with us."

"*We* saved your sorry asses," Flint replied. "Without me and Milo's help, you'd all be outside those gates, looking in. You owe us."

"We owe you *nothing*," Cai shot back.

Eris nodded. "Besides, without magic, your brother would be dead."

"That's not fair and you know it," Kali said. "Why did you come back, if not to free the rest of us?"

"Most of my people are already gone," Eris said. "And I'm starting to think I should leave you here with the hemies you love so sodding much."

Anger flushed through Kali, suffusing Stonewall with its heat. He had to work to shut away the feeling. "Fine," Kali replied. "Run away again. Leave us to be collared and caged while you traipse about the countryside."

"You're deluded," Eris said. "Utterly hoodwinked. Do you think they," she gestured at Stonewall, "care about your freedom, your *life*? They only want what they can get out of you."

Stonewall bristled. He'd been silent so far, but he'd be damned if he let Eris slander him any longer. "If you care so much about mages, why'd you leave the others here? You know what it feels like to wear the collar, yet you ran off and sealed your friends' fates."

The look she gave him could have burned a wart off a mule. "Keep your mouth shut, Sentinel, if you know what's good for you."

"If you threaten Stonewall, you threaten me," Kali said.

Eris glared at her. "Idiot."

"Selfish," Kali shot back. "You always do this! You always run away when life gets too difficult. You abandoned me at Starwatch, and you left me here."

"I had no choice but to leave Starwatch. The hemies hated me–"

"Strange how *your* problems are always someone else's fault," Kali broke in, shaking her head. "Fine. I don't care any longer. Just go."

Eris lobbed another acerbic remark, to which Flint replied this time, and the room erupted in shouts. Stonewall and Drake tried to call for an end to the argument, but their words fell on deaf ears. He shot Rook a helpless look, but she'd slipped to the windows, peering outside.

"Enough!" Serla Natanaree's voice boomed over the quarreling factions, stunning them all into silence. Everyone stared at the Circle priestess, who held herself straight as a scepter and every bit as regal. "Petty quarrels prove fruitless while the storm looms."

"What in the void are you jabbering about?" Cai asked.

"It's an old axiom," Stonewall replied. "From the *Promise of the One*. And she's right. We can argue later. For now, we have to leave."

"You mentioned boats?" Serla Natanaree said to Leal.

"Aye, but I doubt there'll be enough room for everyone," Leal replied.

"How did you even get into the city?" Drake asked. "And where'd you get those clothes?"

Leal glowered and skimmed her hands over the fine livery she wore, while the other mages who'd come with Eris shifted in place.

"That's a story for later," Eris replied.

"It's snowing harder," Rook said. "Wherever we go, we'll need to get there quickly, else we'll be trapped here."

"Or not make it at all." Beacon scrubbed his beard in thought. "But the snow might slow Argent down."

The Circle priestess considered. "There might be another way…" Her eyes rested on Milo, but her gaze seemed distant. "The temple of the One rests upon a hill. Do you know what lies beneath it?"

Surprisingly, it was Aderey who replied. "I have heard…rumors," the Sufani man said slowly, his sharp green eyes studying the priestess.

"Tunnels beneath the temple, buried deep within the earth, that lead... " He spread his hands. "Only the One knows where."

Serla Natanaree nodded. "After Milo and Flint came to me, I did some exploring. I believe I have found an alternate way out of the city."

The room went still. Kali tensed against Stonewall's side, her doubts filtering into his own thoughts. Not that he was without doubt, himself, but between the two of them, he knew he was more inclined to believe the Cipher's words.

"You believe?" Kali said. "Or you *know*?"

The Circle priestess' voice was stern. "Belief is not for the faint of heart, Mage."

"Maybe, but in this particular situation, I'd rather have knowledge." Kali sighed and ran a hand through her tangled hair, and then glanced at Eris. "What do you think?"

Eris seemed to consider the priestess' words before she shook her head. "*I* must meet our people at the docks. They're waiting for us as we speak."

"I'm with you," Cai said. Some of the other mages nodded in agreement, but the ones who'd been in the garrison's detention area looked uncertain.

Drake cleared his throat and glanced at Leal. "You should go with the Cipher," he said. "Take your family and anyone else who wants to come, and take the One's way out of the city. Sounds like it'll be the easier path. The rest of us," his mouth curved in a mischievous grin that Stonewall recognized, "can make our own road on the river."

"This is madness," Beacon said. "You do realize there's a blizzard outside, right? We'll be dead before we get anywhere."

Serla Natanaree withdrew a pouch from within her cloak. She tossed it to the mender, who caught it neatly, examined the contents, and gave her an astonished look. "More hematite?"

Flint narrowed her eyes. "I thought you said you couldn't find any more."

"I was wrong," the Cipher replied.

I don't like this, Kali said through the bond she and Stonewall shared. It was a testament to the severity of the situation that neither of them found the experience odd. *I don't trust her.*

So it's the river for us? he replied in kind.

We don't have many choices. The river, it is. She looked at Sadira. "What do you think?"

"I can help keep the worst of the cold at bay, but I believe that the One has brought us all together for a reason. One thing is certain: our paths lead away from this place." Sadira hesitated, then added, "I do not wish to be underground, although I would like to see the One god's home in this city."

Eris scoffed. "Well, *we* came up with a perfectly reasonable–" Leal coughed into her glove and Eris rolled her eyes, but conceded. "Well, it's *a* plan. *Without* the Circle's aid."

Sirvat cradled a small bundle to her chest. "Eris, I can't get on some rickety boat on a river! Not in this weather." She looked at the Circle priestess. "Will you swear by the One that you mean us no harm? That you'll not see us thrown into a bastion again?"

All eyes fell upon Serla Natanaree, who kept her chin high. "I swear by the One and all the gods: while I breathe, you will not be imprisoned."

"I think it's a grand idea," Leal said, nodding to her father and mother. "Take Dia and the rest of our family and get out of this place."

"You're not coming with us?" Ytel asked, incredulous.

"We'll meet again, but I swore an oath."

"You and your oaths," Ytel hissed. "You're as foolish as your father."

The groups split apart to make last-minute arrangements. Stonewall gathered near Milo with his squad-mates, Kali, and Sadira, who now felt as if they belonged with the sentinels.

"Here," Rook said as she offered Stonewall the sack. Within was not only his gear, but woolen tunics and leggings for all the sentinels to wear beneath their armor. While the others shed their gear and pulled on the warmer clothes, Stonewall began to suit up. His armor felt heavier than he remembered, but the weight was a comfort. As he fastened his greaves, he thanked Rook, who was looking nervously toward the door.

She shrugged and fiddled with her bow. "I'm going to go scout again."

"It's freezing out there," Flint replied, brows knitting. "And you'll be out in it soon enough."

Rook gave Flint a thin smile. "I'll be fine."

Before anyone could object, she slipped to the door. Wind roared inside as she stepped out, but the door closed and battered it away. Stonewall and Flint exchanged glances before the younger woman shrugged. "She knows what she's doing."

"I suppose she does."

As Stonewall buckled on his weapons, he glanced at Kali and Sadira, who were busy adding layers to their own clothes. Kali still looked wretched, but she was smiling at her friend as the two mages spoke in low tones. Though Kali didn't look at Stonewall, the thread of connection that bound their hearts glowed in his mind's eye and love resonated between them. She caught his eye and winked, and his heart soared. Whatever else happened, they would make a bid for freedom. And if he perished, it would be by her side. *We leave together, or not at all.*

"We'll have to wake him to get him dressed," Beacon was saying. Stonewall glanced back at his squad, all suited up, who all now looked at Milo's sleeping form. "He's healing well, but he's not back up to full strength."

"Will he..." Flint chewed her lip. "Will he ever be how he was?"

Beacon exchanged glances with Sadira, who looked grim. "The wound was bad," the Zhee mage said gently. "Milo will survive, but I am uncertain how he will go forward."

"At the very least," Kali added. "He'll need help to recover."

Flint's face set in determination and she nodded. "Right."

Stonewall's attention veered from the conversation when his brother said his name. Drake had come to stand close by him; at Stonewall's look, he jerked his chin away from the others, a question in his eyes. Stonewall frowned and looked away, crossing his arms before his chest to further drive the point home. Drake could take the hint.

One of the civilians who'd come with Eris—a man with an auburn beard—approached and said Drake's name once, softly. Drake went rigid and his face blank, similar to how Stonewall must have looked moments ago. "What are you doing here, Ben?"

"Isn't it obvious?"

"I thought you hated mages."

Stonewall turned back to his squad; this conversation was probably not meant for his ears. Even so, he could not help but notice his brother's hopeful, bewildered expression as the two men slipped off to speak in relative privacy.

"It's odd, isn't it?" Flint said suddenly, catching his attention.

"What is?" Stonewall asked.

She swept a hand across the room before shoving on her glove. "Their common room looks just like ours. Even the kitchens are in the same place. Are their dormitories set up like our barracks?"

Stonewall had only been inside the mage dormitories once before now, and hadn't exactly been studying the layout. He looked around the mages' common room again, seeing it as if for the first time. Although the décor was different than that inside the garrison—a mix of small potted plants and woven wall hangings—the layout did indeed remind him of the garrison.

"More or less," he said.

In his nightmares, he still saw Kali cuffed and bound like a criminal, but he hadn't been treated much differently. His tiny quarters didn't even lock from the inside.

"I wonder if anything else is the same?" Flint said.

A chill passed through Stonewall despite his warm gear. "Maybe more than we know."

32

THIRTY-TWO

Despite everything, a piece of Drake's heart soared at the sight of Ben, wan and hopeful, looking at him with those morning-blue eyes. They stood together in the corner of the mage's common room – a place Drake might have found himself as a prisoner, had his life turned out a little differently.

Drake waited for the inevitable explanation, but Ben only ran slender fingers across a fine, fur-lined cloak trimmed with fox pelt. When Drake could stand the suspense no longer, he exhaled. "What happened to fleeing south?" He tried not to sound as bitter as he felt.

Ben shot him a look Drake could only think of as chagrined. "I…changed my mind. Rather," he nodded to Brice and Rilla, who stood out of earshot but made no secret of watching the two men, "my mind was changed."

Drake nodded to the women, resolving to speak with them as soon as he could. But his former lover had his full attention now. "You had to be convinced to come after me." His own voice sounded flat and monotone, but his heart had sunk back to the earth. "You didn't…*want* to."

"You lied to me," Ben replied. "I was angry."

Something hot stung Drake's eyes and suddenly he was so tired. During the chaos before, he'd been too distracted to notice how exhausted he was, and how much he *hurt*. He wanted to sleep for a decade – at least. He wanted to wake up and realize this was all a dream, with Ben smiling beside him in the golden morning light.

"Why'd you come back here at all, then?" Drake ground out in a hoarse whisper.

Ben thrust the cloak into Drake's arms. "You'll need this."

"Ben–"

"I was wrong," Ben said. "It was dishonorable of me to turn my back on you when you needed my help, and for that, I'm sorry."

Drake gritted his teeth. He knew what was coming. "But...?"

A deep sigh escaped the other man. "But the fact remains that you are a..." He grimaced. "A mage."

"Are you truly so prejudiced?"

Ben went on as if Drake had not spoken. "You lied to me, for the entirety of our...connection. I could maybe learn to accept your...heritage, in time, but I can't abide dishonesty. I can't love someone I can't trust."

No point hiding the bitterness now. The best Drake could hope for was not to shout. "Well, then you're doing us both a favor, because *I* can't trust someone who hates what I am." He dug his fingers in the cloak's fur lining, now damp with his own sweat. "Just go with the others, so you can praise yourself for being the bigger man and showing pity to the filthy, devious moon-blood who–"

Drake's voice failed him; the rest of his words died in his throat. His hands shook and he tossed the cloak to the floor lest he shove it back into Ben's chest. Ben said his name, not without gentleness, but Drake didn't reply. All his focus coalesced into not making any more of a scene.

"I think you should find someplace else to be," Stonewall said as he came to stand at Drake's side.

"I *get* it, Elan," Drake muttered. "You hate me."

"I wasn't talking to you."

Now Drake looked up to see his brother beside him, glaring daggers at Ben. No one could glare quite like Stonewall. Ben glanced between them; if he noted their shared features, he made no comment before he slipped away.

Stonewall did not watch him go, only bent to pick up the cloak. "You're going to need this," he said, offering it to Drake. "Rook couldn't find any gear for you."

Drake accepted the garment numbly, and then met his brother's eyes. "I hated lying to you," he whispered. "It killed me, every day. But so did living as a sentinel. I'm sorry, Elan. I'm so sorry. You're right to hate me."

Stonewall's gaze flickered to some place Drake could not see; for one moment, his brother's expression was strange and distant.

But then he met Drake's eyes. "I can't forgive you yet. One day. But for now..." He sighed. "Blood is blood, *relah*. I love you."

Everything else fell away, even Ben. Drake could only stare at his stubborn, intractable brother, uncomprehending. "You...don't hate me?"

"I never did. I just..." Stonewall sighed again. "You're a royal pain in my ass, sometimes."

"Some things'll never change, eh?" Drake managed a smile. His relief was too big for his body to contain. Surely it would shine out of his skin like sunlight behind a sheet. "I love you, too, *relah*. And you've *always* been a pain in my ass, ever since you were a babe. But I won't hold it against you."

As Drake had hoped, Stonewall grunted at the teasing, but a faint smile curved his mouth. "Suit up as best you can," he said. "I'll give you my sword. It's almost time to leave."

* * *

A familiar weight pressed into Kali's gloved hand; she glanced down to see her battered viol case. She looked up, into Sadira's pale-blue eyes. The Zhee mage offered a tentative smile. "I thought you would not wish to leave it behind."

Kali flipped open the latches and withdrew the viol. Her heart sank at the snapped silver strings that gleamed in the firelight, but otherwise, the instrument was whole. Only because she knew where to look did she notice the seams in the woodgrain from her previous repairs. A brief examination of the viol's particles revealed their true essence: no simple object, but a solid, faithful companion. She glanced over at Stonewall, who was buckling on the last bits of his gear. He did not look her way, but she felt the warm song of his love ripple through her all the same. Everything would work out. She could always get new strings, and if the viol broke again, she would fix it. Carefully, she tucked the instrument back within the padded case, on top of Stonewall's letter.

"Thank you," Kali replied. "And thanks for gathering all my other things as well." She nodded to the traveling pack at her feet, from which she'd already pilfered her warmest clothes. Her knee brace rested on top of the pack; she'd had to remove it to dress in her lined leather leggings.

"Are you...?" Sadira hesitated.

Heat crept up Kali's face and, on a whim, she took Sadira's hand, trying to ignore the persistent, lingering memory of the Fata's hunger for magic. "I was awful to you, before. I'm so sorry. I didn't..." Her face burned like the other mage had lit her on fire. "The Fata wanted your blood—your magic—and I wasn't sure I could control myself. I didn't want you to get hurt."

Sadira looked at their joined hands in bemusement and then met Kali's eyes. "You were not you."

"That's no excuse for my behavior." Kali squeezed her friend's hand. "Please forgive me, Sadira."

The Zhee mage placed her other palm over Kali's, sending a gentle warmth through Kali's entire body. *"Pree, khaar diyah."*

"I hope that's a 'yes,'" Kali managed.

Sadira smiled. "Your hope is well founded."

Gratitude filled Kali's heart, echoing the warmth that her friend had given. She offered what she hoped was a wry smile. "Will you be warm enough in that?"

She gestured to the dyed wool clothes that Sadira wore; her tunic and trousers were shades of brilliant blue, woven in geometric patterns, and her cloak was pale gray.

Sadira, used to Kali's teasing, offered another, broader smile and a bundle of cloth filled with cheese and bread in return. "I will thrive. You should finish preparing yourself for our journey." With that, she went back over to Milo, who still lay sleeping upon one of the tables.

Across the room, Eris watched the exchange. When she met Kali's gaze, she took a single step toward Kali, who rose as well. They had so little time, but she might not get the chance to speak to her old friend again. She gave Eris a small but friendly smile: a peace offering to "Silver Girl."

Then Eris glanced at something over Kali's shoulder, scowled, and turned her back to Kali to speak with the other mages. Confused, Kali went forward anyway, but her knee made her stumble, knocking over her pack. Books, spare clothes, and her knee brace tumbled to the floor. Kali knelt to retrieve her belongings, but her knee screamed in protest, sending her to the floor in a pile of disarray with the rest of her belongings. Tears of frustration and embarrassment pricked at Kali's eyes. She swiped them away as she righted herself and crawled onto the nearest bench, and then picked up the brace. She tried to stuff her knee inside, but the thick layers she wore prevented the brace from closing properly, and when she tried to force it, one of the metal pieces snapped off and clattered to the floor. Knee throbbing, Kali stared at the ruined brace. It was foolish to cry over this, for tears wouldn't solve anything. She swore, hurled the brace away, and ducked her head.

"I knew it'd happen one day," Stonewall said.

"What?"

"You'd get angry enough to chuck something at me." His voice was easy, but Kali could read the concern in his eyes and feel it wavering on the unseen thread that bound them. He stepped toward her, neatly evading the pile of clothes and books at her feet, and knelt at her side, the brace in hand. "What'd I do, this time?"

They were relatively alone in their little corner of the common room and no one paid them any mind. Kali swiped her running nose and managed a weak chuckle. "Quite a lot."

Stonewall began to collect the items spilled from her pack, shooting her another cautious glance. "Are you...all right? I heard... Well, not *heard*, exactly, but felt..." He sighed. "How are you?"

Kali pretended to be engrossed in the food Sadira had provided. "It's Eris."

He was silent.

"She doesn't like you," Kali added.

"Can't imagine why."

She chuckled again, although her humor fled as quickly as it had come. "I don't think she'll ever understand," she gestured to the space between them, "this. Us."

"I suppose I can't blame her."

"Nor can I."

He hesitated. "Do you?"

"Do I what?"

"Understand," he rose to set her pack on the table and took both of her hands, "this? Us?"

Within his words was that warmth she'd felt earlier, although laced with uncertainty, and an idea struck her. She was certain that she was no longer a thrall, but she and Stonewall could still communicate silently, sharing words and emotions along the thread that bound their hearts. Was it a residue of her Fata possession and his Fata blood, or was this connection something more?

Soul-bonded, her heart whispered.

Rather than respond to him aloud, Kali looked into his honey-brown eyes. Concentration was difficult, at first, but she focused on the gratitude that had grown in her heart, and the love that felt as if it had always lived there. With a mental push, she sent the feelings through their bond. His eyes widened before a grin spread across his face, transforming his usual serious expression into one of such joy that Kali could not help but smile too. An answering swell of love filled her to the brim; love and courage, and a resolve for something she could not quite name but recognized anyway.

"I don't understand this—or us—at all," Kali managed. "But I don't care. I suppose our…silent speech is odd, but I don't mind. What about you?"

"I don't think anything between us will ever be normal," he replied. "But I don't mind, either. It could be useful, too. And who knows what's normal, anyway?"

Kali laughed aloud. "Perhaps we'll have to make our own normal."

"That works." Stonewall squeezed her hands again and then glanced down at her feet. He knelt again. When he rose, he held the ragged copy of Fata legends containing *Alem's Wish*. He sat beside her and flipped through the pages carefully, as if wary of accidentally ripping them free of the spine, as his lips moved along with the words he knew.

At last he looked at her again. "Are you certain you're...better?"

Kali closed her eyes. If she concentrated, she could sense Sadira and Eris' different but potent types of magic, and too well did she remember the desperate, driving hunger for that power. Although she could feel no trace of the Fata, how could she be certain the Fata's presence was completely gone?

"I think so," she replied.

His expression was utterly solemn. "What you said in the garden, about the Fata sensing *me*..." He grimaced. "Do you still think that?"

"I do." Her heart fell at the stricken look on his face. "But I think I know why." She laced her fingers with his. "Stonewall, I think you may have Fata blood."

"Did *they* tell you that?"

"Sort of. But much of it is just a sense. A feeling." She sighed in irritation. "I can't quantify how I know, only that I do. I can—could—feel what the Fata felt, and just...know. Sort of like how I can feel you in my mind. The Fata recognized you as their kin." She squeezed his hand. "There's more."

He tensed, as if preparing for battle. "Let me have it."

Kali bit back a smile at the wry humor he emanated and pointed at the little book sticking out of her pack.

"*Alem's Wish*? What about it?"

"I think there's some truth to the glimmer story. The Fata told me they can walk between worlds, and they mentioned something about 'shadow selves.' And I saw *you* vanish in the shadows in the bathing room. You remember our journey from Starwatch, when we escaped the Canderi? How we somehow traveled a great distance in the blink of an eye?"

"Hard to forget that," he muttered.

"The second time we fled the thralls, after we left Riel and Jennet's farm, I tried the trick again. But it didn't work. And I think… Stonewall, it wasn't *my* magic that moved us that first time, but *yours.* I think I gave you energy, but the actual act of getting us *away* was your doing."

She expected him to rebuke this idea, unwilling to believe such a wild notion. But to her surprise, he only nodded, as if she'd told him the time of day. "Well, it's not the strangest thing I've heard lately."

Quickly, he explained his encounter with "Tor," and although Kali was hard-pressed to believe him, she they didn't have time to discuss the matter in depth. Before he'd finished, Kali's thoughts were already racing forward. "If it's true that you *do* have Fata blood, and that you are the reason we could travel so quickly, do you think we could do it again? On purpose?"

"I don't know." He frowned in thought. "You really think that *you* helped *me* send us across the province?"

"I do."

He sat up, shaking his head. "Well, that nearly killed you. I'll not risk it again."

"But doing so could save our lives. *All* of us. Eris' plan is risky, to say the least, and you know as well as I do that we ought to have another plan in our pockets in case hers goes ass-up."

"Right, but I don't know how we could perform such a feat again. Whether I've got any sort of magic or not, I don't know the first thing about it." He sighed and shot a glance across the room, where Drake was speaking to Leal. The Sufani woman was gesticulating at the door, eyes narrowed, while Drake looked grim

Kali shifted so that she could better face him. "We don't have much time, but the most important thing to remember about magic is to *focus* on what you want. Keep a single desire in your mind and concentrated upon it. When we fled from the thralls that first time, all I could think was *away.* I just wanted us to get *away* from them."

"Ea's tits…" He sighed and looked at her. "*Away.* I thought that, too. It was all I could think of to survive."

A hopeful, half-smile crept to Kali's face. "It's worth trying again."

But he was a stubborn lout. "Not at the cost of your life."

"It didn't kill me before. And I've a better understanding of my magic now. I know my limits." She gave him her prettiest, beaming smile. "Have a little faith, Sergeant. We can do this."

He smiled too, but the expression did not reach his eyes. "I hope you're right."

33

THIRTY-THREE

"*Relah,* wake up."

Milo groaned and shifted on his sleeping pallet, which was much firmer than he remembered. Uncomfortably firm. A dull ache throbbed in his chest and gooseflesh prickled over his skin. Sweet Mara, he'd barely set his head down… Was it time to wake, already? He tried to convince his eyes to open, but they ignored him, so he surrendered to slumber, hard pallet be damned. Whoever was pestering him could wait.

"Come on, Mi, wake up. We've got to go."

"I'm sleeping," he tried to reply, but the words came out more like, "Hmm sshleeming." Not good. Maybe he should have been more concerned that his mouth *and* eyes were being insubordinate, but he was just so tired…

"Milo!" Flint barked. "Open your fucking eyes and look at me, you sorry sod!"

"Shut up," he managed to slur, and this time the words sounded a tiny bit like they should have. "What're you doing in the men's barracks, anyway?"

"We're *not* in the barracks, Mi. We're in the bastion."

It was the last thing he expected her to say. Sheer bewilderment made him open his eyes to try to see for himself. Everything was blurry at first, but the world gradually came into focus with a few strong blinks. Judging from the dark circles under Flint's eyes and the sickly tone of her skin, she needed to go back to bed.

"Are you well?" he asked. "You look terrible."

She pulled a face. "You're not winning any hearts right now, either."

"Why am I on a table? And what's−" He tried to sit up, and then hissed as pain stabbed through his chest. Flint called out and several hands gently steered him back down, where someone had bundled fabric beneath his head as a makeshift pillow. Milo looked into the worried faces of his squad-mates, as well as Mages Halcyon and Sadira. There was no sign of Rook.

"You're in pain?" Flint asked him. Without waiting for an answer, she looked between the mages. "Why is he hurting? Didn't you fix him?"

Gods above and beyond, she sounded *worried*. About him? Or had something else happened? His thoughts were muzzy and slow, and he could only call up a vague recollection of the garrison's detention area.

"We did as much as we could," Mage Halcyon replied. "Any more, and neither of you would have survived the process." She swept her dark eyes over Milo. "How bad is the pain?"

"He's all pale and sweaty," Flint answered. "So my guess is really sodding bad. What are you going to do about it?"

The mage ignored Flint. "How bad is it, *Milo?*"

"I dunno." He shifted his left side and was rewarded with another hot stab of pain that made sweat prick along his lower back and forehead. "Not great," he managed through clenched teeth.

"You still have some healing to do, but Sadira and Mage Halcyon took care of the worst of the damage," Beacon said in the soothing way of menders.

Mage Halcyon toyed with her unraveling braid. "I'm not sure either of us could have helped you, Milo, if not for−"

"What matters is Milo's awake now," Flint broke in. "So we can *finally* leave this shithole."

Milo frowned at his sister. "You shouldn't talk to Mage Halcyon like that. It sounds like she and Sadira saved my life."

Flint glanced down at her weapons belt, where only one dagger rested near her sword. Where had the other gone?

Rather than ask, Milo turned to the dark-haired mage. "Thank you, Mage Halcyon."

"Kali." At his confused look, she pointed to herself. "Just call me Kali, please."

"Very well...Kali." Mara's mercy, he almost had to force out the name, and she gave a soft chuckle in response. It wasn't the mocking sort, which he knew well, but rather the sort that encouraged a similar reply, so he chuckled too.

Stonewall put a hand on his right shoulder, drawing his attention. The former sergeant briefly explained their situation—which left a lot to be desired—and then added, "So we've got a boat to catch. Can you walk?"

Good question. It hurt too much to move his left arm, but once the others helped him upright, Milo swung his legs over the table's edge and stood on his own. The pain in his chest built to a dizzying throb and there was a dodgy moment where he slumped against Beacon and Stonewall, but then his head cleared and his legs stopped shaking.

Before he put his shirt back on, Beacon insisted on examining the wound, so Milo relented. "It's fine," Milo said to Flint, who hovered over him like a blue-eyed hornet. "I'm fine. Stop acting like I'm going to keel over."

"You look like five kinds of shit, Mi. Am I supposed to be *happy* about that?"

"No, but I need room to breathe!"

"Both of you, shut it," Stonewall broke in.

"Yes, ser," the twins replied in unison, more out of habit than anything else.

Once Milo was standing, he glanced around the table where he'd lain moments ago, trying to ignore the bloodstains upon the wood. "Where'd my gear end up?"

Beacon pointed to a neat pile of armor stacked under the table. "Can you get dressed on your own?"

Not really, as it turned out, and at first it was humiliating to have his sentinel brothers help him suit up away from the others. But both Stonewall and Beacon were efficient, and soon Milo felt more or less like his old self. Well, maybe less, because his left hand didn't work. No matter how hard he concentrated, he couldn't get his fingers to close around his dagger's horizontal grip. Could he even hold a sword?

"Mi." Flint's gloved hand pressed over his, securing the dagger. When he looked into her eyes, she gave him a faint smile. "Don't mope. Just keep moving."

She knew him too well. His throat tightened, but he nodded and concentrated on at least holding the weapon. Flint squeezed his fingers one more time before releasing him and looking at their former sergeant. "I think we're ready. Are the others?"

"Kali's ready," Stonewall said. "And Sadira."

"Is Milo fit to travel?" a new voice asked.

Milo twisted around, too quickly, for his wound burned, but he didn't care when he met the Cipher's dark eyes. "Naree?"

She was hugging her white and black cloak tight against her body, and her lips were parted in what he thought was surprise. When he said her name, a slow smile spread across her face. "Milo."

He swallowed. "I didn't know you were coming."

"I didn't plan on it," she replied. "But I was summoned to mark a child born on Heartfire, whose parents live near the garrison. When I was done, something pulled me here." Her expression held nothing but wonder. "Sometimes the One guides our steps in unknown directions. We must trust that we're on the right path."

Heat crept to his ears. "I suppose."

"Are you..." She looked him up and down, brows knitted. "Are you truly well?"

"Enough, I guess." He tried to smile. "Thank you. For...well, everything you've done. Everything you're going to do. Has Serla Iban punished you?"

She pulled down the hem of one of her fine leather gloves, so he could see the intricate whorls inked into her dark skin. "My place in the One's world is firm. Iban may become angry with me, but I'm not afraid of him. Ciphers ultimately answer only to the Pillars – and the One, of course."

"Must be nice," Milo said before he could stop himself.

Flint cleared her throat, making Milo start. She stood behind him, fully kitted up, including her helmet. At his and Naree's looks, she jabbed her thumb toward the door, where the others were gathering. "Time to move out, *relah*. Ready?"

Not really, and he wasn't sure when he would be. But there was no time for moping, so he nodded and shoved on his own helmet. "Let's go."

* * *

Eris was the first to emerge from the bastion and into the worst of winter. Snow fell at an alarming speed, blotting out all sound and color, and there was no wind to speak of. She felt no cold, but the air was oppressive and heavy and *wrong*. She could not take a proper breath. As the others crept out after her, she hunched in her cloak and peered upward, squinting through the snow.

"No, you can't fly in this," Adrie said, voice muffled behind a scarf she'd wrapped around her mouth. "It's too thick."

Eris had made the same determination, but when she caught sight of Stonewall helping Kali step out of the dormitories, a flare of stubborn indignation shot through her. "Watch me."

She lowered her gaze, preparing to concentrate, but a strong hand grabbed her shoulder. She whirled to face Cai, staring down at her beneath his knitted cap and scarf. "Don't be stupid. You'll freeze."

She jerked out of his grasp. "I can handle it. Crows are hardier than you realize. Besides…" She glanced at the bastion gates. "I have to scout ahead. I have to know if the others reached the docks."

A strange warmth crept up her back. When Eris glanced behind her again, she saw that Sadira had stepped into the courtyard, a look of concentration on her face. One of the knots of anxiety that had formed in Eris' stomach eased a tiny bit. Perhaps they wouldn't all freeze to death out here. At least, not right away.

But surely Sadira's power couldn't withstand a blizzard. They had to get moving. Eris glanced over at Leal, who held her sister's hand as the Sufani gathered around the Circle priestess, along with the other mages who had decided to brave the tunnels – and trust the Cipher. She caught Sirvat's eye; the other mage nodded and hugged her child close, both wrapped beneath several cloaks. Even so, it would take a miracle for them to reach the temple of the One without losing any fingers – or worse. If the gods did exist, Eris hoped they would watch over mother and child. Having already said her goodbyes to her mage friends, Eris stood by while the Circle priestess offered platitudes to those not accompanying her.

"The One will be with you." The snow muted the Cipher's words as hematite muted the world for a mage. "Have faith in the One, and have faith in each other."

Eris rolled her eyes and strode toward the bastion gates, gathering her strength with each step. They were all wrong; she *could* fly now. "Come on. We have to hurry."

Leal was at her side in a moment. "Let me go first, in case the sentinels are waiting. And no, you shouldn't fly in this."

"I wasn't–"

The Sufani interrupted her with a hand upon her arm. "Don't."

Eris scowled. "We'll need a scout."

"We've got several," Leal replied. "You know, most of us have to make do *without* magic."

With that, Leal trotted toward the gates. Rook followed the Sufani's heels, slinking through the falling snow as easily as a cloudshadow over grass. They disappeared through the gates while the others waited. No one spoke. At last, Leal reappeared, motioning for them to follow. The Circle priestess led her new flock first. The remaining mages came next, then the Assembly folk. The sentinels went last.

"Any sign of Argent?" Stonewall asked as he passed Leal. He and the sentinel mender helped the injured burnie struggle along.

The Sufani shook her head. "None. But this snow will blot out any tracks." She pointed behind them; sure enough, Eris could see no trace of their passage. She shivered, but only in part from the cold.

Drake exhaled in a fog. "Something's not right." He looked over at Rook.

"You're *sure* you saw no sign of Argent? He must be here by now."

She shifted the quiver of arrows upon her back. "I'm sure."

"Maybe the One has truly cleared the way for us," Milo offered.

His twin snorted, but made no comment. No one did, other than a stern, "be on your guard," from Kali's sentinel lover before the group slipped toward the garrison's main gates. Eris pulled her scarf closer around her mouth; her breath had dampened the fabric, which would likely be uncomfortable when it dried, but she had bigger problems now.

Once they reached the gates, the group prepared to part ways. "We'll meet again, I know," Aderey said to Kali, clasping her gloved hands.

Kali smiled at the Sufani man. "Especially since you told us where to find you if we all get free of this city."

Aderey chuckled. "*When*, not if. Let us think happy thoughts."

Eris tried to fight back an irrational swell of bitterness. Save Leal, none of the Sufani had treated *her* or her friends so kindly.

Drake bowed to the Sufani man, who embraced him. When they parted, Aderey said, "Consider your debt repaid."

"Huh?" Drake asked.

"You don't recall the *biri* I gave you?" Aderey clucked his tongue. "Ah, youthful oblivion."

"No one has time for your foolishness," Ytel said, urging her husband along after the Circle priestess.

"Except you, love," Aderey replied.

She took his arm. "Always."

The groups parted ways; Eris stole a few moments to watch the Circle priestess lead the Sufani and a most of the other mages away, into the night.

Seren, watch over them. The thought was as sudden as it was unexpected, and Eris shook it away. Seren was a moon, not a goddess. The gods weren't real. Only magic was real; only what she could feel in her blood and bones. She looked up, into the falling snow that obscured the entire world. Beyond the confines of the bastion and garrison walls, despite the presence of so many buildings all around, the air seemed colder. The snow had even muted the roar of the White River. The urge to fly tore through her like wind, but even if she could fly, she wouldn't get far.

But her frequent reconnaissance trips had granted her a better understanding of the city's layout. She would never get lost again, and when she left the bastion this time, she would never come back.

34

THIRTY-FOUR

Talon's eyes had closed, but she knew every nuance of her father's voice and could picture his earnest, worried expression. "You struck Milo in self-defense," Foley was saying. "Argent will understand that."

Neither of them had moved. She was a prisoner and he would not leave her side, no matter how much she begged, pleaded, or threatened.

"I pray he will." She burned no longer. She had turned into a pile of ashes that would scatter with the slightest breeze. "But if he doesn't..."

She could not finish the thought. A warm hand on hers made her look up. Her sight had adjusted to the dim light in the detention area, so she could make out Foley's face as he peered at her through the bars.

"You're crying," he said.

Only when she swiped at her cheek did she realize he spoke truly. "I've failed you," she whispered. "Everything I've worked for—everything *we've* worked for—will be meaningless if Argent finds you out of the bastion. He'll kill you."

"This province needs mages. Surely the High Commander will–"

"If he finds you–"

Foley squeezed her hand. "I am loyal to you, and to the Circle. Argent is a rational man."

How badly she wanted to believe him, or at least take comfort in his surety. "Perhaps."

Footsteps made them both look up to see torchlight flickering in the stairwell, growing brighter. Heart beating fast once more, Talon pulled herself to her feet in one fluid motion and prepared to face the High Commander. Foley rose as well, although he kept his head bowed.

But it was only Gray, Vigil, and Ferro, swords ready, movements cautious.

The moment Gray spotted Foley, she lifted her weapon and Foley raised his arms in surrender, but Talon called, "Hold! The First Mage means you no harm."

The sentinels looked at each other in confusion before Vigil came forward. Captain Cobalt's second-in-command was a lanky woman, about as tall as Talon, but without Talon's strength. Still, Vigil was as professional as her captain as she opened the lock and then saluted as Talon slipped out of the cell.

"Ser, are you injured?" she asked.

Talon rubbed her side and gave a convincing grimace. "Only bruised, I think. Stonewall caught me by surprise."

"Didn't think the sod had it in him," Gray said.

Talon leveled the other woman with a stern glare. "I was ambushed during an attempt to execute Mage Halcyon, who is indeed a thrall. Stonewall and his squad have turned traitor." She glanced between the sentinels. "You were all near the void when last I saw you."

"The High Commander is here, ser," Vigil replied. "He brought us hematite and sent us to search for you."

"He brought enough for the entire garrison," Gray added, notes of awe and adoration in her voice. "He saved our lives."

"Thank the One," Talon said, despite how her stomach flipped. "Where is he now?"

"In the common room," Ferro said. He cleared his throat. "He said if we found you, he wanted you to go to him at once."

I'm certain he does. Talon nodded. "Of course."

"What should we do with him, ser?" Vigil pointed at Foley with her sword, causing the First Mage to shrink back against the wall.

Talon pretended to consider, though her heart hammered and her tongue felt thick. She had to maintain her role of calm, collected leader if she had any hope of keeping her father safe. "Mage Clementa has remained loyal. He will stay with me, for now." Without waiting for the others to reply, she looked at Foley, who straightened. "Keep close, but out of harm's way," she said. "If there is a fight—"

"I meant what I said, Commander," he broke in. "You have my loyalty, now and always." He added a very credible salute that made the other sentinels glance at each other curiously.

Laying it on a bit thick, aren't you? Talon thought, glaring at her father, who only regarded her in that steady way of his. But no one objected. Gray offered Talon her sword, which the renegade mage had discarded in the corner. Her daggers were nowhere in sight. No matter. She hefted the sword's familiar weight, savoring how the metal hilt already started to warm in her grip, and looked at the sentinels who stood before her.

Be calm, she told herself. *You can both survive this. Have faith in the One.*

"Duty calls," she said, jerking her chin in the direction of the garrison proper.

"Yes, ser," they chorused.

* * *

To Foley's immense relief, the sentinels did not question their commander's orders. Vigil led the way out of the detention area, Talon and Foley following, with the others at their heels. For once, the knowledge that he was under observation did not set Foley on edge. He was by his daughter's side. Everything else, he would face as it came.

Several minutes later, they reached the garrison's common room. Not long ago, every surface had been filled with sick sentinels. Now the space was alive with armored men and women returning from the edge of Nox's void. Creaking leather and jingling buckles interspersed tense conversations, and more than a few narrow-eyed gazes shifted in the direction of the bastion. A tall, broad-shouldered blond sentinel stood at the front of the room, silver-toned gear glittering in the torchlight as he spoke with other, similarly dressed sentinels. The moment Talon and Foley entered the room, the chatter ceased and all eyes fell upon the newcomers.

Foley fought back a grimace but his daughter stood straighter, using every inch of her considerable height to make her presence all the more impressive. How like Isra she was in that way. Isra had never cowed to anyone, even the sentinels. But that pride had drawn the sentinels' ire and ultimately been his wife's downfall. Would it be his daughter's too?

High Commander Argent watched Talon approach with an expression Foley could not read. He was younger than Foley had expected, with an aquiline nose, high cheekbones, and sharp, intelligent eyes that tracked Talon's steps.

Captain Cobalt stood at the High Commander's side. Like most of the other Whitewater sentinels, the captain's eyes were bright as if with fever, and he had the bearing of one who had recently ingested hematite.

"Commander," Cobalt said, stepping forward and offering a salute. "We feared the worst when we couldn't find you. Thank Tor you're alive."

"Thank Tor, indeed." Her salute to the High Commander was a deep bow, deeper than any Foley had seen her use before. "Gray told me how you found the High Commander and brought him here."

Cobalt dropped his gaze to the floor. "I only did my duty, ser."

Bootlicker, Foley thought, mentally rolling his eyes.

"As you can see," Argent said. "The Whitewater sentinels are back to rights – for the most part. A few are still recovering in the infirmary, but my mender assures me they will be back to readiness within a day or so. Unfortunately, there are some who will not rise again, but they will be given proper rites when this business is over."

Talon saluted again. "Thank you, ser. I am in your debt, too. But one of my officers has gone rogue. I believe he has absconded with his squad and at least one mage, if not more. We must–"

"Sergeant Stonewall will be dealt with," Argent interrupted.

"Of course, ser," Talon replied. "Do you have a watch posted at the gates? One of Stonewall's men was injured; if they had to tend to him, they might still be here. There could still be time to stop them."

Argent's eyes flickered to Foley. "The bastion is empty. Stonewall and his allies have fled."

Ice formed in Foley's belly. *Gone.* All his friends; all his extended family. A part of him had hoped—foolishly, perhaps—that the other mages would see reason and remain behind. But now they were all as good as dead.

Like him.

No, he told himself, shoring up his calm. *You're not dead, not yet. You stayed. You are loyal. That's what matters.*

Talon sucked in a breath. "Then we must pursue."

"I have sent a group ahead to wait for them at the docks," Argent replied.

Foley frowned to himself. This was the first he'd heard of Kali and her cohorts' possible destination. How did the High Commander know? The most logical way out of the city was the bridge and main gates.

Talon seemed to feel the same. "Surely they will make for the city gates."

The High Commander shook his head. "No, the docks, although the bridge is well-guarded. In any case, we have the advantage. The storm is upon us and these renegades will not be as well-equipped as my sentinels." He smiled, white and dazzling, and dread curled in Foley's heart. "Do not fear, Commander. Sergeant Stonewall and his mage-whore will not leave this city unless in my custody."

He glanced to the other sentinels. "Prepare to move out. Fain, Spar, and Harper; cover our rear. Commander Talon, Captain Cobalt, and I will take point."

The others filed in quick but orderly lines toward the common room's exit. Foley stood at the room's edge, hoping but not expecting to remain unnoticed. So he was not surprised when Argent looked his way but addressed Talon.

"What is *that* doing free?"

Talon kept her voice professional. "This is Foley Clementa, Whitewater Bastion's First Mage. He came to my aid in the detention area, when Stonewall and his squad attacked me. It was Mage Clementa who informed me of the other mages' escape. He has proven himself a loyal servant of the sentinels and the Circle."

The High Commander lifted a single blond brow. "Has he? Well, we've no time to discuss your claims, so for now, he stays with us."

"I will take full responsibility for him, ser," she said.

"I'm certain you will," Argent replied. A thrill of warning ran up Foley's spine at the soft words. The others had gone now, leaving only Cobalt lingering by the door. Even so, the High Commander pitched his voice so only Talon and Foley could hear. "You should have run, too."

With that, Argent shoved on his helmet and strode out of the room, his armored shoulders brushing the doorframe. Captain Cobalt glanced at Talon and then hurried after the High Commander.

Foley looked at his daughter. "Shall we?"

In hopes of setting her at ease, he tried to keep his tone light. But his daughter had never been one to take the easy path.

"He's right," she whispered. "Gods, I'm such a fool. It's too late to run."

"Yes," he agreed. He should have done many things differently and the ghost of his right hand twinged in agreement. But he'd made his choices long ago, for good, or—more commonly—for ill, so he would bear the consequences as they came.

Because they were alone, because nothing else mattered anymore, he took her hand. "I love you, Talaséa."

"It won't change anything," she replied. "But I love you, too, Da."

He could not recall the last time he had heard her speak those words. Despite the danger, despite the phantom pain that probably heralded worse things to come, he smiled. "Come, child. Let's go to the void, together."

* * *

While the snow made Kali and her friends' journey exponentially more dangerous, it also proved a blessing, as most folks seemed inclined to remain indoors. No onlookers spotted the group, for which Kali was grateful. But slogging through snow-covered streets was no easy task, and by the time they reached the quay, Kali's knee burned enough to bring tears to her eyes.

I'd have gladly carried you, Stonewall said through their bond as the group crept through the dark streets toward the docks.

He meant the offer only as a kindness, but the idea of being toted like a sack of potatoes was worse than the pain. Besides, she wasn't slowing them down *too* much; no one could keep a fast pace through this weather. *I can manage,* she replied.

If there were gods, they were merciful, for the worst of the snowfall had ebbed, revealing how Seren's light fought to break through the cloud cover. The lamps had all burned out and shifting shadows bathed the docks. Cold air, stinking of salt, fish, and smoke, slithered beneath Kali's cloak, making her shiver and wrinkle her nose.

The group converged in a shadowed alley near the quay, where the sheltering buildings had kept back most of the snow. Eris and Cai spoke in hushed, hurried tones before Cai slipped out of the alley, toward the docks.

"He's going to look for the others," Eris whispered.

Drake squinted through the falling snow. "The river's not frozen, thank Tor. Still, we'll probably have a thorny time getting upriver." He looked at Stonewall. "Remember how to paddle?"

"Only just," Stonewall replied, smirking.

Drake chuckled. "Well, this'll be a good refresher."

A warm feeling gathered in Kali's heart at the genial tone between the two brothers. However, she caught sight of Eris, looking between Stonewall and Drake, scowling. Had Eris not known they were brothers? Probably not, for if she had realized Drake was related to a sentinel—let alone that he had *been* one—she'd not have bothered to free him.

"I've never been on a boat," Milo said brightly. "This'll be...interesting."

"That's not the word I'd use," Flint replied.

"The word you'd use probably isn't fit for polite company," Milo said.

"Nothing she says is," Beacon added wryly.

Marcen cleared his throat. "I think our greatest danger is exposure."

"The greatest danger," Leal hissed, "is the lot of you not shutting up.

Unless you *want* every city guard in the area to find us?"

Everyone fell silent as they waited for Cai's return. Kali's heart raced and her breath was still short, but she forced herself to be still. Too many minutes passed while she strained to hear anything other than the drum of her own pulse and Stonewall's soft breath beside her, but there was only the faint lapping of water against the docks. And, of course, the ever-present roar of the waterfall, which the thicker snowfall had muted earlier.

Stonewall did not look at Kali now, but she felt him in her mind all the same: focused on the task at hand; determined to see those he traveled with safely to their goal. He was not reaching out to her, but his presence was soothing. She took a shaking breath to try and quell her nerves, and waited.

At last—at *last*—Cai reappeared at the alley's entrance – alone. Eris straightened from her crouch. "Where are the others?"

Cai gnawed on his lower lip. "There's a nice big skiff out there, with room for all of us," he pointed at the docks behind him, "but no sign of Izell, Davet, or the others. And I found this." He pulled a brooch from his pocket and tossed it to Eris.

"This is Serla Vellis' sigil," she whispered, her eyes wide.

"Aye," Cai replied grimly. "Auda was wearing it. I saw signs of a scuffle, too."

Kali covered her mouth lest she gasp. Eris had told them how she'd taken over an upper-tiered woman's entourage, so Kali recognized the significance of this discovery.

"You didn't see Hazel or Druce, or any of the other bastion mages?" Eris asked.

Cai shook his head. "Not so much as a stray thread."

"Did you see any sentinels or city guards?" Stonewall asked.

"No sign of either," Cai answered after a beat. "But the snow was falling pretty thick for a while."

"Surely this dreadful weather would keep folks indoors?" Kali asked.

Marcen gave her a sad smile. "I'd like to believe that."

"So...this is a trap?" Kali said as dread coiled in her belly.

The others exchanged glances before Eris frowned. "Auda and the others wouldn't have abandoned their post unless under duress."

"Well, we're sodding here now," Rilla replied, gripping her spear. "We can't very well turn around. If this *is* a trap, we'll have to fight our way out of it."

"How?" Ben asked. The Assembly man had been so quiet, Kali had forgotten he was there. Everyone glanced at him and he added, "We have mages, but if this High Commander is nearby with more sentinels, I fail to see how magic would be effective."

"Magic *just* saved my brother's life," Flint shot back. "And Mi's brimming with hematite. So it's not as useless as you seem to think."

Ben frowned at her. "Healing one man is surely different than fighting a small army."

"Kali cured herself of a thrall possession," Flint said.

The Assembly man cast Kali a startled look, but his calm, knowing tone did not change. "Again, that seems a different application for magic than what we need."

"So you're an expert on mages, now?"

Brice lifted her hands. "Everyone, calm down. Eris, the snow has slacked off. Can you fly? We need a better idea of what we're facing."

In response, Eris seemed to melt before their eyes. Even her clothes shifted, and in the next moment, a crow hopped upon a nearby crate and flew off into the night. Kali's heart jumped to her throat and she waited—again—until Eris returned a few minutes later. She shifted back to her human form—clothes and all—and her face was grim. "At least three dozen hemies, along with several squads of city guards, waiting around the docks. The moment we step free, they'll be upon us. I'd be shocked if they didn't already know we were here."

"Shit," Drake muttered. "Ea's balls and bones."

"Some of the hemies had silver armor, if that means anything to you," Eris added to Drake. "I only mention it because it struck me as odd."

Stonewall sucked in a breath. "Argent and Silver Squad. It must be."

"Talon and her insufferable captain are with them," Eris added darkly.

"And Foley's skulking nearby too, naturally."

"Well, that explains why we had no trouble leaving the garrison," Beacon replied.

"Do I want to know if you saw the other mages?" Kali asked Eris.

Eris gave her a withering look. "They're having tea with the hemies, of course." At Kali's frown, Eris blew out a stream of fog. "Prisoners. Again."

"All of them?" Kali whispered.

"I didn't do a head count, but I got a general sense." Eris' gloved hands closed into fists. "They're hemmed in like sodding cattle in a pen. Every one of them cuffed and collared."

Kali's mouth fell open but she couldn't speak. It was too horrible for words.

"What of those who went with that Cipher?" Leal asked.

"I didn't see them, thank the stars," Eris replied. "Though Argent did have the carriage we...commandeered."

"We're fifteen in number," Brice said. "Against over three times that. Surrounded by enemies. There's no hope of sneaking to the skiff or backtracking to rejoin the others."

"Then there's no hope of escape," Rook said weakly, and looked at Stonewall. "We must turn ourselves in. Argent can be reasoned with, but you must first surrender to him."

Everyone stared at her and Stonewall frowned. "Even if surrender was an option, Argent won't let any of us walk away from this. He'll kill us all – and I *won't* let that happen."

Tears trickled down Rook's cheeks and she reached for Flint and Milo, who were closest to her. "No, he just wants the mages. Turn them over, and he'll let the rest of us go. I promise!"

That same sense of dread that Kali had felt now resonated from Stonewall as he stared at his squad-mate. "How do you know that?"

"None of this matters, because I'm *not* surrendering to those metal-blooded idiots," Eris snapped. "Nor am I leaving my fellow mages to their fates. You're all welcome to take your chances, but the entire reason I came back to this sodding city was to free my friends, so that's what I'm going to do." She looked between Kali and Sadira. "Can you do magic on sentinels that *doesn't* involve healing them?"

Kali flushed. "I don't know. Maybe."

"Maybe?" Eris spat. "They've taken our people prisoner – again! What will it take for you to fight back?"

"I *have* fought back," Kali snapped. "Fought – and killed. It's not brave or noble, and I have no wish to repeat the experience – unlike you. Don't look at me like that, Eris. None of you said as much, but I know you killed that Serla What's-her-name, and you're wearing her clothes."

"We left Vellis alive," Eris said.

"In this weather, it'd have been kinder to slit her throat." Kali glanced beside her at Sadira, who radiated warmth and power. On the trip from the bastion through the city, Kali had been able to ignore the urge for more of her friend's magic, but the mere idea of taking some of Sadira's—even in self-defense—made her mouth water and her fingertips ache. She had to make Eris see that what she asked was too much. "Eris, my magic–"

"Aye, your magic is so very special," Eris broke in. "But what fucking good is it if you won't help your own kind? Will you just lie down and accept whatever the hemies deign to give you?"

Fury took hold of Kali, so suddenly she could not keep it from her voice. "At least I'm not blinded by ignorance and hate."

Eris snorted. "You always were *so* melodramatic. I see that hasn't changed."

"That's enough," Stonewall interjected. "Eris, you've no idea the toll Kali's magic takes on her."

"Stay out of this, dreg."

"Focus on getting to the boat," Sadira said suddenly. "Leave the sentinels to me."

"And me," Flint said, drawing a dagger.

Brice, Rilla, and Leal chorused agreement, but Rook shook her head. "There's too many. You'll never survive."

Kali shot Sadira a curious look. "You mean to do them harm?"

The air around the Zhee mage warmed, banishing the cold and sending

398

tendrils of steam from Sadira's fingertips. "I mean to make them reconsider. We need a surprise."

At the others' confused looks, she glanced at Kali. "Distraction," Kali clarified.

Sadira exhaled. "Yes. That." She studied Kali. "Can you help me?"

Kali swallowed the lingering urge to take Sadira's magic for herself. She was *Kali*; she was no mindless thrall, and her friends needed her help. "Yes," she whispered.

More plans were made, these more harried than before. As the warriors—sentinels and otherwise—readied their weapons, Stonewall reached for Kali's pack. "Please don't argue," he said as he shouldered the burden along with his own. "And give me the viol case, too."

"No." She clutched the leather-bound handle.

"You can't run and carry that."

"And you can't fight while carrying *that*." She pointed to both of their packs now slung over his shoulders. "And help Milo," she added, softer. "You're not the only one of us who can be stubborn."

"Too bad," he said with a sigh. Through their bond, he added, *You're certain we can do this...?* The words faded, replaced by a blur of images that Kali recognized as his memories of their first flight across the Aredian countryside.

We will, she replied in kind. *But I'm afraid for you and the others.*

Oddly, this made him smile. *We're all fighters, Kali. We'll manage.* A strange calm emanated from him, setting her more at ease with each breath. He gripped his daggers. *This is why the One brought me into the world, after all.*

Such conviction, she replied, and his smile broadened.

"Stop making eyes at each other, you two," Flint hissed. "We've a battle to win."

Beyond the bubble of warmth that Sadira cast, the snowfall had begun again, thick and silent as ever. Kali's calm faded and she took a shaking breath. "I suppose duty calls," she said aloud.

Stonewall lifted his helmet so he could kiss her forehead. "Not duty." He shoved his helmet back on. "Freedom."

35

THIRTY-FIVE

S tonewall took two paces out of the alley before he caught the gleam of silver in the struggling moonlight. High Commander Argent and his retinue stepped out onto the docks, moving to block their enemies from their escape route.

Enemies. Stonewall shivered. He'd never imagined other sentinels thinking of him in that way, but then, he'd never expected to fall in love with a mage. The gods worked in strange ways.

Hematite be damned; his guts turned to ice and his heart lodged firmly in his throat. What courage he had shored up withered at the sight of High Commander Argent, Silver Squad, and what looked like every crossbow in Whitewater City.

Stick to the plan, he told himself. Except Eris, no one wanted any bloodshed.

"Rook," he said. She flinched and met his gaze, albeit reluctantly. He nodded at the group of sentinels in silver gear, standing in a neat row behind Argent. "Are they as deadly as the rumors say?"

She nodded but said nothing, and her hands were shaking.

What in Tor's name was going on? But he couldn't question her when they had a battle ahead. Even so, he kept his misgivings in the forefront of his mind, just in case.

In direct contrast to Rook's visible fear, Flint pointed her dagger at

Argent and Silver Squad. "Bunch of polished frips. They make Beacon look like a pig farmer."

Beacon, who was helping Drake support Milo, cleared his throat. "First of all, that was rude and uncalled for. Second—and it's just a suggestion—but it's probably not wise to antagonize the deadliest sentinels in Aredia any more than necessary."

Flint grinned. "Oh, I'm just getting started."

They were about ten paces from Argent, Talon, and the others. None of the sentinels who had flanked Stonewall's allies had moved, likely waiting on their leader's command to strike. Stonewall raised his hand in a signal to stop. He felt Kali's presence in his mind, though her focus centered on her own magic. Still, he tried to communicate. *Ready?*

Not yet.

Understood, he replied, and glanced at his squad. "They need a few minutes," he murmured, and then ensured his words would carry through the falling snow. "High Commander Argent. Commander Talon. Captain Cobalt." He gave a brief bowing salute. "Please stand aside so we may leave."

"*You* are a traitor and will be dealt with accordingly," Talon replied, her voice ringing through the docks. "Your mage allies, as well. But your sentinel companions still have a choice. If they return to me, they will suffer no consequences from this misguided attempt at rebellion."

"No consequences?" Milo repeated. "You *stabbed* me!"

"By all rights," Flint added, "you ought to let him stab you back. You know, for balance's sake."

"At the very least, you should apologize," Beacon said. "Perhaps send Mi a nice bottle of wine as compensation."

"For stabbing him?" Flint snorted. "I think five bottles, at least."

"Well, five bottles is a lot, and I don't like wine that much," Milo said thoughtfully. "But five bottles' worth of honey-cider would be nice."

"Oh, yes," Flint replied. "I could drink that stuff all day."

"Who said I'd share any with you?" Milo asked.

Stonewall bit back a chuckle at Flint's huff of indignation. "What about me?" he said.

"You, Beacon, and Rook can all have some," Milo said. "And Kali and Sadira, of course. Flint…well, I'll have to think about whether she deserves any."

"Enough." Argent's grip on his sword had tightened with each word of banter. Now, he stood poised for attack. "You're all under arrest."

"If we are, then Talon should be, too," Flint shot back. "Stabbing one of the men under your command is so much worse than fucking a mage. No offense, Stonewall."

"None taken," he replied. Another brush of his mind to Kali's; she and Sadira were still working on their magic, so he looked back at Talon. "You crossed the line from *strict* to *ruthless* a long time ago."

"Commander Talon is not on trial right now," Argent said. "*You* are under arrest. All of you. However, if you relinquish your weapons, your lives will be spared."

"I'm afraid we can't do that, ser," Stonewall said. "But we still wish to leave in peace. I'll say it again: please stand aside, and we will offer you no trouble."

Silver Squad and their allies chuckled amongst themselves, though none broke formation – nor lowered their crossbows. Stonewall allowed himself an internal sigh.

I'm sure that tactic will work, one day, Kali told him through their bond. *But for now, we're ready to fight.*

Thank Tor.

The High Commander's reply was polished steel. "I don't bargain with murderers and traitors. I have heard of you, Stonewall. How you abandoned your brethren to lie with a mage. How you cast aside your oath of service and betrayed the innocent people you were sworn to protect. I didn't want to believe such heinous accusations…but I see now that Rook's words were true."

Flint sucked in a breath. Stunned, Stonewall risked a glance at the petite sentinel who stood beside him, whose helmet could not hide her stricken expression. That, more than anything else, formed a handful of hard, cold stones in his belly. So it was true.

"He's lying," Flint whispered, voice thick. "Rook...he's lying. Right?"

"It wasn't like that," Rook cried. She ripped off her helmet and grabbed Stonewall's hand. "I just...I had to tell him what was going on in the bastion, yes, but he's twisting it all around!"

Stonewall could hardly wrap his mind around her words. He snatched his hand out of her grip. "I trusted you. We all *trusted* you."

Argent called through the snowfall. "Rook is a valued informant, who has served her purpose and will be duly rewarded." Now he drew his sword, causing Stonewall to rip his gaze away from Rook and look back at the High Commander. "No more games. Stonewall, former sergeant of the Whitewater garrison, you and all those who stand with you are to surrender now, or be sent to the Laughing God."

Despite the frigid air, sweat pricked along Stonewall's spine and his heart hammered behind his ribs. He took a deep breath to try and quell his fear and his anger. It only worked a little. "Go," he said to Rook, speaking through clenched teeth. He jerked his chin toward Argent. "Run back to your master."

Tears streamed down her freckled cheeks. "I'm sorry. I never meant to–"

Gods above, he hated it when his worst fears proved true. Stonewall cut her off with a shake of his head. "Just leave."

Rook looked at Milo, who was silent, and then at Beacon. The mender met her gaze with the same calm detachment he used on his critical patients. "Goodbye, Rook."

She bit her lip, and then took a step toward Flint, who held perfectly still, arms tense as she gripped her sword in one hand and a dagger in the other. "Flint," Rook began. "I–"

"Get the fuck out of here, traitor," Flint snarled.

Rook's shoulders slumped and she trudged across the docks to Argent's squad, who shifted to allow her a place among them. Argent did not watch her, only raised his hand in a silent command. Every crossbow lifted, waiting for their targets to come into range.

"The gods are with us," Stonewall called. He tried to reach out to Kali, but couldn't get a sense of her. Flint was close beside him, trembling with rage, and he added, "But don't do anything stupid."

"She was my friend," Flint whispered.

"I know, but now's not the—"

Flint didn't shriek or cry out, simply charged without warning. Talon met her like a wall and deflected the younger woman's blades with an almost careless swipe of her sword, and then called to her companions. "Take them down!"

"Flint, get back here," Stonewall cried. "You'll be killed!"

"*Relah*," Milo called, and surged forward, gripping his sword in his good hand.

Stonewall swore. Nothing for it now; he had to trust that Kali and Sadira would protect his team. He signaled Beacon and Drake, and they darted forward, Leal and Rilla on their heels. A hail of crossbow bolts fell over them, only to catch fire and burn to ash before they could strike flesh. The High Commander shouted an order, and then the other Whitewater sentinels joined Talon. The world was only falling snow and clashing steel. Stonewall's blood ran hot and his mind took a step backward to let his body lead the way. He'd trained against sentinels since he was a boy. He knew how these men and women fought. But they knew him too, and their numbers were greater. Another volley of bolts rained down and met the same fate as the first. But how long could Sadira manage that? They still had a river to reach.

As Stonewall dodged Vesper and Hornfel's combined strikes, he knew his allies would not win this fight. *But we don't have to win,* he reminded himself. *We just have to survive.*

Instinct kicked in, screaming a warning. Stonewall whirled to block Gray's thrusting sword, and then risked a glance back at the mages, only to see Kali and Sadira standing together, hands joined, eyes closed. There was no sign of Eris or the other mages – had they abandoned the group? Leal fought beside Milo and Rilla, her spear a blur, while Brice lobbed arrows.

"Look sharp, Stonewall," Beacon called.

As another swarm of bolts burned, Stonewall turned in time to see Talon charging his way, sword raised. Her eyes were black as the void and empty as a thrall's. Stonewall's dagger met hers, blocking her strike and leaving them face-to-face. Despite his recent half-dose, he was breathing hard, but Talon's strength had not waned. She bared her teeth in a feral grin and shoved past him, heading for Kali and Sadira.

Stonewall leaped after his former commander. He was taller than she, but not by much. She moved with preternatural speed, no doubt granted by hematite, but sweet Mara's mercy, she must have eaten a handful to move so quickly! The battle had scattered the group and taken him too far from Kali's side; his lungs burned, but he pushed himself harder, faster. *Too late, this time, too late.*

Not five strides away from the dark-haired mage, Talon raised her sword.

Kali's voice reached him through their silent speech, incongruously calm. *Stonewall, get everyone away.*

Kali, what the–

Her reply was less coherent speech and more akin to a slap upside his head. *Message received*, Stonewall thought, and turned to shove Milo and Leal backward toward the alley. "It's time," he called. "Fall back!"

Thank Tor, thank sweet Mara, they all acted immediately. Even Flint followed his order, knocking Gray aside and back-pedaling to stay with her squad-mates. Stonewall scrambled past a bemused Talon, behind Kali and Sadira. The other sentinels shared the commander's confused expression at their opponents' sudden disappearance. A few made to follow, but Argent, perhaps sensing danger, called an order to regroup.

"Kali," Stonewall cried. "Now!"

Kali's eyes flew open; they were dark and human, and held nothing but delight. Sadira knelt and pressed her hands to the cobbled street, which exploded in a spray of bricks and dirt. A wall of fire bloomed up and around Talon and the other Whitewater sentinels, encircling them with saffron and yellow flames that reached above the buildings, well into the night sky. Heat billowed toward Stonewall, sending him stumbling away from the mages, stealing the moisture from his eyes and the air from his lungs. The heat choked; he could hardly keep his eyes open for the force of it, let alone take a proper breath. Someone screamed.

Though his head spun, he could not pull his gaze from the climbing flames, for within them, a pair of golden eyes looked back at him and he heard a voice, as surely as he had heard any sound in his life. *Come, Elan. Come home, my son.*

No sodding way. Stonewall shook away the hallucination. Argent, Silver Squad, and some other sentinels from Silverwood had managed to escape the fire, but barely. They knelt against the cobblestones, coughing and sputtering and trying to scrabble further away from the flames. The rest stood hemmed in, pressed close together in the center of the massive, fiery ring. How close they were to the fire, Stonewall could not say—the flames distorted his vision—but he could not imagine they'd survive more than a few minutes in the maelstrom.

"Ben!" Drake cried. Only then did Stonewall see the Assembly man crawling away from the flames; he'd not reacted in time and his legs were caught in the ring as the fire gnawed his clothes and hair. Drake rushed to his side, but the heat pushed him back, coughing, and he had to stumble away.

Ben shouted; Stonewall saw the movement of his mouth, but the flames took him over and soon he moved no more. Drake collapsed to the street, calling Ben's name, and Stonewall darted for his brother, scrambling through the smothering heat to grab Drake's forearm. His elder brother whirled and Stonewall's heart clenched at the desperation looking back at him. "We have to go," he called, tugging his brother's arm. "Come on, *relah.*"

Drake stared at him, but then nodded and struggled upright, swiping at his face. Someone prodded Stonewall's side. He whirled to see Leal, hood askew and scarf mottled with embers. "Eris and the others made it to the boat," she cried, pointing toward the docks, beyond the fire, where Brice and Rilla had already fled. "Let's go!"

"I'm fine, Stonewall," Drake said, nodding in Kali's direction. "Go help your girl."

Still reeling, all Stonewall could do was grab Kali—and her viol case—and race for the dock. Beacon grabbed Sadira's arm to pull her along, but swore and immediately released her, flapping his gloved hand as if he'd been burned. Thank the One, Sadira could run on her own, though her jerky movements belied her exhaustion. Kali wrapped her arms around Stonewall's neck, clinging to him as he clambered down the rickety ladder. There was no time for them to descend one by one; Flint, Beacon, and Leal leaped into the waiting skiff. Drake followed suit, landing with such force that icy water splashed across the passengers.

Someone had freed the skiff of all but one line tying them to the docks. As Stonewall ensured Kali and Sadira were safely inside, bolts slammed into the skiff's sides with sickening *thwacks.*

"Heads down," Stonewall ordered, and he was gratified to see everyone—even the mages—duck to avoid the onslaught. He cut the line with his dagger and they were off.

"Ea's balls," Flint swore. "Where're the sodding oars?"

Eris' eyes widened and she turned to Cai and Marcen, who exchanged horrified looks. "They were here, I swear," Cai began.

"Argent's people must've dumped 'em," Drake said. "All we've got is a bunch of rope. We're as good as trapped."

It made a grim kind of tactical sense but Stonewall couldn't appreciate the High Commander's cleverness right now. More crossbow bolts fell, but they had no way to get upriver, and the waterfall was fast approaching.

Stonewall's throat went dry. "Paddle by hand! We've got to avoid the falls."

Drake leaned over the side and thrust his arm in the water. "This isn't going to–"

His words died as a crossbow bolt bit into his upper back and he lurched forward, gasping. Stonewall's blood froze; he reached for his brother, but Drake shook his head. "I'm fine. Keep going..."

"We can do this," Cai called.

Another bolt struck, this one hitting the mage's heart. Cai clawed at the shaft of wood jutting from his chest as blood welled from the wound. The other mages frantically tried to reach for him while the skiff wobbled upon the freezing, fast-flowing river. Stonewall looked toward Kali and Sadira; the latter crawled to reach Cai, but Kali sat at the bow, staring at the approaching waterfall.

The skiff could hold their motley crew, but navigation without oars was next to impossible, especially given the storm of crossbow bolts. Stonewall stuck his arm in the icy river and furiously began paddling with the others, trying to coax the skiff away from the center of the river where the current was strongest. They had to get across! More bolts fell like hailstones, striking the boat and the water, and the White River's current seemed fiercer with each second. Stonewall's arm burned with effort, and his fingers were going numb.

Then he heard Kali's voice in his mind. *Let the river take us to the falls.*

"Are you mad?" he shouted, not caring what the others thought.

"All signs point to 'yes,'" Beacon grunted.

Probably, Kali replied through their silent-speech. *But trust me. Our plan is sound, but going upriver isn't going to work. We must follow the river's path.* Her resolve crystallized. *Trust me.*

Gods above and beyond, he did.

"Flint, Beacon," Stonewall called despite the queasy feeling in his gut. "Stop paddling. We're going for the falls."

"Now *you're* sodding insane," Flint cried.

"Just do it," he shot back, ducking to avoid another bolt as Kali turned to Sadira, Adrie, and Eris, who were bent over a groaning Cai.

More bolts struck the skiff and the rushing waters on all sides, but all Stonewall could hear was the roar of the falls pulling them toward the edge.

* * *

Kali gripped the skiff's railing with white knuckles. Inhale. Exhale. She could do this. She already had – in a sense. If she could disintegrate a bridge on her and Stonewall's journey to Whitewater City, surely she could hold a single boat together. But she was weary, not just from her imprisonment and time as a thrall, but also from giving energy to Sadira for that fiery spectacle. Sadira hadn't needed much help, thank the stars, but judging by her ashen cheeks and rapidly cooling skin, the stunt had taken much of her vigor.

"Eris, Adrie," Kali called to the mages crouched over Cai. "I need your help."

"He's *dying*," Adrie cried.

"We'll all join him if you don't help me." More arrows fell around them. One skimmed by Kali's hand on the bow, close enough for her to feel the wind from its passage, but soon they'd be out of the crossbows' range.

The falls loomed ahead, little more than a smudge of mist above the dark water. A thick rope net hung across the lip of the falls, between the two shores; it would stop the skiff, but for how long?

"No, no, *no*," Eris cried. "He's gone! Cai!"

Kali fought back a swell of grief and bitterness—and *longing* for the others' magic; she could not deny the feeling—and forced her words to be as strong and certain as Stonewall's always seemed. "Eris, I can save us, if you help me."

"Shut up, metal-licker," Adrie ground out.

Eris, though, stared at her. "You want our magic?"

Sweet blood. Give it to us.

Kali shoved away the memory of the Fata's litany. "Yes, I need your strength. Now!"

Adrie was shaking her head, clearly prepared to tell Kali to do something rude, when Drake crawled toward them. Kali gasped at the sight of a crossbow bolt sticking out of his back, but he shook his head once. "Hurts like hell, but I'm not dying today. You need magic?"

Kali nodded dumbly. Drake offered his hand; broad, with thick fingers, darker than Stonewall's but calloused in the same places. "Take mine."

No time for hesitation. Kali grabbed Drake's hand and savored the small rush of energy through her veins. All other things fell away. Even the pain in her knee began to ebb. But Drake's magic alone wouldn't be enough and they were nearly at the waterfall. The rope net that spanned the river began to smolder at the center. When Kali glanced at Sadira in surprise, the Zhee mage gave her a weak nod.

Kali took a deep breath and looked between Eris and Adrie. "Eris, I'm sorry we couldn't help the others. I'm sorry Cai's gone. But if the rest of us are to survive this, I need your help."

Green eyes wet with tears, but still sharp as daggers, bored into hers before Eris nodded once. "Do as she says," she said to Adrie as she ripped off her glove and held out her hand. "Hang on with the other," Eris added, raising her voice. "Everyone, tie yourselves down and hang on to the skiff."

Flint looked up, her gaze landing on the falls. "Tie down…? Are you… Oh, no. No, no, no, *no!*"

Stonewall began to crawl toward Kali. "Do it, Flint."

While the others scrambled to fasten themselves down, Eris, Drake, and Adrie each grabbed Kali's arm, while Kali shut her eyes and concentrated. *Sweet magic,* indeed. Oh, it flowed through her veins like fire, like wind, like the waters that licked their craft. She trembled with the force of the raw power surging through her body, making her eyes roll back in her head and her breath come in gasps. No greater pleasure had she ever known, for there was no doubt, nor fear, nor pain. Only magic.

Kali clutched the skiff with one hand as the boat hurtled toward the edge. *I can do this.* She concentrated on the skiff's particles, on the infinitesimal motes of wood that made up the floating vessel. The wood was old, not as old as the bridge she'd destroyed, but weary nonetheless. Without magical aid, the skiff would not survive the trip over the falls, let alone the inevitable crash at the waterfall's base.

But magic was stronger than wood, stronger than water. Drake and Eris' grips were hard enough to staunch blood flow, but Kali ignored the numbing sensation in her arm. She inhaled cold air and river mist, but shunted both from her mind, concentrating only on the skiff's particles, shivering as if with terror as they sidled to the waterfall.

Hold, she ordered the vessel while still clinging to the wooden railing. *Hold.*

The skiff lurched and rattled. Its particles trembled harder as the craft

411

tilted over the fall's edge. Kali's eyes flew open in time to see darkness and falling snow, with nothing but churning waters below. Only magic could break their fall. Stomach roiling, Kali squeezed her eyes shut again and sent her will through the skiff. *Hold.*

Magic pulsed through her veins, sweet and wild and dizzying. In the back of her mind, she knew she was going to faint, but if she lost consciousness, if she lost control, they would all be killed. Someone shouted; another person prayed aloud. A third spoke to her, although she could not piece his words together. Then Stonewall was at her side, wrapping an arm around her waist and saying her name, again and again, aiding her as she fought to retain that single thought that would save their lives. *Hold.*

The skiff canted forward as if trying to buck them loose. A scream cut the air. Kali heard the sound only as the final echo of a call within a mountain pass. Her head lifted from her body, leaving her weightless, but her mind was clear and strong; anchored to the moment by the man who held her fast.

Hold.

36

THIRTY-SIX

Heat caught thick in Talon's lungs and throat as the inferno wrenched every drop of moisture from her body. Her helmet felt like liquid metal, so she ripped it off and hurled it away. Her head swam and the edges of her vision began to fade into blackness. Everywhere, mage-fire closed her sentinels within a wall of flame that danced in mockery while Stonewall and the others fled to the river. Hands clenched, Talon stepped forward—as if she could pursue—but her foot caught on something and sent her to her knees. She landed atop Vigil's lanky form. The other woman had been too close to the flames when they burst from the street; her helmet had fallen away, revealing the charred remains of her face.

Talon scrambled upright and backward, only to crash into Gray, clutching her side, and Hornfel, leaning on Gray, an arrow embedded in his right thigh. He pointed to the flames and shouted something, but Talon couldn't make out his words. No one could speak over the fire's roar; Talon could barely breathe. The Laughing God drew closer. Those who lived gathered at the center of the fiery ring, pressed close together and Talon looked straight up into the sky, where the clouds were finally dissipating.

Mara, have mercy.

A gust of icy air brushed her cheek. She turned to see Foley kneeling outside of and several paces away from the inferno. The cobblestones were gone, leaving only churned earth, into which Foley had buried both his hand and hook. Gradually, as the darkness crept across Talon's vision, the ground seethed, reaching the base of the fire to suffocate a swathe of flames. The resulting path was barely the width of Talon's shoulders, but it was a safe way out of the firestorm.

"Go," she cried, though the word came out as a choking cough. She shoved Hornfel and Gray toward the makeshift path and urged the others after. One by one the surviving Whitewater sentinels stumbled out of the fiery ring. Talon went last, pausing to look at the bodies of Vigil, Griffin, and Jerrod, who would not rise again.

Talon staggered until she could feel no more heat, and then collapsed to the cobblestones, coughing, gasping, each attempted breath a lance of pain in her chest. Although she was away from the inferno, the danger had not passed, for her head was light and she could not think anything other than *breathe!*

"The fire wardens are here," Foley called, and placed a gentle hand on her shoulder. "It will be well, child," he added in a murmur meant only for her ears. "You're safe."

Tears sprang to her eyes – how? There was no water left in her body; she was as dry as old parchment. She could not speak.

Nox bring your spirits safely over the river. Tor guide your steps into the next life. The One keep you in all your days.

Mica knelt beside her and offered a cup of liquid that smelled sweet, like thalo mixed with water, but tasted like nails and hot coals. Talon made herself drink the entire thing, and soon she could take a deep, wheezing breath. In the corner of her vision, she watched more sentinels, city guards, and the volunteer fire wardens dart toward the roaring flames with buckets of sand and water. Gradually, the mage-fire died, bathing the docks in darkness once more.

"The others?" Talon croaked to the mender, who knelt beside her on the cobblestones.

"Vigil, Griffin, and Jerrod died in the fire. Haste made it out of the blaze, but died a few minutes ago. Stout, Shard, Hornfel, and Gray sustained injuries during combat, but should recover. Ferro's unconscious, but Binder thinks he'll live." Mica paused. "Silver Squad is unharmed, as are all of the Silverwood sentinels that the High Commander brought with him."

Talon couldn't summon the strength to be angry, only nodded. Mica regarded her. "How do you feel, ser?"

She took another gulp of mercifully cool air. "Well enough to stand, I think."

"With respect, ser, I advise you to rest a while longer."

But she was already getting to her feet, wincing at the ache that seeped through her entire body. Gods above, her armor felt like it was made of hot lead, and even her slow, halting rise made her lightheaded. She staggered forward, but Foley and Mica caught her before she hit the cobblestones again. When she looked up—and her vision stopped swimming—her heart sank at the sight of the bodies someone had dragged from the circle of desolation.

"That one's not a sentinel," she managed, pointing to one of the corpses.

Mica glanced over his shoulder. "Aye. One of the...others got caught in the flames. A civilian man, by the look of him." He dropped his voice to a whisper. "The High Commander claims the fellow is part of the Assembly – one of the ringleaders, no less."

Was it wrong of her to feel relief at this news? Argent could bring the dreg's body back to the Pillars, and perhaps then their attention would turn away from Whitewater City. But her relief was short-lived. After this debacle, Argent would never let her keep her rank, let alone her posting.

The survivors not involved in putting out the flames had gathered to one side, where Binder and some of the Circle healers moved among them. Argent spoke in low, urgent tones with his squad and a group of city guards. Civilian onlookers filled the streets, gawking at the smoldering remains of the mage-fire. More than a few folks cast dark glances at the sentinels, but thank the One, no one seemed inclined to show more ire than that – at least for the time being.

All for nothing, she thought as she watched Binder wrap Hornfel's injured

415

leg. She looked at Mica. "I'll be fine, thank you. Go help Binder."

"I'll watch her, ser," Foley added.

"I believe it," Mica replied. "Commander, if it weren't for Mage Clementa's quick actions, our brothers and sisters—and you—would *all* be corpses."

"I know," Talon said. "The First Mage's bravery will not go unrewarded."

Foley dipped his chin but said nothing as the mender hurried off. Talon and Foley stood in silence while she focused on sucking in fresh air, although a rasping cough accompanied every other breath. Her eyes itched and her head ached, and the urge to retch rested at the back of her throat. She fought the feeling, lest she expel the healing thalo.

"I wish I could do more for you," Foley said quietly. "But you still burn with hematite."

Yes, she could feel the latent fire flickering through her veins, although in this moment she wanted to be like stone: cool and passive. The clatter of boots on the street made her turn to see Silver Squad and a group of city guards rushing off in the direction of the city's main gates, no doubt to try and track down Stonewall, Halcyon, and their allies.

Except High Commander Argent, who strode up to Talon. Unlike everyone else, not a speck of dirt or ash marred his gleaming armor, and only a few snowflakes had fallen upon his broad shoulders. Captain Cobalt and Rook came with him, each looking all the more wan and disheveled next to Argent's immaculate presence.

The High Commander had tucked his helmet beneath his arm, revealing the grim set of his mouth. "Rook tells me that two mages somehow…joined their abilities to create this destruction," he pointed to the charred ground, "and sent the group over the falls."

"Aye," Talon said, coughing. "One mage is from Zheem, and supposedly gifted with fire. She's powerful, but has never caused any trouble."

"Until today," Argent replied. "And the other? This…Kalinda Halcyon?"

"Mage Halcyon has proven to be the more dangerous of the two," Talon said. Between coughing fits, she began to relate the story of Halcyon's unorthodox transfer, thrall possession, and attempted execution.

But the High Commander held up his hand and stared at Talon, his gray eyes piercing. "I know all of that. What I don't understand is how a sentinel *and* a mage formed such a connection under *your* watch."

"Surely it doesn't matter now," Rook interjected, voice shaking. "Surely they're all dead. No one could survive the drop. Even if they did, the White River's current is swift."

To Talon's surprise, the High Commander did not reprimand Rook for speaking out of turn, only shook his head. "Mages are treacherous and clever. They would not have made for the falls if they did not think they would survive. No, magic aided their escape. Powerful magic, unlike any I've encountered. But Silver Squad *will* find these renegades."

Talon was too exhausted to reply, and simply nodded. Hoping to change the subject, she glanced at Cobalt. "I'm glad to see you unharmed, Captain."

He ducked his head once and removed his helmet, pale eyes sweeping across the docks, resting on the corpses.

"I am in his debt," Argent replied. "Captain Cobalt ensured that I was fully informed of the severity of matters in Whitewater Bastion. And I see," his gaze skimmed over the bodies and landed upon the ring of charred ground, "that he was not exaggerating."

Before Talon could reply, a sentinel she did not recognize trotted up to the High Commander. "Ser, shall we take the mages back to the bastion?"

The newcomer pointed behind her, where a group of Whitewater mages stood in a clump, with bowed heads and bound hands, each one of them collared. Except Foley, who kept close to Talon.

Argent did not spare the renegade mages a glance. "Aye, take them back and deal with them as we discussed."

Foley's head jerked up. "Deal with them, ser?"

Talon turned to give him a quelling look, but Argent merely regarded Foley as one would consider a stray weed in the garden. "They are corrupted and must be destroyed."

"You're mad," Foley said, breath short. "You can't kill them all. It's not fair! They've done nothing–"

"They tried to escape," Argent broke in. "Given this bastion's history, I can't allow these mages to survive. The Pillars agree with me. What if the other bastions hear of such weakness on our part?"

"You can't leave the province with no mages," Foley shot back. "People need us."

"Intractable magic-users are a plague, and the province is better off without them." Argent glanced at Talon. "Well, Commander, it seems the situation is resolved for now. Your garrison is stocked with hematite again, with more on the way."

Nothing in his voice or manner suggested anger. Perhaps she'd been worried for nothing. Hardly daring to hope, Talon gave the best warrior's salute she could manage. "Thank you, ser. I am in your debt."

"However," Argent went on, and Talon's stomach dropped to her knees as he pulled his sword free of its scabbard. "There is one other matter that requires my attention."

* * *

Cobalt should have been paying more attention to Argent and Talon's conversation, but he could not stop scanning the surviving Whitewater sentinels, searching for his own squad-mates. He breathed a sigh of relief when he spotted Vesper and Mica, although that relief quickened into fear at the looks on their faces and the realization that Vigil was not with them. Perhaps his second-in-command was still recovering, or... He followed Mica's gaze to the burned bodies, and his heart sank.

Oh, no. Sweet Mara, no.

"Captain," Argent said, making Cobalt start. "It's best we take care of this now. Restrain the mage."

Cobalt blinked stupidly at the High Commander. "Ser, the mages are being taken to the bastion."

"Except one," Argent said in that same easy tone. He pointed his sword at Mage Clementa.

Talon looked from the High Commander to the First Mage, her blood-shot eyes going huge and round. "Ser, please! Mage Clementa has remained

418

loyal, and–"

"Silence," Argent snapped. "Captain, that was an order."

There was ice in the High Commander's voice; ice on cold steel. Heart hammering, Cobalt turned to Foley Clementa who shrank away from him but did not run – for all the good running would have done. Cobalt had no cuffs, so he took Foley's thin forearm and led the mage to Argent.

Talon scrambled forward to place herself between the High Commander and the First Mage. "Ser, please listen to me! Foley's not done anything wrong." She paused, gasping and coughing. "He had nothing to do with the other mages' escape. He *told* us what they were planning. He stayed. He saved our lives. He–"

"Captain, make him kneel," Argent broke in, gaze fixed on Mage Clementa.

Cobalt's stomach roiled, but he grasped the mage's shoulder and pushed him down to the ashes by the docks. The First Mage trembled but did not resist, nor look down. Rather, he stared directly ahead with unfocused eyes, his lips moving in silent prayer. The sky lightened with dawn's approach. The onlookers that remained muttered and stood on their tiptoes to see better. Behind Cobalt's back, someone was weeping.

"Ser, please don't do this!" Talon shoved past Cobalt to stand before Mage Clementa once more, her eyes wild and red-rimmed, and her face streaked with cinders and tears. Her gear was filthy and her hair had come undone from its habitual neat braid, scorched and dusted with ash. But the raw desperation in her gaze was what made Cobalt's heart sink further.

"*All* of the mages in this bastion are too dangerous to live," Argent said. "But those with…close bonds to sentinels are the most insidious of all."

Talon froze. "Bonds…?"

"Don't play coy, Talon. It doesn't suit you." Argent swept her aside, sending her stumbling. "Besides, you know I keep my promises."

His sword lifted, descended. Foley's head and body fell to the ash and mud with separate, muted *thumps*.

Talon screamed. The sound broke through the air like a cracking whip, then the commander fell to her knees beside the headless body, displacing a flurry of ashes. Cobalt wanted to look away, but he could not tear his eyes from the sight. He'd never seen Talon as anything other than *Commander.* Though she did not weep, he thought something inside of her had broken.

Argent had to know the truth, Cobalt told himself. *You did the right thing.* But then why did he hurt all over?

Argent wiped his blade on the back of the First Mage's coat before sheathing it again. "Talaséa Hammon, because of your incompetence and your attempt at deception, I name you Forsworn. You are hereby stripped of your rank and privileges. You will be sent to the Pillars for their judgment."

He made a signal and four Silverwood sentinels came forward, grabbing Talon's arms to pull her upright. She sagged in their grip and made no effort to rise, let alone walk. One of the Silverwood sentinels muttered a swear and they began to drag Talon toward a group of waiting horses.

"Commander Cobalt?"

It took Cobalt a beat too long to register the rank and his name in the same breath. "Ser?"

Argent nodded once. "Congratulations on your promotion. It's well-earned and long since due."

What else could Cobalt do but salute? He did, but the sick feeling in his gut did not vanish and his voice was weak. "Thank you, ser."

Argent stared at the churning falls, where the first few rays of sunlight brushed the mist. "You've inherited quite a mess. I'll send some replacement mages to tend to the province's needs, but I fear the bastion and garrison will not recover for some time. But you have proven yourself to be an intelligent and loyal sentinel. I pray you have the strength to guide these godly men and women." He turned to leave, tossing the final words over his shoulder. "Good luck."

* * *

Stonewall gripped the skiff's railing with both hands, arms braced on either side of Kali, using his weight to press her against the bow. After securing them both with rope, this was the only way to keep her in place while she worked her magic, for she needed one hand free to siphon power from the other mages.

His blood felt like it was forcing itself through every pore while the White River pounded beside him. Had he reached out, he could have touched the falling water. But rather than pummel the skiff into nothing, the river cradled the vessel, like a mother holding her child close; Kali's magic at work. The White River stretched below Stonewall in a churning, frothing mass, bathed ivory in the predawn light struggling through the cloud cover. The sight struck him dizzy, but he tried not to shut his eyes lest he miss some new threat – even if he could do nothing about it. He shifted his weight again, praying that Kali's viol, which he'd shoved beneath his seat and braced his boots against, would remain in place.

Stonewall's body lifted as the skiff tipped forward and down. Wind whistled past his ears and the wooden planks groaned, both sounds somehow louder and more terrifying than the river's roar. A fine sheen of mist coated his already frosting face and gear. No one spoke. All screams and prayers had stopped as everyone held their collective breath, waiting for the inevitable crash. When he could stand the sight no more, Stonewall ducked his head next to Kali's ear and continued his litany.

"You can do this. Kali, you can do this." He was afraid to risk breaking her focus by using their silent speech, but he couldn't tell if she heard him, for her eyes were closed and her face was tight with concentration. But at least she was conscious.

Flint screamed. The world jolted as the skiff slammed into the river once more, jarring Stonewall's teeth. Freezing water splashed over the vessel, drenching its passengers as the skiff shuddered before the current snatched it forward. Now Stonewall risked a look around. They were in one piece and the skiff skimmed through placid, snow-covered countryside, swift atop the current.

"We're alive?" Flint gasped.

Milo's voice was weak. "I think so."

Stonewall spoke again in Kali's ear. "We made it. We're safe. You can let go now."

At first, he didn't think she heard him, but then she heaved a sigh and slumped into his arms, her soaking hair stuck to her cheeks. She said nothing, but her presence in his mind glowed with relief, satisfaction, and pride.

Kali? he ventured. *Are you...?*

He didn't know what to ask. Fortunately, she replied in kind, though her thoughts were distant. *I'm well, Elan. So very well.*

Tired?

She pressed closer to him. *Not in the least.*

Eyes still closed, she pulled her hand back from the other mages and tucked it beneath her sopping cloak. In doing so, she freed Drake, Eris, and Adrie from whatever she'd had to do to use their magic. The cost must have been great, for Drake groaned and leaned back against the skiff's side, head lolling, the slender bolt still stuck in his shoulder, while Eris and Adrie slumped against one another. But they were all alive.

Thank the One.

Something warm touched Stonewall's arm. He looked to see a shaft of morning sunlight that had pierced the cloud cover. The snow had stopped falling, but now that the energy and excitement had faded, cold started to seep back in. The twins huddled together, teeth chattering, and everyone shivered so hard that the boat shook. Stonewall's armor felt like it was made of ice. If they weren't going to drown or be smashed to bits, they were going to freeze to death. He twisted to find Sadira rubbing her eyes as if clearing them of sleep as she sat upright.

"Sadira, have you recovered?" he asked.

She smiled at him. Within moments, a delicious warmth crept through Stonewall's body, as if he was seated before a cozy hearth and not in the middle of an icy river in the thick of winter. Milo and Flint sighed in relief, while Beacon stared at the Zhee mage, transfixed.

Rilla hugged Brice's shoulders and grinned at the white-haired mage. "You know, I think I like this magic-business. Some of it, anyway."

Eris came to, groaning as she sat upright. She looked at Kali and whispered, "She did it."

"Aye," Stonewall said as he smoothed away a stray strand of hair that clung to Kali's nose. "She's a marvel."

Eris did not reply, instead turned to see Flint and Milo, who had Cai's body braced beneath their legs. "What are you doing to him?" she snapped at the burnies. "What did he ever do to you besides die to save your miserable lives?"

The twins exchanged glances before Flint sat up, making the skiff rock again. "Would you rather we'd have let the river take your friend before you can give him a proper pyre?"

"This was the only way we could keep him from falling in," Milo added in a gentler voice. "Or out, I guess. We meant no disrespect, Mage Echina."

Eris looked downriver. "The sentinels will be on the hunt. We must go faster."

"How can they catch us?" Milo asked. "We're already going so fast."

"Not for much longer," Leal replied. "There's a bend ahead; after that, the river widens and the current slows for many leagues. My family will be waiting where we discussed, but it will take days to reach them if we just drift."

Stonewall took a deep breath. *Kali, it's time. Are you truly awake?*

Dark eyes opened to meet his and her smile was dazzling. *Aye. It just...it feels so good. The magic.*

Along with this silent speech came the heady rush of power he'd only experienced when taking hematite. *We're not out of the thicket yet,* he told her. *We must try to put some distance between us and Whitewater City.*

Yes, she replied, still smiling. *Away.*

She sat up, causing the others to look at her with varying degrees of wonder and consternation. She glanced at Adrie and Drake, still unconscious, and then met Eris' gaze. "I'm so sorry about Cai, and the others," she said softly.

Eris frowned. "Well? What happens now?"

Kali glanced at Stonewall. "Can you tell where we are?"

He closed his eyes, recalling the maps of Aredia that all sentinels were

423

required to learn. "The river's clear of rocks for this portion, though it won't be that way for much longer."

Now *that* was a distressing thought, for he had no idea how much actual *steering* could be done during magical long-distance travel.

"We'll be quick," Kali assured him. Gods above, she felt so calm, so sure of herself. He searched for the same certainty within his own heart, but found only doubt.

"What's going on?" Eris asked. "What does it matter if *he* knows where we're going?"

"I'm wondering the same thing," Beacon added.

Fear seized Stonewall's heart and he shot Kali what was surely a desperate look. *Please don't tell anyone about my...heritage. At least, not now.*

"Stonewall's my navigator," Kali replied, looking between her friend and Beacon, neither of whom seemed impressed with her humor. "Magic's no trouble, but I'm hopeless with directions." It wasn't much of an explanation, but she pushed on before anyone could question her further. "I'm going to use my magic to move us quickly, now, so I suggest everyone hang on. Again."

"Listen to her," Stonewall added. "When Kali says 'hang on,' she sodding well means it."

Confused looks abounded, but once more the others secured the unconscious mages, grabbed hold of the skiff's sides, and braced themselves against the boat's interior. Stonewall did the same, while also trying to concentrate on the singular thought: *Away.* Would this really work?

You can do this. Her thoughts reached his, brushing his mind with a feather-touch.

In another circumstance, her faith in him might have been upsetting—for surely it was undeserved—but now it was a comfort. Perhaps she was right. He nodded, tried to relax, and focused.

Kali made a show of taking several deep breaths before he felt rather than heard her thought: *Away.* The intention resonated between them and plucked the chords of something deep within his heart that he had only just discovered. *We can do this.* The thought was at once knowing and believing; it was magic.

A faint tingle ran through his temples, but otherwise, he felt nothing physical, which didn't seem fair, considering Kali's struggles. Another side-effect of her magic, he supposed. Wind brushed his face, strengthening with each breath. Soft gasps sounded behind him. Stonewall ignored them and focused. *Away.*

The skiff trembled like the rippling wind that even now picked up speed, whistling past his ears, whispering his name. *Elan.* In his mind's eye, he saw the golden-eyed god and felt the power of Tor's presence fill him utterly. *You will come home, Elan. One day. Soon.*

Stonewall? Kali's presence was faint but insistent. When Stonewall opened his eyes, she blinked up at him once; her face now looked drained and pale as it did after bouts of great magic. She whispered his name one more time before she sank into his arms, unconscious.

Holding her close to his chest, Stonewall looked up to see the White River flowing past them, stretched between two shores as it meandered south. The wild ride had ended for now, and the skiff slid over the water as would any non-magical vessel. Judging from the landscape, they had traveled far enough to put them out of Argent's way. Thanks to magic, they would reach safety within hours, not days. More sunlight splintered through the clouds, glittering upon the flowing water. To the east, dawn was breaking.

The saga continues in Surrender (Catalyst Moon - Book 4)

Interested in the immediate aftermath of *Storm*? Click below for the short story, *The Oath*. (You'll also receive updates from me about my upcoming releases - among other goodies.)
https://bf.laloga.com/stormfreebie

Acknowledgement

No story is written in a vacuum. Endless thanks to my amazing, brilliant beta readers: Imke, Isabella, and M.E., my ARC trooper team for catching those last-minute typos, my husband for understanding when my head is in another world, and my friends and family for your endless love and support.

To you as well, dear reader, I send all my love,

Lauren

About the Author

Lauren finds Real Life overrated, and has always preferred to inhabit alternate realities, both self-created and created by others. However, after being burned by certain fandoms one too many times, Lauren decided to focus her reality escape attempts on her own creations. She's much happier now, although she still enjoys fandoms - in small doses.

A believer in love, hope, compassion, and similar squishy ideals, Lauren endeavors to create stories that both gut-punch and elevate her readers. Emotional rollercoasters are what make fiction fun, after all.

When she's not avoiding Real Life responsibilities, Lauren enjoys dancing at music festivals, spending time in nature, and tending to her cat's every whim. She lives in North Florida with her partner and assorted furred critters, but can be found online at laloga.com

You can connect with me on:
- https://laloga.com
- https://twitter.com/lalogawrites?lang=en
- https://www.facebook.com/laloga
- https://www.facebook.com/groups/859225654453729

Subscribe to my newsletter:
- https://laloga.com/newsletter

Made in the USA
Middletown, DE
30 April 2022

65018688R00260